SEARCHING FOR NORIKO

Searching for Noriko

A novel
by

AL DAWSON

Adelaide Books
New York / Lisbon
2020

SEARCHING FOR NORIKO
A novel
By Al Dawson

Published by Adelaide Books, New York / Lisbon
adelaidebooks.org
Editor-in-Chief
Stevan V. Nikolic

For any information, please address Adelaide Books
at info@adelaidebooks.org
or write to:
Adelaide Books
244 Fifth Ave. Suite D27
New York, NY, 10001

ISBN: 978-1-952570-51-3

Printed in the United States of America

To two brothers who did come home,

my uncles Juan and José Baldonado

Contents

Acknowledgments

Inspiration for the novel came from family stories about growing up Mexican American in southern New Mexico, and the nearly miraculous survival and return home of two uncles who were captured on Bataan and suffered for over three years as prisoners of the Japanese Imperial Army. Much credit belongs to my mother Elisa and her sisters for their recollections, and to Father Albert Braun, OFM, himself a POW and missionary to the Mescalero Apache tribe. Father Al died some years ago but he was a heroic figure in my life and the man for whom I was named.

Many friends contributed time, coaching, encouragement and critique as the book developed, including Erwin Adler, Ron Cass, John Stang, Paul Sheridan and Mark Malatesta.

Though he did not live to see it finished, my dear friend and former boss, Dick Barnsback, was a unique influence and cheerleader as the book progressed. He would have loved to see it in print.

Special thanks to George Feifer, a remarkable man, author, philosopher and writer of extraordinary talent. Author of several books set in Soviet-era Russia, his *The Battle of Okinawa*, provided valuable source material for the scenes in this book. He is also a wonderful friend and supporter of my writing efforts.

Bill Greenleaf, a superb editor, worked hard to help me restructure and rewrite what began as *Finding Noriko* and ended up as *Searching For Noriko*.

I can't express sufficient gratitude to a person who inspired the name in the title. Noriko Mooney is a refined lady of Japanese ancestry and a longtime friend who coached me in the intricacies and nuances of Japanese manners, speaking style and cuisine. Without "my" Noriko, I would still be "searching for Noriko".

Finally, and certainly most importantly, I owe so much to my wonderful, lovely Jane who suffered through the frustrating and sometimes aggravating times as the book went from rewrite to rewrite. She is a pillar of strength. *Searching For Noriko* would not have happened without her patient counsel and morale lifting support.

To the many unnamed others who offered suggestions or new directions, or expert advice over the several years of the project, thank you. This book is really yours as well.

PART I

Ghosts and Dreams

Chapter 1

Did I Hurt You?

Friday, October 5, 2001

Mesilla, New Mexico

Frankie opened his eyes, peered into the darkness, and loosened his grip around his wife's neck the second he recognized where he was. "I'm sorry," he gasped, his hands shaking. "Are you okay? Did I hurt you?"

He could hear his wife fumbling for the light switch on the nightstand lamp. He squinted against the sudden glare.

"My God, Frankie! You nearly strangled me," she coughed as she massaged her throat. "I was just dozing because you were doing that jerky thing with your legs and moaning again. I tried to nudge you awake, but you had me by the neck before I could get your attention." Frowning, she threw off her covers. "I'm getting up. Do you want some tea?"

"Please."

Frankie cringed. This was becoming too frequent. First, nightmares about Ramón, now these flashbacks to a terrible ordeal he thought he'd put behind him fifty years ago. Rubbing his eyes, he felt the stubble on his chin, then glanced at his Melanie, grinning sheepishly.

"Didn't I tell you sleeping with me would be exciting?"

"That's not becoming any funnier. I really think you should see someone about these episodes, Frankie." She reached for her robe, found her slippers, and padded toward the kitchen.

She's right, he thought. It wasn't as if he hadn't tried to get help. But the docs at the VA in El Paso hadn't done much for him. Their suggestion that he should join a veterans' support group or at least become active in a local American Legion post had not impressed him. The idea of baring his soul to strangers or wringing his hands with some weepy old farts over wartime events from his teenage years held zero appeal for him. He had crumpled and tossed away the prescriptions for Xanax and Ambien as soon as he walked out the door. He'd have to deal with this himself. The last thing he wanted was to hurt his wife.

Listening to her filling the teakettle, he lay alone for a few moments, debating whether he should try to get back to sleep. Worried that the demons might still be waiting there, he stretched and heaved himself out of bed.

In the kitchen, he caught Melanie studying her reflection in the glass-fronted cabinets, maybe because the worry lines in her forehead looked deeper than usual. Knowing she had a right to be concerned after the difficult last several months, he'd made no fuss about the disappearance of his K-bar knife and .45 automatic from the drawer in his night-table.

The digital clock on the microwave read 3:23 a.m. *Not as early this time*, he thought. Clearing his throat loudly, he limped to the breakfast table. His early morning drink of a steaming cup of manzanilla tea was already waiting for him.

Since he sensed that Melanie wasn't in the mood for small talk, he took the cup through the French doors leading out to the *placita*. Normally he would take a seat on the bench under the portal and listen to the musical sound of the water trickling in the fountain under the old elms, an immensely satisfying daily ritual. During the spring and early summer, honeysuckle filled the courtyard with delicate yellow blooms and near-erotic sweetness. But fall's cool weather had arrived early, and now, at this hour, his only company was cold blue stars.

Life's has been very good, he mused. *Who'd have thought that the son of Mexican immigrants would own the finest territorial-style adobe hacienda in Doña Ana County?*

Grateful Frankie was ever mindful of the good fortune that led to his owning a thriving general contracting business that had blossomed in the postwar years with large housing projects at Holloman, White Sands, Fort Bliss, and even Los Alamos. He raised his cup in a mock toast to the men who had made possible all that he had achieved as a successful builder. *Thank you, Big Ed and Senator Anderson.*

His leg pain—a persistent reminder of that sodden hell in the mud and rain when something very hard and heavy had bounced off his helmet and caromed into a defile before exploding and killing his squad mate, Griffin—was tolerable in the early morning. It was just dumb luck that it hadn't detonated a second earlier. Even so, Frankie had taken some splinters in his right thigh and butt from the Japanese Type-97 fragmentation grenade. The medics had done a nice job patching him up, but there was a bit of nerve damage and several pieces of Japanese metal left inside, a *recordito* of his time in the fire and blood of Conical Hill in May 1945.

He could hear the sound of his wife placing dishes on the table. Melanie would be cutting up some cantaloupe and strawberries. Shivering he decided to go back inside for another cup of tea.

Next Melanie, her lips pursed and eyes looking tired brought the kettle and a fresh tea bag. He'd seen that look during the breast cancer crisis fifteen years earlier: more certain evidence that she was upset. He felt an invisible divide growing between them.

Maybe the nightmares? Was I saying things in my sleep?

He stole a glance at the woman he adored. She still wore her hair long, although it was silver now. Her nose and chin had grown more prominent over the years, but her sky-blue eyes still hypnotized him. Her matronly hips, her graceful manner—she was still beautiful, the blonde cheerleader gringa with Texan roots who had somehow fallen for the caramel-skinned Mexican kid from Las Cruces. More than once, he'd had to fight off Anglo boys who regarded it unseemly that such a gorgeous white girl should be going out with a "beaner." It had helped that Frankie was a good football player, leading the Las Cruces High School Bulldogs to a district championship in the 1943 season. He had more than held his own in several scuffles. After a few bloody noses and a broken tooth or two, Melanie's would-be suitors had declared a grudging truce, in part because the gringo boys themselves were finding female attractions on the other side of the ethnic tracks.

But courting and winning the flamboyant Melanie Bates had been no simple matter. In addition to being gringa, Melanie was a Methodist, not a Catholic, which had been a virtual nonstarter for Frankie's mother, Mama Elena. By contrast and to their credit, despite their unease with the idea of having a Mexican boy as their daughter's suitor, Melanie's parents had raised no objection. It hadn't hurt that Frankie was gifted with charm and confidence and was a born salesman.

Mama Elena had been another matter entirely. She regarded Anglos with the measured disdain of someone whose country had been invaded by *los Norteamericanos* a hundred years earlier on the pretext of defending the US southern border. The actual motive, she believed, was to steal Mexican land, an assumption that had proved correct after a vast swath of Mexican territory was ceded at war's end to the United States.

Mama, Frankie knew, had always imagined that her sons would marry olive-skinned, raven-haired beauties from good Catholic families, and that she would be surrounded by a bevy of brown-eyed babies as she aged into grandmother-hood.

But a gringa and a Methodist to boot! *¡Ay dios mio!* Frankie had been more than mildly concerned that his mother might use her formidable persuasive power in the spiritual realm to influence his patron, Saint Francis of Assisi, to head off this disaster by planting a vocation to the priesthood in Frankie. If she had, the attempt had apparently failed, or the saint himself had overruled the effort, concluding that Frankie would be a rather bad candidate for the Order of Friars Minor. Frankie's stirrings were not of the religious sort.

The ball had clearly fallen into Melanie's court. Frankie wouldn't have blamed her for giving up and walking away. God knew she had enough other, less complicated opportunities with gringo boys. Instead, she had quietly but firmly set about finding ways to win Elena over. First, she learned to speak Spanish, albeit with a broad Texas inflection that reminded Frankie of Charley Pride singing a Johnny Rodriguez song. Then, with the guidance of Josefina, the Bateses' maid and housekeeper, she began learning the mysteries of cooking in the unique New Mexico fashion, so often incorrectly labeled "Mexican" or "Tex-Mex." Before long, she was impressing Elena with her mastery of green and red chile dishes, *Nuevo Mexico* style. And while Melanie had never abandoned her Methodist faith, she would occasionally attend Mass with Frankie, and she allowed their daughter to be raised Catholic.

Grudgingly at first, Mama Elena had felt compelled to admit that Frankie had found a good one. Later, when she thought only her friends were in earshot, she would speak proudly of her daughter-in-law, *la güera*. And even now, watching Melanie place the cut fruit on the table, Frankie couldn't believe his luck.

But Frankie knew that ghosts of his unresolved past were stirring. Was it Faulkner who had said that the past was never dead, that it was never even past? The recent nightmares and an unexpected contact about long-ago events were proof of that. The gnawing feeling in his gut, dormant for so long and aroused so recently, needed to be confronted and reconciled somehow. He owed it to this woman.

But how could he reveal the deep secret that could shatter their world? And how could he make amends for something shameful that had happened a half century ago?

"Thank you, dear," Frankie said after savoring one last strawberry. "That hit the spot. Since I'm up, I think I'll do some paperwork and then meet Ellen at the work site on campus. I want to check on the dorm project this morning." He paused to see if Melanie would respond to this tepid ice-breaking overture. When she didn't, he shrugged slightly and continued. "It's also time I dropped by the cemetery with some fresh flowers for my mother and father."

As he turned toward the office off the kitchen, Frankie tried to remember when he had last felt this distant from his wife.

Chapter 2

The Psychic Angst of a Schoolgirl

Same Day

Shinjuku Park Hyatt, Tokyo

Kume Matsuhata idly stirred the ice in her glass with her finger as she waited for a reaction from Genevieve LaTour, her best friend and business partner. Genevieve was seated across from Kume at the Peak Bar, forty-one stories above street level, reviewing Kume's final plans for the spring collection. Tokyo's endless skyline, visible through floor-to-ceiling windows along the far wall, twinkled in the blue twilight.

Genevieve finally leaned back and lit her Player's cigarette. She blew a ragged cirrus of smoke across the lip of her martini, then smiled at Kume. "It's brilliant."

Kume returned the smile. "I thought you would agree."

When Fashion Week had been cut short in New York the previous month after the World Trade Center attack, all hell had broken loose. The designers and fashion houses had scrambled like crazy to salvage their seasonal collections. A few of the newer studios, already way overextended, had been forced to close their doors. Luckily, Kume's assistants Haruko and Chika had already been in town. While rescue workers had been picking through the smoking rubble of the Twin Towers, Chika had shown great initiative and lined up private showings with the big stores.

"So you'll be traveling to New York with the spring line in late November?" Genevieve asked.

Kume nodded distractedly. September eleven was etched deeply in her mind. She had been scheduled to fly to New York that morning, Fashion Week being a major exposition for design houses. Her young protégés had been working hard preparing for the big event. Kume herself would introduce the spring line in Bryant Park two days later. Much was riding on the success of the spring line, with factories in Vietnam and the Philippines poised to fill orders.

Kume would later learn that Haruko and Chika had been invited to attend a private breakfast for designers at Windows on the World in Building One of the World Trade Center. But Chika, much to Haruko's chagrin, had declined the invitation, deciding at the last minute that they should instead make sure all final preparations for the runway were complete and that the lighting, music, and wardrobe changes would work flaw- lessly—all to impress Kume.

Lucky, indeed, Kume thought to herself. As chance would have it, she had already settled into her seat at the front of the plane with a fresh cup of coffee as the Boeing 747 was taxiing for takeoff at Narita. Then the plane had abruptly halted and, after a brief delay, turned around and returned to the terminal with no explanation from the cockpit.

There would be no flights to the US that day. But in the chaos that followed, Haruko and Chika had deftly secured commitments for private showings before the year end for buyers at Bergdorf, Saks, and Bloomingdale's.

Kume took a sip of water and studied her old mentor and friend. Genevieve still had the looks and bearing of the Parisian athlete-turned-model she had been in her younger days. If it weren't for the tracery of thin smoker's lines around her lips that reminded Kume of cracked china, she could have still passed as a younger Catherine Deneuve. How fortuitous it was all those years ago that Genevieve had been dispatched to Tokyo on a model search for the Ford Agency at exactly the time that Kume had entered a beauty contest during the pageantry preceding the 1964 Tokyo Olympics.

Was it just coincidence that Genevieve had "discovered" her there? *Karma, destiny—call it whatever,* Kume thought. Without it, their paths likely never would have crossed. Kume knew she could well have ended up the wife of a fisherman in Tohoku instead of an international fashion model and the owner of the iconic Tokyo fashion house, Kumiko Ltd. Genevieve had soon become her best friend and business partner. Under Genevieve's inspiration, they had opened Chez Kume, a trendy Franco/Asian restaurant in the Shinjuku skyscraper district. Genevieve had turned it into a culinary destination increasingly popular with an international clientele.

Yes, it has been quite a ride.

"Does your mother know your plans?" Genevieve put the question as delicately as she always did. She was fully aware, Kume knew, of the sometimes frosty relationship between Kume and her mother, Noriko.

Kume nodded with a knowing smile and a slight roll of the eyes. "I told her yesterday. She didn't seem enthused, but I'm not surprised. She's never been good at disguising her feelings about New York—or her daughter's business and other interests there."

"I suppose Gary's name came up," Genevieve said with a mischievous wink.

"Ah, Gary." Kume sighed as she studied the ice cubes in her glass. "It was against my better judgment, but I agreed to meet him. He was persistent—I'll give him that. He wants to have dinner. My mother didn't mention his name, but I can tell she knows I'll be seeing him."

Kume glanced up and away, letting her eyes settle on one of the paper lanterns glowing warmly in the bar, which, even during happy hour, exuded a romantic wistfulness. She could feel the familiar ache at the base of her rib cage—a feeling of anticipation mixed with dread—and wondered if it would ever really end. Times like this made her wish she was more like Genevieve, whose romantic life seemed to consist of a seamless succession of lovers, strangers, and chance encounters, all without strings or apparent emotional hangover. The fact that Gary Masterson still had the power to make Kume feel the psychic angst of a schoolgirl annoyed and embarrassed her.

Genevieve finished the cigarette and drained her drink. "Give my regards to the Great White Way, and good luck with the showings. I'm guessing that New York could use a little lighthearted distraction right about now, and the spring line could be just what the doctor ordered." She turned to Kume and added impishly, in French-accented English, "And when you get back, I expect details. *Details!*"

Kume cringed theatrically. Genevieve possessed a shameless curiosity when it came to matters of the heart, and especially of the body. This had exhibited itself early in their friendship, shortly after Kume had arrived in New York as Genevieve's prized recruit to the Ford Agency modeling stable. Kume had been astonished at Genevieve's indifference to nudity—hers or anyone else's.

Eileen and Jerry Ford had occasionally brought the girls to their Connecticut country home for a summer outing away from the city. Kume remembered her shock during her first time there when Genevieve had stepped out of her shorts, dropped her halter top, and dived into the pool completely nude. After a lap or two, she had emerged, dripping, her nipples firm as thimbles, her pubic hair trimmed in a discreet vertical line.

Kume remembered thinking, *How very French!*

Emboldened, the other girls had followed suit, plunging in *au naturel*, splashing happily, and later lying out to sunbathe without worrying about tan lines.

For a young woman like Kume, who hailed from a culture of strict modesty in a Japanese backwater like Sendai, such behavior had seemed incomprehensible at the time. But even then, Kume had to admit, she had envied Genevieve's absence of inhibitions and self-consciousness. She came to understand the value of those traits in the close backstage confines of runway modeling assignments, where a frenetic tableau of young, unclad female bodies undergoing quick wardrobe changes was unnervingly commonplace. It was something she had learned to accept. But swimming naked at the Fords' country estate was not.

With a look of resignation, Kume replied, "I promise to tell you everything."

Chapter 3

Dos Equis, Iwo Joe, Star Lily . . .

Same Day

Las Cruces, New Mexico

Frankie turned the key, and the diesel engine of the Ford F-250 Super Duty clattered to life. It felt satisfying to be doing something useful like checking on the work site at the university. It was a good job that was likely to keep José and the crew busy for at least another year.

Frankie still felt uneasy about the chilly way in which he and Melanie had parted earlier. He had much to think about, like the letter he had received over the summer from a young man named Andrew Mondragón. The letter had opened old wounds and left him feeling simultaneously nostalgic and unsettled, as though the past was about to overtake the present.

The letter had arrived in late July. A summer rain, as violent as it was fleeting, had come and gone in the predawn hours, gouging rivulets in the back garden and leaving an already evaporating puddle in the front courtyard. Frankie had noticed the puddle after picking up the mail, which had been delivered before noon—about two hours earlier than usual.

He was sorting through a stack of junk mail in the tiled entryway when he'd spotted the handwritten envelope with his name on it.

"Andrew Mondragón," he said aloud, drawing out each syllable as he read the unfamiliar name on the return address.

Sometimes local realtors and other solicitors sent bulk mail dressed up to look like it had been individually sent, complete with a cursive font meant to resemble someone's handwriting. But the blue ink on this envelope had been smudged and was clearly the real deal.

Frankie opened the business-sized envelope and, after reading the opening paragraph of the two-page letter, looked up furtively, suddenly wanting privacy. He could hear Melanie puttering in the kitchen and made a beeline to the adjacent office. Once seated behind his desk, he pored over the letter, rereading it twice. Beads of sweat moistened his forehead. He stood to pace but then remembered his footlocker.

"You want some chopped salad?" Melanie asked as he passed her once again in the kitchen. "I'm going to make some for lunch. Ellen gave me a honey-lime dressing recipe she found online."

"Sure," Frankie said over his shoulder on his way out the French doors. "Just give me a minute."

He made the short trip to the other side of the hacienda and stopped outside the storage shed, a place he seldom visited. After he turned the door handle and flipped on the light, he spied it immediately: the old, olive-drab footlocker sitting off in a corner in dusty silence. He hadn't opened it in years, but he knew what he was looking for. He fumbled around until he felt it: the neatly tied bundle of letters and notes, his mother's file on the search for his brother, Ramón.

It was just where he had expected it to be, tucked away in a corner. After untying the ribbon, he found a list of names of people Mama Elena had tried to contact. Among them was a Porfirio Mondragón from Capitán, New Mexico. Mama's notes indicated that she had never received a response.

It occurred to Frankie that Andrew had gone to some trouble to locate him. Satisfied that the contact seemed genuine, Frankie carefully reassembled the file, placed Andrew's letter on top, and then replaced the file where he had found it. He would have to consider what to do about the letter.

As Frankie was lowering the heavy lid of the trunk, it began to slip from his grasp. He reflexively grabbed the lid with both hands and felt the glued lining on one corner give way. A black-and-white photograph that had been hiding behind the lining dropped out and landed on the floor directly in front of him. He knew his life was about to change.

Frankie slowly lowered the lid and picked up the photo, cradling it carefully. It was a picture of three people: two young American servicemen and a Japanese girl. The men were smiling, but the girl wore a stoic expression. She was lovely. On the back, someone had handwritten the letters *XX-IJ*, with a drawing of a lily and a word in *kanji* and English.

He mouthed the words, *"Dos Equis. Iwo Joe. Star Lily. Noriko."*

The dark past came flooding back, and his hands began to tremble. He felt his face flush.

He'd tucked the photo inside the collection of letters and closed the lid, knowing full well that he had released something that could not be contained by simply shutting an old army trunk.

Frankie's thoughts returned to the present as he reached the work site. He donned his hard hat, hitched up his Wranglers, and walked over to where stalks of rebar were poking upward from plywood forms. Concrete mixers stood by with their cavernous bellies rotating slowly.

Frankie greeted his foreman. "*Buenos días, José. ¿Como estamos?*"

"*Bien, jefe. Casi estamos listos para echar el cemento,*" José retorted, smiling broadly, a gold incisor glinting in the morning sun.

Ellen strode over holding a clipboard. Dressed in a pair of Levi's and a navy-blue T-shirt bearing the company logo, she wore her dark hair in a ponytail that swung side-to-side from beneath her hard hat. Her toned arms glowed golden brown in the morning sun.

"Hey, Dad. I just wanted you to be comfortable with the amount of mud we're going to be pouring in those forms. Damn architectural consultants came up with an estimate that was way low in my opinion—and José's, too. We added another hundred yards for structural strength. Can't have the building collapse on the little darlings, can we?" She held out the clipboard. "Here are the calculations, if you're interested. They'll probably bitch about it, but so be it. You got our back, right?"

Frankie grunted, rubbed his thigh, and waved away the estimate. "No problem. I'll take any heat. Go ahead and pour."

He was so proud of Ellen. She was tough as a hobnailed boot. During her youth, instead of hanging out with her friends or chasing boys, she had preferred accompanying her dad to jobsites around Las Cruces, learning construction from the ground up. Now approaching forty, she ran the show. Worker, architect, supplier—nobody could put anything over on her, and woe betide the poor bastard who tried. She had a special distrust of architects.

Frankie knew he couldn't have found a better project manager anywhere, even if she was his daughter. Four years at the University of Texas-El Paso had given her a solid engineering background and a conviction that she preferred life on a small-town scale.

Frankie smiled at how much she reminded him of Melanie, who often fretted that Ellen had yet to marry. Not that she lacked for male companionship. A serial dater, Ellen was a devotee of western dancing and hard drinking who could also belt out *rancheras* with the best mariachis. And when she wasn't cussing a blue streak at subcontractors or inspectors at the site—or raising holy hell downtown at the building department to speed up permits—she loved taking her Harley Fat Boy out on long rides through the San Andres and Sacramento Mountains. She usually rode with an intimidating peloton of leather-vested and tattooed biker friends, *Los Cruceros*, humming along with Jerry Jeff, Waylon, and Buck Owens thumping through her headphones.

What Frankie admired most was her devotion to her mother and the fiercely protective care she had taken of Melanie during the breast cancer crisis and treatment. Frankie doubted that Melanie or he could have made it without her.

"You don't need me here anymore, do you?" he asked.

Ellen shook her head, grinning. "Nope, we're good."

"Well then, I think I'll take a ride over to the Bataan Monument before heading to Enrique's to pick up some Hatch Big Jim's for your mother. She's doing posole tonight."

"Leave some for me." Ellen spun on her Lucchese boot heel and gave José a fist pump, signaling him to proceed with the pour.

Frankie flashed a thumbs-up and headed back to his truck.

Out on the road, the air was clear and cool, so Frankie lowered his window. From old habit, he cocked an ear to listen. Supposedly the wind working through the cathedral-like jagged spires of the Organ Mountains sometimes made a haunting sound like organ music—thus, the name. But Frankie had his doubts. He had never heard anything, and it was quiet again today.

The peaks pushed skyward ahead of him as he made his way to the monument on the northern outskirts of Las Cruces. Suddenly there they were, appearing as though trudging through the desert: the painful skeletal bronze figures, two American and one Filipino, the middle one supported by the two on either side.

What must that have been like? Frankie wondered as he parked the truck. *Would Ramón have looked like that?*

As he picked up a candy wrapper and an empty red-and-silver Tecate beer can, he couldn't help thinking about those harrowing days so many years ago. His brother, Ramón, had enlisted in a National Guard antiaircraft artillery unit that had been hastily mustered and shipped off to Manila in the fall of 1941 as the crisis with Japan deepened. Four months after the December Japanese attacks, the remaining American and Filipino forces surrendered on Bataan. Frankie's family received no word regarding the identities of the Americans captured. Nevertheless, Mama Elena refused to abandon hope that Ramón was still alive.

Weeks went by, then months. The war news was all about Europe, or Russia, or North Africa. It was as though the Pacific had ceased to exist. Then suddenly there came the unexpected defeat of the Combined Fleet of Imperial Japan in the carrier battle of Midway Island. And the marines landed on Guadalcanal.

But still no word about Ramón.

Frankie remembered how he had felt watching his mother saying her rosaries. He knew he needed to do something. After graduation in 1944, he and his best friend, Bobby Joe Lassiter, decided to enlist. They were itching to get into the fight and hoped the war wouldn't end before they had their chance. Bobby Joe had his heart set on flying and joined the US Army Air Force. He survived nineteen missions as a waist gunner on a B-17 called *Mama's Boy* in an Eighth Air Force heavy bomber group out of Molesworth, England, during the waning months of the war in Europe.

Frankie's conversation with his parents when he told them his plans to enlist in the army was not pleasant. They pleaded with him to change his mind. For all they knew, he was their only son. The family had done its part, they reasoned. Frankie should remain home and let others do the fighting.

But he ignored their pleas.

Frankie joined the army in August 1944—without his parents' blessing. Following basic infantry training in Texas at Camp Hood, he returned home for a farewell visit. That was when Elena placed a small gold crucifix around his neck, kissed him, and said, "*Dios te cuide, mi hijo.*" She turned and hugged her husband, Alejandro, a trickle of a tear tracing down her cheek.

Nearly two years would pass before Frankie would see his parents again.

He deposited the trash in a receptacle and shook his head, realizing he was still wearing the hard hat. He removed it in salute to the haggard bronze figures and said a silent prayer. After popping an Aleve to help dull the ache in his thigh, he limped back to the pickup.

At the cemetery down near the river, Frankie went about the familiar ritual. He took special care to clean his parents' headstones, removing grass cuttings and polishing the smooth granite with his wet handkerchief. As he brushed off an errant cottonwood leaf, Frankie prepared for the customary conversation. He laid the spray of chrysanthemums between the graves and quietly apologized for taking so long between visits.

Would Mama be irritated that he hadn't kept the promise he had made to her on her deathbed? Obsessed by the need to know the fate of her son Ramón, she had implored Frankie to find out what had happened to his older brother. He'd vowed he would.

Frankie took a seat on the grass, hugged his knees, and grimaced at the sharp pain that knifed through his thigh. He closed his eyes as he rocked back and forth.

He was a sophomore in high school when Bataan fell in April 1942. Rumors that Ramón was seen at Camp O'Donnell and then later at Cabanatuan, where thousands of prisoners were taken, had given Mama Elena hope.

"That's where the trail went cold," Frankie said matter-of-factly, as if his mother were still alive and seated across from him in the grass. "Well, until you got the letter from the War Department after the war. Said they found a record at the former camp at Cabanatuan listing a Sergeant R. Castillo among the prisoners who died in 1943."

Ramón had been officially declared dead.

"It must have been crushing to read those words," Frankie continued. "But you never believed it—not for a minute. You never accepted the letter as the final word about Ramón. You couldn't believe God would allow that to happen, not after all your prayers. You were convinced there had been a mistake and another R. Castillo had died."

After the war, Mama Elena had spent five years and a small fortune hunting down former members of the New Mexico 200th

Coast Artillery Regiment, Ramón's old unit. She was sure she'd find someone who could tell her Ramón had found a way to survive and had been moved somewhere else or had escaped. She and Papa pored over the reports she had collected from the survivors. So many blind alleys and dead ends from men whose memories and testimony were addled by their experiences and post traumatic stress. Her disappointment was heartbreaking. She saved every letter, adding her own notes, as though she believed that eventually they'd provide the keys to unlock Ramón's fate.

"Well, Mama, maybe your prayers have been answered after all. I got a letter a few months ago from someone who may have information about Ramón."

Frankie paused, halfway expecting to hear the excited whisper of an old Mexican woman. Or maybe just a giggle. It had occurred to him that Mama and Ramón had very probably been united in the hereafter for many years. As he gazed upward, he suspected that even now they were enjoying the spectacle of Frankie's futile efforts and sharing a fine laugh at his expense. In her wisdom, Mama probably knew that the search for Ramón would benefit Frankie most of all.

But the only sounds in the cemetery came from the mournful cooing of a dove and the rustle of cottonwood leaves being carried away by the fall breeze.

"The person who sent me the letter is a young man named Andrew Mondragón," Frankie said. "His grandfather, Porfirio, died earlier this year, and Andrew came across a bunch of personal items in Porfirio's belongings that led him to contact me. It was one of your letters, Mama, that you wrote to former prisoners. Andrew's grandfather never responded, leaving you at another dead end.

"According to Andrew, his grandfather—the family called him Frío—left behind a handwritten memoir of his time as a young soldier in the Philippines and as a prisoner of the Japanese. Andrew says the memoir contains information about someone who could be Ramón. Andrew sent me the memoir, Mama. I'll let you know if it says anything new about Ramón."

Frankie heard a car door slam somewhere nearby and suddenly felt self-conscious. He picked himself up, took one last glance at his parents' graves, and then crossed himself before limping back to the truck.

Melanie would kill him if he forgot to pick up the green chiles on the way home.

Chapter 4

With Lives
as Complicated as Theirs

Same Day

Midtown, New York

As he gazed bleary-eyed at the city below from his fiftieth-floor office window in the Chrysler Building, Gary Masterson fought off another yawn. The avenues heading north along the Upper East Side glowed with a steady stream of headlights and taillights, each street carving a narrow, luminescent canyon through the never-ending expanse of half-lit buildings. The view usually inspired Gary, but tonight he felt only tired, bone-weary after the long flight from Rio de Janeiro. He stretched and rolled his head around in a circular motion to loosen his neck muscles, which were still rigid from the nap on his couch. If all went well, he'd enjoy a quiet couple of days before the board meeting later in the week.

He was just returning to his leather chair when the phone on his desk rang. He glanced at the caller ID on his private line and was surprised to see Nathan Goldman's name. He picked up the receiver.

"Nate," he said, unable to mask the grogginess in his voice. "What the hell are you doing in your office at this hour? I thought bureaucrats never worked late."

"And good evening to you, Gary. I might ask you the same question."

Gary had known Nate since prep school, although their paths had diverged shortly after graduation. Nate now served as an undersecretary at the State Department, where he oversaw Asian affairs, but his most recent promotion made little impact on their friendship. In fact, the two had remained in regular contact through countless professional and personal adventures over the years.

Gary managed a tired smile. "How did you know I'd be here?"

"Just a guess. Bag a few birds way south of the border? How's Cristina doing?"

"Just fine. She wants me to spend more time down there, but that's just not in the cards." Gary could have offered a longer answer, but he didn't have the energy. "What's up?"

"I may need a favor. Do you have any plans to be in the Far East anytime soon? I mean, being the big cheese in a Fortune 500 company, you probably have some reason to go to Beijing, Hong Kong, Tokyo . . ."

Gary thought a moment. "Tokyo, maybe not so much, but I may have business in Singapore and Seoul sometime soon. What do you have in mind?"

"It's a weird bit of information that our friends in Langley picked up while they were doing some electronic snooping on the Korean Peninsula and the northern Japanese islands. Has to do with gold."

"Gold?"

"Apparently a hoard of it went missing from Japan's wartime treasury during WW II. I'd like to get a better handle on it, but an official US inquiry is out of the question. Might compromise our methods and sources. I think you could be of help just being an American businessman asking some innocent, but discreet questions. Could you come down and talk about it before your trip? Dinner would be on me."

"Fine." The gears were already turning in Gary's brain, but his thoughts had little to do with gold or Japan's wartime treasury. "Let me call you next week."

Gary put down the phone and whipped out a quick e-mail to his assistant, who had already gone home for the evening and wouldn't return until Monday:

> *Set up a meeting in DC with Nathan, and find out how far in advance you need to call to make a reservation for two at Le Bernardin in late November.*

He paused before hitting *send*, suddenly aware that he might be getting ahead of himself with the second part of his message. He felt like a sixteen-year-old with his hormones on fire. Indeed, the prospect of seeing Kume again was all it had taken to overcome his jet lag. And now that rendezvous might occur earlier—during a stopover in Tokyo.

Would she be amenable? Would she even pick up if he dialed her number? He stared at the phone on his desk without really seeing it, his thoughts a jumble of the past and present, of mistakes made and lessons learned, of emotions felt too keenly to be safely indulged. With lives as complicated as theirs, he knew he should just be happy if she answered his call.

Saturday, October 6, 2001

Shinjuku-ku, Tokyo

Kume set down the cup of green tea, her second of the morning, and answered the phone on the second ring. "Hello?" she said from the tidy kitchen of her luxury two-bedroom apartment.

"Hey."

Kume felt an involuntary twist in the pit of her stomach. The voice on the other end of the line belonged to Gary Masterson.

She steadied herself and answered as evenly as she could. "What a surprise. How are you, Gary? And to what do I owe this unexpected call?" Kume could easily visualize Gary. When he was in high spirits, he reminded her of an Irish setter— goofy with delight and practically wagging his tail. She could sense that excitement now.

"We're still on for dinner next month, right? Do we have a date yet? I know a French restaurant that's almost impossible to get into—but worth the trouble." His words tumbled out in an excited stream.

"Whoa, slow down. Yes. Dinner plans are still on. I'm checking my calendar now." She paused to open her leather-bound daily planner, which lay beside a couple of designer pens on her otherwise empty kitchen bar. "Looks like Tuesday, the twenty-seventh of November will work best."

"Great. Listen, you wouldn't happen to be available around October thirtieth for an impromptu visit, would you?"

Kume was taken aback. "Here in Tokyo?" She couldn't mask the mild dread in her voice and knew that Gary would pick up on it.

"I know it's rather spur of the moment," he said. "And I totally understand if you can't, but I have to be in Singapore and Seoul on business. Thought I could make a quick stopover in Tokyo."

Her silence spoke volumes.

She heard him hesitate for a moment and then exhale. "Okay, bad idea."

Kume feigned disappointment. "I'm really sorry, Gary." She wanted to tell him that she couldn't wait for the visit—but feared it, too. Instead, she lied. "I'm actually going to be back home with my parents in Sendai at the end of the month. I hope your trip is a success. I look forward to seeing you in New York." She bit her lip. "Ciao."

Kume put the phone down, mind racing, and tried to process what had just happened. It was unlike Gary to make a random phone call to breezily invite himself to see her on her home turf. That had never happened, not in the ten years since they had last communicated. Why the sudden interest?

She glanced at her watch and remembered she was due for her weekly chat with her mother. It was always a chore, something like going to the exercise studio. She was always happiest when it was over.

Chapter 5

Frío and the Oyabun

Sunday, October 7, 2001

Mesilla, New Mexico

Frankie sat upright in his favorite chair, normally reclined at a more relaxed angle, and watched from his living room as President Bush addressed the nation on television. The AC purred in the background.

"Good afternoon," the president said from behind a desk in the Treaty Room, where he was flanked by an American flag on his right and the deep blue presidential flag on his left. He wore a bold red tie and stared directly at the camera. "On my orders, the United States military has begun strikes against al-Qaeda terrorist training camps and military installations of the Taliban regime in Afghanistan. These carefully targeted actions are designed to disrupt the use of Afghanistan as a terrorist base of operations and to attack the military capability of the Taliban regime.

"We are joined in this operation by our staunch friend, Great Britain. Other close friends, including Canada, Australia,

Germany, and France, have pledged forces as the operation unfolds. More than forty countries in the Middle East, Africa, Europe, and across Asia have granted air transit or landing rights. Many more have shared intelligence. We are supported by the collective will of the world.

"More than two weeks ago, I gave Taliban leaders a series of clear and specific demands: close terrorist training camps; hand over leaders of the al-Qaeda network; and return all foreign nationals, including American citizens, unjustly detained in your country. None of these demands were met. And now the Taliban will pay a price. By destroying camps and disrupting communications, we will make it more difficult for the terror network to train new recruits and coordinate their evil plans."

Good, Frankie thought. *About time those bastards found out that payback is a bitch.* He stood and stretched.

"You're not going to watch the rest of his speech?" asked Melanie, who was standing in the kitchen doorway. She was still brandishing a pair of clippers, having just come in from the back garden, where she'd been tidying a bed of perennials under the late morning shade from the old elms. She wore her long gray hair in a chignon, no doubt to keep it out of her face while she worked.

"I'll wait for the movie to come out," Frankie quipped.

She raised an eyebrow in his direction.

"The president said all I needed to hear," Frankie explained with a chuckle. "I've got some paperwork to take care of."

Once in his office, he closed the door behind him and withdrew a blue cloth-covered three-ring binder from a large envelope. Frío's manuscript. It hadn't been easy to persuade Andrew Mondragón to allow him to read his grandfather's entire original document, but it had finally arrived as promised in Frankie's business post office box.

Frankie opened the binder and studied the handwriting, which was messy but still legible. It was impossible to tell how long ago it had actually been penned, but the condition of the yellow ruled paper and the way the ballpoint ink had bled into it hinted at twenty years or more. According to Andrew, he had come across the binder in the bottom drawer of an old desk that had belonged to Frío.

Frankie read the first several pages and then paused, intrigued. Frío had devoted the opening pages to a description of his family's history in Lincoln County. Those were the territorial days, a largely lawless time when range feuds, cattle rustling, renegade Apaches, and Texas desperados on the run had made life colorful and precarious. Frío's grandfather had emerged as a handyman with a pistol. He had taken sides in the Lincoln County War in the 1870s, had befriended Billy the Kid, and had eventually been ambushed as he rode alone on a mountain road in 1883—an unsolved murder and legacy of the many vendettas spawned during that violent time. Frío had grown up idolizing the larger-than-life image of his grandfather and had wanted nothing more than to become a swaggering *pistolero* like him. He had practiced for hours with his grandfather's Colt and had become a crack shot, blasting away at imaginary Apaches and horse thieves in the high pine country surrounding the village of Capitán.

Frankie thought about how, during his own childhood, some of the old-timers in Las Cruces and Old Mesilla had loved to tell tales about the Kid and their encounters with the famous young gunman. They had greatly embellished their stories, which deserved to be taken with a dash of salt. But the Frío manuscript exuded authenticity. Frankie conceded that it was possible that Frío's grandfather had known Billy the Kid.

Frankie continued reading. When war with Japan appeared inevitable, the New Mexico National Guard was federalized as an antiaircraft artillery unit, the 200th Coast Artillery. Young Frío had welcomed this as an opportunity to see some real action. He joined the unit in April 1941 and spent several months training at Fort Bliss. In September, he was shipped to the Philippines, where the unit was deployed to defend Clark Field.

Frankie was already familiar with much of the history of the 200th and its desperate struggle on the Bataan Peninsula against superior Japanese forces in the months following the attacks on Pearl Harbor and the Philippines. He had also read extensively about the atrocities committed against Allied captives on the Bataan Death March. What interested him as he skimmed Frío's account were the latter's personal experiences, particularly several episodes involving others, including a Private Pablo Padilla, a guard called La Culebra, another guard called El Tuerto, and someone simply referred to as Ramón.

Frankie continued skimming the manuscript for another two hours, pausing once to reheat some leftover soup and once to visit the bathroom. To his great frustration, the memoir described only the events of 1941 to mid-1944, fully a year before the end of the war and liberation of prisoners. If Ramón had survived past that point, the memoir would be useless in establishing his fate. Frankie would have to study the document in detail for any clues that might yield information about what had happened to his brother. For now, it was enough to know that Frío had known someone named Ramón who could very well have been Ramón Castillo.

Frankie felt oddly unfaithful and anxious. It was not like him to keep things from Melanie, but this Frío business had opened a dangerous window on a huge secret from his past with the potential to upend their world. He had no idea where things would lead.

Quietly, he closed the binder and returned it to its drawer in the filing cabinet.

Monday, October 8, 2001

Sendai, Miyagi Prefecture, Japan

"Nori-chan, come, wake up. You should see this." Soichiro Matsuhata was up very early, as usual, checking late weather reports, Tokyo fish market prices, and scanning international news services. "It looks like the Americans are finally going after the people responsible for the attacks in New York and Washington last month."

Soichiro heard the bedroom door slide open, and a moment later Noriko appeared from behind a backlit partition. She pulled a shawl over her shoulders, her thin black slippers shuffling rhythmically on the bamboo flooring.

"God help them," she said as she joined her husband on the couch.

Left unsaid was what she had meant by *them*. But the comment reminded Soichiro of the remark attributed to Admiral Isoroku Yamamoto during the national euphoria following the success of the Combined Fleet's surprise attack on the American naval base in Hawaii in 1941. Yamamoto's sobering words, which suggested that Japan had only succeeded in waking a sleeping giant, prophesized what would become a catastrophe for the Yamato people.

On the far wall directly across from them, the TV in the built-in cabinet showed the American president speaking while a Japanese translation ran along the bottom of the screen.

"Is this live?" Noriko asked, arching her perfectly shaped eyebrows. Her long, dark hair, which she dyed to preserve its original color, accentuated her oval-shaped face.

Soichiro shook his head. "He spoke several hours ago—yesterday afternoon in Washington."

President Bush called the impending military operation Enduring Freedom. His words were measured, but he appeared determined. When he was finished, he closed his address by saying, "May God continue to bless America."

Soichiro turned off the TV with the remote and then wrapped his arm around Noriko, mindful of the effect that news of bombing and the violence of war always had on her. She was strong, this Okinawan girl who had braved the "typhoon of steel" that the Americans had unleashed on her island home in the spring of 1945. Scenes of unspeakable horror and a deeply buried grief over the fate of her parents continued to haunt her, even now, decades later. Soichiro felt the involuntary quiver as she nestled closer to him.

He frowned. "It was only a matter of time. The Americans couldn't stand by and let terrorists attack them on their home soil. There will be hell to pay. I hope they get them. There can be no sympathy for people who murder civilians to make a statement. What do they think they've accomplished? Where's the honor in that?"

The question hung in the air rhetorically.

For Soichiro, this prompted the venting of an old, familiar complaint. "We were called dishonorable for our surprise attack on Pearl Harbor. But there was a difference. We were attacking *military* targets. Besides, we had no choice.

Washington's embargo deprived us of raw materials we needed to survive. We did only what we had to do."

Soichiro knew he was sounding tiresome—that this line of reasoning that had sustained him through all the pain and humiliation after 1945 had worn thin with his wife. Over the years, he had pondered the honor—and even the morality—of LeMay's fleets of B-29s raining napalm, magnesium, and white phosphorus firebombs on tinderbox Japanese cities, incinerating untold thousands of innocent civilians. And then the obscenity of the atomic destruction of two cities having little strategic value. Where was the morality or honor in that? What was the justification, particularly when Japan was all but prostrate and virtually incapable of self-defense against aerial attack?

He wondered whether the Muslim terror networks would ever experience anything like the full might of unrestricted US military power. Would the Americans lay waste to cities in the Middle East the way they had in Japan? Would they kill thousands of noncombatants to punish the guilty?

He decided to change the subject.

"I promised Midorikawa-san I would drop over for a visit today. He's not looking well. I told him years ago that his smoking would kill him, and it seems that my prediction may have been all too accurate." Soichiro paused. "Would you like to come?" he asked hopefully. "He always asks for you."

"His smoking isn't his only problem," Noriko murmured darkly. "It may be that the sins of his life are finally catching up with him. He has a lot to answer for."

Soichiro didn't want to have this argument today. Noriko was adamant in the disdain she held for Kazuo Midorikawa, perhaps with reason. But the *oyabun* was a steadfast friend to whom Soichiro was indebted, and honor required that respect be paid.

The two men had much in common, Soichiro and Kazuo. Both born and raised in Sendai, they had been conscripted as seventeen-year-olds into the Imperial Japanese Army in 1941. Theirs was a storied unit, the Second Division, proudly known as the Sendai Division. Many hours had been spent in Kazuo's beautiful home with the splendid gardens as, over cups of sake, they reminisced about their shared wartime experiences, most notably on the small island of Guadalcanal in the Solomon archipelago.

Soichiro stood and marched toward the *genkan*, where his shoes waited among several others in a tidy wood rack near the front door. He was well aware that Kazuo was a hard man who was not above resorting to cruel means to achieve his ends. He was also aware that Noriko had heard stories, many stories, about black market profiteering in the cold, bitter years following Japan's capitulation. They had argued several times over her inability to reconcile the brutality, extortion, and unsavory methods that attended the making of Kazuo's yakuza fiefdom with what she called Soichiro's uncritical attachment to the man. She said she couldn't figure how a true son of Japan could treat his own Yamato people so pitilessly.

She'd made it clear that if Soichiro felt he had to see Kazuo, fine. She wanted no part of it. Soichiro knew that it especially revolted his wife that the oyabun had always taken a special liking to her, and more than once, she'd had to ward off his unwelcome advances. She was clearly past wondering how her husband—"a good, honest man," in her words—could be friends with such a creature.

"I'll see you later," Soichiro grumbled softly as he reached for his baseball cap.

He would first drive over to Shiogama and pick up some fresh tuna and saury sashimi at the wholesale market. Kazuo loved his fish and had told Soichiro many times that he could always count on his "fisherman friend" to surprise him with the most delectable fresh cuts. Besides, his doctors had advised him to enjoy whatever he wanted to eat. Soichiro suspected that this was a tacit signal that the end wasn't far off, and that the oyabun should partake of what pleasures he could for as long as he could.

It bothered Soichiro that his wife harbored such ill will toward Kazuo. Nevertheless, he rationalized that this occasional visit was only a small mercy, a kindness. Whatever sins Kazuo would have to atone for in the hereafter, it was not for him to judge. Maybe the man had been exceedingly harsh in his business dealings, but Soichiro knew his friend had lost his newlywed wife, the love of his life, to American bombs in a pointless raid over Sendai in the final weeks of the war. Kazuo had been devastated and embittered. He had never remarried and thus had been deprived of the softening influence of female companionship.

Soichiro also knew that, without the help of Kazuo, his plan to build a successful fishing business after the war would have been immeasurably harder.

Once in the tiny driveway, he turned slightly as he reached for the car door, hoping for a conciliatory glance from Noriko through the kitchen window, but she was not there. With a sigh, he turned the key, started the Nissan, and backed out of the driveway.

Chapter 6

Why Take a Chance?

June 8, 1945

Makabe, Okinawa

The air is thick with the smell of cordite, burnt flesh, and blood. Blasted bodies and detached limbs litter the cave floor. The pale face is staring up at him, eyes wide with shock and fear. Her cheeks and forehead are dirt-streaked. She is dressed in what looks like a nurse's uniform. It's drenched in blood—hers or someone else's—he can't tell. She's clutching a Jap grenade. Her hands tremble. The grenade is not armed.

Frankie slings the carbine over his back and reaches for the girl. She tries to push him away, but she's too weak. The grenade falls from her grasp as her body goes limp, and Frankie picks her up, cradling her in his arms.

"Castillo!" his sergeant yells. "She's almost dead. Leave her here!"

Frankie ignores him. She weighs so little—no more than a rucksack of ammo. He carries her out of the cave and into the blinding sunlight, and finds the aid station, where medics are working on several wounded GIs. The medics are just kids, hardly older than Frankie, and their eyes have the glazed look of young men who have seen too much. They glare at Frankie for bringing one of *them* for medical attention. He puts her down on a litter. She squirms and tries again to get away. Frankie restrains her gently, puts his finger to his lips, and tries to calm her. She looks so frail and frightened.

Then, to Frankie's astonishment, she whispers, "Don't go."

One of the medics, a lanky fellow with a face covered in soot, gives Frankie a wry smile. "Got yourself a fighter, huh? She have a grenade?"

"Yes," Frankie grunts.

"You're lucky. We've been picking up pieces of our boys who see a wounded girl, go to help, and find themselves blown up by a concealed grenade. Kind of gives 'booby trap' a whole new meaning, don't you think? Most of the guys just shoot them now. Why take a chance?"

Frankie stares at the girl. She can't be more than sixteen or seventeen. He can't stay.

"You can go," the medic says. "We'll take care of her now."

Frankie turns to leave, but his eye catches the second medic reaching for a .45 automatic resting on a nearby table. Frankie wheels and unslings his carbine. He tries to shout a warning as he hears the pistol's hammer being cocked, but no sound comes from his mouth. He raises his weapon and squeezes the trigger.

Monday, October 22, 2001

Mesilla, New Mexico

When Frankie opened his eyes, the digital clock on the bedside table read 4:05. The dream was fresh in his mind, his pulse was racing, and the collar of his cotton T-shirt felt damp. He turned to where Melanie should have been asleep, hoping he hadn't disturbed her—but she wasn't there.

He rolled out of bed and winced as pain shot through his thigh. He dreaded it, but he knew he couldn't avoid the look of confusion and reproach on his wife's face when he joined her in the kitchen. Would she force a confrontation? It would be very unlike her to do so, but matters were coming to a head. What was he saying in these dreams?

Once in the kitchen, Frankie squinted at the bright light beaming down from the recessed lamps. He paused to glance out the window above the kitchen sink, but, spotting no trace of dawn, saw only his disheveled reflection staring back at him in the darkness. He shuffled over to the table and took a seat.

Melanie had her back to him as she set the kettle on a burner. He felt so foolish. Should he say something? She would be annoyed and expect him to break the ice. She deserved to know the source of his nightmares—they had always shared everything. But when it came to the war, they had an understanding that the subject was off-limits, that Frankie, like many other veterans who had experienced combat, preferred not to discuss the subject. She had respected that for more than forty years.

But things were different now—different in a way that was both puzzling and distressing. He was feeling a powerful need to pour out his soul and relieve the nagging guilt that had been so freshly aroused. He had considered taking it to the confessional, thinking that Father Gonzales might offer some comforting words or advice. But what would he confess to? What was his great sin? Was failing to do something a sin? He abandoned the idea.

He thought perhaps he should say something to Melanie about the communication with Andrew and the Frío memoir. *Would it be enough to satisfy her that his unfulfilled promise to Mama Elena was at the root of his strange dreams and night terrors?* He doubted it, because he'd never been a good liar, and Melanie knew him well enough to discern if he was holding something back.

Melanie brought the teakettle over and poured him a cup. He caught a whiff of her lilac-scented perfume, which still, after all these years, stirred something in him.

She surprised him by being the first to speak. "You were talking in your sleep," she said with a barely detectible sigh. "But no violence this time. It sounded like you were trying to say 'medic.' I couldn't make out much else."

Frankie felt his face flush. He was relieved that Melanie seemed relatively unconcerned about the dream, so he decided against mentioning anything about Ramón and the Frío record, at least for the time being.

"Medic, huh?" He lied to her. "I don't remember dreaming about anything."

He watched Melanie closely to gauge her reaction, but she merely offered a tight-lipped smile and then returned the teakettle to the stove.

Embarrassed, Frankie excused himself and took his tea outside, where the chill caused him to shiver and the pinpoints of a million stars looked down on him like so many accusing eyes.

Chapter 7

The Ersatz Window

Tuesday, October 30, 2001

NMSU Library, Las Cruces, New Mexico

The picture in the footlocker was constantly on his mind. Frankie had tried so hard to forget that part of his life, to pretend it was something from the past that had happened to someone else. But the faces in the old photo were proof certain that he could never escape his past. He couldn't stop thinking about it, even now as he sat quietly at a table on the third floor of New Mexico State University's Branson Library—the one place where he felt sure he could read and be left alone. Only the occasional hushed conversation could be heard as he pulled the blue binder from the envelope.

Frío's memoir fascinated him, the story it told providing Frankie an ersatz window into the experience of his brother, Ramón. It was a tale of resourcefulness and survival in unimaginable places. With every turn of the page, Frankie could sense Frío's frustration that his dwindling cohort of Americans and

Filipinos had been reduced to waging a fighting retreat, always on the defensive.

Remarkably, Frío had decided that it was time to take the fight to the enemy. Using his experience as a boy in the high pine country near his mountain home, he became a solitary, nocturnal warrior. He would masquerade as an Apache, shirtless with face darkened by charcoal as he stalked enemy camps. Every time he calculated when the moment was right, he would rush in, shouting out a war whoop and firing his Colt revolver. In the panic that followed, the Japanese soldiers would scatter, one or two falling to his bullets. He would scoop up provisions and medical supplies and disappear back into the forest.

It wasn't long before he had earned a reputation among the Japs—and a price on his head. The enemy increased their patrols to try to catch the raider savage who they said was taking scalps. Frío found that amusing. He never had the time to take scalps.

After Frío's band of survivors was cornered and forced to surrender, a Japanese major approached the American commander, a Lieutenant Kelly, and offered to provide food and medicine. The catch? The Americans had to hand over the nocturnal raider, whom the Japanese major was sure was in the camp. Kelly denied that such a person was present. In consequence, the captives were forced to endure a long, hot afternoon, with the sick and wounded required to stand at attention, several falling into delirium or unconsciousness.

Frankie, by now oblivious to the comings and goings of the library patrons around him, found himself riveted by the next passage in the memoir:

> *That's when Private Pablo Padilla stepped forward.*
> *"I'm the one you're looking for," he told the Jap major.*

I was stunned. Private Padilla was a wisp of a fellow, a quiet kid who worked as a commissary clerk. He shot me a sideways glance with a slight shake of the head and then stepped toward the major, hands behind his back. The major looked puzzled, like he couldn't believe that the wretched young soldier wracked with fever and standing before him could possibly be the culprit.

Lieutenant Kelly stepped forward with his hands out, ready to intervene on Padilla's behalf, but the major ordered two of his men to hold Padilla's arms behind him and force him to kneel with his head bowed.

Padilla started whispering. I think he was praying. "Dios te salve, María, llena eres de gracia . . ."

The major reached for his sword, wheeled, and with two hands on the grip, brought it down swiftly on Padilla's exposed neck, severing the head cleanly. It rolled a few feet as the body sagged, blood gushing from the neck and pooling in the dust.

I screamed, my blood boiling, and Kelly lunged for the major's throat, but was knocked senseless by the butt of a rifle. We broke ranks and started for our captors until an overhead burst of machine-gun fire from the edge of the clearing stopped us in our tracks.

The major withdrew a clean handkerchief from his pocket and wiped the blood from the blade. "This was for the best," he told us. "You men will thank me, because the outlaw has been discovered and executed,

*leaving no unresolved matters for the guards who will
follow us. Their methods would not be as humane. Your
comrade was brave to come forward, and whether or
not he was indeed the criminal, he died honorably. The
matter is closed."*

*He sheathed his sword and gestured that someone
should bring forward the rations, water, and medicines.
I could feel tears welling as I helped Lieutenant Kelly
to his feet, all the while staring at the headless body of
Private Pablo Padilla.*

Frío's pain over Padilla's personal sacrifice was obvious,
Frankie thought. The worst was yet to come, though, and
Frankie closed the binder with the knowledge that the parts
involving the person called Ramón would be next. He was
finding it hard to separate the mixed feelings he was having.
How would he ever know what had happened to Ramón?

Even as he pondered Ramón's fate, Frankie entertained
another question, which came to him unbidden: *Whatever became of Noriko?*

Chapter 8

Why Don't I Look Like Other Girls?

Same Day, Kumiko Ltd.

Harajuku, Tokyo

Kume stood at a designer's table and fondled the fabric of the spring frock approvingly. It felt delicate in her hands—but resilient, like it could withstand daily wear. Beneath the oversized lamps that hung on long wires from the ceiling, it gave off an almost luminescent quality, which only confirmed Kume's long-held belief that she'd commissioned the perfect design space. Like any fashion house, hers was a reflection of her taste: elegant, airy, and stylish. But it was, at the end of the day, a workplace. Everything was oriented toward design, toward the efficient use of light and space. The marriage of sophistication and utility was the product of accumulated wisdom passed from house to house, one generation to the next. With a long lineage of industry trailblazers to tap into, Kume knew she was on solid ground.

The seasonal collection, on the other hand, was a bit of a stretch. The materials were expensive, and she had worried that the folk art prints on the stretch silk charmeuse fabric that so resembled early work by Kenzo Takada might prove troublesome. To her great relief, Kenzo himself had appeared flattered when she sent him samples and had graciously asked only for an acknowledgement. The great designer's response had been generous, and she could only chalk it up to the fact that she had been his star design pupil in Paris, where she had gone after leaving modeling. It seemed like a lifetime ago.

Kume mused that, in a sense, it really was. It still hurt to think about the times during her youth when the kids at school had made fun of her looks, pantomiming a monkey. With rounder eyes and a slightly darker skin tone, she hadn't resembled other Japanese children. She had often come home from school with hot tears running down her face, retreating to the comforting arms of her parents.

She smiled, recalling how Soichiro had not taken kindly to his daughter's mistreatment and had gone so far as to threaten the parents of some of the worst offenders. But Noriko had wisely counseled him to simply drop it. Children can be very cruel, she had said. Fighting it would only make matters worse.

She was right, of course, and gradually, as Kume grew into adolescence, the issue simply vanished. Not coincidentally, Kume became aware that she was developing into a dark-eyed beauty with height and long legs unlike archetypical Asian women. Her look was at once exotically Oriental, clearly Japanese, but something more, with finely sculpted cheekbones, full lips, and grayish-brown eyes that projected startled innocence. It was a look made for the camera.

Kume looked up to see Chika sidling over to her table.

"Something wrong?" Chika asked.

"No," Kume said. "I was just thinking about the early days, before I became a Ford model, and a conversation I had with my mother. I'm sure it made her uncomfortable, but I was forever asking her why I didn't look like other girls."

"Well, you certainly are taller," Chika said, "and your eyes aren't like most Japanese women's. I'd be curious, too. What did she say?"

"It had to be a conversation she dreaded, but knew was inevitable," Kume replied. "I was thirteen, already becoming quite leggy, and after about the hundredth time I raised the question, she finally relented. She sat me down and told me that Soichiro was not my biological father. She said my father was an American."

Chika gasped and pressed both hands over her mouth. "Oh, my God! What did you say? How did you feel?"

"I remember being strangely calm—as though the news wasn't really news at all. But I could feel a storm of emotions just beginning to brew. I sat there without a word for a few moments."

Chika's eyes were wide now. "Did your mother say who this American was?"

Kume frowned, shaking her head irritably. "No. She became very agitated. I had hardly ever seen my mother cry before. I wanted to know, of course, but she quickly composed herself and said it wasn't important. She said that Soichiro was my father and that, as far as she was concerned, he deserved all the love and respect to which a father is entitled. Mother had said her piece, and now she wished no further discussion of the matter. I learned to accept that I would hear no more about my American father—at least not from her. I didn't understand it at the time, but no doubt she harbored a bundle of hidden feelings she didn't feel comfortable revealing."

Chika made a whistling sound under her breath. "What did you think?"

Kume put the frock on a hanger and took a seat on a nearby stool. "My mind was reeling. I was stunned, of course. Was the American a soldier? Was she raped? If not, why did he not stay with my mother? Who was he? Where was he now? Did he even know he had a daughter? But everything was clear now—why I looked so different. I was half-American! It turned out to be not a bad thing at a time when American looks and style and music were so popular."

Chika took a stool beside Kume and squinted at the south-facing windows, which were pouring bright afternoon sunlight into the office. "Did you ever ask Soichiro about the American?"

Kume nodded. "I did, several years later. He didn't feel comfortable discussing it, but he told me the American was a soldier who looked after my mother during the very difficult time following the battle when the Americans occupied Okinawa. Soichiro thought the soldier grew to care deeply for my mother—and she for him. Soichiro told me he never met the man, and he had no idea why he'd left my mother and returned home. It was clear he did not think too highly of the American. Neither did I. It wasn't easy getting over feeling like I'd been rejected—or forgotten. I eventually got past most of those feelings and grew to appreciate more fully what a good man my mother had married." After a thoughtful pause, Kume wagged her finger. "Enough ancient history. We have work to do before the New York trip. Bring over those two mannequins and let's try some different accessorizing."

Chapter 9

More Fact than Fiction

Friday, November 9, 2001

Washington, DC

"You mind?" Nathan Goldman asked, eying the last strip of spicy beef bulgogi on one of several platters between them.

"It's all yours," Gary said and watched in amusement as Nate struggled to snare the beef with his chopsticks.

Along with losing most of his hair in recent years, Nate had grown an ample spare tire, and Gary could see why, if tonight's meal was any indication of his eating habits. Dumplings, seafood pancakes, and rice and vegetables competed for room on their table.

The beef was the first to disappear as Nate finally gave up on good form and speared the strip with one of his chopsticks. His eyes widened along with his smile. "Man, that's good."

"Told you," Gary said. "You may know DC, but I know Asian food."

More than a month had passed since Gary had received the surprise phone call from Nate. In the interim, Gary's assistant had set up tonight's meeting with Nate in DC, and the two had hammered out the details by e-mail. Gary had let Nate pick the restaurant, insisting only that they go somewhere off the beaten path, and Nate had settled on this little hole-in-the-wall Korean joint in the heart of Penn Quarter, calling his choice "fitting" for what he wanted to discuss. He had needed help with the menu but had been directing the conversation ever since. They'd waxed poetic about women, the old days, and then women again. Now, finally, Nate seemed ready to talk business.

"So let's get down to it," he said before pausing for a sip of water. "Spicy! Anyway, like I said on the phone, I need a huge favor. An old desk hand at the CIA picked up some interesting chatter a couple months ago."

"Something about gold and Japan's wartime treasury," Gary offered.

Nate leaned back in his booth seat. "Right. But that's only the half of it. I'll give you the CliffsNotes version. Rumors have been floating for decades that Japan lost a huge cache of gold during the war, but the prevailing wisdom has always been that those stories are apocryphal. Then the CIA intercepts communication between a Japanese crime syndicate and someone linked to DPRK intelligence."

"Democratic People's Republic of Korea," Gary mused aloud. "North Korea."

Nate brought a stubby finger to his nose, nearly hitting his glasses. "Right again. Our analysts thought they were being pranked at first, but they eventually confirmed through another channel that the communication was authentic. The details are sketchy, but that gold story might be more fact than fiction, after all. Or at least the players in question seem to think so. They've traced it to a mine cave-in on mainland Japan."

"The gold." Gary sat silently for a moment. The story still sounded farfetched to his ears. "So why go to the trouble? Is it really worth that much?"

"Billions," Nate said. "Enough to give a considerable boost to a certain country's nuclear weapons program."

"Is the Japanese mafia group the one that located it?" Gary asked. "I assume they're asking the North Koreans for a cut."

Nate shrugged. "We're still putting together the pieces. At this point, we don't know the exact nature of the relationship."

"So for all you know," Gary said, "the North Koreans are working for the Japanese mafia."

Nate took another sip of water. "I doubt it. But anything's possible at this point."

Their waitress, a petite, no-nonsense woman of Korean descent, stopped at their table. "How is everything?"

"Wonderful," Gary said. He pointed to Nate, who was sweating under his collar and fanning his red face. "But I think we might need a bottle of soju—just to put out the fire for my friend."

The waitress chuckled and disappeared into the kitchen.

"Will alcohol help?" Nate asked.

"Can't hurt," Gary said.

A minute later, the two were raising their glasses in a toast.

Nate stared through his glasses at the clear liquid in his shot glass. "Looks harmless enough."

"It's not," Gary assured him. "It packs a hell of a punch. If you drink it like wine, I'll have to carry you to a cab."

They returned to the subject at hand.

"So where do I come in?" Gary asked.

"Well, this is all unofficial, of course," Nate said. "But we've done a little homework and found someone for you to talk to while you're in Seoul doing business." He slid a manila envelope across the table. "For your reading pleasure. Colonel Park Hong, ROK. He's with defense intelligence. He likes to drink. And he likes to talk."

"Will he know I'm coming?"

"Nope. We need you to play dumb while you go on a little fishing expedition."

Gary shook his head and laughed. He was beginning to wonder if he was in over his head. "What's the hook?"

"Drilling equipment," Nate answered. "We're still working out the details. But when you tell him your story, he's going to want to tell you *his*—assuming he knows as much as we think he does."

Chapter 10

Ghosts of the Solomon Islands

Sunday, November 11, 2001

Sendai, Miyagi Prefecture, Japan

The front door opened, and Soichiro Matsuhata paused long enough to glance over his shoulder at the expressionless "gardeners"—most likely *kyodai*, who he knew were packing concealed 9-millimeter Walther automatics. After entering Kazuo Midorikawa's stately home, Soichiro passed the package of sashimi to Yoko, Kazuo's elderly female servant, and removed his shoes.

Yoko accepted the sashimi with a bow and directed Soichiro to the living room, where he found Kazuo already seated on a plush pillow at a traditional mahogany low table. As frail as he looked these days, Kazuo still emanated the dogged resilience of a survivor. An eye patch covered his left eye. His short moustache—as thick as it was bristly—matched what remained of the silver-gray hair at his temples. He'd suffered male-pattern baldness for as long as Soichiro had known him.

"You really should talk to the gardeners," Soichiro suggested with mock seriousness as he lowered himself to a pillow across from his longtime friend. "Tell them to smile a bit, make people feel welcome."

"If I wanted people to feel welcome," Kazuo snorted, "I'd hire politicians or geishas."

Yoko, who had disappeared only moments ago, entered the spacious living room with tea service, which she set down on the low table. With practiced deftness, she poured small cups, passed them to Kazuo and Soichiro, and bowed to the two men. Then, with silent, small steps, she left the room.

Kazuo pulled a Zippo lighter from his pocket and lit a Camel. For a pensive moment, he fondled the worn lighter with the globe and anchor badge and *USMC* etched on the side. "I guess I should blame the Americans for the cancer," he rasped. "Without this lighter, I probably wouldn't have smoked so much."

Soichiro knew what was coming next. He stifled a yawn and feigned interest as Kazuo began to describe how he had acquired the lighter on that damp October night in 1942. It was a familiar story, retold many times. Sergeant Tanaka had sent Kazuo and three other soldiers of the Sixteenth Infantry Regiment to scout ahead in preparation for Lieutenant General Maruyama's planned Second Division assault against US positions along the Lunga River. It had been hard going, breaking a trail from the Matanikau River through streams, muddy ravines, ridges, and jungle. Kazuo had been bitten relentlessly by mosquitoes—so large that the soldiers had taken to calling them Rei-sens—and leeches had bled him through his leggings.

"All that so the damned artillery could have a six-lane road to carry their cannons to the front!" Kazuo jabbed a finger at Soichiro and cackled smugly.

At this point in the story, it was customary for Soichiro to smile meekly and shrug, all the while knowing that it was patent nonsense. In reality, despite the best efforts of engineers, the Maruyama Road was the barest of tracks through relentlessly unforgiving terrain. The energy required to manhandle the Sendai Division's complement of 75-millimeter Krupp mountain guns, each weighing more than half a ton, through the jungles and mud for five days and nights had so thoroughly sapped the gunners of the Second Field Artillery Regiment—killing and injuring upward of a dozen in the process—that the timetable of the attack was fatally compromised. Soichiro suppressed the urge to disagree, knowing it was folly to object with Kazuo's storytelling under full sail.

"I can still remember the odors that night," Kazuo continued. "After living with the rot of decaying jungle and stench of rancid water, we were intoxicated by the fragrance of smoke from good tobacco. All of us sucked in the sweet aroma—until we saw the glow of a cigarette not ten meters away. It was a US marine standing picket duty on a near moonless night. He appeared to be alone, though we were certain that others were nearby.

"We were just kids—but full of *bushido* and ready to die for the emperor. I was the youngest and signaled brashly to the others that I would take care of the sentry. With hand signals, I warned them to keep a sharp eye out for any more Americans. Then, without a sound, I unsheathed my bayonet, slipped out of my knapsack, and removed my helmet. It amazed me that the marine seemed so disinterested, even bored, as though he were simply pulling barracks duty back home. Generals Hyakutake and Maruyama had brilliantly planned the operation so that the Americans, particularly this marine, were fully unaware of the division's approach.

"I slithered like a snake through tall grass, certain that my breathing would give me away at any moment. But the soldier continued smoking. I could hear him humming softly. His rifle was slung over his shoulder. Suddenly I heard a muffled, hollow sound behind me. It was a canteen belonging to one of my fellows carelessly tapping against a rock.

"The American instantly dropped the cigarette, ground it out, and in a single motion went into a crouch as he unslung his rifle. No one made a sound, and I waited for what seemed like eternity."

Soichiro noted that the story was receiving new embellishments with the retelling. He hadn't heard the part about the canteen before.

"All my nerve endings were on high alert," Kazuo said. "I could just make out the sentry's eyes darting about nervously as he pointed the gun in the direction of the sound. I felt something crawl over my hand and up my sleeve as I lay motionless, but I refused to move a muscle."

Another new wrinkle, Soichiro thought. *A reptile or bug on the arm. Bravo!*

"Finally, warily, the marine slowly stood up and cocked an ear. Apparently satisfied that his mind was playing tricks, he slung his rifle back over his shoulder, reached for his pack of cigarettes, took one out, and pulled his lighter from a pocket. As soon as he flipped it open and cupped his hands to shield the flame, I sprung to my feet and lunged at him with my knife. My hand was over his mouth before he could make a sound. The knife cut his throat cleanly, and his blood sprayed in all directions. I watched his eyes fill with fear and disbelief as he slumped to the ground, clutching at his neck, slack-jawed and choking." Kazuo shook his head slowly with something like regret on his face. "We were taught that the American marines were bloodthirsty warriors, cannibals, larger than life, recruited from Chicago gangs and insane asylums. But all I saw at my feet, with his life draining out, was a frightened boy, much like myself, who didn't want to die."

Soichiro stared at his friend intently.

Kazuo turned the Zippo over repeatedly. "The lighter had fallen from his hands, so I picked it up and took the pack of Lucky Strikes from his pocket. I felt relieved and strangely animated. This was my first kill, but I felt no joy or glory of victory." After a lengthy pause, Kazuo waved the lighter toward Soichiro. "When I'm gone, I want you to have this. Be sure Yoko gives it to you."

Soichiro squirmed at the suggestion. This was no insignificant gesture. He nodded politely. "Thank you. I will honor it as a reminder of our treasured friendship." He paused. "I sometimes think we few who made it back alive are anachronisms. No one today has any real understanding of what we suffered and fought for—or even cares. Who was it that said history is written by the victors? We've probably outlived our time."

"Maybe so." Kazuo grunted. "Too many good comrades died in that jungle hell. An appalling waste. But you're right about history. Legends were created about the Americans—such as that Colonel Puller they called Chesty and Sergeant Basilone, who fought like samurai to defend the airfield they had taken from us. But what of Yamaguchi, Tsuji, Kurabayashi, Tanaka, Watanabe, and dozens more like them who died bravely? Where are the poems celebrating their valor and sacrifice?" Kazuo sighed sadly. "Our young people today have no idea. They play foolish games on their Xboxes and listen to the latest trash that passes for music. Maybe, as you say, we have lived too long."

He crushed out his cigarette as Yoko brought in a serving dish with the sashimi Soichiro had delivered. She set out two exquisite china plates with *onigiri* containing spicy fish roe and soy sauce. Beside the plates, Soichiro spotted two fine pairs of hinoki chopsticks.

The two friends enjoyed their meal, interrupted twice by calls on Kazuo's cell phone, one provoking an impatient eruption of anger. Soichiro judged from the bit he overheard that Kazuo's *shateigashira* had delivered some unwelcome news about a rival yakuza's activities in the area. Kazuo summoned one of the gardeners and whispered instructions. After a hurried bow, the man left.

Kazuo smiled at Soichiro and, with a gesture as though he were shooing away a fly, called for Yoko to break out the special twenty-five-year-old Yamazaki single malt.

Kazuo fixed his one good eye on Soichiro. "Matsuhata-san, you know your visits give me great pleasure. But you never ask me for anything. So I offer. If there should be anything you need, some inconvenience or difficulty that troubles you, it would be my honor to assist you. Only say the word. Has that pirate syndicate from Hokkaido given you any trouble lately?"

"No, my friend. And thank you for the generous offer. Whatever you did to those thieves, it was effective. Now my men tell me that whenever their boats appear on our fishing grounds, the minute they recognize us, they make a hasty retreat."

Soichiro purposely neglected to mention that recently the captain of one of his boats had unexpectedly come upon a bullet-riddled and burnt floating wreck containing human remains. The wreck was clearly from Hokkaido, and the message was equally clear: keep out of Tohoku waters—or else. Soichiro judged it wise to appear ignorant about such things.

"Our challenges are becoming more international now," Soichiro said. "First the Russians, and more recently the Chinese, have been sending fishing trawlers into our waters. It won't be long before we find ourselves in an international clash. The fishery will not be sustainable at the foreigners' current catch rates."

Kazuo coughed as he reached for another cigarette. "I hate to disappoint you, but that's something I won't be able to help you with. Tokyo frowns on gunboat diplomacy by private citizens, particularly when those citizens are people like me."

Yoko had cleared the dishes, and they were well into their second glasses of the superb Scotch whisky from Kyoto when Kazuo leaned forward and asked, "Do you ever wonder why we didn't succeed in defending Guadalcanal? It has baffled and bothered me for years. Our soldiers were the equal of any that the Americans could field, perhaps even more experienced and skilled in hand-to-hand combat. Our naval guns were wreaking havoc on the marines, who were isolated. Our bombers were inflicting serious damage to their ships and troops. Our infantry should have swept the marines away." Kazuo formed a fist as though poised to pound the table.

"Yes, I've thought about that," Soichiro responded. "I believe it all came down to overwhelming resources on their side and bad generalship on ours. From my perspective, I can tell you that wrestling bulky pack howitzers through jungles and over rivers takes more time than we were allowed. The attack had to be delayed for two critical days, but General Sumiyoshi's Fourth Infantry Regiment was not informed of the delay. As a result, his troops and tanks got off the mark too early and were destroyed in the Matanikau, along with any hope of our surprising the Americans across the Lunga River." Soichiro shook his head. "Throwing wave after wave of infantry against well-defended, fixed positions was wasteful and foolish, especially when our field pieces were in no position to support the assaults. In two days, the Sendai Division died, and with it, any chance of retaking Guadalcanal."

Both men nodded soberly.

"So at least I know who to blame for this," Kazuo said, pointing to the patch over his left eye. "Either General Sumi-yoshi or you!" He laughed.

Soichiro knew by heart the story of how Kazuo had lost his eye during a predawn assault. He was relieved when Kazuo stopped to light another cigarette. But Soichiro couldn't push back the sense—a long-festering one—that he had somehow been personally responsible for the failure of the Second Division's assault.

He decided it was time to leave. He bowed expansively to Kazuo and thanked him for a delightful afternoon warmed by a splendid whisky.

Chapter 11

The Cabanatuan Kid

Sunday, November 18, 2001

Mesilla, New Mexico

Frankie pushed his chair back from the desk in his office. Ellen had taken Melanie to El Paso for lunch and an afternoon of shopping, which meant he was enjoying his day of freedom as a result. He now had time to be alone with his thoughts and the Frío manuscript.

He had to admit, Frío's tale was a harrowing one. Other accounts Frankie had read of the forced march to captivity on Bataan and the wretched conditions of the Japanese prisoner-of-war camps paled by comparison. Frío had clearly experienced more as an eighteen-year-old than most seasoned veterans twice his age.

Two incidents in Frío's narrative were of particular interest. Both had occurred at the POW camp called Cabanatuan, and both involved the person called Ramón. According to Frío's telling, the camp had been home to several thousand American and Filipino prisoners. The twin plagues of hunger and dysentery weakened everyone and contributed to a steadily increasing death rate from disease and starvation. Food was always on everyone's mind.

Frío told of restless sleep and dreams in which he imagined scenes back home in Capitán. The sounds of his mother at the wood stove boiling a big pot of pinto beans flavored with a ham bone. The delicious, tangy aroma of red chile posole. The toasty smell of steaming fresh flour tortillas being stacked on a plate. It was enough to drive a person mad. He pictured himself as a boy picking his way through the deep forest ravines, feeling the breeze, taking in the mixed scents of wildflowers and the tall ponderosa pines, and hearing the gurgling of the snow-fed streams, where the water was so icy cold it made his head hurt even in summer, where he might spy the occasional silvery flash of a rainbow trout.

While such thoughts tortured him, they also sustained him. He described how prisoners proved resourceful in smuggling food into camp whenever possible. On one such occasion, Frío was part of a detail of several prisoners returning from the fields, where they were permitted to cultivate turnips, okra, and beans to supplement their diet. However, the food seldom reached the prisoners, most of it being diverted and shipped to the army by the camp commander, who had a thriving little side business going. Frío described how prisoners contrived ways to sneak food past the guards and back to the camp by stuffing such things as they could into their woven hats and loincloths. Some of these contrivances were pretty flimsy, which almost proved to be his undoing.

Most of the guards pretended not to see and ignored the smuggling. But some did not—especially one guard the men called El Tuerto, who was blind in one eye. Frankie thumbed through the journal until he found Frío's account, which Frankie practically knew word for word by now:

I remember the day we got caught. Just like we planned, Ramón wandered to El Tuerto's right. We figured this would distract him so the guy doing the smuggling— that was me this time—could sneak past him on his blind side. But for once he saw through the ruse and turned back in time to catch me. He ordered me to spill my booty, so I removed my hat and a bunch of turnips fell out.

I knew what was coming. El Tuerto always carried a hardwood baton he'd fashioned from a tree branch, and he came at me, baton flying. I covered my head and face, but I hardly had the strength to defend myself. When El Tuerto didn't stop, Ramón wheeled and landed a haymaker on his chin—or so I was told later. I'd love to have seen it, but I was too busy being knocked sense- less. El Tuerto dropped like a stone. The other guards turned on Ramón and were about to nail him to the ground with their bayonets. Fortunately for him, El Tuerto sat up and ordered the guards to let him stand, all the while rubbing what looked like a pretty sore jaw.

El Tuerto was bleeding from the mouth, and I could see that Ramón had taken some blows to his face, too. They stared at each other a moment, Ramón looking so serene in his defiance. El Tuerto had crossed a line, and Ramón had called him on it. Ramón was just a prisoner like the rest of us, but he couldn't let the abuse go unchallenged, regardless of the consequences. It's worth noting that the consequences for striking a

guard typically involved a rather unpleasant death—
quite drawn-out and carried out in the courtyard so the
rest of us could watch and learn.

Instead, El Tuerto wiped the blood from his lips,
smiled, and had Ramón taken to the hot box. Ramón
never uttered a word, but I swear I saw a look of satis-
faction on his face as the guards hauled him away to be
locked up in that hellish little oven. He spent three days
there without food or water and emerged delirious and
mad with thirst but alive. The guards thought he had
died in the hot box. No one else had ever survived it. So
the camp ledger listed Ramón as dead.

No wonder his parents had received the letter, Frankie
thought. Everyone had presumed Ramón dead.

The second incident had involved a somewhat different
problem.

Frío became friendly with Ramón, who was from Las
Cruces, in southern Doña Ana County. Though not an officer,
he was someone who carried authority. The men respected him,
and even the guards were aware that he was something of an
hijo de algo—though not of noble birth, a substantial man not
to be trifled with.

It wasn't long before new prisoners arrived. After the surrender of Corregidor, the surviving defenders were parceled
out to camps in Luzon and Mindanao. A substantial number
were shipped to Cabanatuan, much to the delight of a sadistic
guard the men called La Culebra, who welcomed a supply of
"fresh fish" to torment. The beatings increased, and men were
required to open their mouths to reveal their dental work. Frío
wrote of one soldier whose jaw was broken when Culebra used

pliers and a screwdriver to pry free two gold-filled teeth. Even Ramón was powerless to help.

Over time, the newcomers became wise to the ways of the camp and learned how to keep out of Culebra's way. This only contributed to the guard's paranoid tendencies, but he knew he would be subject to discipline if he succumbed to his murderous impulses without good reason. So he decided to channel his aggression into a more discreet and familiar outlet. Unbeknown to the prisoners and possibly to the other guards, Culebra was a sexual offender and child molester. It was later discovered that before the war he had been convicted by a Tokyo court on four counts of pedophilia. He had already served the first six years of a twenty-year sentence when war broke out. Due to the army's mushrooming manpower requirements, he and other convicts were offered their freedom in exchange for military duty in a battalion being raised to serve as guards for POWs.

He leaped at the chance. He was sent off to the Philippines, where a huge camp held Americans and Filipinos.

This was when Culebra began to take an interest in certain younger prisoners. The Filipinos attracted him, because they tended to be of slight stature and youthful appearance. There was also a young, fair-haired American that caught his notice. Perhaps Culebra could entice some of these to become his sexual playthings in exchange for favors or privileges. And if they refused, all the better. He actually preferred intimidation and physical force, which he found much more stimulating.

Soon Culebra was parading around with one or two hapless young Filipinos in tow, catering to his every whim. But it wasn't enough, and Culebra coveted the blond American.

Frío and Ramón kept an eye on what was happening; they were determined to protect the young Anglo American. He was a kid from Clovis, New Mexico, named Orville Plunkett, a farm boy with a quiet manner, a thatch of unruly blond hair, and sturdy Baptist roots. Clearly he had lied about his age when enlisting and couldn't have been much past eighteen now. Frío described in detail how he almost became another one of Culebra's victims.

One evening, after a day's work outside the fence, Orville was resting in his quarters, a hut he shared with me and about twenty other fellow prisoners. Dinner that night was the usual stew of rice and a few uniden-tifiable bits and pieces. It didn't take long for Orville to stand up with an urgent look on his face. We all knew that look. He made a beeline for the privy shack.

That's when we heard Culebra barge into the shack after him. A second later, Culebra was screaming at Orville. We found out later that he'd ordered Orville to drop his shorts and bend over, and Orville had reluc-tantly complied—and then let loose the explosive diar-rhea he'd gone in there to expel. Anyway, when Ramón and I heard the commotion, we rushed into the shack and found Orville fighting for his life. Culebra was red-faced with rage and swinging a knife at him, and Orville was doing all he could to dance out of harm's way. Ramón got behind Culebra just as I grabbed the arm Culebra was holding his knife with. While I used my other hand to cup Culebra's mouth, Ramón took a sharpened piece of bamboo and punctured the guard's carotid artery. A brief struggle followed while blood poured out of Culebra's neck. Then he shuddered, and that was it. He was dead.

The privy trench was over six feet deep and nearly brimming over. We weighted Culebra's body with stones and lowered it into the mass of liquefied effluent. After a quick cleanup of all the blood, the three of us departed in separate directions.

The only complication was that before disposing of Culebra's body, Orville had slipped off the guard's Seiko watch. Ramón was livid when he noticed it. He knew that if such a thing were found in the possession of a prisoner, it would mean certain death for him and possibly the rest of us. Ramón made sure Orville tossed the watch into the pit to join its rightful owner.

For several days, Frío and the others waited apprehensively. What would be the consequences of Culebra's unexplained disappearance? Soon it became clear that Culebra was not a popular fellow, even among the guards. So his disappearance did not trigger a wholesale search of the camp and interrogation of prisoners. There were stories of other guards who had run off before, either shacking up with a local native girl or being hunted down and killed by guerillas. The guards seemed unconcerned that he was gone. After the third day that Culebra did not turn up, El Tuerto seemed to suspect that there was more to the story and that the prisoners knew what had happened to Culebra—perhaps they'd had something to do with his disappearance. But even *he* seemed disposed to let a sleeping dog lie so long as no proof of prisoner involvement could be produced.

Frankie laid the binder aside and glanced at a photo set in a small wooden frame on his desk. Two boys, grinning with mischief, stared back at him: Ramón and Frankie—two peas in a pod. Frankie had idolized his brother, and Frío's story reminded him of an event that had taken place at about the time the photograph was taken.

Frankie was ten years old when he and Ramón, fourteen at the time, embarked on an expedition. Armed with spades and backpacks containing canteens of water and sandwiches, they left home early one July morning on a hike toward the Organ Mountains. The year was 1936. Tantalizing tales of conquistador gold from the fabled Seven Cities of Cibola buried at the base of the rocky escarpment inflamed Frankie's imagination, and he was sure he and his brother would be the ones to discover it. At the very least, they could probably gather up a few burned-out meteorites that were often scattered across the high, arid plateau outside Las Cruces. They never knew what they might run across in the desert.

By noon, Frankie was tiring from the uphill trek and the merciless beating of the July sun.

"Let's stop and rest," Ramón suggested. He pointed to some shade nearby. "We can split the sandwiches Mama packed."

The large mesquite bush was just big enough for them both to comfortably stretch out beneath it.

In Frankie's weariness, he'd forgotten a cardinal rule of the desert, and so he was unaware that the shade of the large bush had also attracted a five-foot-long diamondback rattler that had curled up to wait out the heat of the day. Frankie didn't notice the snake until it was too late. When Frankie went to flop down in the dirt, the rattlesnake struck without warning. Frankie cried out from the pain of the two puncture wounds on his right forearm, and the snake coiled for another strike, rattles whirring.

Before that second strike, Ramón dispatched the serpent with his spade. Then he grabbed Frankie's arm and set to work tying it off with a shoestring.

"Hold still," he said.

Frankie did as he was told and watched in wide-eyed terror as his older brother used his pocketknife to cut *x*'s on the fang wounds before sucking and spitting out as much bloody venom as he could from the bites. As scared as he was, Frankie took comfort in how Ramón had calmly taken charge.

"I'm going to have to carry you out," Ramón said. "It's the only way."

Frankie didn't protest. He knew he was in dire straits. He let Ramón gather him up piggyback-style, and closed his eyes as Ramón tried to retrace their steps. Every few minutes, Ramón would stop, adjust the tourniquet, pick up Frankie again, and stumble forward.

Within twenty minutes, Frankie felt himself losing consciousness. He couldn't tell what was real and what was in his head anymore. That was when he spotted a solitary rider on horseback. His white collar shone in the bright daylight. He was a priest.

Ramón said something to the priest—Frankie couldn't make out the words—and the next thing Frankie knew, he'd been scooped up and flung across the backside of the priest's Apache pony. With his head hanging over one side, Frankie watched as they galloped through arroyos and around junipers, tumbleweeds, and cholla cacti, the desert shimmering in the heat.

When he awoke the next day, Frankie found himself in his bed at home. Ramón was staring at his bandaged arm and smiling.

"Doc says I saved your life," Ramón said sheepishly.

Frankie remembered the priest. "The padre. Who was he?"

Ramón shrugged. "Disappeared as soon as he dropped you off at the dispensary. Mama's burning candles right now and praying to Saint Francis." Ramón gave him a nod. "Hold out your hand."

Frankie was surprised how weak he felt as he extended his good arm and opened his hand.

Ramón dropped something in it, and it didn't take Frankie long to recognize the tip of the snake's tail, including twelve rattles—a trophy from his brother.

Later that evening, Mama Elena took the rattles, doused them with holy water, and buried them in the yard. No way was she about to allow a piece of *el demonio's* tail in her home!

Frankie took a moment to peel back his sleeve and stare at the old familiar scars on his forearm. He grinned at the memory of his army nickname: Dos Equis.

He was becoming convinced that the person called Ramón in Frío's document was indeed his brother. In a rather strange way, he felt as though he was secretly observing the brother he had idolized. *But to what end?* he wondered. Frankie had always considered his older brother a hero, and nothing in the Frío document had come as much of a surprise in that regard. Whether Frankie would ever learn his brother's ultimate fate—well, that was another matter.

Frankie stood up and stretched, wincing at the twinge in his thigh. A plan was beginning to form in his mind. It involved some risk, but he could no longer ignore the feelings of guilt that were invading his dreams and waking hours.

Chapter 12

Tongue Clicks and Guilt Knives

Wednesday, November 21, 2001

Shinjuku, Tokyo

Kume could hear the familiar sound from the other end of the line. It wasn't as though this was the first time, but whenever Kume had to travel, her mother would click her tongue disapprovingly. Today it was particularly annoying.

"You know you're making that sound with your mouth again," Kume said.

"What sound, daughter?" Noriko asked. "I make no sounds."

Kume set the phone to speaker mode and put the handset down. From her living room on the thirty-ninth floor of her luxury apartment in Tokyo's frenetic Shinjuku ward, she could just make out Mount Fuji's brilliant white cone to the southwest, where it was playing peekaboo behind a wall of skyscrapers. Even from the middle of the city's bustling heart, the sacred mountain soothed. Only Kume's mother had the power to break the spell.

It was useless to be cross with the woman. She was who she was. Kume felt certain that had Noriko been given a choice, she would have preferred that her daughter had graduated from Tokyo University with a business major and returned home to Sendai, where she would have worked with her father and married some local boy.

Instead, Kume had chased a fashion career, starting as a Ford model, and now had a multinational business that took her far, far from Sendai. Why was it that Noriko found Kume's travel to New York so distasteful?

Well, it certainly isn't anything new, Kume mused. From the very beginning, both Soichiro and Noriko had fretted over Kume's living in Manhattan, an urban jungle filled with crime, drugs, and predatory men eager to take advantage of young, unsophisticated women. Over the years, Soichiro had stopped worrying about Kume—or more likely, he'd concluded that Kume was a big girl, wise to the ways of the big city, and besides, worrying would do no good.

But Noriko was another story.

"Never mind, Mother. I shouldn't have mentioned it. I won't be gone more than a week."

Noriko responded with a hint of reproach. "Why you have to go? Can't you just send Haruko and Chika to show the fashions?"

Kume closed her eyes and shook her head. *We've been over this at least a half-dozen times. Why doesn't she get it?* "Because it matters to the buyers that I should be the one to introduce the line. Trust me. It's important. Would I rather skip the trip and have someone else do it? Absolutely. But we need to sell a lot of merchandise, and what does it say to the big American stores if the owner and principal designer decides it isn't worth her time to be present?" Kume hoped that her exasperation didn't sound as strong as it felt spilling out.

"Then go," Noriko said.

Kume could almost see her mother shrugging dismissively. *She's a passive-aggressive expert. She gets under my skin so easily. Next it will be a deflection, as though the prior discussion hadn't happened.*

Noriko went on. "I saw Mrs. Nakajima yesterday. Her son Hiro—you remember, nice-looking man, teaches literature at school in Kyushu—he is coming to Sendai for a visit over *Os-hougatsu*. He's still not married, and his mother thinks it would be nice if you two could meet over the holiday. You do plan to come home for Oshougatsu, no?"

Ah, the twist of the guilt knife, Kume thought. She wanted to tell her mother that the reason Hiro was still single was because he was quite gay and chose to live as far from his parents' home as possible. He was a kind man, strikingly handsome, and Kume had in the past hired him for print ads featuring fashions for the mature male. She had met his partner, a rather artsy and silly younger man, and promised to keep matters mum.

Kume responded matter-of-factly. "Of course I will be home for the New Year. And if Hiro Nakajima is in town, I would be delighted to see him again. Like I said, I'll be in New York for only a week. I don't plan to celebrate Oshougatsu there."

She won't say it, but she's dying to ask if I intend to see Gary. I wish she could understand that it isn't all that simple for me. Clearly she dislikes him. She won't even say his name. Well, I'm not going to help her by volunteering anything.

"Mother, it's time we hung up," she said. "I'm leaving next week, and we have much to do before the trip. Please give Father my love."

She heard Noriko click her tongue as the call disconnected.

Chapter 13

Just Like Her Mother

Thanksgiving Thursday, November 22, 2001

Mesilla, New Mexico

Frankie pushed back his chair at the head of the table and heaved a bleary-eyed sigh. He needed room to breathe, but the top button on his normally loose-fitting Wranglers wasn't cooperating.

"You all right there, Dad?" Ellen asked. "You look ready to blow."

Frankie laughed and then aimed a thumb at his wife. "Blame it on your mother. If she wasn't such a good cook, I wouldn't gorge myself every Thanksgiving."

Melanie, seated to his right, offered a self-deprecating chuckle. "So it's *my* fault, is it? No one made you go back for seconds."

The three of them were seated at the formal dining table, although Frankie hadn't bothered to insert either extension leaf since it was just the immediate family this year. Occasionally, Ellen brought a date or coworker or Melanie invited the neighbors over to help celebrate. More seldom still, one or more sides of the extended family came. But this year it was just the three of them.

The one constant was the food. Yes, Melanie had taken to *Nuevo Mexico*-style cooking like a duck to water, but as someone who knew her way around a kitchen, she could do it all, including a traditional American feast. Every Thanksgiving began the night before with a proclamation that the kitchen would be off-limits for the next twenty-four hours. Then, having secured her domain, Melanie would set to work making a meal big enough to feed a small army. If the turkey was frozen, it had to be thawed. Other staples—yams, potatoes, stuffing fixings—were set out on the counter, ready to be put to use. The kitchen would be just beginning to brighten with sunlight the next morning when the turkey went into the oven, where it would roast all morning and into the afternoon. Potatoes were peeled and whipped. Biscuit dough was rolled and coaxed into proper shapes. Cranberries were simmered on the stove.

So long as Frankie stayed out of the way, Thanksgiving always went without a hitch. But he lurked nearby, inhaling the competing aromas as each new wave hit him: lemon zest from the homemade cranberry sauce, marshmallow from the candied yams, butter and garlic from the steaming mashed potatoes. He wasn't so old-fashioned that he wasn't willing to help out and even take charge of a few dishes. But Melanie refused to delegate. This was her show.

Ellen usually showed up around three o'clock in the afternoon, just in time to help Frankie set the table. She was an excellent cook in her own right but had long since learned to steer clear of her mother's work space. The tables turned when she hosted events at her place, a little ranch style two bedroom in town. Then *she* was in charge. But here she was just a civilian, like Frankie.

"So how are things?" Melanie asked.

The question had been directed at Ellen, whose face reddened visibly. She had her mother's sky-blue eyes but Frankie's olive-toned skin.

Those eyes met Frankie's briefly before she offered a tight-lipped smile to her mother. "Fine," she said, pausing to take a sip of her Garnacha. "Work's keeping me hoppin'. The *Cruceros* are going for a desert ride this weekend." She glanced down at her lap. "And I can still fit into my jeans."

"We haven't had pie yet," Frankie chortled.

Ellen gave Frankie a deadpan stare. "I'm not afraid."

Frankie laughed. His daughter, despite her relatively petite stature and semi-curvy frame, had never had a problem with weight gain, even now as she approached forty. He chocked it up to her speedy metabolism—and the fact that she never stopped moving. She was like a hummingbird, always buzzing, always flitting from one thing to the next. She worked hard. Played hard. She was just like her mother, who, Frankie knew, wasn't happy with her answer.

Melanie brushed aside an errant strand of gray hair. "Are you seeing anyone?"

Here it comes, Frankie thought.

But the eye roll never came. Neither did the sullen sigh.

"Nope," Ellen said in a cheerful tone. She'd obviously been ready for the question and had opted to avoid a confrontation.

It was a sore subject between the two. Her mother wanted her to settle down and was always ready to marry her off to the latest suitor, of whom there had been more than a few over the years. But Ellen had yet to meet Mr. Right. While Melanie made noises about Ellen's dimming prospects as a bride and mother, Ellen shrugged off the concerns. She had more important things to do, whether she was overseeing a new project at work or going skiing with friends.

Ellen artfully dodged any further questions during dessert—pumpkin chiffon pie with homemade whipped cream. Likewise as she and Frankie cleared the table and went to work loading the dishwasher. She even made it to the two-minute warning of the Broncos-Cowboys game before calling it an evening. Frankie was surprised she lasted that long. Ellen was a doer, not a watcher.

"See you around, kid," he said as she offered him and then Melanie a goodbye hug.

Later that night, as Frankie was reading in bed and his eyelids were threatening to close up shop for the night, Melanie broached the topic. "Why do you think she's still single?"

Frankie was tempted to pretend he'd fallen asleep but instead offered the best answer he could come up with at such a late hour. "Maybe she's gay."

Melanie elbowed him in the ribs playfully. "You're awful."

"It would explain a few things," he said with a shrug.

"Don't you think she would have told us by now?" Melanie asked. "She's not gay. She's just . . . picky."

"I know," Frankie said with a mischievous smile.

He had no doubts about his daughter's sexual orientation. He just liked to tweak his better half. Besides, it was nice to engage in a little carefree banter. Things had been icy between them lately. Ellen's presence had brought them back together, if only for a few hours.

Melanie turned off the lamp on her nightstand and rolled over so she was facing away from him. "Good night, dear."

Chapter 14

Hidden Demons

Monday, November 26, 2001

Mesilla, New Mexico

Ellen finished her coffee and set the cup and saucer on the oak coffee table. The late afternoon sun was streaming through her parents' front windows, which meant it was time to get back to work before the men finished their shifts.

"Thanks, Mom," she said as she stood up to leave. "I love the new French press. It's so much better than that old drip coffeemaker."

"Frankie hates it," her mother said. "But you know your father. He's set in his ways."

There was something about her mother's tone that stopped Ellen in her tracks. Then she spotted the look on her face. Brows knitted. Lips drawn tightly. Eyes pointed away. Ellen knew the look well. It brought her back to the mastectomy and the chemo and all the stress and anxiety they'd somehow survived.

She sat back down on the couch. "What's going on, Mom?"

Her mother frowned. "I don't know if I'm just being foolish, but I'm worried about your father."

Ellen tried to hurry her along. "What is it exactly? I mean, sure, he's been a little weird, but that always happens around this time of year. You know, ever since that Thanksgiving when Dad's parents were notified that Uncle Ramón was dead?"

"I know. But I think it's more than that. He just seems so secretive now. I can't get him to open up. The other night he started talking in his sleep again. He was saying, 'medic,' and 'don't,' and a word that sounded like 'Rico.'" She paused as though waiting for Ellen to fill in the missing pieces.

Ellen was used to this, since her mother seemed to know full well that her daughter enjoyed a special closeness to her father. But Ellen could only offer a shrug and a blank look.

"I was willing to chalk it all up to that old veterans' reluctance to talk about their wartime experiences, particularly with their loved ones," her mother said. "But then something odd happened yesterday. José came to see me, almost apologetically, and said he had something he thought I should know."

Ellen hoped that her mother hadn't noticed her immediate focus on the mention of José Contreras, the company foreman and one of its longest-serving and most loyal employees. She tried to mask her surprise, wondering why José wouldn't have come to her first. "What did he have to say?"

"Well, you know, his mother is a Mondragón from Capitán. José had an uncle, Porfirio Mondragón, who died earlier this year. They called him Frío."

Ellen continued with her blank stare. "I don't remember José mentioning an uncle named Frío."

"It gets more interesting. Frío was one of the boys from New Mexico captured by the Japanese in the Philippines at the beginning of the war. He survived captivity, came home, married, had a family, and lived out his life quietly as a Lincoln County deputy sheriff."

Ellen crossed her legs impatiently. "What does that have to do with Dad?"

"I'll get to that. It seems that Frío had a lot of hidden demons—guilt mainly—stuff from the war that he'd kept bottled up and hidden from his family. Sound familiar?" Her mother broke into a wry little smirk. "But he left behind a diary about his experiences as a prisoner. After Frío died, his grandson, a young man named Andrew, was going through Frío's personal effects and happened upon it. It had a lot of information about his time in Japanese captivity and mentioned someone named Ramón."

"Do you mean, like, Dad's brother, Uncle Ramón?" Ellen asked cautiously, her interest piqued now.

Her mother nodded slowly. "It could be. Andrew also found a letter to Frío written by your grandparents many years ago as they searched for information about Ramón. One thing led to another, and Andrew tracked down your father and contacted him."

Ellen finished the thought. "Okay. I get it. So Dad now has the fate of his brother missing in WW II on his plate. Interesting, but old news. Dad told you about this, right?"

"No. And that's the problem. He hasn't said a word about it. José could sense a change in your father and stumbled onto Andrew's involvement. Needless to say, he wasn't happy to hear that his nephew had contacted your father. Since his family was involved, José felt obligated to tell me about it. Didn't think it was right I should be left in the dark."

With a weary wave of the hand, Ellen flashed her annoyance. "Why don't you just confront him? Ask him what's going on and why he hasn't told you about this Frío business. It doesn't really make sense that he'd be so affected by information about his brother. My God! How long has it been? And why keep it a secret, anyway?" Before her mother could answer, she added, "I feel like wringing José's neck for not telling me first."

Her mother thought for a moment, tilting her head to the side. "No. Let it be. I should say something but not just now. At least I can understand part of why he's been acting so strangely. I'll let you know if I need some help."

Tuesday, November 27, 2001

Mesilla, New Mexico

The sun had already dropped below the mountains and a chilly wind was whipping through the parking lot when Frankie spotted Ellen walking to her SUV.

He lowered his window in the Ford truck. "Hey, kid. Got a second?"

She looked surprised—but not displeased, given the cheerful smile on her face—to see him at the work site. "Shouldn't you be kicking back in your comfy chair by now and bugging Mom about dinner?" she asked with a playful wink.

"Hey," he protested, "I cook, too, you know."

"Only if it comes in a can," Ellen countered. She zipped up her fleece jacket. "What's up?"

"Get inside," he said and nodded to the passenger's side.

The smile on her face was fading. "Okay."

As she circled around to the passenger's side, her petite frame all but disappearing behind the Ford's's muscular hood, he felt a tinge of pride. He always did when she was around. She was a good-looking "kid," as he still liked to think of her, and a charming one, to boot. She radiated the same classy presence her mother did—something he acknowledged he'd scarcely played a role in cultivating. She came by it naturally.

She climbed inside and brought with her a whiff of shampoo or lotion or something, clean and pleasant. "What's on your mind, boss?"

She still occasionally called him that, although they both knew she was the one who ran things these days. He could feel his heart rate increasing, which brought on the ache in his thigh, and suddenly wished he'd called her instead of opting for a face-to-face.

"Well," he said, fumbling for a way to begin.

She laughed. "Geez, Dad. Am I going to have to pry it out of you? I swear. Between you and Mom . . ." She let the sentence trail out.

"What's wrong with your mother?" he asked, almost feeling relieved for the distraction.

"Nothing," Ellen said matter-of-factly. "She's just worried about you is all."

"Oh," he said.

"Says you've been acting mysterious lately."

"She does, does she?"

She gave him a no-bullshit stare. "Come on, Dad. Out with it. You and Mom can pussyfoot all you want. People my age don't operate that way. We say what's on our mind."

Frankie was tempted to tell her that wasn't always a good thing, but opted instead to honor her request. He was feeling increasingly claustrophobic in what normally felt like a roomy cab as he stared out at the university campus, which was receding into the blue-black landscape with every passing minute.

"I'm thinking about taking a trip," he finally said. "A long one. It might be for a few weeks. And I was wondering if you might like to come along."

He realized that he hadn't thought everything through. He only knew that he liked the idea of bringing along his daughter, who made for good conversation and a sympathetic ear. How she felt about joining him—well, he figured he'd know shortly.

She cocked her head to the side as she returned his gaze. "What's going on, Dad? Is something wrong? Are you sick? Have you told Mom? Where's all this coming from?"

"No, none of that. And I haven't told your mother. It's . . . well, it's kind of private. It concerns the war and a lot of suppressed issues that've been coming out lately. When I'm not dreaming about the war, I'm thinking about it."

Ellen pursed her lips, looking like a younger, darker version of her mother. "Mom says you've been having a lot of nightmares lately."

"Flashbacks," he said. It was time to come clean—at least partially so. "It all got stirred up by some recent correspondence about my brother, Ramón, your uncle who never came home. I can tell you more about that later. But right now, I've pretty much made up my mind to go to Okinawa, probably after the holidays. I very much would like you to come with me."

She replied without hesitation. "Shoot, Dad. You know I'll go with you. I got your back." She shook her head, as if suddenly realizing the ramifications of her assent. "Wait a second. What about work?"

"What about it? José can hold down the fort while you're gone."

She nodded slowly. "Yeah, okay. I'll need some time to get everything squared away. It'll definitely have to be after the holidays. Maybe mid-January. Is that what you're thinking?"

Frankie heaved a huge sigh of relief. "Sure. It can be flexible to suit your schedule."

He felt like celebrating. This could be an adventure, he thought, a father-daughter road-trip like the one he'd taken Ellen on three decades earlier, when they'd gone trout fishing around Pecos. It would be good to take her mind off work, which he knew had been busy lately—hell, it would be good for both of them.

He tried to ignore the little voice deep in his head that was asking, *How do you plan to tell her about the Okinawan girl?*

Chapter 15

Who's My Dad?

Kume stepped out of the taxi at the West Fifty-Fourth Street entrance to the Rihga Royal Hotel just before noon. After passing beneath a hunter-green awning, she entered the elegant lobby and approached the front desk.

A fresh-faced concierge—young enough to be her son, she thought—handed her an envelope. "Mr. Masterson has left you a note."

She opened the scented envelope and read the message, which had been handwritten on hotel stationery:

> *Hello, beautiful.*
>
> *I hope you managed to get some sleep during your flight. I'll be by to pick you up in the lobby at seven o'clock tonight.*
>
> *Looking forward to it!*
> *—Gary*

The plan, which Gary had shared over the phone, was to walk the three short blocks to Le Bernardin, a chic French restaurant on the ground floor of the sand-and-salmon-granite-clad AXA Equitable Building.

When had she last seen Gary? It had been a long while. She remembered her surprise when he had contacted her unexpectedly and asked to meet her during Fashion Week, which would have made it at least ten years since their last face-to-face contact. Kume had blurted the news to Noriko—something she now regretted. Of course, the Fashion Week plans had never materialized, but Gary had persisted, and she had agreed to dinner.

She thanked the concierge and caught an elevator up to her suite on the forty-fourth floor. A couple of hours later, after a nap and a shower, she was staring out the window at the now colorless and barren trees in Central Park. It was good to be back in New York, she thought. Things had certainly changed since those early days when she'd been just a babe in the woods, a naïve young Japanese Holly Golightly seeking her fortune in the big city.

She crossed her arms and padded softly across the room in her robe and slippers. The recollection of how Genevieve had taken her under her wing and accompanied her to New York to meet Jerry and Eileen Ford caused her to smile. They had been smitten with her look. Before long, it was a marathon of photo sessions and hours upon hours with cosmetologists, hairstylists, and wardrobes.

She remembered, too, that it was during this time when, surrounded by so many Americans, she had begun to think anew about her natural father. She'd imagined him to be in his late thirties, sensitive and handsome, with a face like Montgomery Clift's. She wondered where he lived. Might he possibly be right here in New York, one of the thousands of businessmen in suits hurrying by her on the street or driving a taxi or riding in a police car? Would he be married with a family? If not here, where else might he be? Would he even be alive today? Did he ever think about Noriko, about his daughter? Did he even *know* he had a daughter?

Noriko's stubborn silence regarding "the *Amerika-jin*" only fanned Kume's curiosity. She vowed that someday she would learn more about this man, perhaps even meet him. But she had no idea when—or even how—to go about beginning her search. A part of her wanted to tell her mother she would be doing this, whether she liked it or not.

As she settled into a plush chair with a cup of tea, Kume thought of those early New York days as a sort of boot camp, during which she had learned the modeling trade. Apparently, Eileen's hunch had proved correct. The exoticism of Kume's features proved magnetic, and before long, Kume became used to seeing her face in department store catalogs and print advertising.

Genevieve had confided to Kume that the Fords had bigger plans for their young Asian protégé. She turned out to be right. Soon Kume was being coached on how to handle herself on the catwalk, master proper posture and mannerisms, pose for the camera, and put together a wardrobe. In short order, she was being groomed to become a Ford modeling star along with the likes of Jean Shrimpton, Ali McGraw, and Jerry Hall.

Kume sighed, put down the cup, and strode into the bathroom. She dropped the robe and examined herself in the full-length mirror. The passage of years was a relentless fact, but at age fifty-five, on balance, she realized she shouldn't complain. Yes, the breasts were not as perky as before, but the legs, her prime asset, were still model-perfect, thanks to ceaseless exercise. She lifted her right hand from her midriff to her left triceps muscle and offered a tight-lipped smile to the mirror, satisfied that the extra time spent in the gym had been worth it.

She fretted that travel fatigue was visible in her eyes, but she knew she couldn't relax just yet. Her two assistants would be waiting downstairs within the hour to go over the store presentations. Much was riding on the success of the spring collection, which she had let drop to a reporter for *Women's Wear Daily* was being called "Plumage by Kumiko."

Later, she would decide what to wear for dinner with Gary.

Kume pressed the button for the lobby and took a deep breath. She'd settled on a ruffled white blouse and a tailored gray Chanel pantsuit, set off by three-inch Prada heels and a black Gucci clutch. It amused her that, during the earlier meeting with her staff about breezy spring fashions, she had been pre-occupied with how she would dress for dinner with Gary on a chilly November evening. Unfortunately, her distraction had not gone unnoticed, provoking a round of giggles and knowing glances between Haruko and Chika.

As the elevator doors opened, there was Gary. He was sitting in the lobby and studying his Blackberry.

Punctual as usual, she thought.

He rose to greet her, and she noted that he was aging well—still trim, his stylish hair assuming a touch of silver at the temples. He looked handsome in his gray slacks and Armani blazer. The corners of his mouth turned down in a sup-pressed smile as she held out her hand.

Gary took it and kissed her on the cheek. "You are a vision." He stood back and whistled softly. "I bet those slacks are hiding the same killer legs."

Don't you wish you knew. She squeezed his hand. "It's good to see you, Gary. It's been a long time." She smiled inwardly, pleased that she'd made the intended impression. "Shall we walk?"

After they stepped out onto the sidewalk, Kume rubbed her arms in a vain attempt to ward off the late November chill swirling off the Hudson through the canyons of midtown.

Gary stepped toward a black sedan waiting at the curb. "Why don't we use the car. I'll have James drop us off right in front of the restaurant."

Kume hesitated for a moment, thinking, *Seriously? James?* Then she agreed, climbing into the back of the vehicle.

The Mercedes took them east to Fifth Avenue, where the annual riot of Christmas finery already adorned the various storefronts—Trump Tower, Cartier, Saks.

"I'd almost forgotten how beautiful the city can be during the holidays," she said.

As they turned onto Fifty-First Street, Gary leaned toward her. "The annual lighting of the Christmas tree in Rockefeller Center is tomorrow evening. Laura Bush will be there to do the honors, along with Giuliani and the fire commissioner. There'll be live entertainment." He pumped his eyebrows and leaned back against the seat. "Should be quite the emotional affair, coming on the heels of September eleven." He turned his head toward her. "I've got an invitation from Jerry Speyer to join him in the VIP viewing area. I'd be delighted to bring you as my guest."

Kume smiled faintly. "Why don't we decide on that later? I have a full day of showings tomorrow, as well as the day after, and the day after that." She hoped he didn't think she was blowing him off, but she wanted to see how the night went before making any plans. She hated the term "emotional baggage," but had to admit that it defined their relationship to a tee.

As they entered the restaurant, the maître d' bowed slightly. "Welcome to Le Bernardin, Mr. Masterson, Mademoiselle Matsuhata. Your table is waiting."

Kume pretended to be unimpressed by the exclusive French restaurant, but the ultra-modern, sparse interior was lovely to look at. White tablecloths, exposed beams, and clean, graceful lines pleased her designer's eye. She'd dined at her share of restaurants boasting three Michelin stars, but this one was a delight. She only hoped the food could live up to the elegant ambience.

They took their seats at a private table with a broad view of a mural depicting Van Wyk's famous oil painting, *A Breton Family Fishing Scene*. Gary ordered chilled Belvedere vodka, neat, and Kume settled on a Ramey chardonnay.

"Still like your whites, I see," Gary said with a grin.

They toasted the Kumiko showings, and Gary ordered a bottle of Dom Perignon to have with their dinner. After they set aside their menus, Kume stole a glance at the man who had caused so many complications in her life. The whitish burn scar over his jugular notch was less obvious now but still visible. She felt her hand softly stroking her own neck as she recalled the terrible events of that day at Watkins Glen International, the storied racetrack west of Ithaca.

"Hmm, yes, it's still there," Gary said, noticing her gaze. "Thank God for fireproof suits."

Kume winced at the memory of Gary, surrounded by all that fire and smoke. When the flames had gotten under the balaclava, reaching just below his chin, the crash crew had arrived with foam and carbon dioxide, just in time to save him.

"Still," he said, taking a sip of his drink, "it's a good reminder of why I gave up my dream of becoming the next Phil Hill. Though I gotta say, I don't regret that I had my chance to race with the best. I still can't believe that I ended up turning Colin Chapman down when he offered me a spot as a driver on Team Lotus." He laughed easily at his own expense.

"You were very good," she said, smiling. "A bit wild and reckless, maybe, but I suppose that's to be expected for a race car driver."

Gary shook his head and smiled back. "Your eyes still have that sparkle."

Kume blushed and averted her eyes as the Lalique flutes were brought to the table. She hated that he could make her feel that embarrassing schoolgirl pang.

Before Gary could notice her squirming, she redirected the conversation. "Your dad would be very proud of what you've done with the company. Practically every girl in Japan wants to be a Heloise model."

Gary's father had retired in his mid-seventies, and from that moment on, Gary had made Heloise his life, dedicating himself to growing the company into a cosmetic juggernaut. A decade had passed since the company had gone public. Now the brand was global.

Gary laughed. "She was a fine old cosmetics firm, but stuck in a middle-age niche—and nobody's idea of a sexy, growth-oriented company. When my grandmother died and Dad became CEO, he decided to shake things up. He wanted to change the culture and bring in new lines that would appeal to young professional women. He was certain they'd be entering the workforce in much greater numbers."

Kume nodded. "He was right about that."

"Dad knew that not only would he need new products, he'd need a hook to draw in a younger customer. He shared his plans with Jerry and Eileen Ford. And wouldn't you know, Eileen said she had just the face for the new campaign. It'd be a bit risky—atypical—but Eileen thought it might point the company in a new direction. And that, my dear, is your cue. Enter stage left." Gary's smug smile was irresistible.

Kume shook her head. "I was pretty low on the food chain at that point, just doing shows and shoots on contract for Ford. But I had a hunch that fashion design was where I'd end up. I had no idea what was happening at Heloise."

Gary folded his napkin and slid his chair sideways. "I'm sure you remember the story, but indulge me for a moment. My dad was ready to schlep over to JWT for a bold new creative approach—he used to say that Heloise had been a client of J. Walter Thompson since Jesus was in sneakers—but Eileen encouraged him to consider instead one of the newer, edgier upstarts operating outside the orbit of the big Mad Ave. shops." Gary chuckled. "Dad reluctantly agreed, a decision he nearly regretted. The young Turks of the new agency pressed hard for a '*Hell Yes—Heloise!*' campaign. Thank God we toned it down to the much less defiant '*Hell . . . Oh! Heloise!*' The making of a Madison Avenue legend. Then another legend came along: you, the *Hell . . . Oh!* face of Heloise."

Gary raised his glass to clink against Kume's.

"Of course, who'd have thought I'd find myself in the corner office when Dad 'lost his marbles'—my mother's words—and took up with that young fitness instructor from Jackson Heights. Needless to say, the board members—mostly Mom's relatives—were not amused, and Dad was ushered into an unplanned early retirement."

Kume interjected, "But you proved you were up to the task."

Gary had directed the new product rollouts and a new *Hell . . . Oh!* fragrance package. The campaign, a smashing success, ultimately brought a whole new demographic to Heloise.

"You were the driving force behind Heloise's ads," Kume recalled. "How did *Advertising Age* put it? 'Offering a subtle but unapologetic sexuality and un-pandering sophistication.'"

Gary grinned. "Wow! Surprised you remembered. And thank you. But let's face it. The gamble to use you as the face of Heloise made it all work. It was a break from convention that caught the competition flat-footed."

With a sideways glance, Kume leaned forward theatrically, hardly able to contain her giggles. "My favorite was the near disaster over the musical theme. Remember?"

Gary leaned forward to meet her and loudly whispered, "Remember? How could I forget? The Brothers Gibb turned us down flat. 'We don't do commercials.' Excuse me! So we went after some new Swedish group."

"ABBA!" Kume said with a laugh, still amazed at the timing of it all.

"They were eager to please," Gary said, continuing the narrative, "and came up with a catchy hook. We loved it. It clicked with the mood we wanted. Then Bjorn Ulvaeus and Benny Andersson reworked our little Europop jingle into a hit single."

Kume started humming the melody to "Dancing Queen."

Now Gary was the one laughing. "It could've gotten ugly, but we settled the copyright suit quietly."

"ABBA made out okay," Kume said. "Now *Mamma Mia!* is selling out in London, and I see it just opened on Broadway. Some 'Dancing Queen' indeed."

Gary reached for her hand, and she reflexively pulled away in surprise.

"Sorry," he said. "I can't help it. You just look so stunning this evening. Remember the first time we met? It was at Lever House, and you were doing a commercial for facial cream or something. Dad and I went over there to take a look at you because the Fords had told him you should be the face for the new Heloise campaign. He practically begged me to come with him. I was prepared to be thoroughly bored—if memory serves, I was nursing a brutal hangover—but I humored him. Why he wanted me there, I don't know. Maybe he wanted a second, younger set of eyes on you. My mind was far from cosmetic campaigns, so I was totally unprepared for what happened next. When I saw you, my testosterone level shot up into the red zone. I couldn't stop staring at you. All I could think about was how I could bed that gorgeous body, so help me God." Gary raised both hands in mock surrender.

Kume frowned and sniffed. "Typically blunt and always a charmer. Nice to see you again, too, Gary." She fondled the stem of her glass, feeling pensive. "I remember that day. I was confused by all the attention. Your father seemed intensely interested, like he was about to buy a thoroughbred racehorse. I literally thought he would ask to examine my hooves and check my teeth," she deadpanned with a wink.

Then the dagger.

"And sorry, Gary, but my first impression of you was not so flattering. I saw a swaggering, unkempt young man with long, wild hair. A bit too sure of himself. A pampered, spoiled boy for whom everything came easy. Probably not someone I'd like to get to know."

Gary grimaced and clutched at his chest, pantomiming a bullet to the heart. He sagged in his chair, alarming the sommelier, who nearly dropped the bucket of champagne he was delivering to their table.

After recovering quickly and grinning sheepishly, Gary murmured, "My apologies, Pierre. *S'il vous plaît excusez mon mauvais sens du drame. Je vais très bien.*" He glanced at the Dom

Perignon. "But we may need another bottle. That one could be a bit explosive."

When the graying sommelier departed, smiling thinly and failing somewhat at appearing nonplussed, Kume and Gary both burst out laughing, drawing puzzled glances from several other tables.

"You gotta admit," Gary whispered, "we had a lot of fun."

Kume lowered her gaze. "Yes, we had fun. But it was fun we had no business having, considering you were wearing a wedding band."

She looked up as Gary pretended he hadn't heard the last remark. It was a tiresome subject, and his answer to it had always been that his youthful marriage had largely been arranged as the ritual bonding of two of New York's patrician families. Consequently, it had been a loveless experience in which, by tacit understanding, neither he nor she had asked indiscreet questions about their separate interests and amorous pursuits.

Kume had met Gary's wife, Kim, only once. She was a beautiful, rebellious redhead with a weakness for artificial stimulants and reckless behavior. Her crowning moment was the infamous night at the Juvenile Diabetes Foundation benefit in the ballroom of the Waldorf Astoria. Kim had taken the microphone, stripped to her underwear, and commenced unfastening her bra. Then, to the astonishment of the orchestra and audience—most of whom had thought she was a part of the show—she had attempted a slurred version of "Let Me Entertain You."

Gary had desperately vaulted onto the stage to cover his wife with his tuxedo jacket, but the damage was done. *The Post's* headline read WALDORF ALFRESCO, with strategic, if minimal, masking of the photograph, and New York tittered for days. It was even a sensation on *The Tonight Show*, with Johnny

Carson struggling to keep a straight face during his monologue. Shortly after that, Kim had overdosed and was taken to a secure private facility on Long Island. Several months later, she ended matters there by cutting her wrists.

Kume knew that those bygone memories were now playing in Gary's mind like a bad movie, and she felt sad for him. She struggled to control the urge to hold him and banish the pain.

Gary stared away silently. He changed the subject. "Those were strange times. I probably had no good reason to hang around the office, being generally useless as the campaign evolved, but I really couldn't keep my eyes off you. Technically, I was vice president of marketing, but before you came along, I probably couldn't have found my way to the men's room, never mind make decisions about marketing cosmetics. I learned more about the business in six months watching you and getting a feel for the campaign from the ground up than I ever had previously. It was important preparation for what would come later."

Kume nodded with a self-conscious toss of her head. "It took some time for you to accept your new role. You were only in your mid-twenties, and you'd had some success racing. In a way, it was good that you had the chance to experience Formula One at Watkins Glen, even though it very nearly cost you your life. Without that, you might not have been ready to take the reins at Heloise." She was feeling a pleasant buzz now, and the evening with Gary was turning out better than she had expected.

"Shall we see what's for dinner?" he asked.

"Everything looks fabulous. Do you have any favorites?"

It looked as if Gary, too, was feeling the flush of the alcohol. "Actually, I do. But maybe the staff can tell us if there's anything particularly good this evening." He gestured for the waiter.

Kume opened the menu and noted the interesting Asian influences: hamachi tartare with ginger coriander emulsion and wasabi infused tobiko.

As ever, Gary proved eager to impress her. "Eric Ripert is an amazing chef. He has created some imaginative dishes, some with strong Asian influence."

The waiter glided over to the table. "Welcome, Mr. Masterson. Chef Ripert sends his greetings. He wishes to inform you that he has prepared a special appetizer for you this evening. It is warm baked potato filled with smoked salmon, sour cream, and Iranian osetra caviar. Trust me, monsieur, it is wonderful."

"*Merci, Henri, il semble parfait.*" Gary ordered for both himself and Kume. Then, once the waiter had left, he failed to appear nonchalant when he strained to ask, "So will you join me tomorrow evening at the tree lighting?"

Kume had already decided against it, due to the work demands of the next several days. "I really can't, but thank you anyway. I have to save my energy for the showings. I'm sure it will be wonderful. Perhaps I can watch some of it on television."

Undeterred as ever, Gary nodded. "Your workweek ends after the Bloomingdale's showing on Friday. You'll have no further excuses. So I intend to take you to *Mamma Mia!* at the Winter Garden Theatre that evening."

With a sigh of resignation, Kume capitulated. But she decided that she couldn't let Gary have the final word without a last thrust and parry of her own. "What's been going on with you, Gary? Still unmarried? Hard to believe with an attractive, eligible guy like you." She peered mischievously over the lip of her flute. "Surely there have been opportunities." She was teasing now, but she couldn't hide the fact that she had more than an abstract interest.

The creases in the corners of his eyes deepened when Gary winced in a rueful smile. "Since the first marriage worked out so well . . . I guess I wasn't in a hurry to enter another one. Opportunities? Maybe you could call it that. More like opportunistic women looking for an easy life.

"There's a lady in Brazil I'm fond of. Cristina is a carioca from Rio. We like shooting sports—mostly bird hunting—and working on Amazon rain forest preservation projects. I get down there maybe once or twice a year. And there's a Croatian tennis player I met at the US Open a few years ago. I try to catch her matches whenever the tour comes to the US. Ivanka is a bit young, admittedly, but full of life and athletic as hell. She kicks my butt all over the court. Good fun, both. But we haven't discussed anything long-term." He paused, smiling. "Saved by the bell. Here comes Eric."

Gary introduced Kume to Chef Ripert, who delivered the appetizers himself. He was a striking Frenchman, with thick lips, soulful blue eyes, and a pronounced, beak-shaped nose. They spoke briefly about Franco-Japanese fusion cuisine, and Eric suggested that Kume have Genevieve give him a call.

When the entrees arrived, Kume pronounced her halibut exceptional. As she savored her Sambuca, she checked her watch. "I feel like I haven't slept in three days. Would you mind if we call it an evening?"

"Of course not!" Gary responded as he drained his Drambuie. "But since I've taken a few jabs over my apparent preference for young foreign women, I believe it only fair that next time I be allowed equal time to pry into matters you might consider personal. Deal?"

Kume reached over the table to shake his hand. "Deal."

Chapter 16

Memories of Michiko

Friday, November 30, 2001

Sendai, Miyagi Prefecture, Japan

Soichiro felt strangely ill at ease as he waited beside Noriko at Kazuo Midorikawa's front door. Maybe it was because Kazuo had sounded particularly wretched over the phone. Or maybe it was because Noriko had finally agreed to accompany Soichiro to his old friend's home. Perhaps she, too, sensed Kazuo's time was short. Kazuo had purportedly canceled a business meeting, which Soichiro knew could have been shorthand for any number of sketchy activities, in favor of another visit. How many more remained? Kazuo had seemed unusually stoic lately, even brushing off suggestions by his people that he travel to Sloan Kettering in New York for treatment.

Soichiro exchanged glances with his wife, who wore a frown and an uncertain gaze, just as Yoko answered the door. She, too, looked grim. Exhaustion tugged at the corners of her eyes, and her slender, diminutive hands quivered noticeably. The wrinkles on her face and the stooped angle of her spine suggested she was every bit as old as Kazuo, if not a few years older, but she would no doubt outlive her employer by any number of years.

She ushered them into the ornate study decorated with antique samurai swords and armor. Kazuo was waiting for them, and it was all Soichiro could do not to focus on the oxygen bottle resting beside him. Had it come to that already? Kazuo's cheeks were sunken, and a dark circle showed beneath his one good eye. His decline, so gradual for so long, was finally picking up speed as he neared his final days.

Kazuo stood and offered a crisp bow. "My friend, Matsuhata-san, I am delighted that you have come, and especially that you have brought your lovely wife. Noriko-san, you honor my home with your presence."

Soichiro responded with a bow. "The pleasure is ours. You sounded rather distressed, old friend."

Noriko bowed and smiled briefly, looking unsure what to say. Her long, dark hair tumbled down her shoulders, framing her striking, oval-shaped face.

Kazuo waved them toward the low table. "Please sit. Yoko will bring some tea. I've felt a great need to discuss some things with you. Noriko-san, I hope we old soldiers won't bore you with too many stories from our bygone days. But it's important to talk about such things if we're to understand something about the people we have become." A flicker of mirth sparkled in his one good eye. "Perhaps you'll discover some things about your husband you didn't know."

Soichiro noticed that Kazuo's breathing sounded more labored than it had during their last visit, but he seemed determined to soldier on.

"When last we spoke," he said, "we had survived the defeat at Guadalcanal. I was evacuated to Rabaul for treatment of my wounds. Along with losing my eye, I had several shell fragments removed from my back and shoulders. I was only at the naval hospital in Rabaul for a short time. What about you, So-san? What happened to you after the battle?"

Soichiro stole a glance at Noriko. He found it difficult opening up to others about his wartime experiences, and although Noriko knew much about what had happened on Okinawa, there was a great deal she didn't know of her husband's war before that.

He reluctantly began. "We knew the Second Division was destroyed for all practical purposes and was no longer an effective combat unit. What was left of the division was evacuated to the Philippines. We were told we'd be replenished and refit, but that never happened. What was left of our division was assigned garrison duty for the duration of the war. We were hardly capable of anything else." Soichiro felt himself warming to the subject. "My artillery regiment was detached for duties in the Marshalls and Marianas. I was brought in to support combat operations on Guam. We knew the Americans wanted the island for their B-29s, which would be able to reach mainland Japan. As it turned out, I was transferred to Okinawa before Guam was attacked and taken by the Americans."

Kazuo snorted. "A good thing for you. Otherwise you might have ended up like Sergeant Shoichi Yokoi. You've heard of him, I'm sure. He hid out in the jungles of Guam and lived like an animal before he was discovered in 1972. Now *that* was a soldier. He couldn't believe that Japan had surrendered twenty-seven years earlier and that the war was over."

"We all had a hard time accepting that," Soichiro remarked thoughtfully. "'Enduring the unendurable,' as the emperor put it. And after Rabaul, where were you sent, Kazu-san?"

"The Philippines. Luzon, specifically. With only one eye, I was deemed unfit for combat, so I was assigned to guard the American and Filipino prisoners who had surrendered. They were wretched specimens, hardly requiring guards."

Kazuo paused to cough, and Soichiro tried to ignore the raspy, visceral resonance emanating from his lungs.

"There was a large prison compound north of Manila called Cabanatuan," Kazuo said as soon as he'd regained his voice. "Several thousand of the captives were kept there. I was there from early 1943 until August of 1944. When it became clear MacArthur wasn't going to bypass the Philippines, our commanders decided to move as many prisoners as possible to the homeland. They said they would provide needed labor in the mines and war industries. I accompanied a shipload, and as chance would have it, I ended up in the north at a camp called Hanawa Number Six. It was also known as Sendai Number Six."

"How ironic," Soichiro murmured with a smirk, "a member of the Sendai Division coming home to guard prisoners in a place called Sendai. You never told me much about your time in the Philippines. What was it like?"

Kazuo squirmed noticeably, his hand reflexively reaching for the pocket where he usually kept his Camels, then dropping despondently. "I do that at least a hundred times a day. Never thought I'd miss them so much.

"Guarding captives wasn't what I had enlisted for," he grumbled. "It was lowly work, not befitting a warrior. And it was easy to hold them in contempt. Why had they allowed themselves to be taken alive when so many of their fellows had fought to the death honorably? I had difficulty reconciling that. And there were times, I'm not proud to say, that I acted on that contempt. And I wasn't the only one."

Soichiro rose to refresh his cup of tea. He turned to Noriko. "Would you like more?"

She shook her head and continued to stare at Kazuo with a questioning look in her eyes. Was she warming to him? Reassessing things?

Soichiro chose this moment to interject his own observations regarding prisoners. "I don't recall that we ever took prisoners. I don't know what we'd have done with them if we had. We never were in a position to handle them. We were mostly on the defensive after Midway and seldom had the occasion to capture anyone. If we did, the prisoner was likely a straggler and would probably have been shot."

Kazuo nodded. "Such a shooting would have been merciful—not unlike the machine-gunning of survivors of torpedoed ships on the high seas. They couldn't be accommodated aboard a submarine. Would it be more humane to leave them to the sharks or a slow death of madness and thirst or drowning? Given a choice, I'd take shooting. But I'd also take it over the dishonor of being taken prisoner in the first place."

"You always were a hard case when it came to that," Soichiro said in a scolding tone as he turned a cold eye toward his old friend. "In some ways, I blame the mindless attitude of our armed forces that brainwashed a generation of people like us. It was almost cult-like. A perversion of the samurai code. When we were kids, we were taught *gyokusai*, that honorable death was preferable to the dishonor of accepting defeat, that 'death is lighter than a feather, but duty is heavier than a mountain.'"

Kazuo sat silently.

"We lost an entire generation of young men," Soichiro continued. "Young men who, though terrified and wishing no more than to go home to family and loved ones, accepted a vision of poetic perfection expressed through Imperial sacrifice.

They crashed their planes into ships or charged to their deaths against overwhelming firepower. And when defeat was inevitable, they armed their grenades against their helmets and held them to their chests." For Soichiro, it felt as if the voiceless ghosts of so many dead comrades were speaking through him. "It was a colossal waste of our people, as though merely surviving was somehow shameful. And to what end? The destruction of the Yamato nation and occupation by a foreign power? Was this the glorious result foreseen by Hideki Tojo and his militarists?"

By the time he had finished his rant, Soichiro was shaking. He suddenly felt ashamed at having taken it so far.

Kazuo sat pensively, digesting the harsh indictment. For once, he appeared to have no answer, and as he sat quietly, he fondled the worn Zippo lighter, finally tossing it to Soichiro with a gesture of resignation. "Keep it. I haven't any further use of it." His voice sounded sepulchral.

Noriko had been frowning sympathetically at Kazuo for some time, and he looked surprised when she addressed him directly. "Where did you first meet Michiko-san?"

He brightened upon hearing his wife's name, and his tone softened. "She was the daughter of an admiral. When we were on leave after basic training, I met her on the train taking us back to Sendai for a farewell visit home. She was traveling from Yokohama to Sendai to visit her grandmother." Kazuo sighed. "She was so beautiful and poised, unlike us rustics from the north. I was sure she would ignore me, a mere army private, but I took the chance and introduced myself. She was traveling with a chaperone, a dragon of a woman, who was glaring at me, trying to intimidate me. But I ignored the woman and asked if I could call on her. My heart was in my throat, but when she said yes, I felt like I could leap over Mount Fuji."

"How fortunate, and wonderful, for you," Noriko said gently. "No doubt she had plenty of potential suitors at the naval base, yet she chose an army enlistee. She must have seen something special in you, Midorikawa-san."

"Kind of you to say, but if so, I haven't the slightest idea what it might have been. During my seventy-two-hour leave, I couldn't bear the thought of spending a moment away from her. Thanks to her grandmother, a very wise and noble woman, we were allowed to spend the better part of two days together. I promised her I would write at every opportunity, wherever I might be. At the time, that could have been anywhere, but I didn't care. She told me she would wait and gave me a photo that I carried throughout the war. Would you like to see it?" Kazuo asked hopefully.

Noriko nodded. "Of course."

Kazuo gestured for Yoko to fetch the photo, and she returned a moment later with it in a small gold frame.

Noriko stared for several moments at the fading, cracked photograph before passing it over to Soichiro, who took a moment to study it. The girl was astonishingly beautiful. She wore pale makeup, a simple but well-tailored jacket, and a string of Mikimoto pearls around her slender neck. It was a formal portrait , but she had sabotaged it slightly with the faintest hint of a seductive smile.

"She's lovely," Noriko murmured while Soichiro was still gazing at it. "I can understand your feelings. Was it difficult to communicate while you were deployed on military duty?"

"Almost impossible. The mail seldom caught up with us, because it was always considered less important than things like food and munitions. I read and reread the few letters I did receive until they literally fell apart in my hands. I wrote as often as I could, but Michiko only received three of my letters, all written before Guadalcanal. She had no way of knowing I had lost an eye until later, when I wrote her from the Philippines." He brought a hand to his patched eye, shivering slightly. "I was so worried that she might see me as disfigured, undesirable. I said I'd understand if she no longer wanted to wait for me.

"Then I waited in agony. Weeks, then months went by without a response from her. I was convinced she was no longer interested in me. Perhaps she was repelled by my injury and had found someone else. It was a crushing thought. I cared little for my own life—even tried to talk the camp commander into returning me to combat duty with the army. There was need for more troops, as the Americans were grinding up our garrisons in the Pacific islands." Kazuo broke into a melancholy smile. "Quite properly, the colonel refused my request."

"When did you see her again?" Noriko asked.

Soichiro was surprised at her continued interest.

Kazuo paused, reached for the photograph, and studied it briefly. "It was winter, around the time of Oshougatsu. I had been stationed at the Hanawa camp for several months after the transfer of prisoners from the Philippines."

Noriko interrupted him. "Why were prisoners taken to such a faraway place?"

"To work the old Osarizawa copper mines up in the mountains for Mitsubishi. They made copper for the army. It was ridiculous, of course, because the ore had played out in that thirteen-hundred-year-old dig and the mine had long been abandoned. But Mitsubishi was determined to squeeze every last gram from it. The company asked the army for prisoners of war to act as unpaid laborers. It was dangerous work. I brought over five hundred men from Cabanatuan."

Soichiro frowned as he considered the shameful treatment of those who had suffered so much already. Before he could express himself, the oyabun continued.

"The cold can be bitter in the northern mountains, so I was eager to take a few days' leave to return to Sendai. I hoped to inquire about Michiko and figure out why I hadn't heard from her. I was so nervous when I knocked on the door at her grandmother's house. Nearly three years had passed since I'd been there, and so much had changed. The beautiful trees for which Sendai was famous were mere stumps. They'd been cut down for fuel. The city was dreary with wartime restrictions. Subdued lighting, everything gray, no movement of vehicles. The streets were quiet.

"At first I thought the house was empty, because there was no answer. I knocked again, and this time the door opened a crack and someone asked me in a small voice who I was. I recognized the voice as Michiko's. My heart raced with excitement. When she saw me, she rushed into my arms and held me tight."

Soichiro thought he spotted a tear forming in Noriko's left eye. "Why was Michiko-san in Sendai?" she asked, brushing it away. "Wasn't her home Yokohama?"

Kazuo was clearly tiring. The rasp in his voice had become a croak. "I just need a moment to catch my breath," he said and held up his hands, insisting that he wanted to finish.

Soichiro took the opportunity to ask Yoko to bring sake and three cups, plus one for herself. She nodded, arching an eyebrow at being included, and quietly left the room. Then Soichiro took a seat, cross-legged at the low table, chin resting on his folded hands.

"Thank you, So-san," Kazuo said approvingly. "I believe a taste of good sake will refresh spirits and memories."

As soon as she returned, Yoko set out the cups and poured the Ginjo Urakasumi.

"Nori-chan, you asked why Michiko was in Sendai," Kazuo said. "Her father had sent her there during September to stay with her grandmother, who was ailing. But I believe his true motive was to remove her from harm's way. He thought his daughter would be safer in Sendai than Yokohama. With bases on the Marianas, American B-29s could reach the Japanese heartland, and Yokohama was sure to be a high priority target because of the city's defense industries." Kazuo took a deep, wheezing breath and continued. "When I arrived, Michiko was in mourning. Shortly after packing his daughter off to what he had hoped would be safety in Sendai, her father was ordered by Admiral Nishimura to prepare his warships for battle. It was a desperate gamble to prevent the Americans from landing on Leyte. The fleet left the inland sea for a fateful encounter with Nimitz's carriers and battleships. During that great battle, Japan lost essentially what was left of the Combined Fleet. Michiko's father went down with his flagship, the battleship *Yamashiro*. It was sunk by dive bombers and torpedoes. The loss was more than the grandmother could bear, and she followed her son in death several weeks after receiving the news."

Soichiro shook his head sadly. "Poor child. Losing her father and grandmother at the same time. She was alone and far away from everything familiar. Where was the chaperone?"

"Michiko's father had dismissed the woman and told her to return to her family in Osaka when Michiko left for Sendai. He knew a terrible time was coming and thought she should be with her own people."

"Did Michiko-san say anything about your eye?" Noriko asked. "Or why she hadn't replied to your letter?"

Kazuo sipped from his cup and chuckled. "Oh, yes. She had quite a lot to say, the first being that she had in fact received the letter. Second, that she had been insulted—*infuriated*, actually—that I could think she was so shallow that the mere loss of an eye would be sufficient excuse to change how she felt about me. She regarded my letter as a self-pitying whimper, unworthy of response. So she decided to punish me and let me think she'd lost interest. If I was the right one, she concluded, I would return to try to win her again."

"And you did return." Noriko offered a faint smile.

"I did indeed," the oyabun replied with relish. "And I was not about to risk losing her again. Nori-chan, it was the pivotal moment in my life. To me, she was all that was desirable and good. Life without her was unthinkable. In my dreams, I thanked the blessed fortune that had brought her to me. I felt . . . unworthy of her." Kazuo's good eye glistened with emotion. "We tracked down a city magistrate, who kindly agreed to perform a civil marriage service. There were no blossoms or paper lanterns, no religious ceremonies at ancestral shrines. We dressed in our best finery—an army uniform and a lovely kimono that had belonged to her grandmother. For a wedding feast, we had some rice with tai, which I persuaded a shopkeeper to part with in exchange for a book of counterfeit ration coupons. He threw in a bottle of cheap sake. It was the most wonderful meal I've ever had."

Kazuo smiled self-consciously and nodded to Noriko. "Our wedding night was awkward but sweet. We were innocent, like two kittens discovering a new toy. But as the Americans say, practice makes perfect. Two heavenly days and nights were all we had before I had to return to Hanawa. As the hours ticked away, I seriously considered deserting. I figured I would take my beloved Michiko far away to the northern mountains of

Hokkaido and leave behind the world of war and duty." Kazuo's face darkened. "She's the one who put an end to such
thinking. She told me that it would be the greatest dishonor to
abandon my responsibilities when the nation so badly needed
her sons to defend the sacred Yamato land. She began to weep
as she spoke of the sacrifices made by her father and so many
others. So I reluctantly returned to the task of guarding prisoners of war in the cold mountains of Akita."

Soichiro turned the Zippo lighter over in his hands. Kazuo's breath had become a hoarse whisper. And it was clear that
Noriko had been moved by the story of his love and courtship
of Michiko.

But before he could begin again, Soichiro rose from the
table and walked over to his old friend. He pressed the lighter
into Kazuo's palm. "Keep this. When the time is right, I will
accept it, but now is not that time. You're tiring and should
rest. Noriko and I will return soon, and we hope to hear the
rest of the story of Michiko-san."

As they picked up their coats to leave, Soichiro caught a
glimpse of Yoko gently picking up and staring at the framed
photo of Michiko. He was sure he saw tears on the old woman's face.

Chapter 17

Step No. 2

Same day

Mesilla, New Mexico

After outlasting another night of disorienting nightmares, Frankie was relieved when morning came. As usual, Melanie was already out of bed by the time he entered the kitchen. He glanced out the window above the sink and noted the pockets of frost, just visible in the early morning light, that had formed overnight. As chilly as the late November air looked, it was likely balmy compared to the cold shoulder his wife had been giving him lately. She'd just rinsed out her new French press and seemed determined to angle her back toward him no matter where he stood.

"Want some coffee?" she asked.

"No thanks," he said, hardly bothering to open his mouth in reply. He could be just as frosty as his better half, he told himself.

Of course, even as he entertained the notion, he knew it was a lie. He'd never been one to hold a grudge, much less

keep score. Besides, this was *his* problem, not hers. Sooner
or later—hopefully sooner—he'd drum up the courage to tell
Melanie everything. For now, though, he was merely counting
down the weeks until his trip to Okinawa, which, had he been
a moth, might as well have been a 400-watt streetlamp. It was
tugging at him every day, and he was doing nothing to resist
its lure. Whatever he had to work out was going to be worked
out there, on that island, where he'd once longed to escape
and where he now returned every time he drifted off to sleep.

He was staring at a row of cereal boxes in the cupboard,
contemplating which high-fiber marketing gimmick would
determine his breakfast, when he heard a knock at the front
door. Melanie didn't react, which told him it fell to him to do
the honors.

"I'll get it," he said, stating the obvious as he shuffled to
the tiled entryway.

"Hey, Dad," Ellen said as soon as he opened the door. She
was holding a box of donuts and looked awfully peppy with
the low-hanging morning sun shining brightly behind her.

"Morning, kid," he said as she breezed past him toward the
kitchen. "What brings you to these parts?"

"Just figured I'd surprise you and Mom with something
naughty," she said without looking back.

Frankie followed his daughter into the kitchen and found
her and her mother drooling over the contents of the box, now
open and sitting on the breakfast table.

"What is this?" Melanie asked with a gasp.

Frankie couldn't remember the last time she'd sounded
so tickled. "There better be a maple bar in there," he quipped.

"What—you think I'm a rookie?" Ellen nodded to a cru-
elly tempting assortment of donuts that bulged with all the
classics, including a bear claw and a pair of apple fritters.

Frankie spotted at least three maple bars. "Hot damn."

"Better get that coffee going, Mom," Ellen said.

"I'm way ahead of you," Melanie replied and grabbed a short stack of medium-sized plates from the cupboard.

Between the sight of so much sugar on the table and the spontaneous visit from his daughter, Frankie felt himself momentarily paralyzed. It wasn't as if Ellen didn't drop by on a regular basis. It was just that she rarely brought treats when she wasn't up to something. Was she trying to melt the icy relations between her parents?

Frankie only needed a moment to compose himself. "I'll be right back," he said. "I wanna grab a quick shower before I sit down to debase myself."

Barely five minutes had passed—Frankie had mastered the art of a quick shower in basic training, and the skill had never left him—when he joined the ladies at the breakfast table. All he wanted was that maple bar.

"So," he said, reaching into the box for his favorite donut, "to what do we owe the pleasure?"

Ellen shrugged. "It's Friday. I figured I'd stop by on my way to work. You coming in today, Dad? I can give you a lift if you want."

"Sure," he said. "But what's this *really* about?" The hacienda was hardly on her way to work.

Ellen shot him a quick glare that told him to quit while he was ahead. "Does there have to be a reason?" she asked.

"Absolutely not," Melanie answered. "We're just glad you came by."

Frankie offered a halfhearted grunt and went to work on his maple bar, which he gripped gently between his right thumb and forefinger. There was no way to eat one without getting sticky fingers, he conceded. Nor did he have any shot at figuring out his daughter's motives. It was possible her visit was a spontaneous one, born solely out of her love of her parents and the occasional descent into gluttony. But it seemed more likely that she was trying to encourage some kind of détente between her parents, maybe get them talking openly. He knew the way she operated. First, she'd give them room to sort it out themselves. Then she'd gently—or mischievously, if that was what it took—prod them toward resolving their problems. Then, when all else failed, she'd knock their heads together and get the dialogue rolling herself. Presumably she had only reached Step No. 2, but there was no telling when she'd tire of waiting for her parents to start communicating effectively.

Then there was Melanie. She was obviously long past resenting the nightly interruptions to their sleep and the daily conceit that everything was normal. It wasn't. He knew that. He just wasn't ready to go there yet. He was tempted to steer the conversation toward Melanie's favorite topic—Ellen's love life—but knew that way, too, was littered with landmines. The last thing he wanted to do was draw his daughter's ire after inviting her, albeit only partially, into his dilemma. He had yet to tell Melanie about their trip to Okinawa. He wanted her to hear it from *him*, when the time was right, not from Ellen during an angry outburst.

Better to keep a low profile, he thought, and enjoy his maple bar.

Chapter 18

The Lid to Pandora's Box

Same Day

New York City

Gary Masterson produced a bottle of Veuve Clicquot brut and two plastic cups. "To a successful showing!" he said after filling the cups.

Kume, still making the transition from a frenetic day of meetings and last-minute preparation, feigned a smile. "To a successful showing," she repeated as she tapped her cup against his.

They sat together in the back seat as their driver, dressed incongruously in a formal top hat and a faded jean jacket, guided their white carriage toward Central Park. The lone horse, a chestnut mare, seemed too disinterested to keep more than a lackadaisical pace.

Kume, though, was still elsewhere. She felt like a load had dropped from her shoulders, thanks to Chika and Haruko and their amazing work, which had resulted in a fat book of orders from Saks and Bloomingdale's for the spring "Plumage" collection. It had been a gamble, but the trip had been worth it. She was tired from the stresses of the showings and would have liked nothing better than to enjoy a hot bath, put on her pajamas, order room service, and watch an old movie on TV. But she had agreed to meet up with Gary, who had arranged a carriage ride through Central Park before dinner at a little Hell's Kitchen Thai place that was a favorite of his. From there, they'd take a short stroll to the theater.

At least she hadn't been forced to bundle up. With the mercury holding in the mid-fifties, it promised to be a pleasant excursion.

"Your modeling name is still a door opener," he said with a genuine smile. "It gets you special access others could only dream about. So . . . when do you think you might return to New York."

Kume, whose modeling name was simply her first name, tried not to look thrown by the question. "I don't have any plans for the near future," she said, determined to keep things casual between them.

The hollow clop of the horse's hooves on pavement, the merry rhythm of the sleigh bells adorning the harness, and the pleasant buzz from the bubbly induced a hypnotic warmth and tingle in Kume as they entered the park. She waved at passing joggers and strollers, who looked up and smiled, no doubt assuming the handsome couple was celebrating an anniversary or a much-anticipated tryst.

She was mildly surprised when Gary said, "Okay. Now it's your turn." He had mischief in his eye.

Kume stared at him. "My turn for what? To try to top your romantic entanglements with an Amazon queen and Croatian tennis goddess? Sorry, but I concede. Between the fashion house and the restaurant, I haven't had much time to flirt with the jet set. Of course, I guess you'd have to count that Aussie professional golfer who had me thinking about slowing down and letting him help me improve my swing."

Gary winced, which told her she'd scored with that dart. "Golfer, huh? I didn't know you played."

"I don't, but Greg told me I had great legs and turned my hips well. Said I might be a natural."

"Okay, okay. Too much information." He held up both hands and laughed. "Let's change the subject. It's been so long, and there's so much to catch up on—and so little time. I wish you could stay another day or so."

"That's just not possible. I leave for Tokyo tomorrow." Kume knew that what Gary really wanted was more than just her company; he wanted to revive old memories of the past. And in another life, she might have submitted. But she also knew that she was already testing the limits of the window she had felt safe in allotting to Gary Masterson. Their history was too complicated to hazard reopening carelessly, and Kume had no desire to revisit those memories.

They finished the champagne just as they exited the park at West Eighty-Sixth Street and clopped on down Columbus Avenue. At Fiftieth Street and Eighth Avenue, Gary had the carriage drop them in front of an unpretentious door with peeling signage that READ *SEEDA THAI II*.

"I guarantee you'll love this place," he gushed. "It's not fancy or beautiful, but the food is wonderful. John Kennedy Jr. used to come here a lot and even had a favorite dish. The offices of his magazine, *George*, were just down the block. They have a plaque with his name over at that booth."

Kume looked around the dark restaurant and glimpsed the Kennedy plaque and the obligatory aquarium, where several fat koi lazily drifted in bluish light. The aromas were delicious, heavy with onion, ginger, curry, and wok-prepared fish and pork. Kume ordered the panang curry and Gary the chopped pork with basil, onion, and chile-lime sauce.

Kume tried to sound animated when she said, "You're right. The food is great," but her tone betrayed fatigue and flagging enthusiasm.

Gary picked up on it immediately. "Listen, why don't we skip the show? It's not like you haven't heard ABBA before. Suppose we just take a walk and have an early nightcap somewhere? We aren't far from the hotel."

Kume felt relief easing its way through her. "Thank you. I hate being such a poor companion this evening, but this week took a lot out of me."

After dinner, they strolled slowly east and crossed Broadway and Seventh, turning at the lighted fantasy of Avenue of the Americas and Radio City, finally settling into a cushioned banquette at the Halcyon Bar in the Rihga Royal Hotel.

"You were very thoughtful to change plans for me this evening." Kume reached over to grasp Gary's hand. "I've really enjoyed seeing you, and if it were possible, I would gladly put off my return trip." That was a lie. She saw Gary's eyes glimmer and thought about how she had missed the funny dimple that appeared when he was getting serious.

"The pleasure has been all mine," he said. "I hate to admit it, but I've missed you very much. Our self-imposed separation and lack of communication hasn't been easy for me. I guess I'll always carry a torch for you. I'd have fueled up the jet and set course for Tokyo at least a dozen times in the past ten years if I'd felt there was even a remote chance that I'd have been welcome. But I do understand. I guess time doesn't heal all things."

Kume could tell that the conversation was about to take a turn she wanted to avoid. She decided to tack strategically into safer waters. "Being in New York invariably brings back an old yearning that I first experienced when I joined the Ford Agency. Surrounded by so many Americans, I couldn't help wondering about my biological father. Who was he? *Where* was he? Why did I never know him? Why did he leave my mother? All those questions. It bothers me even now, but I guess I'll never know."

Gary's expression radiated surprise. "You've never mentioned that before. Haven't you done anything to pursue it? I'm sure you know there are amazing resources today for tracking and locating missing persons." He changed his tone to one of mock seriousness. "Or might it be that you really don't want to know who he is—or *was*? Maybe you're afraid of what you'll discover. Maybe he's a wanted criminal or serving time in prison. Or was married eight times and has twenty-three children."

Kume had to laugh in spite of herself. Gary could always amuse her with his absurdities. She paused to arrange her thoughts. "No, I haven't done anything to find my American father. It's not an easy subject. I used to worry about what it might do to my mother if I were to locate the man—or even if she knew I was looking for him. And what about my dad, the man my mother married and who has been the only father I ever knew? How would *he* react?"

The dimple was back. "Do you still feel the same way?"

Kume frowned and looked away. "Honestly, no. I don't want to hurt my mother, but she's been so obstinate about the subject despite my pestering her over the years. All I want to know is who my dad is. Am I a terrible person for wanting that? Do you think I'm being selfish? Is wanting to know so wrong?"

A note of exasperation crept into Gary's voice. "No, you're not being selfish. Could anything be more natural than wanting to know where we come from? And particularly if that requires learning the identity of an unknown parent? If it were me, you can bet I'd do anything I could to find that parent, and I wouldn't worry too much about my family because I'd give them enough credit to understand my need to know."

Gary pulled himself closer to Kume and placed his arm around her shoulder. She did not withdraw from his contact.

"Having said that, I do understand the delicacy of the matter. What if someone else did the digging for you? Someone who promised to be discreet, someone you could trust. Someone like me."

The proposition surprised her. *Interesting but perplexing*, she thought. Certainly not something she had bargained for. Gary didn't make idle offers, but would she want to invite him back into her life when it had taken so long to get over the painful memories? On the other hand, it might be a way to come to terms with an unhappy void in her life without leaving telltale tracks. The last thing she needed was for her mother to find out that she was looking for her natural father—and that the person actually doing the looking was none other than Gary Masterson. So it would have its risks. Would the payoff be worth it?

"Let me think about that. It's very generous of you to offer, but I don't know if I'm ready for it. And I'm not sure you realize what you'd be getting yourself into. You know practically nothing about my family. And what about wartime records in Okinawa? Would such records even exist? We're talking about things that happened over fifty years ago." Part of Kume was hoping to give Gary a graceful way to withdraw his offer.

Gary dismissed her objections out of hand. "All that means is that I'll need your help in getting some basics. Then leave it to me." He was clearly warming to the idea. "You can e-mail me what you know, like your mother's family name, where she went to school, her husband's name, and whether or not she had any military record. Anything you can give me. I have a friend in the State Department who can help open a few doors, if you really want to pursue this."

Kume could sense that she wasn't likely to discourage Gary, and secretly she loved that he seemed willing to take this on for her. All her instincts told her to nip the idea in the bud right here and now and tell Gary that she wasn't ready to expose her family—or even the American soldier's family—to such a startling revelation.

But she astonished herself when her mouth formed the words, "I do. I think I need to know, and waiting may just make it harder. Gary, it means the world to me. Thank you for offering to help."

She leaned over and stared into the eyes of the man she had tried to erase from her past. She took his face in both hands and kissed him long and full on the lips.

The next morning, in the car on the way to JFK, Kume wondered to herself whether she had just cracked open the lid to Pandora's box.

Three nights later, Gary entered his brownstone on Sixty-Third Street and tossed his coat into the den, just missing his office chair. He grabbed a bottled water from the fridge and returned to the den, not bothering to turn on the light. Instead, he unslept his computer and waited for an Internet connection.

A few seconds later, he was scrolling through his e-mail. There at the top of his inbox was a message, only five minutes old, from Kume. He glanced at the clock on the lower right-hand corner of the monitor and then paused a moment to do the math in his head.

"Thirteen hours ahead," he muttered tiredly. It had been another long day at the office. "That means it's almost nine o'clock tomorrow morning there."

Kume had likely written the missive from her design studio—or was just now leaving for work.

He unscrewed the top from his water bottle, took a long, refreshing swig, and then settled into his chair to read.

Hello, Gary.

Thanks again for your kind offer to help me track down my biological father. It was awfully sweet of you. Please don't feel obligated to follow through on your end. I was halfway home on the plane when it dawned on me that this might end up being more trouble than it's worth, at least for you.

But if you're still game, here's some information to get the ball rolling. I guess I should start with my mother. Her family name is Ota. They were originally from a small island called Kume-jima. I think it's about sixty miles west of Okinawa, give or take. Her father's name was Tomeji, and her mother was Misaki. They only had one child together. A daughter. Noriko (my mother).

Like I said, Kume-jima was quite small. Not much of an economy, other than sugarcane production and some fishing. When my mom turned thirteen, her parents decided to move to Okinawa, where she could attend Okinawa Daiichi Girls High School. After that, she went to Okinawa Shihan Girls Teachers College. Both schools were considered Okinawa's most prestigious, the yin to the yang of Normal School (an all-male school that sits at the base of Shuri Castle in the old capital of Shuri.

Anyway, Tomeji got a job in the prefectural government. Neither he nor Misaki survived the battle. But back to Mom. She excelled in high school and became acquainted with another student, a distant cousin named Masahide Ota, also from Kume-jima. He went to Normal School and was a member of the Blood and Iron Scouts (an Okinawan regiment made up of students from the Normal School) for the Emperor. The unit basically served as messengers for the Imperial Japanese Thirty-Second Army, which had been assigned the island's defense. Everyone knew an invasion was imminent. Masahide survived the battle and later went on to become Okinawa's prefectural governor.

Mom served in the Student Medical Corps. She was one of 155 students and staff of the high school and teachers college who were recruited, trained, and assigned duty with the corps. They were called Star Lily Girls. The Japanese word is Himeyuri. Basically, nurses' aides. She tended to military casualties in army hospitals and infirmaries that were being set up deep underground.

Shoot. I'm out of time. I'll write more when I get a chance—assuming you're still feeling like you want to do this. I won't blame you if you change your mind.

Ciao,
Kume

Gary leaned back and took another swallow of water. He felt oddly energized as he wondered where all this would lead. Somehow he'd have to track down Kume's American father while keeping his commitment to Nathan. He smiled at the thought of the two projects dovetailing. Years of juggling a hectic schedule had taught him how to keep two or more balls in the air at once.

In any case, Kume's e-mail constituted a good start. There would certainly be some record of Noriko's father as a governmental official, and the well-known legends about the heroic sacrifice of the Himeyuri Girls in a desperate cause had provided sentimental fodder for a generation of books and movies in Japan. There would have to be some trace, anecdotal or official, of Noriko and what had become of her at the end of the battle. The difficult part would involve finding the American soldier, who remained nameless.

Chapter 19

Fires of 1945

Friday, December 7

Sendai, Miyagi Prefecture, Japan

Soichiro was in the middle of his morning ritual—reviewing the international news and fish prices—when Noriko stepped into his studio.

"I'm ready," she said.

He shut down his computer and then turned to face his wife, who was dressed in a simple but elegant black shift dress with a hemline just above her ankles. A powder-blue chiffon jacket covered her arms and shoulders. To his astonishment and delight, she had again agreed to accompany him to Kazuo's home after the oyabun had invited them back to resume their conversation of the previous week.

As it happened, the date marked the sixtieth anniversary of the Combined Fleet's attack on the US bases in Hawaii. Each year Kazuo and Soichiro would traditionally observe the anniversary by raising a glass in honor of their fallen comrades.

This year, Soichiro had planned a special surprise. He would bring a special bottle of Old Grand-Dad whiskey. It was an ancient bottle of a not particularly good bourbon that he had received from a US Army captain in exchange for a pristine Nambu sidearm at the end of the Okinawa battle. He'd kept it unopened all these years and now could think of no better use for it than to share it with his old comrade. He feared Kazuo would not be alive to observe the next Pearl Harbor anniversary.

They drove in silence to Kazuo's estate and were once again greeted at the door by Yoko, who escorted them into Kazuo's study. Ancient samurai swords gleamed from behind glass cases on the wall.

Soichiro set the American bottle of whiskey on the low table and smiled mischievously.

"I remember you telling me about this, my friend," Kazuo said as he removed the oxygen cannula from beneath his nostrils. "Am I to take this as a sign that the end is near?" he teased in a hollow voice.

"I should have expected you'd say something ridiculous like that," Soichiro said with a snort. "Actually, it represents a closure of a different kind. On this date sixty years ago, Admiral Nagumo launched an air assault on the US fleet in Hawaii. Thus began a terrible war that claimed many lives. Three and a half years later, that war ended after a horrific battle on another island, Okinawa, where I acquired this bottle." Soichiro paused and accepted the glasses from Yoko. "We few are becoming fewer every year, so it's appropriate that we the living should honor those who gave their lives and now sleep at the bottom of the Pacific or in unmarked jungle graves."

Kazuo nodded solemnly as Soichiro twisted the top of the bottle, nearly breaking the brittle cork. *Not a good sign*, Soichiro thought as he poured a dram for his host and himself.

Noriko and Yoko both declined.

"To the warriors who fought and died for sacred Yamato. We salute you!" Soichiro quaffed his drink and watched as Kazuo sipped his.

"Not too bad for being so old," the oyabun said, still grimacing after swallowing the deep amber liquid. "Still prefer our Yamazaki." He motioned to Yoko to bring out the Japanese whiskey. "I should have known the American spirits would leave a bad aftertaste."

Soichiro hissed through his teeth as the warmth worked its way down his chest. He kept a wary eye on Noriko, whose fragility was cause for worry anytime the discussion returned to wartime. He noticed the slight tremble, while understanding that she genuinely wanted to know the full story about Michiko. It was as though she was determined to understand how a man like Kazuo, so rough and cruel, could have been so loved by a girl like Michiko. What could she have possibly seen that seemed so invisible now?

Before Soichiro's amazed eyes, Noriko broke the ice.

"Midorikawa-san, your story touched me deeply. Michiko-san must have been an exceptional woman. Please tell us more about your life with her."

Kazuo squinted as Yoko poured the Yamazaki. "Probably more accurate to say my life *without* her. It seemed we hardly had any time together.

"When I returned to the Akita detention camp, the prisoners seemed hopeless. Several had died in my absence—complications of the cold, overwork, and malnutrition. The way duties were divided, we Imperial soldiers were responsible for the prisoners while in camp. But the mines were a good distance away and high up on a mountainside. Getting there required climbing up a steep incline, sometimes in deep snow.

Mitsubishi employed special guards to deal with the prisoners once we got them to the mines."

Soichiro, stubbornly sticking to the Old Grand-Dad, took a long sip and shuddered as he swallowed. "Why use hired guards? Why wasn't the army in charge?"

"Probably because we soldiers knew nothing about mining. But I also suspect the company men were trusted to work the prisoners much harder than we soldiers. The contract with Mitsubishi was lucrative, and the company was determined to get the most out of the laborers. There was also the fact that the army's demand for manpower had stripped most camps bare of able-bodied guards. Hanawa Number Six was not spared."

Noriko pressed her question further. "Were you able to get away to Sendai at all during that winter? You must have worried about your young bride. Certainly you would have been granted leave."

"Leave was a luxury that was becoming exceedingly rare. By then the prisoners could sense that the tide of war had turned. Many hoped for rescue, I'm sure. We were warned to watch for any signs that might suggest escape plans or even revolt. We heard rumors from our senior officers that Imperial Headquarters would order the execution of all prisoners before allowing them to be liberated. Everyone was on edge."

Kazuo took a sip and gestured futilely with his hands. "In fact, the war was going badly. During the early part of March, Tokyo, Nagoya, and Osaka had all been firebombed. The raids caused thousands of deaths and burned huge parts of those cities to cinders. But I believed that Sendai would be spared due to its northern location and its lack of strategic importance.

"I did manage to steal away for a two-day leave in late March. Conditions were grim. Very little food was available, and blackout conditions were in effect. I brought a haversack stuffed with as much as I could scrounge of our army rations for Michiko. I could see she was becoming thinner. Everyone I saw was gaunt—on the verge of starvation.

"Again I considered deserting and taking her away, and again she refused. That was when she told me that she was expecting a child. I felt like I'd been struck by lightning. I hardly thought it possible. We'd had so little time together. But she was certain. I was overjoyed and conflicted at the same time. She urged me to return to my duties because deserters were being hunted down and shot. I promised to come back to her as soon as humanly possible." Kazuo paused, his voice choked with emotion. "As I kissed her goodbye, I had a dreadful feeling that even today I find hard to describe. How could I have known that it would be the last time I would ever see Michiko?"

Soichiro watched his wife as a tear traced a trail down her cheek. He was sure the story of Michiko was bringing back memories of herself, abandoned in a ruined land by the father of her unborn child, her parents and most of her friends dead.

He decided it was time to take the conversation in a different direction. "What would it have mattered if the prisoners were left unguarded? The war was all but over. What was so special about the Hanawa camp?"

Kazuo heaved a long sigh. "In hindsight, all we knew was that orders were orders. The work in the mines was exhausting and dangerous. Prisoners were often injured due to the unsafe conditions. That plus illness brought on by the cold and poor rations resulted in seldom more than half of them being available for work at any given time." He shook his head in disgust. "Of course, this didn't sit well with Mitsubishi's mine personnel, and there were frequent beatings administered to those prisoners suspected of malingering.

"But something strange happened a week after I returned from Sendai. I was told by the commander that a large number of heavy wooden crates had been delivered one night by several army trucks. These crates were to be moved by the prisoners into the mine, where they would be stored deep inside. He did not say what the crates contained, but I naturally assumed it was a shipment of explosives to aid in the tunneling. Only later did I learn that the boxes contained a far more interesting cargo.

"The mine shafts were very old and had not been tended for many years. They'd become unstable as a result. Supporting trusses were lacking in some of the newer digs, and timbers in the older areas were rotting and buckling under the pressure of the mountain. Even Mitsubishi declined to send their own men into the most dangerous areas.

"A crew of prisoners was ordered to drag the crates deep into the mine. That work was well underway when the ground shook. I felt the tremor even several kilometers away at the Hanawa camp. I scrambled up to the mine and found a scene of utter chaos. Some prisoners had emerged coughing and covered with dirt. They were crying and shaking in terror. The civilian mine workers were cursing and striking them, demanding that they go back to work.

"I drew my sidearm and ordered the beatings to stop. One of the mine foremen came at me with a pickax and challenged me. Before he could take a swing, I took him down with a blow from my pistol.

"When I was finally told what had happened, I asked the mine personnel to accompany me back into the mine shaft and guide me to where the collapse had occurred. When they refused, I turned to the prisoners and immediately had a volunteer. Together we entered the dark hole carrying a single carbide lantern. The dust was so thick it was difficult to breathe." Kazuo coughed as though to embellish the scene he was describing. "We could only go perhaps two hundred meters before we were blocked. The tremor had evidently triggered a whole series of cave-ins, and the shaft was sealed by thousands of tons of rock and dirt. It was clear that no one could have survived the collapse, and even if they had, rescue would be impossible.

"As we made our way back out, the prisoner motioned for me to follow him into an abandoned lateral. I wasn't sure what to expect and wondered if he planned to try to overpower me. The vulnerability of having only the one eye was a constant worry, but the pistol in my hand gave me confidence to follow him. We came to an area where a solid slab of granite formed one of the walls. On the slab, prisoners had scratched inscriptions with dates, names, and drawings. They were written in Spanish and English, so I couldn't read them. I assumed they were messages to loved ones." Midorikawa paused, spent by his long monologue.

Yoko approached silently with concern tugging at the corners of her mouth. She inquired if Kazuo would like his Yamazaki refreshed, but he declined, asking instead for a glass of ice water.

Kazuo turned to Soichiro and met his gaze with his one good eye. "So-san, I've done most of the talking. While I was freezing my ass off in the northern mountains, you were where? In the near tropical glory of lovely Okinawa?"

Soichiro wasn't about to take the bait. Okinawa was, by the fall of 1944, anything but a paradise. Okinawa would be Japan's Alamo, *jikyusen*, an ultimate attrition battle. When Soichiro arrived, the island was crawling with military activity. Under its new commander, Lieutenant General Ushijima, it was being converted into a sophisticated fortification, bristling with artillery and linked deep underground through a maze of interconnected tunnels.

More important to Soichiro, this was the place where Noriko had suffered her deepest wounds, both psychologically and spiritually. Soichiro noticed how merely the mention of Okinawa caused his wife to stiffen. No, this was not the time to unlock the past with its bloody memories.

"Kazu-san," Soichiro said, "I can understand you're tiring after such a long story. But to give Okinawa its due would require far more time than we can spare today. May we plan another time? I'm sure Noriko would much prefer to hear the rest of the story involving your lovely Michiko-san, if you feel up to it."

Kazuo nodded, replaced the oxygen cannula under his nose, and bowed slightly at Noriko. "Indeed, it was for that very reason I asked for your company. If you'll allow me a few moments to breathe with this infernal device, I'll be pleased to continue. Yoko, would you mind bringing tea and some of those sweet confections you've prepared? Then come join us for the rest of the story, in which you play an essential role."

Soichiro watched the old woman bow hesitantly and quietly leave the room.

Kazuo also watched her go. Then he turned to Noriko, cupped his hand to his mouth, and whispered, "You probably already know this, but my history with Yoko goes back a long time. She was Michiko's chaperone when I first met her. After Michiko's father graciously released her, Yoko went home to Osaka, where members of her family worked in small shops making aircraft parts.

"At that point, no one expected what would happen to that city on the night of March 13, 1945. Osaka was attacked by more than two hundred B-29s that dropped hundreds of tons of firebombs—mainly napalm and white magnesium incendiary clusters. They targeted civilian housing. More than four thousand men, women, and children died in the inferno.

"Yoko witnessed some terrible sights. The combination of jellied gasoline and magnesium clings to whatever it touches and burns fiercely. Once it's on you, it can't be rubbed off or extinguished. The resulting firestorms reached temperatures that melted steel. People attempting to flee ignited like torches, and the water in ponds and rivers boiled from the heat. Yoko lost her entire family—two brothers, their wives, a sister, and both parents. Much of the city was reduced to ashes. With nothing left for her in Osaka, she made her way to Sendai, where she hoped to find Michiko."

Noriko shuddered in revulsion as she left to help Yoko set out the refreshments.

Soichiro finally gave up on the fifty-six-year-old bourbon and set the glass down. "I had no idea. But I always suspected there was a great bond between you and Yoko-san. Now I understand why. I can't wait to hear the rest of the story."

"And you shall, So-san. But it was important that you should first have some appreciation of that good woman and her own history of suffering and loss."

Kazuo stood as Yoko and Noriko entered the room with the refreshments. When all were served, he resumed.

"By now, it was April. The bombers from Guam, Tinian, and Saipan were coming daily. We had no aerial defenses to speak of because so many planes had been lost in the Marianas. The bulk of the remaining aircraft were being used in kamikaze attacks against the US fleet at Okinawa. The American fighters based on Iwo Jima could escort the bombers deep into Nippon practically unopposed. Fighters and bombers from American aircraft carriers also ranged over the home islands with near impunity. It was no contest.

"I worried constantly about Michiko. And although I didn't know it at the time, Yoko had finally made her way to Sendai." Kazuo gestured toward the old woman. "Please, Yoko, if you feel able, would you tell our guests what you experienced in those last weeks of the war?"

Yoko slowly looked up and, with hesitant hands, brushed aside a few stray white hairs from her eyes. Her glance at Kazuo suggested that she would have preferred to remain silent.

Noriko reached for and held her hand, encouraging her.

"Michiko-sama was overjoyed to see me, and I her," Yoko finally said. "I'd known her since she was a little girl, and it was clear that she would soon have a baby of her own. She wanted nothing more than that she might join her husband and find somewhere to live in peace and raise their child together."

As she spoke, Soichiro realized this was the first time he'd heard Yoko string together more than a few words. She had the voice of a little girl: diminutive, meek, and bell-like.

"Life in Sendai was harsh," she said. "There was no fuel left, and food was scarce. Every day was a struggle to find enough to eat. And the American planes . . . Every day, the air raid sirens wailed as fleets of aircraft flew overhead. Sometimes a fighter plane would make a low pass. It was all very frightening, but with each passing day, the planes would fly on, and no bombs would fall. We became complacent, often ignoring the sirens. I frequently would leave Michiko-sama for much of the day, foraging for whatever vegetables and fish I could find for us to eat. Rice had become a luxury. One evening, I had heard a rumor that a fishmonger with a supply of fresh haddock had set up a small stand about ten kilometers away. I left Michiko-sama at home, determined to barter a ring that had belonged to her grandmother for some fish.

"I set out on foot to find the fish seller, and after a long walk I located him. Then the familiar rumble of heavy engines and the shrill sirens and searchlights lighting the sky warned of an attack. As was our habit, I ignored the alarms, but this time the bombs fell. I could see the fires erupting in Sendai and could hear the explosions. In panic, I ran all the way back, only to find the city engulfed in fire.

"By morning, most of the flames had abated, and I tried to find the house, but it was gone, along with Michiko-sama and her unborn child." Yoko turned away to hide the deep sorrow etched in her face.

Kazuo rose to put his arm around Yoko. "The raid took place on the night of July tenth," he said. "Over a hundred B-29s came. Nearly three thousand died, and twelve thousand homes were destroyed. And to what purpose? Certainly it wasn't to further the war effort, because Sendai had no military value. For all practical purposes, the war was coming to an end."

Soichiro detected an acid edge in Kazuo's tone. The decades had done nothing to soften his anger.

"I'll tell you why," Kazuo thundered in a shaky voice. "It was a stunt to impress the Russians—nothing more. The bombers had come from the Marianas, which meant it was the longest bombing mission of the war to that point—something LeMay could strut about as he puffed his cigar and sipped brandy with General Arnold. Together they could imagine Stalin's alarm at the reach of American heavy bombers. They were already thinking about the next war. Meanwhile, thousands of innocents died for no reason other than the vanity of the American air commander. Good thing for him that only the defeated are tried for war crimes."

Kazuo turned to the window and slammed his fist on the sill. "When word reached me about the raid, I abandoned my post in Hanawa, commandeered a truck, and rushed to Sendai. I found Yoko wandering as though in a daze, combing the ruins for any sign of my wife and child. Alongside hundreds of others looking for their loved ones, we dug through the rubble with our bare hands. We never found any remains we could identify as theirs. I took Yoko into my care and swore from that moment that I would do all in my power to make the Americans pay for their crime. And over the next forty years, starting with the occupation, I made good on that vow by organizing black markets, counterfeiting, and causing 'accidents,' sabotaging them at every possible turn. Even today, when the big container ships from the US arrive in Nagoya, Kobe, and Yokohama, strangely significant portions of their cargos often turn up missing. And in the process, I became a very rich man. What is it the Americans say? 'Revenge is a dish best served cold?'"

Soichiro found himself speechless.

Noriko gave Yoko's hand a final squeeze. She rose and strode over to the oyabun. She touched his shoulder and murmured, "Thank you. Now I understand. Michiko-san loved you, and clearly you loved her. Be thankful for that, because it is a gift denied to many. She would be pleased that you so cherish and honor her memory."

She turned and smiled at Yoko. Then she nodded to Soichiro that it was time to go.

Chapter 20

The Korean Colonel

Thursday, December 13, 2001

A Bar Near Gimpo International Airport

Seoul, South Korea

Gary Masterson hunched his shoulders and tugged at his lapels as he hurried toward the door.

Damn. Nathan might have warned me how cold this place would be.

The meetings with the cosmetics distributors in Gangnam earlier in the day had gone well. It never ceased to amaze him that, these many years later, the enduring image of Kume had practically made Heloise an Asian brand. Korean sales were booming.

But now it was time for business of another sort. Nathan had told him about this bar that was known to be an after-hours hangout for fancy women and high-ranking officials in Korea's defense ministry. They had rehearsed a role for Gary to play.

Once inside, Gary shivered and surveyed the dimly lit room. Cocktail waitresses in outfits reminiscent of the Playboy Mansion were languidly delivering drinks to several tables of quite soused men. One waitress slipped her arm around his and teasingly rubbed her hip against his crotch. She asked if he was having anything special. Gary smiled and said if he was, he'd be sure to let her know.

Then he slipped away to a banquette against the back wall, where a solitary man with a cigarette in one hand and a martini in the other had caught his eye. At their dinner meeting back in DC, Nathan had provided Gary with a photo of Colonel Park Hong, a senior defense intelligence officer, and this was the guy. Same stout neck. Same pugilist's nose. Same sleepy-eyed gaze.

Playing the part of a bumptious American businessman, Gary strutted toward him. "Mind if I join you?"

The man gave a desultory wave of welcome and slid over slightly to make room.

Warming to his role, Gary theatrically checked his watch. "This is my first trip to South Korea. Been here a few days now on business."

Park shrugged. "What line of work are you in?" he asked in near-flawless English.

"Drilling," Gary said with a smug nod of the head. "Tunneling, to be specific. I'm with a startup firm that's about to unveil groundbreaking—pun intended—technology. We're looking to give Schlumberger and Halliburton a run for their money."

The colonel drew on his cigarette and stared idly at Gary. "What brings you to South Korea? The last I checked, we had no proven oil reserves."

Gary laughed—too loudly, drawing attention from several tables. "I said the same thing. But the boss said to go anyway. Said there was a foreign buyer interested in our drill." He paused conspiratorially and then drawled in his best West Texas accent, "Hell, we could drill a four-lane hole from here to Tokyo with our high-speed bits."

Park frowned and then recovered and offered his hand. "Forgive my poor manners. I'm Colonel Park Hong. You are?"

"Ian Mooney. Pleased to meet you. I'd give you my card, but I checked the briefcase with that pretty young coat check girl. My company is Advanced Carborundum. It sounds like abrasives, but we're actually diggers. You'll be hearing about us—mark my words. Keep an eye out when we go public." Gary gripped Park's hand and shook it vigorously. "What say I buy you a drink, Colonel? I could use one or three myself." Gary was beginning to feel like Henry Gondorff in *The Sting* as he rubbed his hands with relish.

"Very kind of you, Mr. Mooney." Park waved over the waitress who had greeted Gary and tapped his glass, pointing to Gary. "Her name is Moon. Interesting. Moon. Mooney. Perhaps you're related." Park cackled at his bon mot.

Gary tried hard not to roll his eyes. "Could be," he joked good-naturedly. "Ma told me I had a world-traveling uncle in the merchant marine who had a girl in every port." He sized up Moon's figure with a top-down once-over and declared, "We could be cousins, but I sincerely hope not."

Park laughed. It seemed as if he was beginning to feel at ease with his new friend. They clinked glasses to Gary's good fortune in locating a heretofore unknown cousin.

"So, Colonel, don't tell me you're one of those tough military guys that the Democratic People's Republic of Korea is so worried about. Do you command a regiment?"

Park smiled at the intended compliment and straightened in his seat as the second martini arrived. He squinted, his eyes nearly closing while he lit another cigarette. "No, Mr. Mooney. My work is in military intelligence."

Gary pretended to nearly drop his vodka Collins. "No shit! No offense, Colonel, but back in my country, that's called an oxymoron. No. Really, I'm impressed. I can't believe I came across a military espionage expert." He poked Park in the ribs with his elbow. "I bet you have some stories. Is it true that you have sources in the North Korean military that give you the goods before even Dear Leader hears it?"

Park nodded ever so slightly, flicking the ash from his cigarette as he responded. "As I'm sure you appreciate, that's information I'm not at liberty to share. But we do have assets in the north, as you'd expect."

"Sheez!" Gary whistled with mock amazement. "I knew it! I bet your guys are really good."

"They should be, Mr. Mooney. I personally cultivated those internal sources and trained the people we planted in Pyongyang."

Gary shook his head in wide-eyed wonder, raised his glass to Park, and said, "Please. Call me Ian. Colonel Park, you're a gentleman and a patriot. Here's to you!"

Park accepted the toast and drained his martini. Gary summoned Moon over and pointed at Park's empty glass. Moon leaned over the table to reveal her ample cleavage and rubbed Gary's thigh as she retrieved both their glasses.

"Thank you," Park said. "I think she likes you. But be careful. She's an agent for DPRK intelligence."

Gary just shook his head. "Bummer. What a buzzkill. Don't you think she just wants to jump my bones because I'm a cool-looking dude?"

Park burst out in uproarious laughter.

Two hours and three drinks later, Park was clearly feeling the alcohol. Gary was trying to hold his own while pretending to get merrily drunk.

Park slid closer to Gary. "I'm interested in hearing more about your high-speed drilling equipment," he said in an earnest whisper, "and who might be interested in buying it."

Gary shrugged. "I was told it's an import firm named Daejong something-or-other. I'm supposed to expect contact information waiting for me at my hotel."

At this revelation, Park nodded knowingly with a faint smile. "Daejong International is one of several front companies licensed in Seoul that DPRK uses occasionally to acquire items prohibited under UN sanctions. Fissile material, certain types of metals, and drilling equipment are among those prohibited items."

Gary looked up blearily and feigned ignorance. "Why drilling equipment?"

"Because of its uses by the Korean People's Army in tunneling under our border. They've done so before, but the tunnels haven't been sufficient to move large quantities of men and equipment. They would dearly love to launch a surprise invasion in such a way. If your drill is as good as you say, it could be just the thing they need."

"Wow!" Gary exclaimed, assuming a wide-eyed look of disbelief.

"It could be that, or it could be something else. Kim will manufacture crises when it suits his purpose, but DPRK seems content to leave us alone for the time being. I believe the drilling equipment may have a different intended use." The colonel winked.

Gary did his best to appear befuddled and in awe of the South Korean officer's perceptiveness. "What might that be, Colonel?"

Park paused and peered into Gary's eyes. "Normally, I wouldn't share what I'm about to say with an outsider. But since your company unwittingly may have stumbled into a situation that could develop into an embarrassment, if not an international crisis, I think it only fair that you should know."

Gary noted how clumsily Park lit his eighth cigarette.

"It's no secret that Pyongyang has been working to develop a nuclear weapon," Park continued. "It's also no secret that they're well along the road toward perfection of a multistage ballistic missile capable of reaching targets thousands of miles away. Both projects are very expensive, and DPRK has—what is it you Americans say?—maxed out their credit card with Beijing."

A polite chuckle escaped Gary's lips.

"The Chinese want no part in enabling Kim to miniaturize a warhead. And they especially don't want to support development of a third-stage booster for an ICBM that the Korean People's Army has been calling 'the America Rocket.'"

Gary took a deep breath and exhaled loudly. "Well, I can understand that. But what does this have to do with my drilling equipment?"

Park smiled and leaned forward, conspiratorially glancing to his right and left.

Past the colonel's shoulder, Gary noticed Moon talking to two younger Korean men, gesturing with a tilt of her head toward Gary and his new friend.

"This is where it gets interesting," Park whispered. "And you may have just added a dot to a chain of dots that connects some important pieces together."

"How so?" Gary asked while trying to keep an eye on Moon's friends, who appeared to be muttering to each other as they glanced his way.

"DPRK needs hard currency to pursue its projects. That money may be buried deep in a mine shaft in northern Honshu."

Gary cocked his head and frowned. "Money? In a mine shaft?" Even in his inebriated state, he could feel his heart thumping wildly in his chest. This conversation was leading exactly where Nate had hoped it would go.

"Let me back up. Over the years, there'd been persistent rumors about a trove of gold bullion from Japan's Imperial treasury that went missing toward the end of the WW II. It was supposedly moved for safekeeping to a mine in the northern mountains of Akita and then lost in a disastrous cave-in. It would be a windfall amounting to several billion in today's dollars to anyone who could recover it. For a government as cash-starved as DPRK, it represents an irresistible temptation. Sources tell me that the North Koreans are actively seeking a collaboration with underworld elements in Japan to get at that gold."

Gary perked up. "Okay. I get it. So all they need is a super-drill to tunnel down into the mine where the gold is, right? And that's where I come in."

"Yes. That may be the missing dot. I know that Kim's government first tried the Russians, but their drilling equipment was found to be inadequate. I also have been informed of the activation and movement of an elite KPA commando unit whose mission is currently unknown. Our military has gone on alert at the demilitarized zone in case this signals an incursion, but I suspect the two matters are related."

The two men Gary was watching began to move toward the door. Moon slipped over to the table and asked if Gary needed someplace to stay for the evening. Gary smiled but declined the offer. Park was fading fast, and Gary was worried that he might be easy prey for an "accident" outside the bar.

He paid the check and hustled Park out the back door. Around the corner of the building, Gary saw no one. He half carried Park to the Audi S8 he had rented, strapped the colonel in, and started the engine. He wanted to take Park to someplace safe. Just as he maneuvered the big sedan out of the parking lot, the headlights of a waiting vehicle flashed on. A black SUV followed him out and took a position behind the Audi.

Okay, he thought. *Let's have some fun.* He jammed his foot on the accelerator, and the Audi leapt forward with a roar. Gary worked the shift paddles as they entered the expressway to the Han River and downtown. The other car tried to keep pace, but it was no match for the training of Gary's youth. Maybe he'd never carved out a career as a professional race car driver, but tonight he found himself disappointed at the lack of competition.

When he felt he'd lost the tail, he drove back toward the airport, found a police station, dropped off Park, and suggested to the desk sergeant that the police keep the colonel overnight. He could explain matters in the morning. Gary drove on to where the Gulfstream was waiting at the private air terminal, climbed aboard, and ordered the pilots to spool up the engines.

No question. Nathan would owe him big-time for this one.

Chapter 21

Motherly Voodoo

Monday, August 6, 1945

Main Island, Okinawa

Frankie was soaked to the bone in spite of the waterproof poncho. Rain dripped off his helmet as he kept a watchful eye on the ragged procession of sick and injured civilians being herded toward an open field overlooking the East China Sea. Their destination was a makeshift camp that had been hastily erected by the Seabees and army engineers. Orders had been handed down to keep a sharp eye out for Jap soldiers who had traded their uniforms for civilian clothes and were trying to blend in among the throngs of refugees. Some of these were diehards who had not surrendered. They could be armed and dangerous—and not afraid to blow themselves up along with anyone nearby. "Shoot when in doubt," was the order.

Frankie had had enough of shooting. He just wanted this god-awful war to be over so he could go home and leave these wretched people and their ruined land.

Then he heard the commotion and a few rifles being fired. He unslung his M1 and pulled the charging bolt. But he soon realized that the shouts and shots were in celebration of something. A lanky NCO raced past with the news that a devastating secret bomb had been dropped on Japan. The war would be over soon.

Frankie was stunned. Could it mean that he might actually live to celebrate his next birthday? Would the plans to invade the Japanese home islands be canceled? Cheers of relief and jubilation echoed across the grass field.

Then he saw her face. She was alive. Barefoot and wearing the same stained uniform, she shuffled forward numbly. Her hair was matted against her head, and she was shivering in the rain. She looked emaciated.

Frankie fumbled in his pockets for a Hershey's bar, and stepped forward to press it into her palm.

She looked up at him warily and then recognized him. Her smile warmed him. She bowed appreciatively.

A second later, an ill-tempered MP brandishing a .45 pistol rudely pushed her forward, knocking the chocolate out of her hand. "Feeding the damn Japs ain't your job," he growled at Frankie.

Frankie dropped his rifle and took a swing at the barrel-chested military cop . . .

Frankie woke up with a yelp in the living room and glanced at the fireplace, where three or four *piñón* logs were still crackling. He inhaled deeply, hoping the scent from what he liked to call "desert perfume" would steady his nerves. He had started the fire less than an hour earlier after waking up to frost on the bedroom window. Christmas had come and gone, and now, three days hence, he found himself startled by another dream in which he'd confronted one of his own comrades over the girl.

No such event had occurred. Or had it? Surely, such an armed confrontation, no matter how justified, would have resulted in house arrest and some serious time in lockup. Then again, he thought, he *had* been in a war zone, where all kinds of strange things had occurred. People had often looked the other way—except when serious transgressions had been committed, like shooting an officer.

Still wrapped in his robe, Frankie steeped a steaming cup of manzanilla in the kitchen and then gingerly walked it outside to the placita. Perhaps the chill would help clear his mind. The dream had been so vivid. Normally after waking he couldn't remember the details of the dreams he'd just had, but this one was crystal clear.

Her face. That dirt-smeared face with the haunting eyes and the perfect skin would stalk his dreams forever.

After much effort, he had located her in the hastily deployed tent city that was going up near the wreckage of what had been the port of Naha. It was makeshift and chaotic, but at least it was reasonably safe. The army clearly had underestimated what was needed to house and feed several hundred thousand refugees after the battle.

She was cleaned up and looked much healthier than before. Her Red Cross clothes were at least two sizes too large. Though technically still in effect, the anti-fraternization orders issued before the invasion were largely being ignored. That, plus the bottle of scotch and extra carton of Luckies slipped to one of the MPs on guard, had given Frankie pretty much free access to the camp.

Why did I care? Frankie wondered. She was one of hundreds—thousands—who had had their lives torn to shreds by the battle. What made her special? Was it because she could speak English? Many kids educated at Okinawa's schools learned basic English. Was it because she had pleaded with him not to leave?

Or was it because he was probably the single reason she was still alive? Mama Elena had told him that a person who saved a life was inextricably bound to that life and assumed responsibility for it. Where she had come up with that one was anyone's guess. It was the typical motherly voodoo he expected from her, but Frankie had to admit that there was some truth in it. He felt responsible.

He also knew that there was something else besides a sense of duty. The girl had been tender, vulnerable, fragile. And beautiful. There was no denying he had been drawn to her. Even now, he felt a pang of loss . . .

No. No. Even if he were able to go back in time, he wouldn't have been able to change things. She was Asian, someone on the enemy's side. He had a girl back home. He couldn't possibly be entertaining feelings for this poor, wretched, vulnerable, beautiful victim of the carnage that he and the US Tenth Army had brought to the island.

Frankie shivered and reached for his manzanilla as the cold crept between the folds of his robe. He sipped the rapidly cooling tea and frowned. The thigh was starting to hurt like a son of a bitch, and the twist he was feeling in his gut didn't help. He decided to go back inside, where the fire from the burning logs was warming the room and filling the air with that fragrance that reminded him of sandalwood incense.

Friday, December 28

New York City

Gary pushed the redial button and then turned away from the window as he propped his feet up on his desk. The late afternoon sun, so low on the horizon this time of year, was reflecting off a nearby building and beaming straight into his study. As if not to be outdone, his old-fashioned banker's lamp cast a golden glow in his work space. Scattered across his desk were dozens of loose sheets of paper, each one a testament to his growing research into Kume's past.

Denny Townsend, just less than four hours away at the National Archives in College Park, Maryland, picked up on the seventh ring. "Not you again."

Gary leaned forward, switched off the speaker phone, and cradled the phone to his ear. "Missed me, didn't you?"

Townsend, whom Gary had never met in person, chuckled on the other end of the line. Between his husky laugh and his southern twang, he sounded like a good ol' boy fresh from the hills of West Virginia. But he sure seemed to know his way around the byzantine maze of military records Gary was hoping to access. He'd been invaluable to Gary's hunt thus far, never mind his early protests that he wasn't Gary's private assistant. "Every time I see your phone number on my caller ID, I age another year."

Now it was Gary's turn to laugh. He'd taken a few days off after Christmas to look into the mystery that was Kume's biological father, but the quest had proved difficult so far. Holiday hours had conspired to slow everything down. Thankfully,

Townsend, an archivist and an old friend of a colleague on the Heloise board, had foolishly agreed to guide Gary's research.

"Next time I'm in the neighborhood I'll buy you a drink," Gary offered.

"I don't drink," Townsend said. "But you could inspire me to start."

"So what do you have for me?"

"More than you can handle. I'm going to snail mail you some records—and a bill for ink cartridges."

Gary ignored the joke. "Records?"

"Disciplinary records. From the army. It's not comprehensive. Some of this stuff is still classified. But I was able to hunt down a stack of disciplinary records involving American soldiers caught fraternizing with Okinawan women from April 1945 through 1946."

"Why only army?" Gary asked.

"Well, your gal's mother says he was a soldier, right? A marine would never identify himself as just a soldier. Got to be someone who was with an army unit. He probably took on occupation duties and stayed on Okinawa for some time after it was secured."

"He was a grunt," Gary said, nodding.

"Most likely. He probably fought in the three-month-long battle. The Tenth Army did almost all the fighting on land under Lieutenant General Simon Bolivar Buckner. It was a hefty force—180,000 troops from four army and three marine divisions."

Gary stifled a yawn. "I guess this is a start."

"It's the best I can do," Townsend said. "If you're serious about finding out this soldier's identity, you're probably going to have to go there."

"Okinawa?"

"That's what I said."

Gary thought a moment. He'd done quite a bit of dig-ging on his own this week, as well, but none of it had opened any doors. He had learned that Ota, Noriko's maiden name, meant something special in Okinawa, owing to the fame of the prefectural governor, native of Kume-jima and survivor of the battle, Masahide Ota. There were records at the prefectural government in Naha that could be accessed to aid in identi-fying survivors, both Okinawan and Japanese.

But the work would be tedious and would best be pur-sued with local help. Besides, he already knew where Noriko was. Townsend was right: it would be better to approach it from the other side.

"Okinawa," he repeated as the sun disappeared behind a building.

"You need someone on the ground there who can open doors and maybe put you in touch with survivors who might remember a Himeyuri Girl who got involved with an American," Townsend suggested. "There can't be *that* many. You'll have the records I'm sending you. One of those soldiers might be your man."

"Talk about a needle in a haystack," Gary mused. "Thanks, Denny. I owe you one."

Townsend got in one last dig before hanging up. "Don't I know it."

Gary set down the phone and rubbed his tired eyes, his mind racing. He still owed Nathan Goldman a visit. They'd yet to go over everything he'd learned during his recent trip to Seoul. He was eager to find out what had happened to Colonel Park after dropping him off at the police station. Nate would probably know. Plus, Gary had done Nate a huge favor, and Nate had offered to repay it.

Gary's gaze settled on the calendar on his desk, and he made a mental note to remember to text Kume before Oshougatsu, the Japanese New Year festivities, kicked off. It would be good form to wish her and her parents a New Year filled with good luck and benign spirits. He would also ask to be remembered during the *Hatsumode* shrine visit and *Joya no Kane* ringing of the temple bell.

Chapter 22

Everybody Loses

Monday, December 31, 2001

Mesilla, New Mexico

As the clock drew closer to midnight, Frankie felt the familiar throbbing in his leg and inched closer to the front door.

He was stuck in a tedious conversation with a middle-aged sales rep for a newfangled roofing material. Soft in the middle, gabby, and eager to talk shop even at a holiday party, the man had clearly come to the company party to network, not socialize.

"No one offers a guarantee like ours," he said with a slight lisp. "Even the shingles they sell over at the hardware store—you know the ones with the thirty-year warranty—don't cover damage during installation."

"Uh-huh," Frankie said and searched the crowded living room for José, the company foreman, who had graciously offered up his modest home for the party.

When he spotted Ellen walking past, Frankie excused himself and followed his daughter outside to the back deck, which overlooked a ditch, or *acequia*. She'd come to the party solo and was nursing a brown bottle of some microbrew.

"Hey, Dad," she said when she spotted him.

Frankie closed the French door behind them and stuffed his hands into his pockets. "Gonna be another chilly night."

Ellen took up a position at the railing and gazed up at the night sky, which was littered with twinkling stars. "Beats hanging out in a stuffy room with a bunch of salesmen. You were a good sport to show up."

Frankie chuckled softly, steam escaping his lips. He knew he didn't have to explain himself to his daughter. She was built the same way he was: competent in social situations but a natural introvert who tired easily of small talk. "Your mother made me. She's in there listening to Angelina blab about the latest gossip." Angelina was José's effusive wife, a drama queen who loved taking center stage. "I snuck away from that conversation just in time to be cornered by someone who wanted to give me the hard sell."

Ellen rested her elbows on the railing and her chin on her fists. "So when are you going to tell Mom about our little trip? The clock is ticking, you know."

Frankie felt his shoulders slump. "Soon."

Ellen sighed but said nothing.

That silence—he knew it well—was her way of stating her disapproval. Frankie had been dragging his feet. But prodding, even from his daughter, only inspired him to dig in his heels further. He knew he had to come clean soon, but he was still waiting for the right moment. Melanie would have questions—lots of them—and he wasn't yet sure how he'd answer them. The best option, he knew, was to just tell his wife everything and then take his lumps. But something was holding him back. Was it guilt? Shame? A fear of dredging up the war in all its grisly glory? His betrayal of Noriko, now decades old, still gnawed at him. And so did his ongoing betrayal of his wife, who knew nothing of that Chapter in his life. She didn't know how deeply he'd felt for Noriko. Hell, even *he* was still coming to grips with those feelings. And she didn't know how close he'd come to staying put in Okinawa—or to dragging Noriko home with him.

But what if he had? Then what? How would he have reconciled one love with the other? Loyalty and duty had compelled him to sever ties with the vulnerable girl in Okinawa and come home to his American sweetheart. But love, too, had weighed into it. As torn up as Noriko had made him feel at the time, he'd longed for home, for the young woman he'd left behind.

"You in there somewhere?" Ellen asked as she turned to face him.

Frankie smiled at his daughter. Even in the faint glow from the porch light behind them, her sky-blue eyes sparkled. Not a day went by that she didn't fill his heart with pride. "I'm here."

"What was it like?" she asked.

"What was *what* like?"

"Okinawa."

He drew in a breath. "What do you want to know?"

"Did you have to kill anyone?"

He nodded.

"Did you lose anyone close to you?"

This was why he didn't like talking about the war, especially with someone like Ellen, who went straight to penetrating what mattered most.

"I did," he finally said. "We all did. War doesn't choose sides. Everybody loses. Victory is for the politicians, for people back home, for those lucky enough to never have to choose."

"Choose?"

"Between death and survival." Frankie took his daughter by the shoulder. "I'll tell your mom. I promise. And maybe someday when I'm ready, I'll tell you a story or two about the war. Okay, kid?"

She maintained the same stoic expression she'd assumed since turning to face him. "Okay."

Frankie hurried back inside, past the revelers readying themselves for the countdown to a new year, and grabbed Melanie by the arm. "C'mon," he whispered out of the side of his mouth as he hustled her toward the door. "I gotta get outta here."

Chapter 23

Iwo Joe

Tuesday, January 1, 2002

Outside Kadena Air Force Base, Okinawa

Joseph Petrini opened one eye, blinked, cleared his throat noisily, and rolled over. The headache would be nuclear today. He hoped Ayaka would keep the grandkids at bay while he endured a well-earned hangover on the first day of Oshougatsu, the three-day-long Japanese New Year's celebration. His snoring began anew, but he awoke with a jolt as Ayaka's sharp elbow and muttered displeasure put an end to sleep.

Bullshit, he thought. *I need coffee.* He half fell out of bed. Then, gaining his feet, he staggered unsteadily to the tiled bathroom. The image in the mirror was frightening to behold. A once formidable man with bulging biceps and a chest to match, he sometimes found it hard to believe he had ever contended for the fleet cruiserweight boxing title. Staring back at him now was a balding, chunky man with flabby skin drooping down his chest, man-boob style, and rippling down the backs of his arms. *Not pretty*, he thought.

Joe was feeling his age. And no wonder. An ex-Seabee, he was now approaching his seventy-seventh birthday. He glanced approvingly at the tattoo on his right shoulder. It was a beauty, if he did say so—his own design, featuring a scrolled *IWO JOE* superimposed over a honeybee in a navy seaman's cap. The bee was attacking Mount Suribachi and was underscored with *133rd CB*. Crazy days, going ashore with the marines to take the airfield and using a bulldozer with the blade elevated like a shield to advance on and destroy two enemy pillboxes. He had damn near gotten himself killed, but the exploit had earned him the Silver Star and his nickname, plus the ebullient gratitude of the half-dozen marines—only two of whom got off Iwo Jima alive—who had followed his charging Caterpillar.

Ayaka was still in bed, sawing logs.

"And she complains about *my* snoring?" he grumbled.

He pulled on his dungarees and wandered out for a smoke on the back patio, a small, brick-paved space beneath the cool shade of three towering royal palms.

As the owner of several eponymous tattoo parlors catering to US servicemen, Iwo Joe was something of an institution on Okinawa. After retiring from the navy just as Vietnam was ramping up, he had decided to learn the intricacies of body art from an old local expert who couldn't keep up with the burgeoning demand of the youngsters of the Third Marine Division. Joe proved a quick study.

They teamed up, beginning with a single shop over by the Marine Corps Air Station near Futenma. But after the old man died and the political winds began to blow in favor of closing Futenma and moving the marines to a place farther north near Henoko, Joe decided to open two new establishments near

Kadena and one over by Yomitan. It had proved an inspired decision. Now he had thriving businesses to pass on to his six sons, three daughters, and thirteen grandchildren, some of whom were already developing a cult following due to their exceptional artistic skill with ink and needle.

He shook a Winston from the pack, flicked open the old Zippo lighter, and drew the first lungful. He had reason to be thankful for the coming year. Life had been good to him. A tough kid from Pawtucket who was always getting into trouble, he had found a way out by joining the navy. And being good with his hands, he had been drawn to the Seabees. He'd seen enough fighting in the islands to last a lifetime.

Thankfully, the fighting had been mostly over by the time he arrived on Okinawa in June 1945. But what a nightmarish hell it had been. The countryside was one festering cemetery of half-buried corpses, destroyed ancestral tombs, and starving figures, including a few desperate Japanese soldier holdouts clinging to a bare existence while doing their best to avoid capture.

As for shelter, there was none. The whole island had been pulverized by the rain of millions of explosive shells and bombs—what the locals had called "the typhoon of steel." The towns and cities were in splinters. Left in their wake? A couple hundred thousand native refugees who desperately needed food, clothing, medicine, and shelter. In addition, the army had designs on using the island as a bomber base and a stepping-off point for the invasion of the Japanese home islands expected later in the year.

So the work had been monumental. Iwo Joe and fifty thousand other men from navy and army construction units, joined by thousands of servicemen from the occupation forces, were tasked to clear the debris and provide a modicum of habitable living spaces for the native survivors. At the same time, the Kadena runway was widened and lengthened, several new airstrips were added, and hundreds of structures were erected for the expected massive influx of military personnel.

Joe recalled working his Cat D8 around the clock, practically living on caffeine and nicotine. At night, the kids from the refugee camps would trickle in to beg for sweets and whatever food they might coax from the sailors. Joe was always a sucker for those kids. He cleared a field, laid out a diamond, and organized a baseball game. It wasn't hard getting the Seabees to contribute bats, balls, and gloves. The Okinawan children, most of them orphans, were ecstatic. Most didn't know that baseball was played with three bases and a home plate.

One boy, Takeo, proved to be a gifted player, and it wasn't long before Joe noticed that Takeo's sister, a beautiful teenager named Ayaka, would frequently come to watch her brother play. One thing led to another, and the rest, as the saying went, was history.

Joe ground out the cigarette on one of the brick pavers, squinted up at the royal palms for a moment, and then went back inside to start a pot of coffee. He was feeling better now and would let Ayaka sleep a bit longer. Normally about now he would be heading over to the Okinawa Prefectural Peace Memorial Museum in Mabuni, where several times a week he greeted visitors and conducted tours as a volunteer. Being fluent in Japanese, Okinawan, and English, Joe found his services much in demand at the museum and the nearby Cornerstone of Peace Memorial.

But today, both would be closed. In fact, nearly everything would be closed for the next three days. Everything except, of course, the flight line at Kadena. He had also heard that SEAL teams were training with light assault craft in the

Kerama Islands for planned operations against Muslim extremists in the southern Philippines. Rumors of deployment to the Middle East for certain air force squadrons were circulating as the crisis with Saddam Hussein's Iraq deepened.

Joe hardly reacted as an F-16 streaked overhead with a buffeting roar that made the house shudder. He just shook his head. He had seen it all. From the Pacific to Korea to Vietnam, his little island, Okinawa, had had an unenviable front row seat to history, a history that seemed doomed to repeat itself in perpetuity.

He poured himself a cup of steaming Folgers and placed it and a second cup on a tray, which he delivered to his groggy wife, still in bed.

"Happy New Year, Aya-chan," he said with a smile.

Chapter 24

You Are the Master, Son

Tuesday, January 8, 2002

Old Angler's Inn, Potomac, Maryland

"And that's it? You just dropped him off at a police station?" Nathan Goldman stared through his glasses at Gary Masterson with an incredulous look.

Gary had joined Nate for a fireside drink just north of the Beltway at one of Nathan's favorite restaurants, a half-timbered inn with checkered tablecloths, weathered plank floors, and a crackling fireplace. The nineteenth-century inn boasted a storied past and had attracted its share of larger-than-life visitors over the years, from Union *and* Confederate soldiers to Teddy Roosevelt. Tonight, it was occupied by a largely sedate mix of tourists and regulars, the latter distinguishable by their casual dress and indifferent attitude toward their fellow diners and their surroundings.

Gary grinned sheepishly as he sipped his Marimar Torres chardonnay. "Yes, I'm afraid so. It was that or bring him back in the jet. I didn't think you'd want that. I wasn't about to just leave Colonel Park back there, drunk, with those two North Korean goons and Mata Hari Moon. Don't think it would have ended well."

Nate laughed and pointed at Gary. "You're right about that. As it is, Seoul is searching high and low for an American businessman named Ian Mooney."

Gary nodded and pretended not to be enjoying his moment of triumph.

"Supposedly this Mooney is working on a deal to sell high-speed drilling equipment to Pyongyang," Nate continued. "Mysteriously—and this is where it gets weird—Mooney then kidnaps a senior defense intelligence officer, who manages to escape and goes directly to the police. Mooney vanishes without a trace. Even the car used in the kidnapping was rented through a phony corporation."

Gary tried hard to suppress a grin. "Park probably told his boss he'd been kidnapped to avoid revealing that he was pretty blotto and had gotten himself into a dicey situation. Give him credit. It made for a plausible alibi. But I imagine he still will have some explaining to do."

Nate raised his glass to Gary. "I have to admit, you managed to pull it off—and without any fingerprints or diplomatic debris to deal with. At State, we have no idea who this Mooney guy is, and he certainly wasn't working for us."

"I was worried about Park," Gary said and raised his glass in return, "and I'm glad he's okay. But the matter of that Japanese gold appears to be real, and if Park is right, the North Koreans have a real incentive to go after it."

Nate lowered his voice and surveyed the room. "Yes, you played that perfectly. That story about missing bullion from Japan's wartime treasury is something of an old chestnut that makes the rounds in the cloak-and-dagger division every ten years or so. It isn't as well-known, but fits in the same category as the story of Yamashita's gold that supposedly was looted by the Japanese army in Indochina and hidden somewhere in the Philippines. Or the tale of the *Awa Maru* that was sunk off Singapore with five billion dollars in gold and platinum." He eyed Gary over the rim of his glasses. "No one ever puts much stock in the story of the missing treasury gold because it sounds so preposterous. But when CIA starts picking up new chatter between a Japanese crime syndicate in Hokkaido and a shadowy character with known connections to DPRK intelligence about a big trove of Imperial gold from a mine cave-in—well, people in NSA and State begin to sit up and take notice.

"What you found out during your little adventure was passed up the chain. The trouble is, with Secretary Powell working twenty-four-seven on shoring up allied support in the Middle East, anything short of a full-blown North Korean invasion of the south just isn't going to get too much high-level attention, no matter how messy it could become. Still, I owe you a big one for this."

Gary nodded in amusement. This was fun, and he was enjoying Nate's company in this picturesque little inn away from Foggy Bottom.

Gary's friendship with Nate had begun during prep school at Andover. Nate had gone on to Columbia, where he had excelled, and then had joined the family investment bank. Gary had been astonished to learn that Nate's great-great-grandfather was none other than Marcus Goldman, the German immigrant who had founded Goldman Sachs. Upping the ante, Gary had been moved to inform Nate that his own great-grandfather was Bat Masterson—a complete fabrication.

After a successful career at the firm, where he had specialized in emerging markets in the Asian Pacific, Nate had felt the pull of government service. Like many Goldman alumni, he had started at Treasury and moved on to State. As undersecretary, he now had overall responsibility for Asian affairs, ever alert for anything that might upset the always delicate balance of tensions between China, Japan, and the two Koreas.

By contrast, after an undistinguished prep school academic record—and much to his father's dismay—Gary had decided to skip college for the allure of motor racing. Still, the two friends had remained close, and Nate had become a trusted adviser to Gary during Heloise's meteoric growth in Asia.

A young waiter brought in another bundle of uniformly cut wood, which he deposited at the foot of the slate fireplace, only two tables away from where they were seated.

"You said you had a favor you needed," Nate said. "Lay it on me. Whatever you need, I'll do my best to help."

Gary pursed his lips. "Yeah, Nate. I've gotten myself in a pickle, promising to deliver something I may not be able to. It's about Kume. She wants to find out about her birth father. The trouble is, she doesn't want her mother to know she's searching, so I offered to do the legwork. Do you have any idea how hard it is to locate someone from fifty-five years ago when you don't have a name or anything else to identify him?"

Gary watched Nate's bespectacled face soften as he processed the question. Gary had told Nate about Kume, but Nate had never met her. Gary had also kept Nate up-to-date on the highlights and lowlights over the years. That meant Nate was aware that Gary had been smitten with the supermodel for years, that they had been estranged, and that Gary would do anything he could to bring them back together.

"So she won't give you much to go on," Nate muttered. "No name. Nothing."

"Right. She's pushed her mother as far as she can, but the woman refuses to talk about it. Kume says it's a sore subject between them. She's even talked to her stepdad, but he's too smart to step into that minefield. And who knows? Maybe he hates the thought of the guy and hopes he's dead."

Nate nodded and signaled the waiter for another scotch and water. He paused to stroke his neatly trimmed salt-and-pepper Edwardian beard—a new look for him, and one that gave his face more character while complementing his balding head. "I see your dilemma. But how do you think I can help?"

"I've decided I should go to Okinawa and do some of my own detective work. There has to be something—a person, maybe, who remembers them, the Himeyuri woman Noriko and her American soldier. Maybe there are some records from that time. I've been in touch with the National Archives and got my hands on some disciplinary records involving American soldiers and native women in Okinawa in the 1945-46 period. But it's not much to go on. A lot of those records are still classified, apparently. I guess that subject may be tender even after all this time."

"'Tender' is hardly the word for it. I'm sure you've heard about the recent cases of rape committed against Okinawan women by US servicemen. Tempers have gotten very hot. The folks over there are demanding the US pack up and go home. But that's not going to happen—not with an ascendant China stirring up trouble just across the water. Cooler heads among the islanders understand that. They also understand that the island economy is hugely dependent on our military bases there.

"But I'm digressing. You want to know how I can help clear the way for you to get information about a subject that Okinawans may be a little reluctant to discuss."

"That's pretty much it." Gary mugged his best Jack Nicholson smile.

"Well, for starters, I have some connections—mainly in Tokyo—but they'll get you access to prefectural officials in Naha. If there are records of incidents involving American soldiers from that time, or archives concerning the population after the battle, you may find something about Noriko and her American soldier." Nate took a sip from the just-arrived scotch. "Not promising that you'll get any real satisfaction, though. Remember, we're talking about 1945, and any hint of a liaison between an Okinawan woman and an American serviceman wouldn't have been welcome by the military *or* the Okinawans themselves. And as you already know, the US military records are nearly useless without a name or something else to narrow the search down."

"I hear you, but I have to try. I'll let you know when I plan to make the trip. Is there anything else I should know about the lay of the land?"

Nate's Blackberry buzzed. He paused to look at the screen. "Beth says hello. Wants you to come over for dinner next time." He put the phone down and shrugged. "There's nothing much more to say. In recent years, a fair number of veterans groups have made the pilgrimage, and they've done much to heal the old wounds. There's a Prefectural Peace Memorial that was dedicated not too long ago in a park overlooking the ocean. Supposed to be quite an impressive place—very moving. Contains hundreds of thousands of names of those who died from all sides. My advice is, just be your usual, charming self. If anyone can get people to relax and open up, you are the master, son." Nate winked at his use of their familiar old wordplay. "And please don't get involved in any more car chases, Mr. Mooney."

Two hours later, back in his suite at the Ritz-Carlton, Gary studied his calendar. He would try to block out a week later in the month to spend in Okinawa, followed, he hoped, by a stop in Tokyo.

Chapter 25

What Else Haven't You Told Me?

Monday, January 14, 2002

Mesilla, New Mexico

They were in the living room—piñón logs popping in the fireplace, late morning sunlight streaming through the shades—when Frankie finally blurted out the truth. "I'm going to Okinawa."

Melanie looked up from her knitting, dumbfounded. "What?"

Frankie felt like he did in the dentist's chair right before a root canal. He just wanted to get it done. "Next week. Ellen's coming with me."

Melanie shot him a sideways glance, her bright blue eyes smoldering with anger and disbelief. "So that's it. That's what you've been hiding from me all this time. While I've been walking on eggshells around you, you've been planning a trip to Okinawa! With our daughter!" She shook her head. "Well, I hope to high heaven it's worth it and you can purge your soul of whatever it is that's causing you these awful nightmares."

Frankie could see that Melanie was about to burst into tears—so unlike the tough persona she presented to others. The funny thing was, he hadn't had a dream for at least a week. But the trip was drawing near, and Ellen had been threatening to spill the beans if he didn't come clean with his wife about their plans.

Melanie's lip began to quiver as the anger on her face gave way to a look of genuine hurt. "You could at least have told me sooner. How long have you been planning this? And why didn't you ask me if I'd like to come with you?"

Frankie scrambled for a good answer. "Honestly, I didn't think you'd want to."

"Why drag Ellen into your little conspiracy?" Melanie sounded almost as mystified as she was wounded.

"I thought it would give us a little bonding time. And I'm not even sure how I'll feel once I'm there." He tried not to look directly at Melanie's eyes, afraid she'd see that he was only telling her part of the truth. But as uncomfortable as he felt, he wanted to console her and tell her everything would be fine.

She wiped her cheek with the back of her hand. "Does this have anything to do with the recent business about Ramón? Funny. You never mentioned *that* to me, either. I had to find out about it from someone else."

Frankie could feel the prickly heat of guilt warming his ears. He knew he'd had no good reason to keep that from Melanie. She was well aware that Mama Elena had contacted many people over the years in her search for news about Ramón's fate.

"I should be furious with you," Melanie continued. "Sneaking around like some child with a nasty little secret. Well, let me tell you something: I found out what was going on because of the good sense and decency of José, who didn't think it was right that I should be in the dark, especially since his family was involved. He told me that his uncle left a memoir with a bunch of information about the war and POW camps and that his nephew sent it to you. Andrew was his name. Andrew put two and two together after he read the parts about someone who sounded like your brother. He decided to answer the letter from your mother that the grandfather had ignored years ago." Her eyes narrowed in anger once again. "So what's so damn hard about that? Why the secrecy? Why couldn't you have just trusted me? What else haven't you told me?"

Frankie stood mute, feeling overwhelmed by the barrage, trying to sort out an answer. "First, the trip has nothing to do with Ramón. I've finished reading the document, and I'm pretty sure the person that Porfirio—Frío—described is my brother. Unfortunately, the document ends with events almost a year before the end of the war and provides no clue about what eventually happened to Ramón. I don't expect to find out anything about Ramón in Okinawa—"

Melanie cut him off. "Fine. It still doesn't answer what you need to resolve in Okinawa. It sure must be a big deal to cause you so much guilt over all these years. I can only imagine what it might be."

The conversation had spun out of control, and Frankie desperately needed to put the genie back in the bottle. "All right. That's enough!" he barked, surprised at the harsh sound of his own voice. "You know very well that what happened in the war is not a subject I want to discuss with my family. War is ugly, worse than your wildest nightmare. It does no good to dredge it up. You've been understanding of that for fifty years and have respected my wish not to discuss it. Can we just leave it at that for now?"

Melanie turned away, looking furious that he'd said something that she couldn't deny was true.

Frankie sighed. "I don't know what will happen or what good will come of this trip. All I know is that I can't go on like this, fighting wars in my dreams. I want—*need*—to reconcile myself with the past and find an inner peace. Just give me that chance, okay?"

He reached to take Melanie's hand, but she pulled away and left the living room.

Chapter 26

Who Is This?

Kume gratefully accepted the ginger saketini from Asahi, the slender young man behind the bar, and then went to work stirring the lemon peel and fresh ginger in her clear martini glass. One of the advantages of co-owning a hip restaurant in the skyscraper district was being so well understood by all the bartenders. At Chez Kume, Kume usually had a drink in her hand—and just the right one—the moment she claimed a stool at the bar.

Currently, she was mid-conversation with Genevieve, who was catching up on the past several weeks. Kume was eager to vent about her mother, whom she'd finally persuaded to come out for a long-overdue visit. Enough time had passed that Kume had forgotten how frustrating a visit from her mother could be. Each time she would approach it with eager anticipation, thinking that this time would be different. And each time, by the third day, she would be checking her calendar to see how many days were left of her mother's annual visit to Tokyo.

Thank God, Genevieve was a good listener.

Genevieve, though, wanted the tabloid version of Kume's rendezvous with Gary Masterson. "You can't be serious!" she exclaimed after Kume told her they had *not* slept together during her stay in New York. "You'd better not play too hard to get, or else Gary will find other, more accommodating fish in the sea." Genevieve stabbed her Player's cigarette in Kume's direction. "A good-looking, rich man like him will have no trouble attracting *la jeune femme*." She giggled. "Maybe even an old hen like me."

Kume smiled and wagged her finger at her friend. "To-morrow my mother leaves for Sendai. I feel so guilty saying it, but it can't come too soon. I'm so tired of hearing how she feels seasick from the swaying of the building. And the noise from the traffic thirty-nine floors below. And the crowded streets and subways filled with rude people. And the kids, dressing like tramps and behaving in a vulgar way—no respect for their elders."

Genevieve nodded knowingly. "So she hasn't changed her mind about big cities. At least she's consistent."

Kume noticed they'd attracted the attention of two fair-haired Scandinavian-looking men, whom Genevieve was pre-tending to ignore as she sized them up.

"Sometimes it seems that she comes from another century," Kume said of her mother. "Always judging things. Never seeing the wonder and beauty of the amazing city around her."

Genevieve shot an expressionless glance at the two Nordic men, as though she were looking past them, and shrugged. "But didn't you say she likes the old Imperial Gardens at

Shinjuku Gyoen? Doesn't she take walks through the conservatories? And what about the other day, when she came to the studio in Harajuku to make pretend fashions with Chika and Haruko? She must have enjoyed that."

Kume looked up toward the ceiling. "Yes. My mother likes the peaceful and ordinary, away from the pulsing, maddening city. In quiet times, she can be charming and interesting, speaking of her girlhood in Kume-jima. She grew up in an ordered, simpler time. Everything exploded into chaos and horror when she was just a teenage girl. I can't imagine what that must have done to her. I try to remember that when she starts really getting on my nerves. I think my dad must be a saint."

Genevieve put out her cigarette, stood, pulled her shoulders back, and adjusted her skirt. "Well, tomorrow it will be over, and you have done your duty as a good daughter. Now I believe I should introduce myself to those blond businessmen who are probably here for the first time. We must make sure they have a positive first impression."

Kume shook her head as she picked up her purse. *"La belle dame sans souci . . ."*

The Next Day

Kume was dripping sweat as she hurried past Hiro, the doorman. Still feeling her pulse pumping, she headed for the elevator. The morning run had invigorated her.

She turned the key in the lock and braced herself for the last few hours of living with her mother. It hadn't been a bad visit, but she was tired of her mother's clear disdain for all things Tokyo, New York, and big cities in general. That her mother still refused to budge on the subject of her biological father wasn't helping things, either.

She walked through the door and into the ergonomic kitchen, setting her keys on the counter. "Mother?"

"In here," her mother called from the guest room.

Something in her tone triggered an alarm bell inside Kume. She hurried down the hall and into the last room on the right. "Mother, are you—"

She was sitting on the bed, her face pinched—and as pale as Kume had ever seen it.

"What?" Kume asked. "What's wrong? You look—"

Her mother slowly lifted the familiar three-by-five black-and-white photo and held it up for Kume to see. "Who is this?"

Kume felt her head spin suddenly. She stared at the picture for a long moment, searching her mind for some way to explain. But there was no way to skirt around the truth. She backed into the bathroom for a towel, slipped off her running shoes, and padded across the hardwood. She sat on the bed next to her mother. Her eyes filled with tears as she took the photo and gazed down at a solemn little face with bright eyes and a thatch of dark hair. "Where did you find this?"

Her mother shook her head. "It does not matter." In an uncharacteristic move, she grasped Kume's free hand. "You can tell me, daughter. I am stronger than you think."

Kume pulled free, exhaling and chuckling softly. "Despite what you might think of me, I have never thought of you as weak, Mother. Not for one minute."

"Okay," her mother said, tapping at the photo. "Then tell me."

"He was my son." Kume handed back the photo and stood, turning her back to her mother as tears coursed down her cheeks. It had been so long since she had allowed herself to look at the picture of her son, and it still hurt just as much—perhaps now more than ever. "His name was Henry," she explained. "He was born September 20, 1972, and he only lived thirty-six days." She bowed her head. "He had a congenital heart defect."

Her mother cleared her throat. "The father?"

Kume turned to face her but said nothing.

"The American, yes?"

Kume bit her lip to keep her anger in check. "His name is Gary, Mother. I think you know that."

Although her mother was trying to hide it, Kume could see it in her face: the judgment.

Her mother broke eye contact and looked down at the photo. "This Gary. Did he stay or . . ."

"Are you asking if he left me?" Kume snapped. "Is that it? Like your American left you? The answer is no. He stayed. He stayed until I walked out on him."

Her mother, obviously chagrined, looked up. She nodded almost imperceptibly—her usual understated apology.

Shaken by the exchange, Kume crossed the room to the dresser. She paused there, shoulders slumped, and then without looking back, left the room. In her own bedroom, behind closed doors, Kume felt the deluge begin. The tears flowed anew. She sobbed, sensing again the black abyss of grief she had fallen into so long ago. Along with the tears came the flood of memories she had kept from her mother.

When her pregnancy had become known, she was dismissed by the Ford Agency. But the Mastersons were good to her, and Gary arranged to secure Kume's exclusive services for Heloise, buying out Ford's rights. In the aftermath, Kume threw herself into her work with a single-minded, nearly frantic dedication to establish the new Heloise image. The harder she worked, the less she had to think about it. But it wasn't long before she realized her heart was no longer in it. The death of her infant son had taken an unbearable toll on her.

Gary, poor Gary. He had tried so hard to console her. He had asked Kume to marry him, to try for another child, but she had turned him down. She had needed to get away, to find a change of scenery, to turn the page on her life.

Kume walked over to the large window and looked out over the Tokyo skyline. Thank God that Genevieve had invited her to stay with her in Paris. It had been the tonic Kume had desperately needed, and she had gratefully accepted. Paris proved to be her salvation. Her interest in fashion returned, and she was introduced to Kenzo Takada, who, in due course, took her under his wing as his protégé.

But now, here she was, devastated over events of nearly thirty years past. Perhaps she had been too hard on her mother. She didn't deserve the implication that the American had left her behind due to some failing on her part. But words could be cruel and, once uttered, impossible to retract.

Kume heard her mother's halting, shuffling steps, followed by the sound of wheeled luggage rolling past her door. She couldn't be seen in public like this. She quickly changed, tied her hair back, and put on dark glasses. Her mother was waiting in the spacious living room.

Kume approached, reached for her hand, and held it until her mother withdrew. "The JR Tohoku Shinkansen leaves in an hour and a half. We should leave for the train station."

"No need to bother," Noriko responded flatly. "I can take a taxi."

"Nonsense, Mother. It isn't far. I'll walk with you." Kume paused and added, "I'm sorry I spoke like that."

Noriko looked at her daughter briefly before waving her hand dismissively.

From a bench in the terminal waiting room, Kume watched the clock. On the other side of the wall, busy Tokyo Station no doubt pulsed with the same frenetic energy as it always did. But here, in a windowless room with stark, fluorescent lighting and drab gray carpet, the minutes passed slowly.

Kume caught a whiff of cologne—or was it deodorant?—from someone sitting a few rows ahead of her and her mother. The average Japanese person, male or female, didn't bother with heavily scented body spray, lotion, deodorant, or perfume. Instead, the Japanese preferred to wrinkle their collective nose at the "stinky foreigners," so conspicuous by the various odors that trailed them.

The automatic doors slid open, and the station's cacophonous medley—brakes squealing, robotic-yet-soothing voices floating from the public address system, bullet trains howling like ghosts as they whipped through nearby tunnels—entered with a young couple and their baby.

Kume glanced at her mother, who had closed her eyes and was silently, gently rocking in her seat, head bowed.

"Is everything okay, Mother?"

Noriko looked up slowly. "That photo of your son. It reminded me of a dream I had two days ago."

"A dream?"

"I was in an underground military hospital, probably Haebaru. Horrible sights and smells—young men with no arms, legs, screaming in pain. Surgeons barely able to keep up. Constant shelling."

"But you said . . . was there a baby?"

Noriko exhaled a long sigh and brushed her dark hair back from her eyes. "Yes—more than one. Although the hospital was military, many civilian refugees from the shelling had begged to come inside. We had no room. Already we were overwhelmed by the number of our wounded soldiers. A young mother, clearly pregnant and nearly full term, was carried in. She had lost both legs in the bombing. She was delirious and bleeding badly. I could do nothing more than hold her hand while she cried and her life slipped away. One of the doctors performed a caesarean. It was a healthy baby boy . . ."

Kume reached for her mother's hand. This time they held on tightly until a familiar, bell-like melody chimed overhead and was followed by an announcement for the Sendai bullet train.

PART II

Frankie's Journey

Chapter 27

Hit by a Velvet Truck

Wednesday, January 23, 2002

Chatan, Nakagami District, Okinawa

Frankie's body clock was a mess, and his thigh hurt like hell. He turned toward the digital alarm clock on the nightstand to his right and frowned when he saw the oversized numbers. It was almost midnight. He'd been tossing and turning in his hotel bed for a solid hour. Less than two hours had passed since he'd said good night to Ellen, who, for all he knew, was sleeping like a baby in the suite next door.

The trip from El Paso had begun almost thirty hours earlier and had included stops with layovers of several hours at Denver International and Narita. Just before the ANA flight from Tokyo to Naha, Ellen had asked to trade seats, and he had happily obliged. By then, he'd been too rummy to enjoy the view from his window seat anyway.

As late as it was here, his brain told him it was midafternoon. Sleep was out of the question. He threw back the covers, shuffled into the bathroom, and fumbled through his Dopp kit for the Advil. Then he slipped out the sliding door to the balcony, where he was greeted by a curtain of dampness—the same one that he'd never gotten used to as a kid from the high desert of New Mexico. He'd nearly forgotten what it felt like.

From his perch on the fifteenth-floor balcony of the Beach Tower Hotel, Frankie could barely make out the dark expanse of water below. By contrast, over his shoulder, the city lights of this town on the outskirts of Kadena Air Force Base seemed almost otherworldly.

How could it all seem so different? He would have to wait for first light to get his bearings. But for now he tried to imagine what it must have looked like that April morning in 1945, when the sea was carpeted by 1,300 ships, all part of a massive US invasion force. To the poor inhabitants of Okinawa, it must have been an awesome sight.

He could still hear the raspy klaxon shriek of the ship's loudspeakers as it assaulted his ears, warning the troops to expect stiff resistance from the defenders during the landings. This was Japanese soil, and it wouldn't be surrendered without a fight. Frankie remembered that the confession lines were long, and services on board had been unusually well-attended that night of March 31, which happened to be Holy Saturday.

The memory of the mind-numbing fear as he climbed down the netting into the amtrac with all his gear on that Easter Sunday morning had never left him. The smell of exhaust, the humidity, the lurching boat, and the deep, gripping dread combined to make him lose his breakfast over the side. While aboard the motorized landing craft with his platoon mates, carving nauseating circles in the sea, awaiting the signal to head for the beach, he had said a final act of contrition and kissed the gold crucifix given him by his mother. After churning through the water in a mad dash of several thousand yards, they would come ashore just a bit north of where he now stood, near the village of Hagushi.

God willing, he would reach the beach alive.

Fatigue overcame Frankie suddenly, like being hit by a velvet truck. Tomorrow would be here all too soon. He stretched out on a chaise lounge, crossed his arms, and floated away into deep sleep on the balcony.

Chapter 28

A Dinosaur in Okinawa

Thursday, January 24, 2002

Okinawa

Frankie woke up to the sound of someone knocking on his hotel suite door, but he needed several seconds to make sense of the noise. After a brief moment of disorientation, it all came rushing back: the long flights and layovers, the late evening check-in at their hotel, and the restless night's sleep.

Okinawa. He was finally here. Never mind that he had slept on a hotel suite balcony.

He hoisted himself up from the chaise lounge, opened the screen door, and shuffled to the front door. After taking a moment to secure his robe, he flung open the door and found Ellen waiting in the hallway, bright-eyed and looking disgustingly rested.

"Jesus, Dad," she said, giving him the once-over, "you look like death on a soda cracker."

He waved off the comment and invited her into his suite. "Whatever, kid. Make yourself at home. I just need five minutes."

"Good," she said, eyeballing his bed, which he'd stripped of its comforter in the middle of the night. "That gives us just enough time to grab breakfast downstairs before we meet our guide in the lobby. So . . . what's wrong with your bed?"

He followed her eyes from the bed to the chaise lounge—and the comforter—out on the balcony.

"Don't tell me you slept out there!" she protested. "Are you crazy? You could've fallen right over the side. How would I explain that to Mom?"

"I'm fine, aren't I?" He started for the bathroom. "Like I said, I just need five minutes."

Despite struggling with the shower knobs—some genius had installed them backward—he made quick work of his time in the strangely configured bathroom. After a quick shower, he brushed his teeth and combed his wet hair in front of the mirror, which only showed traces of steam at the edges. He'd have to let the stubble on his chin proliferate another day before attacking it with his razor. All he could think of at the moment was breakfast. Hopefully he'd be able to scrounge a Danish and a cup of tea downstairs before their guide arrived.

What I wouldn't do for a cup of manzanilla, he mused.

To his amazement and delight, Ellen had one waiting for him when he emerged from the bathroom.

"How'd you manage this?" he said as he gratefully accepted the steaming cup of herbal tea.

She nodded to the coffeemaker and small sink in a corner nook opposite his suite's balcony. "I brought the tea. The hotel provided the rest."

"Wonderful," he said.

After making sure he had the key card to his suite, he followed Ellen to the elevator and, tea mug in one hand, pushed the button for the lobby. He could smell the aroma of fresh coffee and bacon as soon as the door opened.

Their guide, a young marine with a chiseled chin and perfectly erect posture, arrived just as Frankie and Ellen were polishing off the last of their traditional American breakfast, which had included all the essentials: eggs, bacon, sausage, fried tomatoes, and an endless supply of toast. Frankie spotted the marine talking to someone on the hotel staff at the entrance to the dining area, which was separated from the rest of the lobby by a loosely assembled wall of room dividers and large indoor plants in huge ceramic pots.

"I assume you're the Castillos," the marine said in a deep baritone as soon as he arrived at their small table for two. "I'm Major Gregory Jamison. I'm assigned to be your guide today."

"Pleased to meet you, Major," Frankie said and stood to shake the hand of the handsome and strapping young marine.

Ellen smiled at the officer in his dress uniform but said nothing. She appeared determined to play it cool.

"I'm part of Headquarters Battalion, Third Marine Division, Camp Courtney," Major Jamison explained. "Last evening, the XO called me in, all excited because of a message he'd received from the Marine Barracks, Washington. He said that two special visitors to Okinawa were to be treated as guests and extended the full professional courtesies of the Third Marines, including guiding them to battlefield sites." He turned to Frankie and added, "I was told that one of the visitors fought in the Battle of Okinawa. That's all I had to hear. A salute, *OO-RAH!* and here I am, at your service."

Frankie shot Ellen another look of surprise. First the tea, now the welcoming committee. "You didn't say our guide was a marine."

"I made a few phone calls before we left home," she said coyly. "I figured you'd prefer a marine to some civilian tour guide."

All Frankie could do was chuckle. His daughter knew him so well.

"Thanks for making us feel so welcome," Ellen said, addressing the major. "I'm Ellen, and this is my father, Francisco Castillo. Just call him Frankie."

"Glad to meet you both. And please, call me Gregory."

Frankie gave Ellen a discreet nudge with his elbow. With any luck, while he took in the sights, his daughter might make a new friend in the dashing major. He appeared to be only a few years younger than her and, along with boasting All-American good looks and a deep, mellifluous voice, was undeniably charming.

"So let's see," Gregory said. "How to begin? I guess it's pretty obvious the island has changed a lot in fifty-seven years, Frankie. I understand you were in the Tenth Army's Ninety-Sixth Infantry Division. Can you fill in the particulars for me?"

"Sure, Major . . . uh, Gregory. I was a rifleman in Charlie Company, Second Battalion, 383rd Infantry Regiment."

"Pretty impressive. That unit saw a lot of action. Kakazu, Nishibaru, Charlie Hill, Dick Hill, Conical Hill, Yuza, Kunishi—those places mean anything to you?"

Frankie nodded. "Now *I'm* impressed. How do you know so much about the army units that fought here?"

"Good question to ask a marine," he said and smiled, revealing a gleaming set of perfectly straight white teeth. "I've always been fascinated by the Okinawa battle, particularly the Japanese side of it. I decided I needed to learn everything I could about it. After the Naval Academy, I managed to get a master's at Harvard with a specialty in World War Two military history. I did my thesis on the strategies and tactics of the Japanese generals Ushijima and Cho. That meant becoming familiar with virtually every major unit formation in both armies."

Frankie whistled under his breath.

"So after Desert Storm, it probably should have come as no surprise that I would find myself in Okinawa." Gregory shrugged.

"Are you married?" Frankie wasn't embarrassed to ask, although the question earned an immediate reaction from Ellen, who was staring daggers at him. "Any kids?"

The major revealed another picture-perfect smile. "No, and no. Well, let me qualify. I married a Harvard classmate, but it didn't last. She couldn't understand why someone like me wouldn't want to get into politics or study law. My mother, bless her heart, wondered the same thing. I guess they couldn't grasp that a guy who was born only a few days after his father was killed at Khe Sanh might feel a special kinship with the marines." He added, pointedly, "Thankfully, there were no children."

Frankie offered a sober nod as he studied his daughter's face, searching for clues. Was she as impressed with the major as he was?

"Can we order you something?" Ellen asked, seemingly determined to steer the conversation back toward more neutral territory. "Some coffee?"

Gregory shook his head. "I'm fine. Since you're here for such a short time, I've laid out a route to a few places that might be of special interest. We should probably get started soon. I have a car and a map. I hope you won't be disappointed, Frankie, but the island is very different from what you probably recall. Many sites are no longer recognizable." He took a deep breath. "Still, it's worth the effort. Shall we go?"

Frankie rode shotgun and was entrusted with the map, now a partially folded mess in his lap. He tried to match his memory of blasted hilltops and ruined fields with the civilized, mundane sights that were flying past his window as they sped through Naha. "You're right," he finally told Gregory. "It isn't the Okinawa I knew."

Gregory glanced over at Frankie. "What I was saying before about everything changing—the sad thing is that there are lots of caves and tunnels, especially on the southern end of the island, that are only just now being explored. Every so often, a bulldozer cuts into a spider hole or a sniper's nest. They often find bones and live ammo. They always attempt identification, though not always successfully. Now and then the remains of a long-missing American turn up. The cave systems alone are mind-boggling. Some of them went for miles underground. It was impressive defensive work." He grinned. "But I suspect that the marines and soldiers of 1945 would describe it a little differently."

Frankie lowered his visor to block the morning sun. "You know, we couldn't believe that we got ashore without so much as a shot being fired. We started to think it would be a cakewalk."

Gregory nodded. "Ushijima had other plans."

Indeed, Frankie thought, General Ushijima had understood exactly what he was up against. With no air or naval support to draw on—notwithstanding kamikaze attacks on the invasion fleet—he had wisely opted not to fight the Americans on the beaches. Thus Frankie and the others, rather than face a replay of Tarawa, Peleliu, or Iwo Jima, were allowed to get comfortable while the Japanese forces remained concealed in a system of defensive underground positions farther inland, from which they could grind the enemy down, yielding yard by yard, hill by hill. Experienced artillery gunners calibrated overlapping fields of fire, and the Americans found themselves in a different predicament altogether. Ushijima had hoped the killing zones would result in a stalemate on Okinawa, giving the home islands time to prepare for the expected American invasion. Or even motivate the Americans to offer peace terms.

Frankie shook his head as they drove past high-rises, parking garages, and fast-food joints. "I feel like I'm in some kind of time warp. It's like, what battle? Everyone hast just moved on. I might as well be a dinosaur. Does the younger generation even know what happened?"

Fifty-five years had passed, and the carnage Frankie remembered was long gone.

"It's not just the younger generation," Gregory replied as he adjusted the settings on their Honda's air conditioner. "Some of the older locals who survived the battle act like it should be forgotten." He pointed to a Starbucks sign up ahead. "I imagine this is all pretty disorienting."

Frankie resisted the urge to grab the steering wheel. "It doesn't help that you're driving on the wrong side of the road."

Ellen laughed from the back seat. "Not wrong, Dad, just *left*."

Gregory slowed the sedan as they approached a green hill topped by a water tower. It rose perpendicularly from the street, courtesy of cement retaining walls a few stories high.

"Recognize it?" Gregory asked.

Frankie stared at it through the passenger's side window. "Afraid not."

Gregory flashed those perfect teeth. "Sugar Loaf Hill."

Frankie let out an involuntary gasp but said nothing. He barely felt Ellen's hand on his shoulder as he fought off the lump in his throat. All he could think of was the marine blood that had been spilled there in what was some of the fiercest fighting of the war. Now? It was an inglorious lump wedged between duty-free shops and apartment buildings. "It looks smaller," he finally said.

"That's because it is," Gregory said. "Much of it has been hauled away to make room for development. There are plans in the works for a shopping mall and a movie theater."

The tour continued at a dizzying pace. Next up was Kakazu Ridge—now a pretty little park with a rusting blue observation tower at its center.

"The whole damn place looks like Los Angeles now," Frankie said as they descended a wide cement staircase on their way back to the Honda.

Once back on the road, Frankie felt the bitter irony gnawing at his gut. It was on Kakazu that his battalion had faced the enemy's powerful antitank gun, which had shot the hell out of their armor. The Japanese had set up their machine guns and mortars so they could support each other and cover the routes the Americans tried to move through. The Americans called in airstrikes and artillery, but the Japanese would just disappear back into their caves and dugouts until the coast was clear. Then they'd come out and blast the Americans all over again.

Frankie still dreamt about trying to take the ridge. His squad, caught in an open area on the facing slope, took cover in a ditch. The mortar fire from the back slope and machine-gun fire from concealed positions in front of them were overwhelming. That and a talented Japanese sniper had them pinned down.

A replacement named Sidney Thoresen had recently joined the squad. He was a wiseass and full of himself—someone who had no discipline or appreciation for just what a dangerous enemy they were up against. At Kakazu, Frankie ended up picking pieces of Thoresen out of his face and neck after Thoresen lost his cool and got blown to bits by a mortar round.

Frankie's heart raced as he remembered his first kill. It was April twelfth—or maybe the thirteenth. He could never remember the exact date. The Japanese counterattacked. A Jap captain, brandishing a sword in one hand and a Nambu pistol in the other, had emerged from a cave mouth and was charging toward the squad. He was followed by six soldiers screaming, "Banzai!" They advanced in a crouch, their rifles tipped with long bayonets.

Frankie aimed and pulled the trigger, but the Garand was empty. He stood to take the second charging soldier by the neck and dug his fingers into the enemy's throat. Frankie strangled the guy. At least he thought he had. More Japanese were pouring out of caves and Frankie's squad was about to be overrun, but a flame-throwing tank had arrived in the nick of time and sprayed the area with napalm. Frankie had vomited from the smell of burning flesh—something he would never forget. That was just before a Japanese 47-millimeter gun turned the tank into a fireball and cooked the crew.

"Huh," Frankie grunted under his breath. He hadn't thought about that day in a long time. Everything had bogged down after several weeks of awful weather. The mud and the stench of the unburied dead had been all but unbearable. Then his squad was tapped to lead a breakout.

As they drove past Kakazu and Nishibaru Ridge, Gregory pointed to a Burger King next to a car wash, and Frankie remembered what had once been there: a little saddle just before Tanabaru where his battalion had broken through. They took a lot of machine-gun and grenade action from the heights. The lieutenant to his right had his lower jaw blown off by a rifle bullet, and a few yards away, Frankie saw one of the medics lose a leg to a mine. Frankie got hold of a BAR and ammo from a dead gunner and emptied seven or eight magazines at the ridge. He and the others fought back with everything they had. When night fell, the shooting stopped. Frankie dug in along with the rest of the battalion and waited. When the fog lifted the next morning, the Japanese were gone. They had pulled out during the night.

"We're almost at our next stop," Gregory said a few minutes later. "Can you make out Conical Hill?"

That evening at dinner, Frankie didn't feel much like talking. It had been a day of alternating disappointment, recognition, and emotion. Gregory had dropped them back at the hotel, promising to pick them up in the morning for a second escorted trip. They would proceed to the southernmost parts of Okinawa, finishing at the peace memorials.

"You're awfully quiet, Dad. Something bothering you?" Ellen picked at the sashimi plate. She was nursing a cup of sake.

Frankie stared at his untouched linguine with white clam sauce. He looked up, turning the question over in his mind.

"You don't have to talk about it if you don't want to," Ellen said with a sympathetic look.

"Thanks," he said, suddenly feeling grateful for her presence. "I'm just thinking about those places and the memories of young guys I saw die back then."

Ellen reached across the table and took his hand. "It can't be easy to live with all those memories."

He nodded grimly and tried to think of something he could share that wasn't too personal. Then he remembered

Ernie Pyle, the famous wartime correspondent. "I didn't say anything while we were there, but we passed the spot where I actually met and spoke to Ernie Pyle. You've probably never heard of him. He was a famous reporter back then, and the brass bent over backward for him. The war in Europe was finished, and he wasn't about to miss the Pacific finale."

Ellen sat back in her seat and raised an eyebrow. "How did you meet him?"

"Well, here he was, scurrying around getting bits of interviews with grunts. Most guys were happy to oblige, because he might mention their names in his column. Everybody back home read Ernie Pyle. Most of the old breed ignored him, though. Said he wasn't even close to describing the reality of the shit we were facing. Pegged him as a puppet for the War Department propaganda machine. Keep Mom and Dad from worrying about their hero son, who was having a wonderful war with dry socks and clean sheets. But Pyle, who was from Albuquerque, was like a letter from home. I remember thinking what a skinny-ass little gringo he was."

Ellen smiled.

"I only had a few words with him," Frankie continued. "I gave him my name, and then some colonel yanked him aside and said he was going to Ie Shima, some island up north just a few miles off the coast. Wanted to know if Ernie wanted to go. Couple days later, we got word that Ernie Pyle had been killed by a sniper on Ie Shima. My name never made it into his column. I guess the lesson is don't accept offers for a ride from a colonel."

"That's a terrible story, Dad."

"I know."

The waitress, a waif of a young woman with a shiny black bob, paused at their table. "May I get you anything else?" she asked in a heavy Okinawan accent.

Frankie nodded and ordered a shot of Patrón Reposado and a bottle of Dos Equis. As soon as the waitress left, he scooched his chair back from the table so he could stretch out his leg and rub the thigh.

"Giving you trouble?" Ellen asked.

"It seems to know that we're near the place it happened. Been hurting like a son of a bitch all day. Maybe a little liquid painkiller will help."

Frankie stared at his daughter, silently wondering if this was the moment to bring up the real reason for coming to Okinawa. *How would she react? Would she be angry? What would it do to our relationship? Could I just pass it off as the foolish but harmless curiosity of an old man who wanted to know what had become of a refugee he had tried to help so many years ago? Or would that sound ridiculous? What better time would there be? Should I put it off and rehearse, or should it be spontaneous, like right now?*

He threw back the shot of Patrón, felt the scald as it met the back of his throat, and grimaced, hissing as he inhaled through his teeth. *What a pleasant hurt*, he thought as he motioned for another. He decided that the mood was all wrong. Now was not the time. He would bring the subject up later, maybe tomorrow after the tour.

Ellen produced an Advil and handed it to him. "This might help, too."

He chased it down with a swallow of beer. "Thanks, kid."

She studied him with affection in her eyes. "I don't remember you ever talking about Okinawa. Certainly not in detail. What else do you have bottled up in that memory vault?" She tapped her temple.

He chuckled softly, feeling simultaneously sleep-deprived and restless. His eyes felt heavy, but his memory had become electric, with sharp details coming to the surface.

"Did you see any civilians?" Ellen asked.

Frankie downed the last shot of tequila. "Yes. That was the worst part. The bombing and shellfire had saturated the place. People caught out in the open were blown apart or maimed. I saw a bearded old man without a leg crawling toward God knows where. A few yards away was a mother lying dead, face-down in a mud puddle with a crying baby on her back. Kids were shaking in fear as we Americans approached. These are things I want to forget, but I don't think God will let me.

"Then there were the caves where families were hiding. They were handed grenades and told by the Japanese military to use them to kill themselves. They were warned that the Americans would roast them with flamethrowers, or rape the girls, or bayonet babies and mutilate children. Would you believe many Okinawans actually bought that shit? What we saw in those caves, where mothers blew themselves and their children up—" Frankie had to pause. He took another swig of beer. He felt his eyes filling up. "For some of the more experienced GIs who had become so hardened, it was nothing special. They shrugged it off. One of the sergeants liked saying that the only good Jap was a dead Jap, and Okinawans were just southern Japs. But it made me sick. I think the ones who listened to our bullhorns and gave up and came forward were amazed. They received food and medical care, not torture. Camps were set up to house them. I helped with those camps after the fighting ended." He drew a deep breath and slowly exhaled. The memory flood hadn't crested yet. "We were dirty, wet, and bone-tired. But there was no letup. We had to keep attacking. On Hacksaw Ridge, fighting got very personal. Grenades, bayonets, even fists. We became like robots, killing machines. We had lost all sense of mercy and humanity. Between the flame-throwing tanks and the gunning down of fleeing enemies . . ." He looked at Ellen and shook his head wearily.

Ellen took his hand once again, this time more firmly.

Frankie continued. "I saw some amazing things. Like this weapon the Japs had called a spigot mortar. Big as a battleship shell at 320 millimeters. I don't know what the thing weighed, but when it came down, the explosion made a hole five feet deep and fifteen feet across. Usually we could see them in flight and scoot to a safe place. But I watched one erase a group of six guys. They literally vanished—gone. Nothing but a smoking hole and a few scattered bits of bloody cloth."

Frankie fell silent and stole a glance at his daughter across the table. She looked strange in the hotel restaurant's ambient lighting. The wounded look in her eyes suggested profound sadness, but the upward arc of her tightly drawn lips hinted at something else. Gratitude, maybe?

Ellen scooted over and wrapped him in a one-armed hug. They sat silently for a moment, and Frankie let himself bask in the tenderness.

Ellen had barely returned to her place across the table when an American stopped at their table.

"Mind if I join you?"

Frankie, figuring Ellen would shoo him away, hardly bothered to look up at the guy, who was sporting a rugged beard, thick eyebrows, and shoulder-length, dark brown hair.

"We're kind of in the middle of something," Ellen said.

Good girl, Frankie thought.

"I know," the man said. "I've been watching you two for a while from the bar."

Ellen frowned. "Great. So you're a stalker?"

"No, just an admirer. I don't think I've ever seen someone so captivating." He turned partially toward Frankie. "Is this your father?"

Frankie felt his face flush. He was too tired—and too old—for this shit. "Look, son. Just move along, please."

The man, who looked to be in his late thirties or early forties, did the exact opposite and sat down beside Frankie. "I apologize if I've offended you, sir. Unless I'm mistaken, you're a member of the Greatest Generation and fought here in WW II. You probably came back to visit the old haunts. No doubt you don't recognize the place." He extended his hand. "The name's Anthony Wagner. I'm an environmental attorney from LA, here on business."

"Oh brother," Frankie muttered, ignoring the man's hand.

"Do you make a habit of interrupting people's private conversations?" Ellen asked. "Or is this a new thing for you?"

Frankie tilted his head toward Ellen. Her words were combative, but her tone was accommodating. So was the curious smile on her face.

"Definitely new," he said. Was he blushing? "I'm not sure what's gotten into me. I might be a little drunk."

Ellen shook her head in amusement. "Well, Anthony Wagner, you're bold. I'll give you that."

"My friends call me Tony," he said and offered his hand.

Unlike Frankie, Ellen accepted the handshake. "Oh? Are we friends now? What do your enemies call you?"

Tony's face darkened. "The same, I guess. But that's another story. Let me buy you two the next round."

Frankie motioned to the waitress for the check. He'd heard enough. "No thanks. We're calling it a day."

"Maybe I can take you two out for dinner tomorrow," Tony suggested. "My treat."

Frankie frowned. "Yeah, buddy, I don't think—"

"We're touring the south end of the island tomorrow," Ellen said. "You can tag along, if you want." She locked eyes with Frankie. "Assuming it's okay with you, Dad."

Frankie sat upright in his chair, his buzz suddenly waning. *What was happening? Did Ellen see something in this joker? And had she just invited him along on our trip tomorrow?*

"I don't want to intrude," Tony said, suddenly sounding like the reasonable one.

Frankie glanced at his daughter, whose eyes were pleading with his, and threw his hands up in defeat. He'd dragged her to Okinawa and kept her mostly in the dark. Now she was asking him for a return favor. He thought back to Thanksgiving and all the times Melanie had all but begged her to land a serious boyfriend. Now here she was, in Naha of all places, smitten with some stranger who was full of himself and had all the social dexterity of a bull elephant.

"What the hell," Frankie finally said. "The more the merrier."

Chapter 29

Impeccable Timing

Later that Same Evening

**Thirty Thousand Feet over the Pacific,
Approaching the Marianas**

Gary Masterson gazed out the window beside him and saw nothing but blackness, except for the occasional tracery and flash of lightning illuminating an entire cumulus cloud in the distance. It was a beautiful sight that Gary never tired of. The cabin was quiet with only a muted hum as the jets roared away outside in the frigid atmosphere six miles over the Pacific. Chasing the sun for the better part of the past twenty-four hours had made for a grueling first day. Fortunately, the Gulfstream V would touch down at Naha International Airport in only a few more hours.

Just as his eyelids grew heavy, Gary felt his cell phone vibrate and was grateful for the distraction. He glanced at the caller ID and saw Nathan Goldman's name on the display.

"Nate," he said. "Good timing. I was just about to throw myself out of my plane."

"That bored, huh?"

"And then some."

"Well, good. We've got lots to talk about."

Gary liked the sound of that. "Oh yeah?" he said, pulling himself upright in his chair. "Hit me."

"Since our meeting at the Old Angler's Inn a few weeks ago," Nate began, "I've been wondering whether there wasn't something more I could do to help you with your research on Kume's American father. So I decided to call in a favor with the US Customs director—strictly off the grid, of course."

"Of course," Gary said with a smile. Nate never failed to surprise. The guy had more connections than an A-list celebrity.

"Well, anyway, I asked for any information he could find on Americans age seventy and over who've cleared customs in Okinawa in the past twelve months. It was a long shot, but I figured, hell, maybe Kume's father was a veteran and recently made a sentimental journey to the island. If so, maybe we'll get a name.

"I'll tell you what: I wasn't prepared for how many files— nearly ten pounds of 'em—that arrived in a cardboard box at my office. Turns out nearly a thousand aging vets and curiosity seekers have traveled to the old battleground just last year. And that doesn't count everyone who's flown out since the New Year. I had two interns sift through the files, and they flagged several names for extra attention, although four or five were ruled out due to insufficient service records or the wrong branch or what-have-you. Then yesterday I asked for an update from the director—I figured it was worth the trouble since you'd be arriving there shortly—and he faxed me a current list of everyone in our bracket who's traveled to Okinawa so far this month. One of them looks pretty promising: a Francisco Castillo, age seventy-three, from New Mexico, formerly of the US Army's Ninety-Sixth Infantry Division. He fought in Okinawa and returned home in 1946."

Gary hurriedly jotted down the information on the back of a magazine he'd been reading earlier. "And?"

"*And,*" Nate said, drawing out the word, "let's just say you have impeccable timing, old friend."

"How so?"

"Mr. Castillo and a younger Castillo—maybe a daughter or a sister—arrived in Okinawa yesterday."

Chapter 30

Dragons and Faded Scars

Sunday, April 22, 1945

Nishibaru Ridge, Okinawa

"Holcombe!" Frankie whispered.

He waited for a response, but none came. The rain was intermittent—just enough to warrant donning his hooded poncho once again. He hated being trapped inside the thing, which felt confining, claustrophobic even. Hunkering down in a foxhole on a starless night only made him feel more trapped.

He tried once more. "Holcombe!"

Several hours had passed since nightfall, and the broken ridge laid out before him had long since receded into darkness. Distinguishing features had been lost. So, too, his sense of direction. Nighttime was the great equalizer. Any advantage gained during the day—such as taking a ridgeline—disappeared with the sun. That was when the hallucinations came. Tree stumps became men. Depressions became whole squads of soldiers slithering forward on their bellies. Frankie's squad—the survivors, anyway—had become impervious to the little tricks of the imagination. They were hard men now. Professionals. And that was why Frankie didn't like the silence emanating from the foxhole to his left. Either Holcombe had fallen asleep while on watch, or . . .

Frankie sat still and listened. Nothing. No sound of movement. No clanks of metal or machinery. No bayonets being fixed. He was, as far as his straining ears could tell, alone. It would be risky to leave his one-man foxhole. Indeed, he was just as likely to be killed by friendly fire as by a round from the enemy, but this wasn't like Holcombe. The guy was a regular who didn't make mistakes.

With his knife gripped in his right hand, Frankie crawled out onto the exposed parapet, hugging it tightly. He moved as quickly and quietly as possible toward where he thought Holcombe's foxhole should be and, sure enough, found it within seconds. He slid down inside and landed directly where Holcombe should have been standing watch.

"Holcombe?" he whispered.

Inside every foxhole was a deeper depression, a place to crouch when the Japs started shelling, and that was where he found Holcombe dead and bathed in his own blood, his throat slashed.

Friday, January 25, 2002

Chatan, Okinawa

As Frankie shook himself awake, it struck him. The sound and the smell. It was the rain that had brought it all back. Would he ever forget the misery of the rain? It had a familiar odor to it, only lacking the pervasive stench of the rotting dead and the vast compost of human waste that was the battlefield. Ernie Pyle, may he rest in peace, had neglected to inform the moms and dads from Spokane to Jacksonville that their boys were fighting and dying in a noxious sea of shit.

Frankie's body clock was still off-kilter. He had tossed fitfully for much of the night. Images of faces long forgotten had crowded into his head, and his thigh had ached mercilessly. At one point, while drifting off into the twilight world before dawn, he had jerked awake and sat bolt upright, peering into the gloom for signs of any movement, ears alert for the slightest sound.

Lying quietly now in his Egyptian cotton sheets and waiting for his alarm clock to sound, Frankie let the images slide through his mind. He remembered the afternoon he and two other men had used a canvas bag to gather up what was left of Private First Class Gabriel Chavez from the crest of Hacksaw Ridge. The heroic little bastard from Socorro had conducted his own private banzai charge into a Jap machine-gun nest, armed only with the grenade that killed the three-man crew and himself. Real recruiting poster stuff. Could anyone really understand why people did things like that? He thought of the bizarre Japanese assault with grenades and spears on his company position in the early hours one April morning.

Spears! Not funny to someone who had seen one of his buddies impaled in the gut and crying for his mother as the life ebbed from his eyes.

Frankie rolled over on his side and realized he was covered in sweat. That was when he noticed the silence. His suite's AC unit had died sometime during the night, which was why he could hear the rain falling just beyond the balcony. It seemed only fitting.

Same Day

Kadena Air Force Base, Okinawa

"Nice work, Mizu-chan. The dragon eyes are amazingly vivid. So reptilian! You've become as good as your brother."

Iwo Joe beamed with pride at his granddaughter, who was about a third of the way done with an intricate tattoo of a writhing dragon that showcased fierce reds, blues, greens, and grays. Her customer, a young lance corporal from the Third Marine Division, sat patiently on a hydraulic chair as Mizuki toiled away. The tattoo would eventually wind its way along the marine's upper arm and shoulder and across his upper back to his other shoulder. It was an ambitious project that required the sure hand and patience of a Michelangelo—with needle and ink instead of pigment and brush. Finishing it would require another three or four sessions.

Mizuki's eyes brightened. "Thank you, Grandfather," she responded in the Okinawan dialect with a delighted smile. "My father is a good teacher."

Joe had dropped in unannounced at his son Vincent's shop just outside Kadena's main gate. He had a few design ideas that he wanted to discuss with Vincent. "Is my son around?"

"No," Mizuki said. "He's out running errands."

Joe nodded and walked across the red-and-black tiled floor toward the far wall to study a painting of a brilliant sunset. Like everything else in the shop, the watercolor was bold and colorful. Joe then plopped down on a nearby bench to watch Mizuki work. He could feel a cool breeze on his skin, courtesy of the ceiling fan whirring above them at full speed.

After observing his granddaughter's artistic efforts on the young marine for twenty minutes, he grew tired of waiting for his son and decided to leave for the Prefectural Peace Memorial at the southern tip of the island. Given how gloomy the weather was outside, he figured it would be a light day at the memorials. That meant he could bring along his sketchbook and try drafting some of the concepts he hoped to share later with his son.

"I'll be back later," he said and stood up to leave.

Once behind the wheel of his Jeep Cherokee, he made a mental note that he had to leave the memorials in time to pick up Ayaka's brother, Takeo, who would be flying in from Tokyo at three p.m. Takeo had half a dozen business interests that kept him in Honshu, although he was beginning to talk about retirement. Joe admired that he always took time to visit his sister, with whom he shared an uncommonly close bond.

The thought of his successful brother-in-law, whom he had first met as a hungry, skinny orphan in the internment camp outside the wreckage of Naha, always made Joe smile. The boy with the dazzlingly quick hands and strong right arm would go on to enjoy a superb career as a star third baseman, annually batting .330 for the Hanshin Tigers of the Central League.

Palm trees drooped in the rain as Joe sped by them on Route 507. He loved telling the story about the amazing day when the call came. The Detroit Tigers of the American League wanted to have a look at the young phenomenon who was already being called the Brooks Robinson of Japan. No less than the great Al Kaline had taken Takeo under his wing during the kid's brief career with the Detroit ball club.

Well, so a career in the US major leagues didn't pan out. Takeo was happy to return to Japan, where he resumed his celebrity and ended his career as one of the most revered players in the postwar period. His baseball fame allowed him to launch a string of fast-food restaurants, and he became a distributor for Suntory Liquors and Sapporo beer. Among other things, that assured a virtually unending supply of liquid refreshment in the Petrini household.

The dirt field that Iwo Joe had carved out of the rubble with his bulldozer so many years ago was now Petrini Field, a first-rate ballpark with regular stands and dugouts on the outskirts of Naha. Weather permitting, Takeo would want to spend a day there, teaching the latest generation of kids in this baseball-mad country the finer arts of hitting and fielding. Who knew? Maybe some of those kids would go on to play for Japan in the Little League World Series in Williamsport. Other Okinawan kids coached by Takeo had done so. No rock star could match the devoted following Takeo had as a hometown hero.

When Joe arrived at the Peace Memorial Park, the main parking lot was empty, except for a single Toyota. Joe wondered if they'd even open today, considering the weather. He hurried through the park's grounds, holding his windbreaker over his head, and was greeted by Ken Sonohara, the curator, under the covered entrance to the museum.

"Joe-san, I'm so glad you came today." Ken nodded to the sideways rain, which was threatening to soak them even under cover of the roof. "Didn't expect it, really. I doubt there will be many visitors, so I told the rest of the staff to stay home. But I got a call from the marines this morning, and they specifically asked to open the museum and memorial for a couple VIP guests who'll be escorted by a marine major. It seems one of the guests was a soldier in the Ninety-Sixth Infantry Division and was in combat here in 1945. They were hoping you would be available as a guide."

Joe grimaced slightly and grumbled. "I was hoping you'd say the place was closed. Just what I need: babysitting a brass hat and a couple of old vets trying to recapture their lost youth by reliving the terror of being nineteen in the South Pacific." He shrugged. "All right. I guess I'm stuck. Did they say when they'd be here? I have to be at the airport to pick up Takeo at three o'clock."

Sonohara smiled broadly. "Please give him my regards. He was my favorite player growing up. If I had known, I'd have brought a baseball for him to sign. No, I wasn't told exactly when to expect them, but I'll be sure you're free to go to the airport in time."

"Thanks, Ken. I probably shouldn't be so cynical about it. It's a real effort for some of these old guys to make the trip here. I'll be sure to give them the blue ribbon treatment." Joe turned and went inside for a cup of coffee.

Same Day

Chatan, Okinawa

"I hope you slept well, Frankie," Major Gregory Jamison said as he deposited a Starbucks latte in the cupholder, "because we've got a big day ahead of us. Even though the weather isn't cooperating, I'd like to pick up where we left off yesterday near Conical Hill. Is that okay with you?"

"Sure." Frankie fumbled briefly with the seat belt before latching it properly. "And don't worry about the weather. It's pretty much like I remember it."

Rain fell in sheets, leaving the road slick in front of them. The Honda's window wipers had already settled into a monotonous rhythm.

"Did it rain the whole time you were here?" Ellen asked from the back seat.

"More or less," Frankie replied without looking back. He was trying his best to remain on good behavior, but Tony's presence beside Ellen left him somewhere between flummoxed and cantankerous. What did she see in the guy? More importantly, why had she invited him along? Revisiting the landscape of his nightmares was an ordeal in its own right. Bringing Tony along felt like an invasion of privacy. Indeed, it was hard enough to do this in front of Ellen and the major, let alone a complete stranger. Frankie fantasized about leaving Tony behind at their first stop, but he reminded himself that Ellen had extended herself for him; he could do the same for her—or so he told himself.

Gregory, who was dressed in civvies but somehow still looked thoroughly military, glanced up at the rearview mirror. "So what brings you to the island, Mr. Wagner?"

"Call me Tony. I'm doing consulting work at the base."

"Kadena?"

"You got it. I'm helping the air force comply with the latest string of environmental regulations issued by the Japanese government. Everything from storage and disposal of old chemicals to obtaining building permits for new construction—it's all affected by the latest provisions of Japanese environmental law."

"You an environmental attorney?"

"I am."

A barely detectable frown appeared on Gregory's face, which made Frankie feel better. At least he wasn't the only one annoyed by their new passenger.

"He's from LA," Frankie added. Why not bust the inter-loper's balls a little? It might make the trip more enjoyable.

Gregory nodded knowingly.

The drive over toward Yonabaru was mercifully brief, but Frankie was disappointed that nothing looked familiar. Even the rise known as Conical Hill was unrecognizable, covered by dense vegetation. In Frankie's memory, the hill was still craggy and bare of all but a few blasted trees and bushes. Gregory parked the car in an adjacent parking lot, where they took advantage of a break in the rain squalls to approach what appeared to be a path leading uphill.

As Frankie followed Gregory up the rise, he searched both sides of the path for any telltale landmarks. The regiment had been ordered to take Conical Hill on May 10. A day later, his company had attacked Charlie Hill just to the west. From what Frankie could tell now, most of the hill had been leveled.

"See anything familiar?" Gregory asked.

Frankie shook his head, already lost in thought. The fighting had been more like a gang rumble than an organized battle and had ultimately come down to who had the best grenade chuckers. Mere yards had stood between Frankie's company and the Japanese. Frankie had held on to his BAR, which he'd used to keep the enemy's head down. He could still see his platoon moving up close to throw satchel charges and grenades over the top to the reverse slope, where the Japs had set up their mortars. Of course, all that did was piss them off, and soon enough a counter barrage of grenades came from the defenders in caves and on the crest. Frankie found cover in a narrow defile and thought he was well-protected, but a second later he felt something hard hit his helmet. Certain someone had dislodged a rock from the hillside above, he looked downslope just in time to see the damned Jap pineapple bouncing past him.

He yelled, "Grenade!" but it was too late. The explosion killed one guy in his squad and wounded two others, including him. He had turned partway to protect his face, but the blast sent shrapnel back up toward him and into his right buttocks and thigh.

"You okay, Dad?"

Frankie realized Ellen was standing beside him now and had locked arms with him.

"Yeah," he said. "Just trying to decipher the landscape. I don't recognize a thing." He patted the old wounds thoughtfully. "I got hit somewhere around here—I think."

He could still remember the ringing in his ears. The blast had blown off his helmet, which had left him feeling exposed. Then he'd felt the warmth of the blood running down his leg. That was when he'd known something was wrong. Then came the pain. A medic had patched up the wound and given him a shot of morphine. From that moment until he woke up at a battalion field hospital, his memory was sketchy.

He turned and saw Tony studying him with big brown eyes. The look of compassion on the guy's face was disarming.

"Was that the end of the war for you?" Gregory asked.

Frankie shrugged off his stupor. "No, not nearly. I was classified as walking wounded. No ticket home. Surgeons picked a bunch of metal out of me and found no serious damage. Basically I was fit—and happy for the two-week vacation off the line while the wounds healed." He managed a sheepish grin. "Probably saved my life, because my company took a lot of casualties cleaning out the 'Charlie Pocket' over the next two weeks."

Gregory looked over the now incongruously green fields dotted with buildings. "You were one of the lucky ones to come home practically whole, Frankie. And what happened here was a huge turning point."

True enough, Frankie thought. The path had been made clear for the push south through the corridor opened up by the Ninety-Sixth Division. The marines broke through at Sugar Loaf and Dakeshi Ridge in the west. The Shuri Line was finally broken.

Once back in the car, they followed signs to Mabuni.

With one hand on the wheel and his other on the stick shift, Gregory assumed the role of a professor challenging a class. "So put yourself in General Ushijima's shoes. You have a real problem. Thirty-Second Army headquarters and five thousand of your best soldiers are about to be encircled and trapped. What are your choices? Would you barricade your remaining forces in the tunnel complex under the ruins of Shuri Castle and make like the Alamo, hoping to draw in and kill a thousand marines? That's what General Cho and his aggressive commanders wanted. It would be *bushido*, a glorious battle to the finish, standing in place and refusing to surrender, taking as many of the enemy as you could."

He took a hard left down a narrow road, and they zoomed past a guardrail that was all that stood between them and a tangle of lush bushes and small trees. The landscape offered no hint that they were nearing the sea.

"But maybe you're thinking more like Ushijima," Gregory continued in his baritone voice. "You wish you hadn't decided to waste so much manpower and artillery in that ill-fated counterattack on May fourth. If only you had listened to yourself instead of Cho and Fujioka, who insisted on taking the fight to the Americans, which had been a disaster. General Ushijima knew what his commanders didn't seem to understand. He accepted that his role in Okinawa was a suicide mission, a last ditch to provide the home islands time to prepare for an American invasion. He calculated that he could best accomplish that mission by dragging matters out, not committing to an Alamo-style defense at Shuri."

Ellen, who had been mostly quiet in the back seat, played along. "Can I be Ushijima?"

"Sure," Gregory said and smiled up at his rearview mirror.

"Okay," Ellen ventured, "then I'm thinking I need to draw things out, right? So maybe I tell my troops to withdraw quietly to another fortified position farther south."

Frankie exchanged grins with Gregory.

"You're right on, General," Gregory said. "Around the last two or three days of May, Ushijima ordered a stealthy withdrawal from Shuri to the southernmost tip of Okinawa, a rugged area of coral cliffs riddled with caves. It was well-stocked, and he believed the remnants of his army could hold out much longer there, bleeding the enemy and giving the home front more time. He set up his final headquarters in a cave near the village of Mabuni, overlooking the sea."

Now Tony was engaged in the discussion. "Did the move surprise the Tenth Army?"

"It sure did," Gregory said. "It caught General Buckner flatfooted. He was convinced that the Japanese would make a final stand at Shuri. Consequently, columns of IJA troops and trucks towing field pieces made their escape by night to the caves of the Yaeju-Dake and Yuza-Dake ridges. Some were caught in the open by spotter planes and destroyed by artillery and strafing fighters, but a good many made it to the southern defensive line."

Gregory glanced up ahead. "Where I'm taking you now is the largest memorial on the tip of the island. It sits right over the cave complex where the Japanese commanding officers committed suicide. It's an impressive park and includes the Okinawa Prefectural Peace Memorial Museum and the

Cornerstone of Peace Memorial, which contains the names of over two hundred thousand people—Japanese, Okinawan, Korean, American—who died during the battle." He paused and offered an apologetic smile to Frankie. "I know I'm talking a lot. I tend to run on when I get going about the battle. I hope I haven't bored you with things you already know."

Frankie spoke up. "Not at all. When you're a PFC, seventeen years old, all you know is 'Yes, sir. No, sir.' We did what we were told. It was much later when I learned what had actually happened here. You've obviously done more reading than me."

The history, though, felt disconnected from Frankie's memories. It was as if there was the official version of events— the one written down in books—and *his* version, which was personal, narrow, visceral. His version felt far more real.

As they sped through the rain, he remembered how strange he'd felt when he rejoined his company in early June near the village of Yuza. The Japs were on their heels. There were a lot fewer of them than before. Somehow, though, they had managed to get some artillery up in the Yuza-Dake, and the Americans were still taking fire.

But there was another difference. Something had come over the guys. Frankie had sensed a reluctance among many, especially the veterans, to put themselves in harm's way. Their whole mind-set had changed. Where before they had believed all of them—or at least *most* of them—would never make it home, which had resulted in a lot of risk-taking, now, with the end so near, no one wanted to be the last casualty on Okinawa. Understandable, maybe, but not a healthy attitude for a victorious army, especially when the enemy wasn't done fighting.

Frankie was lucky his platoon leader tried to keep him out of the worst action. But he still saw a good many guys killed and wounded trying to root out the Japs. It came down to flame-throwing tanks and satchel charges—and flooding tunnels with gasoline and then igniting it. They sealed up cave entrances and left hundreds to die inside.

Somewhere to the south—they had to be close by now—was a small village called Makabe. Under it was a huge cave where the Japs had set up their last field hospital. After it was secured, Frankie went down inside. It was ugly. Lots of dead soldiers and medical staff—most from self-inflicted wounds, apparently. Lots of others dead from burns or asphyxiation.

Frankie felt the icy fingers of the past beginning to close in around him.

As if on cue, Gregory said, "We're not far from the Cave of the Virgins—*Itokazu*. It was named for the student nurses' aides, most of them high school girls, who died there. There's a memorial there now."

Frankie stared straight ahead, hoping his trembling at the memory wasn't noticed. He said as evenly as he could, "Imagine that."

Moving curtains of rain were now sweeping off the gray waters below and up the cliffs of Mabuni as Gregory pulled into the main parking lot and parked next to a Jeep Cherokee. With Ellen and Tony sharing an umbrella, the four of them scurried to the museum, which, Frankie quickly learned, required a mad dash through the sprawling, park-like grounds. By the time they reached the entrance, where the frail-looking curator was waiting to greet them, Frankie's thigh was talking to him.

Once past the enormous lobby, they stepped into the first exhibit room, and Frankie looked around uncomfortably at the artifacts, maps, and photos. Someone handed him a towel, and he looked up to thank the man, a burly Caucasian wearing a billed cap with the Seabee emblem. Frankie's eyes wandered from the emblem to the man's red vest and the two words stitched in kanji and English across the right breast: *Iwo Joe.*

Frankie was speechless.

Gregory smiled and shook the volunteer's hand. "Good to see you, Joe. I'm glad you came on such an ugly day." He turned to Frankie and the others. "Iwo Joe is a legend in Okinawa—and not just because of the tattoo parlors, of which he has several. Incidentally, they're very good ones from what I hear, in case either of you wants to go home with a spectacular example of body art. But I digress. Joe is a living link to the past and a fountain of information on the history of Okinawa in the time since the war. He came as a Seabee in 1945 and helped rebuild the island, starting with a ballfield near Naha. He served during the occupation, and he's been here ever since. He married the lovely local, Ayaka Fuchida. I've lost track of how many kids and grandkids they have."

"Nine and thirteen, so far, at last count, Major," Joe responded gamely. He was thicker than Frankie remembered—and had lost most of his hair—but he still had the same bulbous nose and toothy smile.

Frankie, rallying from his initial shock, stepped forward, rolled up his right sleeve, and extended his hand so Iwo Joe could see the scars. "It's been a long time, Joseph. I never thought we'd meet again."

A clearly flabbergasted Joe appeared to recognize the scars on Frankie's forearm. He looked up at Frankie's face. "Dos! Dos Equis! Is it really you?" He took Frankie into a crushing bear hug.

Frankie felt tears welling in his eyes, and soon both men were shaking with a mixture of sobs and laughter. Frankie heard Ellen gasp and could sense the others hovering nearby, obviously intrigued.

Gregory was the first to speak. "You two actually know each other? How is that possible?"

Smiling through moistened eyes, Frankie pulled himself together and turned to the group with his right arm hanging over Joe's shoulder. "Iwo Joe became my closest friend on Okinawa. After the fighting was over, so much had to be done to clear away the wreckage and rebuild. The army and navy sent in thousands of workers. Soldiers like me who had nothing better to do and weren't going home anytime soon were more or less encouraged to pitch in."

Joe loudly blew his nose into a handkerchief. "Truth be told, most of the army and marine 'volunteer' workers weren't worth a damn. Lot of them were green replacements. They'd screw around and goof off. Half the time they were drunk. They'd do foolish things, get hurt, and cause problems. But not Dos Equis here. He seemed interested in operating equipment and learning how to build, so we hit it off right away. At night, when he wasn't pulling guard duty, we'd sit around, have a few beers, and talk about what we planned to do when we got home. He had some definite ideas, and building seemed to have a powerful pull on him."

Gregory's phone vibrated, and he turned away and cupped it to his ear.

Ellen stared at her father, looking as if she was struggling to process what she had just witnessed. "You mean you two never communicated all these years? As close as you were? Dad, you never mentioned Iwo Joe—"

"Excuse my daughter, who hasn't properly introduced herself. Joe Petrini, meet Ellen Castillo. And this is her friend Tony Wagner." Amid handshakes and nods, Frankie tried to explain the remarkable reunion. "Back then, it wasn't uncommon to have friends like us go their separate ways. There was a deep desire to put things behind and turn the page. That included some of the people you felt close to. We'd seen so much that we'd have nightmares for the rest of our lives. Besides, Joe stayed in Okinawa after I went home."

"What your dad says is true, Ellen. We never thought we'd see each other again. But now that we have, we have a lot to talk about."

Gregory finished with his call. "That's a pretty good cue for what I have to say. That was my boss, and it seems he needs me back at the base this afternoon. I can't think of a better person to leave you with than Iwo Joe. Would you mind taking our guests back to their hotel in Chatan? I think it's on your way home, Joe."

"Not a problem for me, Major, although I'll be picking up my brother-in-law on the way. Believe me, we won't lack for conversation between now and then."

Ellen took Frankie by the hand. "You two obviously have a lot to catch up on. Tony and I can grab a cab at the base." She turned to Gregory. "Do you mind if we tag along?"

"Not at all."

Frankie's eyes darted from his daughter to the shaggy attorney standing just behind her. "You sure about that?" he said in a voice barely above a whisper.

She laughed. "I'll be fine, Dad. I'll see you back at the hotel."

Before Frankie could protest, she turned and took Tony's arm, and the two sauntered toward the door. As he watched his daughter and her new friend follow Gregory out of the exhibit room and into the lobby, Frankie experienced a chill that made him shiver involuntarily. The exhilaration he felt upon discovering his old friend was accompanied by dread that the time to face his past had arrived.

"If you'd like, I can give you a tour, Dos. Or we can just sit down with some coffee and talk." Iwo Joe looked like he was hoping Frankie would choose the latter.

"I've seen almost everything I needed to," Frankie said quietly. "How about we talk?"

"Sure, old buddy. I wish we had something more appropriate than a cup of coffee to toast the occasion." Joe chortled. "Perhaps we can do something about that later."

Frankie followed his old friend to a small office. After telling the curator that there was no need for him to stay and that he would take care of locking up, Joe brewed a pot of fresh coffee. He hunted down a couple of cups in the staff room, filled them, and finally sat down with Frankie, smiling wearily. "I'm so glad to see you. So long ago, but it seems like yesterday. You'd been wounded, and you were hobbling around—I saw you limping back there. Still gives you trouble?"

"A little. When the weather changes, you know. But nothing I can't handle with a little Advil. How is Ayaka? Thirteen grandkids?"

"Love of my life, most beautiful woman in Okinawa, best thing ever happened to me—and still a pain in the ass. She's great and will want to see you. But I should warn you that she still holds it against you, leaving like you did." Joe paused and remarked, almost wistfully, "I've had a good life here, Dos. Sometimes I've thought that it would've been a good life for you, too."

Frankie squirmed. "I know. But I couldn't stay. I'd blame it on my folks, but that wouldn't be fair. They had already lost one son and couldn't bear losing another, so I felt an obligation to come back home for their sake. But the real reason involved a woman—a girl, actually—the one back home in New Mexico. Her name is Melanie."

"I remember that. And Ellen is your daughter with Melanie?"

"She is."

Joe stroked his chin. "What are you doing here, Dos? For years, no letter, no cards. Then all of a sudden you show up with your daughter in sunny Okinawa? Just an old veteran's pilgrimage? I've seen a lot of those. Guys come back to confront old demons or reconcile with something in the past. The shrinks like to call it 'closure.'" Joe leaned back in his chair and looked into Frankie's eyes.

Frankie felt the hairs on his neck standing up. "It's nightmares. About the fighting. And about her. You know who I mean."

Joe snickered and stood up to stretch. Then he took Frankie's cup for a refill. "Yes. I know. And I thought as much. Guilt can be a bitch. And you never told your family, am I right?"

Frankie nodded somberly.

"So you decided to bring your daughter to the place it all happened, figuring that you can ease her into this big revelation. Might even salve your conscience by asking about her, trying to locate her, maybe even contact her. Sound about right?" Without waiting for an answer, Joe muttered under his breath, loud enough for Frankie to hear, "Christ. *I'm* the one who should be a shrink. I'd have made a fortune if I had a nickel for each of these tales of guilt and remorse I've heard from old vets over the years."

Frankie accepted the refill.

Joe rummaged around in his pocket for his cigarettes. "Not supposed to smoke here, but what the hell. Nobody here but us chickens." He offered one to Frankie, who declined.

"You're right," Frankie said once he'd found his voice. "About everything. I tried hard to put that part of my life behind me. I was just a kid. I went home, married the high school sweetheart, made a good living as a home builder. Created a different, happy world away from the fire and blood and destruction. But lately, her face keeps coming back to me in my dreams. And it's making me crazy. Yes, it's guilt—and a feeling that I owe her something. I can't tell Melanie about it. It would feel like a betrayal, even after all these years."

Joe lit up and blew a stream of smoke high overhead as he stared at the ceiling. "Trust me, Brother Dos Equis, I'm not judging you. But maybe there's some karma in your suffering over this. What you did back then, you did for your own good reasons. No one can blame you. But you broke her heart. She loved you, you know."

Frankie suddenly found it impossible to hold back the tears filling his eyes and streaming down his face. His shoulders shook.

Joe sat impassively, flicked an ash, and watched. Then he spoke. "For what it's worth, she got over it. Turns out you weren't the only fish in the sea. She took up with a Japanese soldier, who apparently was a real fine guy. They married, and after a time, they moved away."

Frankie could imagine how he must have looked in that moment, his eyes red from tears, a picture of inexpressible sorrow. The double X scars on his forearm glowed a pale white in the artificial light. Thunder rolled outside, and wind-whipped spray pelted the windows.

"Listen, old buddy," Joe said. "Let's head for the airport. I promised Takeo—you remember him, right? Ayaka's brother? I promised I'd pick him up this afternoon. He's flying in from Tokyo, assuming the plane can make it through the weather. We can hang out at the bar."

Joe crushed out the Winston in a saucer and took the cups to the kitchen, looking back over his shoulder at Frankie. Then he returned, and Frankie was grateful when his old friend threw his arm around him. Together they dashed through the sideways rain and climbed into Joe's Cherokee.

Chapter 31

Her Name Is Kume

Friday, January 25, 2002

Naha International Airport, Okinawa

Gary Masterson sat glumly on the barstool. He ordered a Belvedere, neat. The day had been a waste. It had started with the crazy, nearly sideways landing last evening as his jet had careened against a quartering wind blowing off the East China Sea before skidding to a stop with only yards to spare. Gary had been sure they would end up in the water. Even Captain Sam had come back to the main cabin with a screwy half-smile and looking like he could use a change of underwear.

Next came the day-long monsoon rain. Worse, the government contacts Nathan had set up, although unfailingly cordial and polite, either had no idea how to help him or were not inclined to make much of an effort.

Maybe tomorrow will be better, he thought. Of course, being Saturday, most government offices would be closed. His Plan B would involve going to the peace memorials, where someone might have an idea what to try next. Would anyone still be alive who might remember a GI and his Himeyuri girlfriend? Would the name Francisco Castillo mean anything?

Gary looked around the bar, which, like the airport terminal itself, felt cramped and too crowded. Between the cafeteria-style décor and lighting and the baseball banners hanging side by side above the kitchen window, the place was painfully free of anything Gary might have considered ambience. With nothing left to do but people watch, he decided to study the crowd. Faces were invariably interesting. Most were Asian, although he spotted a sprinkling of Caucasians among them. Many travelers with flight delays were clearly massaging their frustration with liquid relief. Some, like Gary, were scowling over their gin and tonics. Others, marines mostly, were laughing loudly, chugging beers, and dealing with delay as though it was just another reason to party.

To be young again. He smiled ruefully. *Not a care in the world.*

He nearly missed seeing the two men arrive, soaked to the skin and heading for a banquette near the back of the room. One was an older, heavyset guy with a red vest and a billed cap. The other was a fellow with a limp and a vague resemblance to Anthony Quinn. *Perhaps a couple of interesting Americans? Beats sitting alone and sucking vodka.*

He'd give them a moment and then drop over and introduce himself.

"I'll bet you don't get rain like this in New Mexico, Dos," Iwo Joe said as they settled into a booth at the crowded airport bar.

Frankie gingerly removed his windbreaker, now soaked, and set it next to him on the bench. "You'd be surprised. Desert thunderstorms can be pretty impressive. They don't usually last this long, though."

"I think you'll enjoy meeting Takeo. Not only was he a great baseball talent; he's one of life's good guys. He gives a lot of himself to the kids here. You'll see if it clears up tomorrow and we go over to the ballpark."

"You did good with that, Joseph. Creating a baseball field gave the kids something fun to look forward to and soldiers like me with time on their hands something useful to do."

Joe signaled the waiter, a young man with a slight build and perfectly coiffed short black hair, and the two men ordered.

"I feel like I owe you an apology," Joe said. "I was pretty hard on you back at the memorial."

Frankie waved his hand absently. "I deserved it. From the moment I first laid eyes on Noriko, I felt this incredible need to protect her. I've had dreams where I've actually fought our own guys when I thought they were planning to hurt her. I wake up in a sweat, and Melanie thinks I've lost my mind."

Joe chuckled, accentuating the crow's feet fanning outward from the corners of his eyes. "Maybe you have. Reminds me of the joke about the dog who likes to chase cars. What's he plan to do with it if he catches one?"

Frankie smiled wanly. "I just can't believe how I left her after caring for her and protecting her as I did. Somehow I tried to make myself believe that I could pack away that period of my life in a neat little box, stick it up on a shelf, and pretend it never happened."

Two bottles of Dos Equis arrived, and Frankie, after lifting the closest one to his nose, enjoyed a lusty whiff of its malty aroma.

They clinked longnecks.

"To my friend, Dos Equis." Joe grinned at his double entendre.

"I just need to know she's okay," Frankie said. "And to tell her face-to-face how sorry I am that I left her like I did."

Joe cleared his throat and put down his bottle. He gave a look—head to the side, mouth twisted into a sad smile—like he'd been waiting for just the right moment to share something he was dreading having to share. "I think you mean *them*, Dos."

Frankie frowned. "What do you mean?"

"I mean that when you left, Noriko was pregnant. You have a daughter. Her name is Kume."

The bar swam unsteadily in his vision as Frankie struggled to fix his mind on Joe's words, which hung in the air like a thundercloud.

"I know," Joe said. "It's a lot to process. I figured you didn't know. But that day on the dock in Naha when you were about to climb aboard that liberty ship for home, do you remember what you did? You took that gold crucifix on a chain that you said had given you so much luck . . . you took it off your own neck and put it around her neck. She looked numb. She already knew she was carrying your child, but she refused to tell you. She didn't want that to be the reason you stayed. You took out a camera, and we had a sailor take our picture. Remember?"

Frankie was feeling as disoriented as he had when the Jap grenade exploded just downslope of him. The chatter in the bar, so ubiquitous only moments earlier, sounded far away, like it was coming from another room. A wave of nausea threatened to pull him under.

Joe motioned for a glass of water. "Let me finish telling you everything I know. Ayaka and I took Noriko in. She had regressed into that dark place that you had helped pull her out of. After the baby was born—a beautiful girl, I might add—she stayed with us briefly and then moved to a group home with several other women. Ayaka tried to keep in touch, but Noriko seemed determined to sever connections with anything from her past. The last we heard, she had met a soldier, a Japanese survivor of the battle. They married and moved away from Okinawa."

The world had suddenly, profoundly changed. The barking dog had finally caught the car. *Now what?* Frankie needed some time to think—alone.

An announcement crackled over the airport intercom that all incoming flights had been indefinitely delayed due to the weather.

Joe sighed and checked his watch. "I might as well take you back to the hotel. Sounds like Takeo's plane won't be landing anytime soon."

Frankie nodded numbly. He had all but forgotten about Ellen and Tony.

As they rose to leave, a tall Caucasian man from the bar approached them with a smile, clearly signaling a desire to join them.

Joe intercepted the man. "Not right now."

The man said something about the badge stitched onto Joe's vest—Frankie could hardly make out the words; he was so lost. But it sounded like the man wanted to know if Joe worked at the peace memorial and if it would be open tomorrow.

"It will," Joe said. "I'll be there if you want to drop by."

Frankie felt Joe's hand on his shoulder, and the next thing he knew his old friend was hustling him through the bar and out into the rain.

Chapter 32

A War Hero of
Uncommon Modesty

Saturday, January 26, 2002

Sendai, Miyagi Prefecture

"So-san, why are you so upset?" Kazuo's breathing sounded shallow as he inhaled air from the oxygen tubes. "You became a grandparent. To me that would be very good news."

Soichiro sat quietly in the oyabun's study. He had hoped for at least a gesture, just a glimmer of understanding from his friend. A bit of empathy, perhaps. Since Noriko had told Soichiro the shocking news upon her return from Tokyo, he had tried to conceal his own feelings from his wife. But after a week of brooding privately, he had decided to visit his friend and tell him about the baby Kume had lost. He had thought he could open up to Kazuo, but now he regretted sharing anything. The oyabun evidently regarded the whole matter as being too remote in time to be of current interest or consequence.

As he rose to leave, Soichiro hesitated. Kazuo looked dreadful. He'd grown thinner, and, according to Yoko, who was hovering nearby, whatever the doctors were giving him had made him so violently ill that he was having difficulty keeping in nourishment. While he withered away, his eye patch appeared bigger than it ever had above his sunken cheek.

Kazuo gestured for him to stay. "Things are not looking good for me—in case you haven't noticed. The vultures are circling, and I'm doing my best to make sure there will be no disturbance, no loose ends, once I've passed on. I'm arranging for Masashi Tomonaga to succeed me as oyabun. He's younger, full of energy, bright, and experienced. He's also trustworthy, and he's earned it. The Yamaguchi-gumi Tokyo Kai's board members agree with my choice. Please sit. There's much more you need to know. And I haven't been entirely candid with you about certain dangers."

Soichiro did as he was asked and took a seat directly across from an antique samurai sword with cloth binding and a gold *kashira*, or end cap. Like the others in the room, it was mounted on the wall and illuminated behind glass.

Kazuo broke into a violent cough before finally catching his breath and continuing. "I have strong reasons to believe that yakuza interlopers from the north will try to use my current incapacity as an opportunity to move into Tohoku and take over our territory. They're a rogue syndicate headed by the Tsuchiya brothers. You know from experience how they covet the fishing ports on our coastline. And they haven't forgotten the beating we gave them in the not-too-distant past."

"How do you know all this?" Soichiro asked slowly.

"Not important, but the information comes from reliable sources. There's another thing: the matter of the gold I mentioned during your last visit, the gold that went missing from the Imperial treasury in the final months of the war. We know that the Hokkaido yakuza has made contact with the North Koreans. Together they hope to recover the gold from the old mine where it lies buried." Kazuo paused and drew a rasping breath as he searched Soichiro's eyes for a reaction. "Yes, I know it sounds farfetched, but there's a certain logic to it. The Koreans need the money, and the northern bandits want our territory. The plan would require the elimination of our organization. I won't allow the Hokkaido thugs to succeed. As we speak, Tomonaga is making plans to preempt the threat. My advice is that you await word from him about keeping your fishing boats in port. I say this because your name has come up as someone they would like to make an example of."

Soichiro nodded soberly. This was quite a lot to digest. His first thought was Noriko and her safety. Would it be prudent to leave Sendai for a while until things settled down—perhaps take that vacation to Hawaii they'd always talked about? He wanted to ask if there was anything he could do for Kazuo, but before he could speak, the oyabun responded to the unasked question.

"So-san, when the time comes, I will trust only you to handle the arrangements for my cremation and memorial service. I want my ashes to be taken to the Gokuku shrine. I've given detailed written instructions to Yoko. She'll pass them to you at the appropriate time." Kazuo waved his hand in a gesture of resignation. "I wish that Noriko were with you today. Her presence is always a source of comfort and peace for me. But perhaps it's for the best, because there's one other thing I wish to ask of you, and you might be reluctant to comply, were she present. You have never spoken of it, and I would like to hear of your service on Okinawa and how you met your wife."

"Are you sure, Kazu-san?" Soichiro couldn't disguise the exasperation in his voice. He had avoided any mention of his experiences during the battle to anyone, Noriko included. "Those things were so long ago, and my memory isn't what it used to be."

"Rubbish!" Kazuo said, wheezing. "There are only two events in life about which memory will always be crystal clear: one's experiences in wartime and in love."

Soichiro signaled to Yoko that he would like a cup of sake and that she should bring cups for Kazuo and herself. Then he cleared his throat and began. "Very well. I arrived in Okinawa in August 1944. Several of the ships in our small convoy were sunk by American torpedoes as we made our way from the Marianas. We were lucky to get through. When I arrived, the island was already buzzing with activity. General Ushijima had assumed command of the Thirty-Second Army. He immediately judged the terrain of the southern third of the island ideal for defensive operations. He could envision tunneling and establishing killing zones with overlapping fields of fire.

"The island was also bursting with armaments. Many weapons that had been earmarked for the Philippines and elsewhere ended up piling up on the docks in Naha because there were no ships to move them. There was so much artillery that a separate command was organized. Together with several other experienced artillery veterans who had served in China and French Indochina, I was assigned to the new command. For the next several months, the labor was backbreaking. Almost everyone on the island was involved in digging or enlarging mazes of tunnels deep within the hills. I supervised the location of large mortars on the reverse slopes of ridges likely to be attacked from the front. I also worked with engineers on tunnel design and camouflage. We placed howitzers inside caves where they could be rolled out and withdrawn after firing. Defensively, the plan had elements of genius."

Yoko returned with the sake on a tray, which shook ever so slightly in her grasp.

Kazuo was right, Soichiro thought as he accepted his drink. The recollection of his deeds in wartime remained embedded with startling clarity in the recesses of his memory. How ironic, he thought, that the things he wished most to forget were the ones least likely to be forgotten.

He resumed. "By March, there was no doubt that we would soon be in the fight of our lives. The sea was covered with enemy ships, and the sky was swarming with our kamikazes and their fighters. We knew it would only be a matter of time. When the shelling began, it beggared description. 'Typhoon of Steel' doesn't do it justice. To be outside or anywhere but deep underground was insane. Day after day, American fighters, battleships, and heavy cruisers carpeted the island with thousands of tons of high explosives. Then, on April first, American troops landed on the western beaches. According to plan, we offered no resistance."

Kazuo, clearly captivated, raised an eyebrow. "What was your role in combat operations?"

"I was put in charge of an excellent gun, the best I had encountered throughout the war. It was a field gun based on the French 75 Schneider design. It could fire a variety of munitions over a range of fifteen kilometers. As a standoff weapon, its high-explosive round with airburst capabilities was devastating against infantry, and we inflicted grievous punishment on the US Marines when they began their assaults on the fortified hills leading to Shuri. But it really came into its own as an antitank weapon due to its high muzzle velocity and armor-piercing ordnance. I can say with certainty that my crew alone destroyed or disabled seven Sherman tanks during April and May. Combat was almost continuous for us during that period.

"When the Americans finally broke through the defense lines at Shuri, my command was ordered to retreat to new lines. As it turned out, these would be our final positions at the southern end of the island. Fortunately we were able to commandeer a truck to pull our gun through two nights of hard going to a coral ridge, where we dug in. My gunners were exhausted. By then, few entertained any thought of survival, let alone victory. After two months of relentless fighting, our divisions were tattered remnants of their former selves. Only the delusional could imagine that anything but sacrifice and death awaited what was left of the Thirty-Second Army. I, too, was convinced I would die. But unlike many others, I never considered taking my own life. I would do my utmost to defend our homeland, and if that meant being killed by the enemy, so be it. But I saw no point in killing myself.

"We set the gun up in a cave on the side of a hill just south of Maesato Ridge. From there, it was possible to observe and range in on flame-throwing tanks and infantry facing the coral ridges at Kunishi. We were not alone. There were several pack howitzers and one large 120-millimeter piece positioned nearby. My crew had become quite skilled at using deception, conserving ammunition, and firing sparingly to avoid being pinpointed by enemy spotters.

"By the second week of June, aerial bombing and counter battery fire had destroyed or disabled nearly all but my French 75. We were nearly at the end of our rope, and had already received orders to destroy our equipment and begin an exfiltration to the northern part of the island. Somehow we were expected to link up with other surviving units and continue fighting as guerillas. We were down to our last few rounds of ammunition when one of my spotters, Corporal Akanishi, signaled that I should come quickly. He handed me his binoculars, and from his concealed vantage point, I could make out what appeared to be a gathering of important American officers at a forward position near Maesato."

Uncomfortable with what was coming next, Soichiro hesitated and stole a glance at Kazuo. His friend sat erect—at least as erect as his frail body would allow him—and appeared eager to hear what came next.

Soichiro reluctantly continued. "It was within easy range—about a thousand meters—so I ordered the gunners to prepare to fire five high-explosive rounds at the small clearing bounded by boulders where well-pressed officers were busily scanning the ridgetops through field glasses. At one point, it appeared that a middle-aged officer with stars on his helmet and I were staring directly at one another through our eyepieces. Once our gun fired, I knew we could expect a ferocious response, so I ordered the crew to leave as soon as the last shell left the tube. I would stay behind to spike the gun. The crew did as I ordered, and with their usual rapid efficiency, they fired five projectiles and scampered away from the cave. I watched as, within seconds, smoky blasts erupted on the target." Soichiro looked down at his hands, interlocked his fingers, and closed his eyes. "As I had anticipated, the American artillery homed in on our area and covered the hillside with fire. I was placing a thermite grenade in the breech of the gun when a blast at the cave mouth lifted me and threw me back against the rocks. When I came to, I was lying on the ground outside the cave, bleeding from the ears, nose, and mouth—and practically deaf. A US Marine sergeant was pointing his Thompson submachine gun at my head. I believe he said something like, 'Congratulations, you Jap son of a bitch. You killed General Buckner.' Then he cracked me on the head with the butt of his weapon, and I lost consciousness for a second time. He probably would have shot me right there if a US Army captain hadn't arrived and ordered that I be taken alive."

Mouth agape, Kazuo stared at Soichiro in admiring disbelief. "You mean to tell me that you were the gunner who brought down the American Tenth Army commander? Why did you never mention this before? What an incredible feat! Had the war ended differently, you would have been decorated by the emperor himself. Matsuhata-san, you're too modest."

Soichiro pursed his lips and shrugged. "No one's sure whose artillery shell caused the death of the American general. It could have been one of mine, but another gun was also in action. After my wounds were treated—concussion, a few shell fragments, and a broken collarbone—I was grilled at length by US Army intelligence officers, who seemed convinced that it was my gun. There was no way to prove it. Besides, what did it matter? By that point, the battle of Okinawa had already been decided. It was just bad luck for the general. I felt sorry for him and his family."

Kazuo squinted at Soichiro with what looked like newfound respect. It was obvious he'd underestimated Soichiro and now sat ready to lionize his old friend.

Soichiro smiled meekly. "The captain who had captured me came by to check on me later. He said he owed me for the virtually unused Nambu Type-14 pistol he'd taken from my holster as I lay unconscious. He handed me a bottle of Old Grand-Dad, the one you and I tried to drink. I thanked him. He didn't have to do that. Just a considerate gesture, one officer to another.

"In due course, life settled into a routine. I was a prisoner of war, but it was a war that had ended. After I was screened and cleared of being a war criminal—no small consideration, given the anger over the death of General Buckner—I was more or less free to move about. Along with other survivors, I busied myself with clearing the huge quantities of rubble that were left in the aftermath. I missed home and wondered how and when I might return to Sendai. The Americans, for their part, turned out to be decent captors. They seemed relieved that the war was over and that they had survived. American soldiers wanted to go home as badly as I did. It was constantly on my mind."

Kazuo fidgeted impatiently. "When did you first meet Noriko?"

"I was walking back to camp from a work site, probably daydreaming of going home. There was a young Okinawan mother and her infant child being treated very rudely by a group of older women. I knew a few epithets in the Okinawan dialect, so I understood they were accusing her of being a whore for the Americans and saying that her child was a half-breed mongrel. Several of the women had picked up stones to throw at her. I found a sturdy-looking barrel stave and advanced toward the women. They immediately dropped the rocks and scattered. The young mother was Noriko. She shyly introduced herself and thanked me. She told me her daughter was three months old and that her husband, a *Boetai* soldier in the Japanese army, had taken his own life several months earlier. She was becoming accustomed to being treated poorly by other women who had lost relatives and perhaps envied her for having a child. Even in her ill-fitting clothes and grimy appearance, she was a beautiful woman.

"She didn't know that I understood what the women were saying to her, but I went along with her story and asked her if I could help her and her daughter in any way. She politely declined, but I insisted. She clearly had no way to support herself and her baby. I suggested that we locate a place where she could feel secure and live with her child. I promised to bring her food and such necessities as she and her daughter might require. She was at once grateful and wary, wondering what I expected in return."

Kazuo pursed his lips and chuckled. "And what did you expect in return, So-san? A gold star on your heavenly ledger for humanitarian service? A samurai's reward for rescuing the damsel in distress? Or was it something, shall we say, more practical?"

Soichiro clenched his fists. It offended him when the oy-abun's observations about his wife took a tasteless turn. True, Soichiro had found himself attracted to Noriko's considerable beauty, but that was none of Kazuo's business. Soichiro had for many years silently endured Kazuo's suggestive remarks that so repelled Noriko. Despite resenting them, over the years he had chosen to let them slide.

Not this time.

"Kazu-san, you know that your friendship is something I've always prized. And for that reason, I've refrained from objecting whenever you have spoken inappropriately about Noriko. But it has to stop, if for no reason other than the respect and love you had for Michiko-san. Understand that mine for Noriko is no less." Soichiro's voice had dropped to a steely whisper.

Yoko nodded with raised eyebrows and glanced approv-ingly at Soichiro. "It's about time that you spoke up, Mat-suhata-san. I've wondered all these years how you could let Kazu-san's occasional vulgarities and unwelcome flirtations go unchallenged. He's not a bad man, but like a naughty child, he needs to be kept in check. Good for you. Now please continue. I am intrigued by your story."

Soichiro exchanged glances with Kazuo and then turned to Yoko in stunned silence. The quiet, unassuming little woman who had so ably, nearly invisibly, attended Kazuo over five decades had, like a mother admonishing a misbehaving brat, put Kazuo in his place. Soichiro gazed at her in sheepish but admiring wonder—and then noticed Kazuo doing the same. Finally Soichiro composed himself and continued.

"With the aid of several other prisoners, I was able to construct a shelter, barely more than a shack, for Noriko and the child. It was enough to keep the rain out, and I added a small stove for heat and cooking. She was fearful of further threats and harassment, so she asked if I would stay with them, which I agreed to do. At that point, we were not intimate. But in time, she became my lover and wife.

"I let Noriko tell me in her own good time the truth about the baby's father. She admitted that it was an American soldier, not Okinawan. He had been good to her, saved her life, and made her believe life in the future would be better. Her American had an older brother, also a US soldier, who had been captured when our forces took the Bataan peninsula in 1942. He was thought to have died in captivity. When her Amerika-jin returned to the United States, she felt utterly abandoned. She told me he didn't know she was carrying his daughter. But his departure was a fact, and in time she grew to accept it. Personally, I thought the man was a coward and a fool. She would never tell me his name, and I didn't press her to reveal it.

"Life in Okinawa was not pleasant. The American occupiers and their administrators weren't necessarily evil, but they were feckless and, in some cases, incompetent or corrupt. And once Okinawa was no longer needed as a base for the invasion of our home islands, the allocation of resources for rebuilding diminished noticeably. Nori-chan and I grew ever closer to one another. She confided to me her own hellish experiences as a student nurse's aide, including the mercy killing of so many wounded patients at the Haebaru military hospital. At Makabe, she was handed a grenade and told she should use it on herself if she wished to be spared being raped and tortured by the American marines. She very nearly did so, such was her despair at the end, but she couldn't bring herself to arm it. Despite everything, she was a fierce protector of her child, whom I grew to love as my own daughter. Eventually I managed to secure passage for the three of us on a decrepit steamer headed toward Honshu. And you know the rest." Soichiro sighed, relieved that his story was now finished.

"So-san, thank you," Kazuo said solemnly. He was fading visibly. "Thank you for sharing your remarkable story, and thank you for your steadfast friendship. I apologize for offending you by my rudeness."

Soichiro rose and bowed to the oyabun and Yoko. He was feeling strangely upbeat. Having reminded himself of his life with and love for Noriko, he couldn't help but consider the tragic loss of an infant grandson so long ago as very remote indeed.

He whistled as he drove home, eager to see his wife.

Chapter 33

Snapshots from the Edge

Saturday, January 26, 2002

Chatan, Okinawa

He was standing on a cliff overlooking the ocean. Below him, bobbing in the water, were seven bodies. Three of them were small children. The waves were lazily lapping the base of the coral cliff, moving the bodies languidly to and fro, arms outstretched, in a macabre rhythm. One arm flopped slowly from side to side, as if waving goodbye.

Suicides. First Saipan, and now here. Mothers holding their children and throwing themselves into the sea rather than risk torture by the American devils.

She appeared out of nowhere on a small promontory just twenty yards away. She held a bundle in her arms as she picked her way gingerly along the cliff.

Frankie opened his mouth to shout, but all he could manage was a strangled snarl.

She took a step toward the edge and turned his way, her face a stony mask of resignation, like the face in the photograph. "No!" he screamed. "No! Don't—"

A persistent knock at his door woke him from the nightmare.

Ellen's morning greeting, delivered in a sing-song voice, sounded from the hallway. "Dad, wake up!"

Frankie sat up and rubbed his eyes, overcome by a flood of relief, his shirt clinging to his clammy spine. It hadn't been real. But he knew that the time had come to tell his daughter.

He threw on a robe, shuffled stiffly to the door, and greeted her. "You never stopped by last night." He delivered the subtle admonishment matter-of-factly, careful not to sound controlling or overly protective—two tendencies of his that Ellen had trained him over the years not to display in her presence. She'd long been a grown woman, but he still worried about her almost as much as he had during her youth. Only exhaustion had enabled him to drift off to sleep the night before.

Ellen wore her dark hair pulled back in a ponytail and was dressed in a pair of low-riser jeans and a plain black T-shirt that showed off her toned arms and her olive skin. She marched straight to the sliding door that led out to the balcony and opened the blinds. "It was late. I didn't want to wake you."

Frankie, after taking a moment to adjust to the bright light pouring into the suite, hastily made his bed while his daughter fussed with the coffeemaker in the corner nook. He sensed a strange tension and realized he wasn't the only one who needed to get something off their chest. Should he be the first to speak? Or should he let her go first? He decided on the latter. Ellen seemed happy—almost bubbly—as she prepared his manzanilla.

"You sure spoil your old man," he said and gratefully accepted the steaming cup of herbal tea. "So I take it you made it back okay. Were you able to get a taxi from the base?"

Ellen nodded and took a seat on the armchair that sat diagonally from the bed. "We ate dinner at some restaurant Tony knew about. They served only traditional Okinawan food. I had no idea!"

Frankie eased himself down on the edge of the bed, careful not to spill his tea. "No idea?"

"I had assumed people here just eat sushi or whatever," she gushed. "But the food's totally unique. We had goya champuru, umi budo, rafute—oh my god, the rafute! As much as you love pork, Dad, you have to try it. It melts in your mouth!"

Frankie laughed. He was tickled to see his daughter so enthusiastic about something. "So what did you do after dinner?"

"We talked," she said, her eyes growing wide. "Till two in the morning! I told him all about home, you and Mom, work—everything. And he told me about his life. You wouldn't believe his story. I know he comes across all intellectual or whatever, but the guy's actually a bit of a rebel."

"Oh?" Frankie tried not to sound as guarded as he was feeling.

"He's a genius with numbers, but not in a nerdy way. When he was younger, he used to live in Atlantic City. He was a 'card counter' or something like that—a whiz at systems. He had a system for beating the tables. He got a reputation as someone who was too smart for the house. It wasn't long before a local don, one of Nicky Scarfo's, put the word out that Tony Wags—that's what they called him—was no longer welcome in the casinos. That's when Tony decided a career change was advisable and went to college."

Ellen was talking a mile a minute, and Frankie was having a hard time keeping up. *Tony Wags?* His daughter was hanging around with a guy who had a nickname like a "made man"?

"College?" he managed.

"Penn State. That's where he says he found his conscience. He went on to law school at Stanford and came out multilingual and an attorney specializing in environmental law. But that's not the half of it. He plays drums in an old-school jazz trio! They play all over LA."

Frankie nodded in bewilderment. Ellen was positively giddy, which made him happy—and nervous. "I don't think I've ever seen you like this," he said warily.

She raised an eyebrow at him. "Don't freak out, Dad. I just met someone interesting—that's all."

"Uh-huh," he said skeptically as he sipped at his tea. *Tony Wags* . . .

"Dad, I'm so glad I came on this trip with you. I know I've been a little grumpy about it, but that's just because you've been so distant lately. And Mom—she's a nervous wreck. I just hope you can find some closure and finally put whatever it is that's haunting you in the rearview mirror."

That's my cue. Frankie took a deep breath to steel himself and then fixed his daughter with his gaze. "Ellen, I'm glad you're sitting down, because there's something I need to tell you."

Ellen drew back slightly, her sky-blue eyes narrowing in concern. "What is it?"

Frankie heaved a heavy sigh. "I haven't been honest with you about this trip. Truth be told, I haven't been honest with *myself* for nearly as long as you've been alive. I was planning to tell you, but it all came to a head when we met Iwo Joe back at the memorial."

Ellen, clearly bracing for bad news, frowned at him. "What was it, Dad? Did you kill someone?"

Frankie squirmed at the end of the bed, the old wound shooting a ripple of pain down his thigh. "Yeah. Probably more than one. That was what I was here to do. It was hard, but I learned to live with that. No, it's something else. I met a woman after the battle. She was Okinawan, young and fragile, a casualty of war as much as any soldier could be. I took her into my care, totally against regulations, and against my own common sense. I became her friend and confidant. She spoke passable English. She had been a nurse's aide . . ." Frankie's voice trailed off. He suddenly felt the overpowering need for a cigarette. He hadn't smoked since Melanie's breast cancer, but the craving for nicotine was causing his mind to feel vacant. He shook his head in puzzlement, refocused, and picked up the thread. "Her name was Noriko. Her parents were killed during the battle. She had experienced horrors you can't imagine. I found her half alive in a large cave and preparing to kill herself with a grenade. I saved her."

Ellen exhaled with visible relief. "So? You saved a girl. Good for you."

"That's not everything. In the following months, we became close. *Extremely* close. I was her protector, and she came to depend on me. In time, the closeness became intimate. She fell in love with me, and I fell pretty hard for her. What changed everything and brought me back to reality was the letter I received around Christmas from your mother. We were just boyfriend and girlfriend when I joined the army, but she promised me she would wait. In the letter, she told me how happy she was that I was safe and how she thought of me every day and was hoping the army would let me come home soon. She said she had talked to her parents and told them she intended to marry me."

Ellen nodded guardedly. "Okay, but you had Noriko. Did she know you were planning to leave? Or were you having second thoughts?"

"Truthfully, I might have been entertaining crazy thoughts about staying, like Iwo Joe did. I was living in this little fantasy world far from home with a beautiful, delicate girl who depended on me. But I think deep inside, Noriko knew that I couldn't stay. I didn't tell her about the girl back home, but I'm pretty sure she sensed something. And as for bringing her home with me? That just wasn't going to happen. I doubt it would have been allowed. Can you imagine—bringing home a Japanese woman when the whole country was still toxic with Jap hatred? It wouldn't have been possible."

Ellen's brow furrowed. "So why does it bother you so much that you left her behind? Had you promised her anything?"

"No. But I feel like I bugged out on her in her time of need and left her helpless in a terrible place." Frankie let his shoulders sag, no longer attempting to maintain a stoic front for his daughter.

She brought her hand to her mouth, clearly trying to sort out why this Noriko person mattered so much to him, especially considering so many other people had been left helpless in that terrible place. "Do you know where she is?" she asked. "Or even if she's alive? In all these years, did you ever try to contact her or find out anything about her?"

"No." The word hung in the air with a leaden sound.

"Then help me understand—"

"Noriko had a daughter," Frankie blurted out. "*My* daughter. I didn't know until Iwo Joe told me yesterday."

"My God, Dad," was all Ellen could manage as her eyes registered shock.

"I tried to pretend Noriko had never happened for so many years. But I was living a lie. I came here to find Noriko and make my peace over leaving her that way. And now I learn that I have another daughter." Frankie shook his head and stared down at his hands.

For several long minutes, neither of them spoke.

Finally Ellen stood and walked over to the sliding glass door. The day had dawned clear and bright. The monsoon rain had passed, and the East China Sea was a deep azure. She turned to Frankie. "Well, you really know how to spring a surprise. I guess Iwo Joe didn't tell you where she—*they*—are."

"No. All he knew was that she married a Japanese soldier who survived the battle. The three of them moved away—I'm guessing to mainland Japan."

Ellen stared at the ceiling and released a breath through rounded lips. "So this is where the journey ends? Is there any way to find out more? If not, don't you think it's about time you forgave yourself? You've done what you could, traveled halfway around the world. At least you know she ended up okay after you left. What more is there to do?" She turned to Frankie. "Except, of course, tell Mom."

Afternoon, Same Day

Mabuni, Okinawa

Gary Masterson sat in the rented Nissan for just a moment after parking in the main lot at Peace Memorial Park. An ocean breeze blew through the cracked window next to him, bringing with it the salty scent of the sea. Yesterday's gloomy rain had given way to cobalt-blue skies and a beaming sun, but the improvement in the weather had done nothing to rally his mood. He felt discouraged about the prospects for learning anything new about Kume's mysterious American father. It didn't help that the fellow in the bar yesterday had seemed a bit gruff and dismissive. Gary hadn't even gotten a chance to introduce himself before the guy and his friend had elbowed past him on their way out the door. But he *had* caught the name of the man stitched on the vest: *Iwo Joe.*

Well, maybe "Iwo Joe" was here today, he thought. There had to be a story behind a name like that. And maybe Gary would learn something helpful. At the very least, he could take a pencil tracing of the names of Kume's grandparents on the stelae commemorating the dead. According to the park map, there were more than a hundred of the upright slabs of granite arranged neatly in parallel rows forming a concentric semicircle containing hundreds of thousands of names. He would need help locating the right one. He reminded himself to bring along the piece of stationery he'd filched from the hotel room and a number two pencil with him as he opened the car door.

After a long, leisurely walk through the park grounds, Gary approached the museum, an enormous gray structure with a busy roofline, a medieval-looking tower, and a long, covered walkway out front. The edifice's countless orange roof tiles contrasted sharply against the clear blue sky.

Gary entered the museum's cavernous lobby and let out an involuntary gasp. The feeling was church-like—quiet and reverential. He took the stairs to the second floor, where most of the materials concerning the 1945 battle were housed. As he strolled from exhibit to exhibit, he was moved by the scenes in caves, dioramas, and actual battle implements. There were large naval shells and artillery pieces. Gary stopped to examine a Japanese Type-92 heavy machine gun on a tripod.

"Pretty impressive collection, don't you think? That gun killed a lot of marines."

The voice came from over Gary's left shoulder. He turned and found himself face-to-face with the man from the bar yesterday.

Balding. A few decades Gary's senior. Too much heft around the middle. Despite all that, the man still looked formidable. He held out his hand. "My name is Joe Petrini. People call me Iwo—hey, don't I know you?"

"No, but we almost met—at the airport bar. Gary Masterson." Gary reached out and shook Petrini's hand.

"Yeah, you're the guy who asked me if we'd be open today. Glad to meet you. I apologize for being in such a hurry yesterday. My friend was having a bad day."

"No problem." Gary paused and scanned the large room. "I agree. It is impressive. The battle must have been something."

Joe nodded. "Lasted nearly three months. Largest seaborne invasion in history, bigger than D-Day. Navy lost a whole bunch of ships to kamikazes, Japanese lost over a hundred thousand soldiers, and about a third of the native Okinawans died. The army and marine casualty counts are probably what triggered 'Give 'em hell Harry's' decision to use the Bomb."

Gary moved to the next exhibit, a Japanese mortar tube, and turned to Joe. "Were you here in Okinawa then?"

"If you mean during the actual fighting, no. I arrived just as it ended. We Seabees had a huge job getting the place ready for Operation Downfall, the invasion of the home islands. Of course, that never came to pass."

"You must have known a lot of soldiers, seen a lot of bad stuff."

"Amen to that. After the surrender, we did our best to put up shelter for the surviving native population. It was pitiful, awful. So many orphans . . . What brings you to Okinawa, Mr. Masterson? Business? History buff? Have a relative who fought here?"

"Something like that. I'm trying to identify a US soldier who was here during the battle and stayed on with the occupation for a while."

Joe scratched the stubble on his chin. "Do you have a name? That shouldn't be too hard."

"Well, no. Not actually. The man is a mystery. He had an Okinawan girlfriend. She became pregnant, had a child. I'm not clear if he even knew about it. But he left for home, and the girl stayed behind. She had a daughter who now wants to know who her American father is . . . or was."

The look on Joe's face, which fell somewhere between puzzled and intrigued, suggested he was experiencing a sense of déjà vu. "That's a long time ago. And what's your interest in this American soldier? Are you related?"

"Yes . . . well, no," Gary replied. "Not by blood. I'm a friend of his daughter."

"Why didn't this girl get the information from her mother?"

"Believe me: she tried over many years. The mother refuses to budge."

Joe glanced sideways in both directions. Then he pulled out a pack of Winstons, shook one out, and lit up. "Tell me about this mother. Survivor of the battle?" He squinted through the smoke.

Gary nodded.

"Her name wouldn't happen to be Noriko, would it?" Joe asked, blowing a large billow from the side of his mouth.

It was Gary's turn to register shock. "You are shitting me!" he stammered incredulously. "Yes. It is. Did Nate Goldman put you up to this?"

Joe chuckled and then erupted in a hearty guffaw. "I don't know any Nate Goldman. But I have a feeling I do know someone who can answer all your questions. And wouldn't you know, you came this close to meeting him yesterday. Back in the day, we called him Dos Equis. But now he goes by Frankie Castillo."

Chapter 34

We Have Quite a Lot
to Talk About

Sunday, January 27, 2002

Sendai, Japan

Soichiro paced the living room's bamboo floor in his slippers. He was never good at breaking bad news to Noriko. He usually hemmed and hawed as he skirted the problem. But the phone call from Midorikawa was troubling and serious. It seemed that matters involving the rival syndicate were becoming dangerous more quickly than expected.

As he turned to face his wife, he watched her fondle the small gold crucifix she always wore. It reminded him of those early, awful days in Okinawa when he had first noticed it around her neck. She had told him it was a gift from the Amerika-jin. She regarded it as a charm that had brought her the good luck of meeting Soichiro. A Catholic himself, one of a shrinking minority in Sendai, Soichiro could claim a religious heritage in his family dating back nearly four hundred years to when the daimyo Date Masamune had established diplomatic relations with the Vatican. He found it impossible to object to Noriko's wearing the gold amulet.

"Nori-chan, your crucifix catches the light in a special way this morning. Is it a sign you will be coming to Mass at the cathedral with me?"

Noriko waved her hand dismissively. She hadn't been religious since the summer of 1945, and Soichiro knew it. But occasionally she would accompany her husband to Sunday Mass. She often said that she liked the peace she experienced with the ancient ritual in Mototerakoji Cathedral, where she would always light a candle for her lost Himeyuri companions. "No. Not today. I would like to stay home and read. Say a prayer for me."

Soichiro nodded thoughtfully, braced himself, and began. "I spoke with Kazu-san last evening. He called to warn me that the business with the rival syndicate in Hokkaido could be coming to a head soon. He expects there to be violence. Apparently my name has been mentioned as someone the northerners would like to deal with specially. Kazuo believes it may be wise for us to go away for a while."

Noriko snorted. "Why is it that anytime there is a mention of violence, somehow Midorikawa is involved? And what right does he have to be ordering us around? I'm staying put, thank you very much." She sat down on the two-piece sectional and ostentatiously reached for the Sunday paper beside her.

Soichiro heard that clicking sound she made with her tongue. He would go to Mass alone and pray for inspiration on how to reason with an obstinate wife.

Same Day

Chatan, Okinawa

Frankie sat with his daughter at a small bistro table for two on his hotel suite balcony. The morning breeze had a chill to it, but the sun, which had already risen level with the balcony, was warming his face and hands.

"Dad, I told Tony I'd be spending the day with him. You're welcome to join us . . ." Ellen let the sentence trail off unconvincingly. "I didn't know if you had other plans."

Frankie half grinned as he sipped his first cup of tea. "No, it's fine. Go out and have some fun. Iwo Joe said he'd come by. We might go down to the ballpark and watch a baseball player hold a clinic for some kids. Other than that, it may be time to think about heading home."

"Okay. I'll go down to the lobby. He'll be arriving soon." She stood up to leave and then paused and sat back down. "Are you okay with me seeing Tony?"

"Why wouldn't I be?"

"Well, for starters, he's not exactly your type. I'm not even sure he's *my* type."

Frankie chuckled and set his teacup on the glass tabletop. "Ellen, I'll admit, when I first met him, I found him arrogant, clueless, and annoying as hell. But . . ."

Ellen's shoulders rose as she squinted at him sheepishly. "But?"

"But if this trip has taught me anything, it's that I don't know half as much as I thought I did. I came here to find

Noriko, maybe make some peace with my past, and instead found out I have another daughter out there somewhere. I was gung ho to find out what had happened to Noriko after I left her, but it turns out I didn't even know what was going on with her before I said goodbye." Frankie took Ellen's hand, which was resting on the table. "Who am I to tell you how to live your life?"

Ellen stared at his hand a moment. "You were just a kid. Don't beat yourself up about something that happened half a century ago."

Frankie groaned. "Now you're just reminding me how old I am!"

"Look, Dad. Not everything works out like how we imagine it will. Maybe it's enough that you made a pilgrimage here. Now you can focus on getting right with Mom."

"Maybe," he said, although he doubted he'd accomplished anything worthwhile. He gave Ellen's hand a squeeze. "Get outta here. Go be with your new friend."

Ellen smiled and stood up. "Thanks, Dad. I'll try not to stay out too late tonight."

After Ellen left, Frankie shuffled back inside and got comfortable on the bed, determined to decipher the TV remote. He'd just figured out how to turn on the TV when he heard a knock at the door. He sat up and swung his legs to the floor. It was too early for Iwo Joe to be dropping by—unless he'd decided to take Frankie to breakfast.

Frankie opened the door to a tall Caucasian stranger with his knuckles bent in mid-knock. "Can I help you?" As he said the words, he thought there was something familiar about the man.

"I hope so," the man said with a slight smile. He was dressed in an expensive-looking suit, sans tie. Silver streaks highlighted his full head of hair. "I apologize for showing up unannounced.

We nearly met two days ago at the airport. My name's Gary Masterson. Are you Frankie Castillo?"

"Oh yeah. You're the guy we walked past on our way out." Frankie stopped smiling. "How do you know my name, and why did you go to the trouble to find me?"

"May I come in? I believe we have quite a lot to talk about."

Frankie glanced past the man and, leaning forward, looked up and down the hallway. He was tempted to tell the guy to buzz off. But he didn't look outwardly suspicious. Frankie waved him into his suite. "Can I offer you some coffee? Tea? I'm expecting to have to leave soon—a friend is picking me up."

"I think Iwo Joe will be arriving quite a bit later," Gary replied with a wink. "Mr. Petrini told me where to find you."

Frankie felt his face reddening as he silently cursed Joe for not giving him a heads-up. *Who is this guy, and why hadn't Joe called?*

Gary took a seat next to the coffee table in the small living room, which, until now, Frankie had barely set foot in. "If you're wondering why Iwo Joe didn't contact you, it's because I asked him not to, and he agreed. Let me cut to the chase. You and I are here on roughly the same mission. Each of us is looking for a missing person. I'm pretty sure the one I'm looking for is standing right in front of me. And the one you're looking for is someone intimately connected to you. A woman you once knew back in wartime days. And I know how to reach her."

Frankie blinked twice and raised his eyebrows. He circled warily behind where Gary was sitting. "Why should I believe any of this? You show up at my door with a fantastic story that may or may not be true. Who sent you?"

Gary turned his head slightly. "Your daughter, Kume Matsuhata."

Frankie reached down to the back of the sofa where Gary was sitting to steady himself. His head was swimming, and the room swirled in his vision.

"Sit down, Frankie," Gary said quietly. "I've known Kume for many years. She was raised by her mother, Noriko, and the man her mother married, Soichiro Matsuhata. Did you know your daughter was once a world-famous fashion model? I'm here because she asked me to find her biological father." Gary paused and smiled, a faint dimple creasing his cheek. "Truthfully, I was about to give up. No leads and no path to find the American soldier. And then I met Joe Petrini at the peace memorial. He was able to tie up a lot of loose ends."

Frankie managed to navigate around the sofa and took a seat opposite Gary. "You said you know where she is. Noriko. How can I contact her?"

Gary raised his palms. "Hold your horses, cowboy. One step at a time. For one thing, I need to see Kume and tell her the news. For another, Noriko has no idea any of this is happening. Kume asked me to do this on the QT, and who knows how her mother might react? I'm sure Kume would want to meet you, but Noriko? Hmm. Big question."

The thigh pain was becoming unbearable, so Frankie rose to get an Advil. He ran his fingers through his hair as he limped toward the bathroom. "Mr. Masterson—"

"Please, call me Gary."

"Gary, you haven't told me why you're doing this for Kume," Frankie said from the bathroom. He caught a glimpse of his wavy white hair in the mirror above the sink before he threw back his head and swallowed the pill. "What's she to you? Did she pay you to hunt me down?"

Gary sighed. "Long story, Frankie. Too long to tell here. Let's just say that Kume is extremely special to me. I took it on as a favor."

"Ah. You love her." Frankie beamed at this deduction as he limped back to the living room. "So you could be my son-in-law."

Gary squirmed uncomfortably, crossing and recrossing his legs. "Another long story."

"Do you have a picture of her?"

Gary twisted in his seat and pulled out his wallet. He handed Frankie a snapshot that had obviously been taken many years before. It showed a younger Gary and a tall young woman standing next to a race car. She had delicate features, long legs, and a medium-length pixie cut.

Frankie felt his heart jump. It startled him to see his daughter for the first time. "She looks like her mother." He studied the photo longer, and it stirred a vague recognition—Frankie felt sure he'd seen that face before. Maybe in a cosmetics ad. He handed the photo back to Gary. "She's beautiful."

Gary stood and gathered himself. "I need to be leaving. I'm flying to Tokyo to see Kume. I promise I'll tell her you want to see her and her mother."

Same Day

Petrini Field, Naha

"That's how you left it? Masterson goes to Tokyo and arranges for you to meet Noriko and Kume?" Iwo Joe seemed delighted at how he had played a role in furthering Frankie's quest.

Frankie had joined Joe at the ballpark, where the two were watching Takeo coach a large group of children. The setting was glitzy enough—far more than a sandlot wedged between busy streets. Indeed, the chalk lines were straight, the outfield grass was green and perfectly manicured, and the ad-lined outfield fence boasted a small warning track. Even the dugouts looked sleek and well-built. As for Takeo, it was clear the man had a gift for teaching. He was animated, authoritative, inspiring—and still moved well for a man past his prime. The kids stood at attention while he demonstrated proper fielding technique, temporarily taking over for the shortstop.

Frankie, seated beside Joe on the bleachers in the gleaming park, experienced a shiver of satisfaction in the knowledge that he'd contributed, albeit briefly, at the very beginning to what had resulted in this ballplayer with these children in this ballpark on this day. "Yeah, that's about it. And I'm still pissed that you didn't tell me I'd be having a visitor."

Joe grunted. "It was better that way. I wish I'd been there to see your face."

Frankie made a feint as though to pop a left hook at Joe's chin.

Joe pretended to cover and parry the punch. "Ayaka expects you to come over for dinner tonight and meet the family. Actually, you and Ellen both."

"Forget about Ellen. She's out with Mr. L.A. Wonderful, and I doubt she'll be coming back to the hotel this evening. She doesn't know what happened today. Probably just as well. I don't want to spoil her evening. She probably thinks we'll be going home shortly."

"What if Noriko says she doesn't want to see you?"

"I'm not sure. I'll cross that bridge when I hear from Masterson."

"Well, if you do decide to go up there, they won't be talking a lot of English, not like down here. You'll need someone to help you with the lingo. I'd do it, but I can't get away. Takeo says he can call in a favor from a friend named Takashi Kojo, who's bilingual. He can go with you."

Frankie thought a moment. Bringing Takeo's friend along meant there would be no need for Ellen to invite Tony, who obviously had command of the Japanese language if he could do legal consulting for the US military. "Good. I may need him. But first I have to tell Ellen that we may be taking a detour on our way home."

Chapter 35

Consummations

Same Day

Shinjuku-ku, Tokyo

Kume fretted as she watched the late afternoon shadows lengthen on the tarmac. Gary's message had been terse, but he'd told her to meet him at the airport. She was waiting for him outside at the private aviation terminal in Haneda as the big Gulfstream rolled to a stop.

When the cabin door opened, Gary bounded down the steps and hugged her, whispering urgently in her ear, "I found your American father!"

Kume struggled to contain her emotions. She was both elated and terrified.

They grabbed a taxi and hurried to Kume's apartment, and on the way, Gary related the story of his trip to Okinawa and the extraordinary experiences of the previous three days. He finished just as the taxi was pulling to a stop outside Kume's building.

Kume waited until they were alone in the elevator and almost to her floor before she started peppering Gary with questions. "Does he look like Montgomery Clift?"

"No. Not at all. But he's a pretty good-looking old dude. He could pass for Anthony Quinn."

"And he wants to meet my mother?"

"That's what he says."

"What gives him the right . . . ?"

"No rights involved. He says he needs to apologize."

"Apologize?" Kume rubbed her forehead wearily as they exited the elevator on the thirty-ninth floor. She felt like her head would burst. Part of her had never expected that Gary would succeed in locating her father. But now that he had—in Okinawa, no less—she was faced with a serious dilemma. "I don't know what to do, Gary. I should talk to my father. He will know whether this is a good idea. I can't talk to my mother about it. My mother . . . You know, she wrote the American off when he left. The shock would push her over the edge. She wouldn't know what to do with an apology." Kume dabbed at the corner of her eye. "What's his name?"

"Francisco Castillo, but he goes by Frankie." Gary dropped his overnight bag in the entryway after they stepped inside her apartment. "He's not alone. His daughter came with him. I didn't meet her. Her name is Ellen. She's your, uh, sister."

"Did Frankie ask about me? Does he even *know* about me?"

"Yes. He had just learned about you, literally hours before I saw him. He asked to see your picture, so I showed him the one I keep in my wallet. He said you look like your mother."

At that, Kume's composure evaporated. She took a seat on the living room couch.

Gary hurried over and sat next to her, wrapping an arm around her.

She could feel her mascara streaking down her cheeks. His steady grip on her shoulders, meanwhile, was the only thing keeping them from shaking uncontrollably.

"God help me, Gary. I'm sorry to be such a wreck." She rose and walked briskly to the bathroom to compose herself. "Help yourself to a drink," she called out to him as she dabbed at her eyes. "There's Belvedere in the bar. Make me one, too."

Later, after he stretched and rolled over, Gary noticed the fog of the alcohol beginning to lift. The lights of the city cast soft shades of purple and pink on Kume's bedroom ceiling.

He cupped himself against her bare bottom and, feeling aroused once again, whispered in Kume's ear, "Well, that was unexpected. But still the greatest of great legs."

Kume turned to face him. She was smiling. She pushed herself closer to him and giggled. "At ease, soldier. You've exhausted me. I'm getting up to make some coffee."

Gary groaned and, propping himself on his elbow, watched Kume leave the bed and stand in silhouette against the violet sky framed by the window. "You're a goddess," he murmured.

She turned and blew him a kiss. "I need to call my father. He'll know best what to do about Frankie meeting my mother. I think I know what he'll say, but I need to hear it from him." She slipped on her robe and left for the kitchen.

Gary lay quietly, thinking to himself how, strangely and improbably, he had simultaneously found both Kume's American father and the way to her heart. They'd left a trail of clothing from the dining room to her bedroom, where their lovemaking had been fierce and deep. He spied his Armani shirt on the floor in the doorway. It was missing several buttons.

Not bad for an old boy like me, he congratulated himself. *I think I'm in love.*

From the kitchen, Kume announced that the coffee was on.

Gary got up and found a robe in her closet.

She greeted him with, "I have my dad's cell number. I've texted him and asked him to call me when he can talk privately. I expect he'll be calling soon."

Gary nodded. "Good move."

"But there's something else I should tell you, Gary," she said in an apprehensive tone as she poured the coffee. "My mother knows about our son."

"What?" Gary sputtered. "You didn't tell me that."

"I know. I should have told you. It was quite accidental—and very recent. When she last visited, she found an old picture of Henry that I've held on to. It was a shock—it shocked *both* of us. And as usual, it provoked a scene between us. Still, it was really emotional for me—and probably for her." She paused before asking, "Do you ever think of Henry?"

"Hardly a day goes by that he doesn't cross my mind." Gary closed his eyes and shook his head. "What a capacity we humans have for inflicting pain upon ourselves. I had a hard time getting over blaming myself for his death—I know, senseless—but I was helpless to support you in your grief. And that's when I felt that I lost you."

"Gary Masterson, you never lost me. I probably lost myself. The death of a child is brutal—heartrending when you've already experienced the magic of staring into the wise little eyes, feeling the touch of the soft fingers, and watching the tiny mouth as it seeks the breast. I didn't blame you. How could I?

We were so young. I thought that leaving you and New York would help me leave the loss behind. Little did I understand back then that all I did was compound the loss." Her eyes glistened with tears welling at the corners.

Her cell phone buzzed.

"Hello, Father," she answered. "Are you alone? Okay. I have news, and I need your advice."

Restaurant Hamaya, Chatan-cho, Okinawa

"What do you think?" Tony's big brown eyes twinkled beneath one of the restaurant's bright fluorescent tubes hanging unceremoniously from the ceiling.

How, Ellen wondered, could someone look that handsome in such awful lighting? She nearly choked on a noodle before mustering a reply. "It's wonderful."

Tony sat back in amusement. "You okay?"

"Sure," she said, eyes watering. "Just tried to inhale my dinner is all."

They sat at a table for two in what was purported to be the best soba restaurant in all of Okinawa. The humble eatery, which sat less than a hundred feet from the sea wall, was crowded with locals, US servicemen and women, and scuba divers, the latter congregating around tables outside, where their wet suits weren't apt to drip on the shiny hardwood flooring. Blond wood paneling adorned the walls, along with the signatures of Japanese celebrities. A handful of traditional low tables sat on raised flooring along the walls, but most of the tables, like Ellen and Tony's, were of the Western variety.

But according to Tony, people didn't come here for the ambience. They flocked to this family-run restaurant to partake of the pork soba, a noodle soup that overflowed with green onions, strips of scrambled eggs, and of course, pork. Ellen had mistakenly ordered a large bowl and was currently staring at more food than she could possibly stuff away. Not that she wasn't going to try. Normally on a date with someone she'd only recently met, she felt too nervous to overeat. But something about Tony and her connection with him invited relaxation, not to mention a little overindulgence. She wanted to savor his ornery smirk, his mischievous gaze, and that long, dark hair of his.

The soba, meanwhile, continued to capture her attention. "I think my eyes are too big for my stomach," she said, not quite ready to give up.

"Save some room," Tony said as he tapped a bottle of chile vinegar over his soup. "You don't want to miss the Chinsuko cookies."

Ellen shook her head in defeat. Her next sentence had barely escaped her lips before she instantly regretted it. "I hope you like your girlfriends in plus sizes."

Girlfriends? Whatever they were doing—sightseeing? dating?—hardly constituted a relationship. She was thankful no power tools were near.

He didn't miss a beat. "In your line of work, you can probably afford the extra calories."

She smiled timidly, her face still burning with embarrassment.

"So here's a question for you," he said, pausing to take a sip of beer. "Is it just me, or does your dad hate me?"

"*Hate* you?" she said with a laugh. "I don't know about *hate*. But you gotta admit: you were a little pushy when we first met."

His shoulders sagged. "I don't know what came over me that night. I saw you and I just . . . flipped. I haven't been able to see straight since."

Ellen felt embarrassed again—but this time in a good way. "Just give him some time. He'll come around . . . eventually."

She was doing it again—hinting that their future might stretch beyond her father's trip to Okinawa. But she was beginning to sense he was thinking the same thing. She didn't know whether to be excited or frightened to death.

Tony, it turned out, was right about the Chinsuko cookies. Shaped like fat fingers with ridges, they tasted like shortbread, long a favorite of hers. Like Tony, they struck her as both familiar and exotic. Somehow she made room for several.

Back at the hotel, she led Tony to her door, which she made sure to open as quietly as humanly possible. He opened his mouth to speak, but she brought a finger to his lips and pulled him inside. She hated the idea of sneaking around with her father next door, but dinner and dessert had done nothing to diminish certain other appetites.

Chapter 36

The Whole World Changed

Same Day

Chatan, Nakagami District, Okinawa

Frankie lay on top of his bed in his hotel suite, TV on, balcony door wide open. A refreshing breeze cooled his bare feet. He hadn't bothered to call the front desk about the AC unit. So long as the East China Sea kept churning out there in the darkness, he figured he could make do.

The TV, on the other hand, remained a confounding mystery. He'd figured out the remote—and had found the mute button—but the endless parade of cooking programs and talk shows were another matter. It didn't help that Frankie wasn't much of a TV watcher, anyway, or that he didn't know more than a few words of Japanese, much less how to decipher the Okinawan dialect.

He felt a surge of relief when his cell phone rang on the nightstand next to him. Although he didn't recognize the number on the caller ID, he had a hunch he knew who was calling. "Hello?"

"Frankie, this is Gary Masterson."

Frankie propped himself up and switched the phone to his other ear. "Gary. What have you learned?"

"Bad news, I'm afraid."

Frankie said nothing and waited for Gary to continue.

"Kume spoke with her father. He told her he always knew there'd be a chance that sooner or later she'd try to contact her American father. He had no problem with that, although, as you can imagine, he has a pretty poor opinion of you, given how you left."

Frankie grimaced. "No surprise there."

"I suppose not. Anyway, here's the bad news: he doesn't want you coming anywhere near Noriko. Says she's suffered enough. He wants the past left in the past."

Frankie silently absorbed the news. What had he expected? He hardly understood what had compelled him to come all this way in search of Noriko. Why should he expect her husband—the man who had looked after her and Kume in his absence—to humor him? It probably looked to her husband like Frankie was doing nothing but stirring up trouble. Who would welcome that?

"You still there?" Gary asked.

Frankie heaved a long sigh. "I'm here." He opened his mouth to concede he'd made a mistake and then stopped himself. Something in him refused to let it go. He'd come too far, waited too long to be stopped dead in his tracks.

"Maybe it's for the best," Gary suggested.

"Maybe," Frankie said without believing it.

"On the positive side, Kume wants to meet you. But not just yet. She'd like to wait for a better time."

Frankie tried to take solace in that bit of news but couldn't help feeling chagrined. Even his daughter was putting on the brakes. "Where's Noriko now?"

Gary hedged on the other end of the line. "Sorry, Frankie. I can't share that information with you."

"Yeah, I get it." Frankie suddenly no longer felt like talking. "Thanks for calling. I appreciate it."

"You bet. We'll be in touch."

After hanging up, Frankie set his cell phone on the night-stand and rubbed his jaw. He had some serious thinking to do.

Same Day

Shinjuku-ku, Tokyo

Kume drew a shallow breath. Lying beside Gary on the bed, she'd been close enough to hear her American father's voice, which had sounded rugged and gruff but vulnerable somehow. Had she heard warmth in his responses? Regret?

Gary wore a wistful smile on his face, his dimple once again appearing on his cheek in the soft glow of the bedside lamp. "I guess that's that."

"I guess so," Kume said, feeling deflated, like she'd been cheated out of something important.

Gary had relayed her father's wishes to Frankie in typical diplomatic fashion. In fact, during Kume's phone call to him, Soichiro had bristled at the suggestion that Frankie pay a visit to Noriko. He had called Frankie "a shadowy presence from the distant past" and had said he considered the man "craven" and "irresponsible." Though Soichiro claimed he bore Frankie no ill will, he had sounded dubious, to put it mildly, where Frankie's motives were concerned. Why fly across the Pacific to find Noriko? Was he going to apologize? Was he hoping to satisfy a guilty conscience? Whatever Frankie's motives were, Soichiro had declared it far too late. He had refused to subject her mother to an unwelcome source of stress just to alleviate the American's anxiety.

"Hey." Gary, who lay beside her, turned on his side to face her and touched her cheek. "Are you okay?"

She met his gaze and nodded. She wasn't okay. But what could she say?

Gary's eyes were full of tenderness as he took her hand in his. "Marry me."

Kume felt her heart do a giddy dance in her chest. "Did you just . . . ?"

He nodded resolutely.

If the past few days had been an emotional roller coaster, this had to be the ride's final plunge over the edge. She couldn't believe Gary's awful timing, the sheer audacity of his proposal. The only thing more absurd was her response. "Okay."

Monday, January 28, 2002

Chatan, Nakagami District, Okinawa

When Ellen arrived at his suite for tea the next morning, Frankie noticed that her mood had changed from faintly glowing to downright radiant. She was wearing a yellow sundress and strappy, low-heeled sandals, sporting a playful look that, Frankie had to admit, agreed with her. Sometimes he forgot that her wardrobe included more than jeans, work boots, and T-shirts decorated with the company logo.

They sat down for the last time on his suite's balcony, which was just beginning to warm in the morning sun. For the first time since their arrival, the air was dead calm.

"Change of plans," Frankie declared as he stared down at his tea, still too hot to drink. "We aren't going home yet."

Ellen cocked her head at him, and her lips parted slightly. She looked hopeful but wary. It was obvious she was thinking about Tony. Perhaps she thought this meant they could spend more time together. "What do you mean? What happened?"

"The whole world changed while you were out with your friend."

Ellen rolled her eyes. "You can say his name, Dad. And stop being so cryptic. What changed?"

Frankie took a moment to describe Gary Masterson's visit to his hotel suite the day before.

Ellen's eyes narrowed with concern. "And did he call you back?"

"He did," Frankie said with a tight-lipped frown. "He called late last night and told me that Noriko's husband, speaking for his wife, says that under no circumstances will Noriko wish to see me. I get the feeling that they're protecting her and that she has no idea we're here or that I wish to talk to her, face-to-face. He also told me that Kume feels differently. She would still like to meet me—just not right now."

"So what are you going to do?"

Frankie shook his head angrily. He could feel sweat forming on the back of his neck. "Damn it! We traveled too far not to finish what I came to do. I still need to see Noriko."

Ellen eyed him skeptically. "Okay. So for starters, do you know where she is?"

"Not exactly. Masterson wouldn't tell me. But Iwo Joe and Takeo recalled that the Japanese soldier who married her was a fisherman. Joe remembered hearing that he had served in the IJA Second Division, known as the Sendai Division. Sendai is a city north of Tokyo with a large fishing port called Shiogama. Chances are that's where the soldier and Noriko headed for when they left Okinawa. At least we have a name: Soichiro Matsuhata. We should start there." Frankie set his jaw so Ellen would know the matter wasn't up for discussion.

Ellen took the hint. "Fine. Have you called Mom to say we'll be heading to Japan to see your old flame?"

Frankie glared at her. "A few extra days won't be such a big deal. I'll call your mother when we get to Sendai."

Chapter 37

Secrets and Lies

Wednesday, January 30, 2002

Shiogama Fish Market, Miyagi Prefecture

Frankie stood with Ellen at the end of a concrete dock and watched while Takashi Kojo, the interpreter Iwo Joe had arranged to accompany them, approached a man unloading his catch. Kojo and the fisherman made for a stark contrast. Kojo, dressed in black slacks and a white dress shirt, complete with black tie, looked like a businessman ready to clock off early. He wore dark aviator sunglasses and had rolled up his sleeves, exposing slender forearms and an expensive Rolex on his left wrist. The fisherman, meanwhile, was still dressed in his grimy coveralls and was at least a head shorter than Kojo. He had forearms like Popeye's and, despite the graying at his temples, appeared every bit as fit as his younger interviewer. Behind the two men, a forty-foot fishing trawler bobbed in the water. It looked top-heavy and unwieldy, but, judging by its salty, weathered veneer, was plenty seaworthy. The business end of an enormous rusty anchor protruded from its bow, which, like the stern, had been secured to the dock by a pair of thick ropes.

"Wish I spoke Japanese," Frankie said as he watched the two men talk.

"I don't think it would help," Ellen said, squinting in the bright light at the two men. "They're practically whispering."

The weather so far in Shiogama, Sendai's fishing port, had been cooler but drier than Okinawa's, which Frankie appreciated. A steady onshore breeze buffeted the dock.

The conversation, like the half dozen or so that had preceded it, was brief. The fisherman's face darkened as he pointed at Frankie and Ellen, and a minute later, Kojo returned to Frankie and Ellen as he had after his other encounters with fishermen at the docks—shaking his head.

Two days into their excursion, they had so far learned only that their mere presence elicited suspicion. Kojo's questions seemed to confirm the locals' fears, whatever they were. And so far Frankie had spotted, among other things, the shape of an AK-47, which had been partially obscured beneath a tarp among a trawler's dockside supplies. Clearly things around the port were tense. Lips were tight. Eyes were guarded.

"We're becoming quite popular," Kojo said as he rejoined Frankie and Ellen.

Frankie didn't like the sound of that. "What do you mean?"

Kojo smiled nervously. "Word is spreading about a couple of gaijin strangers who are poking around." He pointed at the fisherman with his eyes. "He knew we were looking for Soichiro Matsuhata before I even mentioned the name."

Less than forty-eight hours earlier, Frankie had been feeling optimistic during their flight from Naha to Sendai. Kojo, Takeo's bilingual friend, had met them at the airport, and his value had become immediately apparent in this part of Japan where little English was spoken. Matsuhata, Kojo had informed them, was a fairly common surname in the area, so they'd begun their search by making inquiries at the docks. But the sleuthing had gone downhill from there. No one wanted to talk. And everyone seemed to resent their presence.

Ellen, Frankie could tell, was quickly tiring of the hunt. "Anyone hungry?" she asked in a peevish tone. It wasn't so much a question as a request.

"Do you like sushi?" Kojo asked with inquisitive eyes.

"I love it!" Ellen gushed before Frankie could object.

Kojo smiled. "Then I know just the place."

They walked a block inland and stopped in front of the Shiogama Fish Market, an enormous covered warehouse-like structure that, Kojo explained, sold fresh seafood at wholesale prices. The air was thick with smoke from vendors grilling oysters just outside the covered entrance, and Frankie's senses went into overload the moment they passed through the over-sized doors. He felt like he'd entered a big box store. Only instead of selling tools and building supplies, this one specialized in the ocean's pungent bounty. Merchants in one hundred and forty stalls hawked everything from shellfish to octopi.

Kojo directed them past several sushi stands, and soon they were seated at a small bistro table in one of the market's open-air restaurants.

Less than ten minutes later, Ellen was looking up from her plate of sushi and rolling her eyes heavenward—or at least toward the steel rafters above them. "Dad, you really should try it. You'd love it. So fresh and delectable. I've never seen so much great sushi under one roof in my entire life."

Frankie cast a baleful glance at his daughter, tried picking at his bowl of rice and noodles with his chopsticks, and gave up. "I don't know how you can eat that stuff raw. I doubt I could keep it down. Right now, I'd give my right arm to have a bowl of your mother's posole or a green chile enchilada. I'd starve if I lived here."

Kojo laughed as he gulped down something slippery-looking. "You don't know what you're missing."

At least the sake was superb. Frankie made sure to nurse his. "Does it seem a little strange to you how people stare at us and then quickly turn away?" he asked after a time. "Every time Takashi here asks about Noriko's husband, he gets the big freeze-out, like maybe we aren't exactly welcome here."

Ellen nodded in unison with Kojo. "Yeah, hard not to notice that. Things do seem very tense. It may not be a bad idea to pack up and leave. I sort of get the feeling the locals aren't fond of outsiders." Ellen had insisted to Frankie that the trip to Sendai be brief—no more than three days. She had asserted that this was long enough to finish his quixotic search, and she appeared eager to cut the trip short.

Kojo set down his own cup of sake. His eyes were fixed on a group of several large men standing near a sushi stall about thirty meters away. They were dressed in suits and stood protectively around a somewhat smaller man. The larger men were acting exceedingly deferential to the smaller man, nodding and saying, "*Hai hai*," frequently.

The smaller man was very well dressed, trim, and clearly the leader. In an almost theatrical way, he reached into his pocket for a silver cigarette case, and one of the large men hurriedly produced a lighter. After a few moments, the group moved away, but the smaller man lingered behind, staring thoughtfully over his sunglasses at Frankie and Ellen.

"Did you see that?" Kojo murmured under his breath. "You were getting the once-over from the yakuza. The smaller man is obviously the oyabun or *wakagashira*. They seem very interested in you." He shot nervous glances at Frankie and Ellen. "Is there something I should know about you that you haven't told me?"

Ellen tossed him a sardonic grin. "Come to think of it, Kojo-san, there is something. My father and I are both undercover operators for the CIA, and we've been sent to investigate activity by sushi terrorists in the Shiogama Fish Market."

Kojo frowned as he fell for the bait. Then he brightened and laughed hysterically when he realized he'd been had. "Very funny, Ellen-san. But we may not find it so funny if we keep asking questions. Rumors are circulating about an expected clash between the local yakuza and a rival syndicate from Hokkaido. I think we should go back to the hotel and talk this over. It may be time to decide how or even *whether* we should continue our efforts here."

As Kojo drove them back to Sendai and the Westin Hotel, Frankie decided to share his own thoughts with Ellen. "Something just isn't making sense. Those fishermen at the docks are too tight-lipped, damn near hostile. Why is that?"

"Maybe they know this Matsuhata guy and think we mean to do him some harm," Ellen replied. "You heard what Kojo said about a mob war about to break out. Maybe they think we're working for the other side."

Frankie pumped his eyebrows and agreed. "That may be it. And maybe the bad guys have it in for Matsuhata for some reason. Everything considered, we might be wise to change our plans." Frankie hedged, not willing to abort their plans when he felt they were this close to locating Noriko.

"You haven't talked to Mom yet. What are you going to say?"

"Well, I'm sure as hell not going to tell her the truth. Not yet. I plan to blame you. I'm going to say you met some hippie environmentalist in Okinawa, and he wanted to spend a few days with you in Tokyo. I'll say I decided to come along and keep out of your way by taking a tour along the northern coast."

Ellen shook her head. "You're something else." In the hotel lobby, she suggested they play tourist to kill some time: go up to Sendai castle, see the famous zelkova trees, visit a Shinto shrine or two.

Frankie gave her a sour frown. He hated the idea.

"At least it would give you something honest to describe when you call Mom," she said.

Frankie went to his room, picked up the phone, and to his immense relief heard an English-speaking voice on the other end. He ordered a *wagyu* beef hamburger and fries off the room service menu. It was still too early back home to call Melanie.

Ellen had just hung up her cell phone when it rang again. Had Tony forgotten to tell her something? They'd just spoken for more than an hour. Then she saw the number on the caller ID.

"Mom?"

"Hi, honey."

Ellen glanced at the clock. It was eleven o'clock—bedtime. "What's up?"

"I just had an interesting conversation with your father."

"Oh." Ellen stifled a yawn. "What time is it there?"

"Eight in the morning," her mom answered. "I was making breakfast when your father called. He says you two are in mainland Japan. Gave me some cock-and-bull story about you hooking up with a man in Okinawa and following him to Tokyo to go sightseeing. Your dad claims he's just being a tourist along the coastline to give you some space. Sounds like hogwash to me."

Ellen slipped off her bed to pace the small room. The carpet felt plush beneath her bare feet. "Mom, I really did meet someone. He's amazing."

Her answer seemed to take her mom off guard. "You're kidding me."

"His name's Tony. He's an environmental attorney, of all things. He's from LA."

"You sound smitten."

Ellen could hear the smile in her mother's voice. "I am. We just spent the last hour talking. I've never met anyone—male or female—I could be so open with. I mean, there's plenty of chemistry between us. But I feel so comfortable with him, like I can tell him anything."

"He must not be with you right now."

"No, he's in his room." That was true, as far as it went.

"So he's a gentleman, then."

"He is." Also true. Ellen couldn't stand keeping anything from her mother, but so long as she kept redirecting to Tony, she figured she could keep the outright lying to a minimum.

"And your father's just being a tourist?"

"As best he can," Ellen replied. "I guess he went to a sushi place with his tour guide today, but he just ate noodles. You know Dad; he doesn't like to try new things."

"Exactly," her mother said, returning to her suspicious tone. "I know that man like the back of my hand. I'm sure there's something else going on. I can't imagine him taking a tour. He hates tours. I'm half tempted to fly over there and surprise him. I would if I had any idea where to find him. I mean, it's one thing to go to Okinawa and spend a few days revisiting the places he fought. But now it's going on two weeks. What the hell is your father up to?"

Ellen took a deep breath. "Mom, I wouldn't worry about it. I think Dad just has a lot to process. His homing instinct will kick in soon."

"What about you and your new beau?"

The question threw Ellen off-balance. She'd been trying not to overthink things. Tony had said his job would keep him in Okinawa another week or two. After that, he said he wanted to visit her in New Mexico. He'd even hinted that he might take a sabbatical—or even open his own private practice. The latter, he'd said, was something he could do anywhere.

"I'm not sure," she finally said. "We're taking it one day at a time."

Her mother was silent a moment. "I'm glad for you, honey. It sounds like you've met someone special. As for your dad, all I know is he'd better be home soon, or I *will* take a trip to Japan."

Chapter 38

Why the Hell Were
We Brought Here?

Thursday, January 31, 2002

The Westin Hotel, Sendai

The rap on the door was loud—too loud for four in the morning.

Frankie groggily rubbed his eyes and stumbled out of bed. He was prepared to scold whoever was responsible as he opened the door, but he was greeted by two hulking Japanese men in dark suits, telltale bulges under their jackets. He tried to scramble to the bedside phone, but they had him restrained before he could move more than a few feet. One of the bruisers gripping Frankie stood so close Frankie could smell his breath, which reeked of cigarettes and coffee.

The strangers made it clear through hand signals that Frankie should dress quickly, and he complied, realizing too late that he had put on mismatching shoes. A moment later, two more toughs brought a wide-eyed Takashi Kojo to the room. The first two men left and returned a few minutes later with Ellen in tow, her arms bent behind her. She had apparently taken exception to being so rudely disturbed at such an early hour and had put up a futile resistance before being frog-marched to Frankie's room.

The sight of his daughter being manhandled sent Frankie into a rage. He turned to Kojo. "What the hell is going on? Who are these assholes and what do they want?"

"I don't know, Frankie-san," Kojo stammered through clenched teeth. "They aren't saying much. Just giving commands. They want you to give them your cell phones and passports. They said to tell you to just do what they say, and no one will get hurt."

Ellen gave Frankie a reassuring nod. "I'm okay, Dad. Do what they say."

Frankie nodded, grimacing as he rubbed his shoulders to restore circulation. He thought he recognized a couple of the men from the fish market. They were acting like they wanted to take the three of them somewhere. If they'd come to kill them, Frankie reasoned, they would have done so by now. It was best to play along—at least until he could figure out what they wanted.

Phones and passports collected, the four men in suits hurried Frankie, Ellen, and Kojo out through the hotel service entrance, where two black Mercedes G-Class SUVs were waiting. The three of them were ordered into one of the vehicles, with Frankie taking the middle seat. Before he could get his bearings, one of their captors pulled a hood over his head, and with that, everything went black. All he could do was wince as he was bound to Ellen and Kojo via several zip ties, one of which pinched the back of his wrist as it was tightened.

Frankie felt the SUV tremble as two of the men, ostensibly their driver and whoever was riding shotgun, ducked inside. He strained to listen for clues but heard nothing more than doors being slammed shut.

He had to work hard to stay upright as the car lurched through the predawn streets of Sendai.

"One of them just used his cell phone to report the 'packages' have been picked up and will be delivered within the hour," Kojo whispered.

There was little banter between the men in front. Frankie noticed their captors hadn't tightened one of the zip ties around his wrist but didn't bother to wriggle free. The last thing he wanted to do was endanger Ellen further. He had no choice but to sit back and wait. He rode on in the dark, blindly wondering what was in store for them.

Adrenaline made the time pass quickly, and soon Frankie noticed the car gaining altitude. He could hear the engine straining and thought he felt a chill on his skin.

Ellen must have noticed the same thing. "Kojo, are there mountains nearby?"

They made another in a long series of twists and turns, but Kojo didn't answer.

"Kojo," Ellen whispered, this time with more urgency in her voice, "are you okay?"

The Japanese interpreter remained mute.

Same Day

Izumi Ward, Northwest of Sendai

Half an hour later, the tiny convoy came to a stop. Frankie heard the sound of a muffled voice and the metallic creak and squeal of an electric gate opening. A short distance later— Frankie reckoned it at about a half mile—they came to a final stop. Someone opened both passenger doors, starting with the one to Frankie's left, and cold air invaded the SUV. After his hood was removed, Frankie blinked at the bright, early morning light. The man with the bad breath cut the zip ties from their hands and ankles, and they were assisted out of the Mercedes, with Frankie exiting last.

Ellen's hunch had proven correct. They were surrounded by mountain peaks, the rosy dawn painting them in pale pastels.

Their captors escorted them to a heavy metal door, where two stern-faced guards stood aside and allowed them to enter.

"What is this place?" Frankie asked no one in particular. The cramped ride had left his thigh feeling like it was full of needles. He wished he had his Advil. He looked around and up at the ceiling, where a remote video camera was tracking their movements.

They were ushered through a corridor into an inner room that opened up into a larger room with comfortable leather chairs and a large fireplace with a crackling log fire.

Seated in one of those chairs was an older balding man with a toothbrush mustache and a patch over one eye. He appeared rather frail and was taking oxygen through a nasal cannula. Standing beside him was a younger man, very stylishly turned out, who smiled faintly at their arrival. Frankie recognized him from the fish market. Kojo's face was ashen as he tried to avoid eye contact with the two strangers.

With a curt motion, the younger man dismissed the two large escorts, who bowed crisply and left. He then turned to address Frankie, Ellen, and Kojo in flawless English. "First, I must apologize for the unceremonious manner in which you were brought here. It was necessary to avoid any unpleasantness or official embarrassment. My name is Masashi Tomonaga. The gentleman seated next to me is Kazuo Midorikawa. We are businessmen with extensive interests in this region of Japan."

"Well, happy to meet you, son," Frankie snarled. "But where are we, and why the hell were we brought here?"

Ellen and Kojo each shot him a cautionary glance.

"Ah. Right to the point. Very American. You must be . . ." Tomonaga glanced at Frankie as he riffled through the two passports the guards had handed to him. "Francisco Castillo. I understand that you are called Frankie. If so, may I?"

Frankie responded sullenly. "Sure. *¿Como no?* Everybody else does."

"*Entonces, te voy a saludar*, Frankie-san." Tomonaga's riposte through a teasing smile caught Frankie by surprise. "Yes, I speak Spanish, Mandarin, and Russian, as well as English— and, of course, Japanese, although among the foreign tongues, English is my favorite. Consequences of a Harvard education, I suppose.

"But, as you suggest, let's get down to business. You have asked quite reasonably where you are. You are on one of the lower slopes of Mount Izumiga Dake, some kilometers north and west of Sendai. It is a popular area for winter sports, so in the event you should ever plan to return to our lovely region, I think you will find the skiing quite good in January." Tomonaga gestured expansively. "This building is not in any official guidebook, because it does not officially exist. It was designed and built by the Imperial Japanese Army in the early 1940s and intended as a safe refuge for the emperor and his family, far from the Imperial Palace in Tokyo in case of air attack. Of course, that never became necessary inasmuch as General LeMay was ordered to avoid the Imperial Palace as a bombing target. The building and its underground facilities are not unlike structures built in America during the Cold War as a refuge for the essential elements of government in case of a nuclear attack on Washington. The underground bunker at the

Greenbrier Resort in West Virginia comes to mind. I believe that bunker is preserved as an historical artifact. By contrast, this facility fell into disuse in the postwar years, and it passed into private hands. It now serves as a secure corporate retreat."

Tomonaga's chattiness was starting to get on Frankie's nerves.

The man with the patch over his eye signaled an elderly woman and said something to her in Japanese. Another hasty communication in Japanese followed, this time between the old man and Tomonaga.

Tomonaga then advised the Castillos and Kojo to be seated. "Considering that you are our guests, your host, Midorikawa-san, wishes to extend you our hospitality. Tea and a light breakfast will be served."

Upon the mention of tea, Frankie brightened. "Have any manzanilla?"

Tomonaga nodded. "Of course." He requested that the woman bring Frankie several bags of chamomile.

Frankie caught Ellen smiling to herself. No doubt she was beginning to find this whole charade amusing. She had never lacked for moxie or grit. For his part, he was starting to feel better about his abductors. But there was something about that guy with the eye patch, the *tuerto*. He reminded Frankie of Frío's description of a camp guard. Frankie had quietly been trying to piece together a reason for their abduction and transfer to such a remote location. If it had to do with suspicions over their possible affiliation with a rival mob, it seemed excessive. There had to be something else at work here. He looked over at Kojo, but the poor fellow seemed frozen in fear.

As he enjoyed his steaming cup of chamomile, Frankie could feel the pain in the thigh easing, the warmth of the room so very welcome after the long, cold drive without coats. He looked over at Ellen and gave a half shrug. These yakuza guys didn't seem so bad, after all.

The unmistakable aroma of frying bacon filled the room. Within moments, the elderly Japanese woman had set out on a conference table a full spread of bacon, scrambled eggs, and toast. Frankie, who had endured one too many breakfasts of strange fish and rice so far on their trip, felt like he had died and gone to heaven.

Kazuo Midorikawa stood, removed the oxygen tubes, and approached the table. He spoke in Japanese to Tomonaga.

Tomonaga nodded and turned to Frankie and the others. "My chairman, Midorikawa-san, has something to say to you, and it will provide answers to many of your questions. I will translate for him."

Kazuo took a seat at the head of the table, and soon Tomonaga was relaying his words in English.

"We thought you might enjoy more typical American fare. I can't say it appeals to me, but I hope you find it satisfactory."

Kazuo paused for the expected appreciative nods, and looked on as Ellen and Frankie sat down to breakfast.

Tomonaga resumed his translating. "For several days, I have received reports about two Americans and their interpreter making inquiries in Shiogama about a particular person. Normally such a thing would not be of interest, but circumstances of which you are probably unaware gave us reason to look into the matter further. The person you are trying to locate, Soichiro Matsuhata, is a man who owns a prosperous fishing business. He happens to be a good friend of mine. May I ask what your business is with Matsuhata-san?" Kazuo's breathing was becoming more labored.

Frankie set his fork down and took a moment to organize his thoughts. Then he nodded to himself and addressed

Kazuo directly, making sure to speak slowly so Tomonaga could translate. "First, thank you for your hospitality. The breakfast is superb—and thoroughly appreciated. The reason for our being here arises from events more than a half century ago on Okinawa, where I served as a young soldier in the American army. After that battle, I met a young woman, an Okinawan woman who I cared for deeply. When I returned home to the US, alone, I lost contact with her. I told no one about her, but I never stopped wondering what had become of her. I knew I needed to find out for myself. I invited my daughter Ellen to come with me. While in Okinawa, I learned what had become of the woman, whose name is Noriko. I also learned for the first time that she had borne a daughter—*my* daughter. I was informed she had married a Japanese soldier named Matsuhata and that he was a fisherman, possibly from Sendai. I determined then and there that I couldn't return to the States without attempting to contact Noriko. My daughter and I didn't have much else to go on, so with Kojo-san's help, we began asking questions around the waterfront in Shiogama. Apparently that wasn't very smart, since we met with what could only be described as suspicion and hostility."

After patiently listening to Tomonaga's translation, the old man leaned forward, cleared his throat, and spoke once again in a raspy voice.

Tomonaga translated. "Yes, it was unwise—but for reasons that have nothing to do with you. Many of the fishermen are on edge due to the threat posed by a rival organization from the northern island. Accordingly, they are very distrustful of strangers. They were uncooperative because they wanted to protect their friend, Matsuhata-san, and they didn't know you or what your intentions were."

"I understand," Frankie said. "But there is more. Several days ago in Okinawa, I was approached by a man named Masterson, who said he knew how to reach Noriko. But he would not help me unless he made sure it was Noriko's wish to be contacted by me. Later, I received word from Masterson that, according to her husband, Noriko didn't wish to see me. But I couldn't accept that after going to such lengths to find her. So I decided to try to find her despite being told not to do so."

Tomonaga explained Frankie's response to Kazuo, and the old man's eye glistened with mischief as he let out a rumbling cackle.

"So it seems my old friend Matsuhata-san is in for quite a surprise," Tomonaga said, translating for him. "But what you say does sound like him. He is sometimes overly protective of Noriko-san. Believe me, I know. This should be interesting. I should tell you that Soichiro is an old army comrade who I regard as a brother. He and Noriko are very dear to me. If I had discerned anything but noble motives in your search for him, I wouldn't have hesitated to order a different sort of welcome."

Kazuo reached for his cell phone, and Tomonaga told Frankie and the others that Soichiro Matsuhata would be arriving within the hour.

Same Day

Sendai

Kume accepted the shot of whiskey from her father and then poured one for him in return. Whether a guest or the host, it was customary in Japan to never fill one's own glass. Her father, though, had surprised her with the offering.

Whiskey before breakfast, she mused.

Then again, Gary, too, had been full of surprises. They'd made the short flight from Tokyo to Sendai in his Gulfstream and had gone straight to her parents' home, where Gary so far had performed admirably. His halting Japanese greeting, rehearsed at length during the flight, had charmed her parents, and Kume had noticed an expression of tacit curiosity on her mother's face. Did she know this was more than an impromptu visit? Did Soichiro? Kume was grateful for her dad's hospitality, which contributed to a welcome thaw in what she had feared would be another frosty encounter with her mother. She could tell by her mother's surreptitious glances at Gary that she was trying to compare Gary's features with the face in the photograph she had found in Kume's apartment.

Gary raised his glass as the four stood together in the living room. "May I toast this, my first ever meeting with Kume's father and mother? It is my good fortune, and I wish good fortune and health to all present."

Kume answered, "Hear, hear," as they clinked glasses and exchanged smiles and bows.

The whiskey went down smoothly, despite the early hour. Soichiro rarely drank, Kume knew, but he typically had only the best on hand, should the occasion arise.

Soichiro's cell phone rang before Gary could finish. After closing the liquor cabinet, Soichiro signaled to Kume's mother that he would need to take the call privately and then answered his phone as he left the room.

Kume noticed her mother's oval-shaped face darken and saw the whites of her eyes as she glanced away. She'd seen that look before. Something was worrying her.

Soichiro returned before Kume could ask what was wrong. "That was Midorikawa. A car will be arriving to pick me up shortly. I apologize." He offered a curt bow to Gary.

"What's this about?" Kume asked.

"I don't know," her father answered. "The oyabun only said it was important—and that there were two people that he was sure I would want to meet."

Gary cocked his head to the side and gave a knowing smile. Did he know something Kume didn't? He turned to her father. "I'd like to join you, Matsuhata-san."

Soichiro raised both hands in protest. "Out of the question."

Gary, though, was adamant. "I think I have a pretty good idea what this is all about, and I won't take no for an answer."

Kume grabbed him by the arm and whispered into his ear, "I really don't think you should go. There's danger whenever the yakuza is involved. My father will be safe because of his close relationship with the oyabun. But you don't even know the language."

She should have known better.

"No way," Gary whispered back. "I'll be fine. And what better way to set the stage for our big announcement than to do a little male bonding with my future father-in-law?" He winked and reached for her hand, kissing her on the cheek. Before she could protest, he followed Soichiro toward the genkan.

A black Mercedes arrived moments later, and Kume watched from the front porch as the two large men occupying the car appeared to balk at Gary's inclusion. After studying him with suspicion, one of them got on his cell phone and, satisfied with the response from whomever he'd just called, grudgingly motioned Gary inside.

Kume exchanged worried glances with her mother and then waved goodbye to her fiancé.

Chapter 39

The Subject Is Gold

Same Day

The Bunker at Izumiga Dake

As the minutes passed, Frankie began to grow uneasy. How would Noriko's husband react when he arrived? Would he agree to let Frankie see her? What kind of a temper did the man have? Frankie vainly wished he'd been chauffeured to Noriko's home instead of left to argue his case here, isolated in the mountains and surrounded by well-armed muscle. The windowless bunker's sterile lighting, notwithstanding the warm glow from the fireplace, left him feeling cut off from the rest of the world.

He turned to Ellen, who sat silently beside him at the conference table. "How are you doing?"

She brushed her dark hair out of her eyes and offered a tight-lipped smile. It was clear she'd had about enough adventure for one trip. "Fine." She nodded to his thigh. "How are *you* doing?"

That was just like Ellen, he thought. Even when she found herself out of her comfort zone, she was still looking out for others, including her old man.

Frankie raised his cup of manzanilla, which he'd neglected after sitting down to breakfast. "I could do without all the drama, but the leg's holding up all right. I imagine you'd rather be back in Okinawa with Tony."

She drew back, her lips curling into an amused smile. "You actually said his name. I'm impressed."

Frankie allowed himself a small chuckle. "He's not so bad—for a lawyer."

"And an environmentalist," Ellen said with mock alarm, clearly needling him.

"Don't forget about his mob ties," Frankie replied.

The playful look on Ellen's face disappeared at the sound of the metal door opening on its squeaky hinges and then, a second later, slamming shut.

Frankie heard footsteps in the corridor and then in the anterior room just outside. A second later, an older Japanese man walked through the door. Trim, fit, with a broad nose and square jawline, he wore a baseball cap over his full head of silver hair. Towering over his right shoulder was Gary Masterson, dressed in an expensive suit as usual. Gary's eyes brightened when he recognized Frankie. The Japanese man, meanwhile, looked bewildered as he surveyed his surroundings. He'd obviously never been in the bunker.

That's got to be him, Frankie thought.

The man noticed Kazuo Midorikawa seated by the fireplace and gave him a questioning gaze.

Kazuo greeted Soichiro in Japanese.

Kojo, seemingly relaxed enough to finally do his job, translated. "He's telling him about you and how we've been looking for him down at the docks."

Kazuo addressed Frankie and Ellen directly in halting English. "Frankie-san and Ellen-san, this is Soichiro Matsuhata, my friend and the husband of Noriko." His next words were in Japanese. But Frankie recognized Gary Masterson's name.

Frankie rose to offer Soichiro a proper bow and then nodded to Gary.

"You know him?" Ellen said after joining her father and giving both men a bow.

"This is the man I told you about: Gary Masterson." He eyed Soichiro. "And this is Noriko's husband."

Soichiro's bushy eyebrows nearly met as he angrily rattled off a long string of sentences in Japanese.

Kojo intervened. "May I translate for you? Matsuhata-san is expressing great displeasure at your being here when it was made clear to you that your presence would not be welcome. By what right do you think you are entitled to come and disturb Noriko, a woman you abandoned more than fifty years ago?"

Frankie exhaled loudly. "I realize that I have no right to cause anyone discomfort. You are correct: I *did* leave her. And I was told by Gary that Noriko doesn't wish to see me. But maybe I'm becoming more stubborn in my old age. Noriko was very special to me many years ago. And I know I didn't do right by her. I came here in humility to tell her, myself, how terribly sorry I am."

Soichiro sputtered in English, "And you want her forgiveness?"

"If she is willing to bestow it, yes."

Soichiro removed his cap and slapped it on his thigh. He shook his head. "You ask too much. You should go back to America with your daughter. There is nothing for you here."

"And what about Kume?" Frankie wasn't about to back down. "Does she feel the same way?"

Soichiro's eyes widened in shock. Fists clenched at his side, he took a step toward Frankie.

Tomonaga, Kazuo's right-hand man, stepped between them, a scowl on his round face. "Please, gentlemen. Let's try to remain civil. Maybe this is not the way anyone imagined that you two would finally meet. But here we are, and we should be able to resolve this peacefully." Then, facing Soichiro, Tomonaga asked pointedly, "Does your wife have any idea that any of this is happening? Have you told her that Frankie-san has made a very long trip to find her?" He followed up the question in Japanese.

Gary, meanwhile, took Frankie by the arm. "These guys are armed to the teeth. Not exactly the welcoming committee I was expecting."

"You and me both," Frankie said with a grunt.

Kazuo raised his hand to silence the room. "Enough of this kabuki soap opera. If you men wish to have it out, please do so some other time and somewhere else. We have much more serious matters to attend to, and we haven't the luxury of time." He turned toward Soichiro. "My friend, Matsuhata-san, this place is alien to you, I know. You have never been here, and there are reasons for that. I just ask that you trust me and allow Tomonaga-san to explain." He gestured for Tomonaga to take over.

Tomonaga ordered everyone to gather around the fire-place, beside which Kazuo was already seated.

Frankie waited for Ellen to take a seat in a plush-looking chair across from Kazuo and then eased himself down in the chair beside her. Kojo remained standing but drew closer. Gary and Soichiro took seats to the left of Kazuo and the fireplace.

Tomonaga ran a hand over his shaved head. His scowl softened as he did his best to convey his boss's words. "Two days ago, we received information from an informant within a rival organization in Hokkaido that an assassination attempt would soon be made against Midorikawa-san. The purpose would obviously be preemptive: to behead the Midorikawa organization and take advantage of the absence of leadership to move into our territory. The same source reported that an attempt would also be made against Matsuhata-san's life to serve as an example to anyone who would dare defy the Hokkaido organization, as he did in the recent conflict over the fishing grounds."

Gary turned toward Soichiro in alarm, but from where Frankie sat, Noriko's husband didn't appear surprised.

"Disagreements like this between two groups that have for many years coexisted within their respective spheres of influence can usually be resolved," Tomonaga continued. "What makes it different and more dangerous this time is the introduction of foreigners into the equation. Our sources tell us that North Korean manpower and arms have entered the picture on the side of the Hokkaido syndicate. It is no secret that Pyongyang loves to find ways to subvert and embarrass Tokyo. What better way to do so than by exercising a shadowy influence over our northernmost prefecture?"

The oyabun, wheezing slightly, interrupted Tomonaga in English. "What Masashi-san has not told you is that there is also a more practical side to the picture that requires a bit of historical background. This will take some time, so if you will permit me . . ." He drew deeply from the oxygen mask. "The subject is gold."

Frankie, never one to give a good poker face, couldn't hide the incredulity he was feeling. Here he was, locked away in some bunker in the mountains, listening to a one-eyed crime boss spin a tale about rival gangs and . . . gold. He let his eyes drift from Ellen, who was wide-eyed and apparently just as flummoxed, to Gary, who, in stark contrast, had just uncrossed his leg and inched forward on the edge of his seat. Did he know something? Kazuo had certainly gotten his attention.

The old man continued with his story, this time in Japanese.

Tomonaga translated. "Several years before the attack on Pearl Harbor, the Bank of Japan shipped more than six hundred tons of its gold reserves to the United States. This was seen as prudent at the time, to move the bullion to a secure location like Fort Knox, where other nations also keep their reserves. Ironically, that gold ended up serving as collateral for the costs of preparing for war against the US. Of course, after 1941, all Japanese assets in the US were frozen, but Japan still had adequate domestic reserves of bullion for the war effort. During the war, some of that gold was transported by sea to the Third Reich in exchange for technology and scientific assets, like jet and rocket engines. Substantial amounts were lost when some of those ships and submarines were sunk by US ships. Most of the gold has never been recovered.

"In late 1944, the war cabinet decided that what remained of the Imperial bullion should be taken to a hidden repository for safekeeping. An old mine shaft in the mountains of Akita was selected to house it, and an elite unit of the emperor's own guards was entrusted with the transfer. A truck convoy was assembled under strict secrecy and a heavy escort. The commander in charge was Colonel Hiroshi Tsuchiya, a decorated combat veteran but one who had concluded that the war was lost and had plans of his own for a portion of the shipment. Thousands of kilograms of ingots were loaded in wooden crates and driven overnight to the mine. I know this because I was there when it arrived. I knew the mine foreman, an unpleasant man and a relative of Colonel Tsuchiya, who was responsible for accepting the gold and having it placed in a secure location deep underground. To all outward appearances, the mine was being operated by Mitsubishi for the sole purpose of extracting copper ore for the war effort, and a number of American captives had been brought from the Philippines to provide labor. I was there to guard those prisoners. So the cover was perfect. No one would guess that a fortune in gold was being buried there."

Tomonaga paused, apparently tripped up by something he was translating, and then picked up the pace, having fallen behind.

"While en route, some say Colonel Tsuchiya managed to divert over five hundred kilograms of bullion to this very building where we are standing. I suppose it's possible, since this was what I believe you Americans call a 'black site,' and he knew very well that only he and a select few others were aware of its existence. As the story goes, the gold stash remained hidden in one of the interior chambers until Tsuchiya managed to return and collect it during the confusion at the war's end. Supposedly it served as seed money to finance his own yakuza enterprise in Hokkaido."

Kazuo's strength was clearly flagging. He paused to take some oxygen, and waved Tomonaga off when he looked concerned. "Let me finish," he said before reverting to Japanese.

Tomonaga continued with his translating. "Colonel Tsuchiya died years ago, but his sons, who succeeded him as leaders of the Hokkaido yakuza, had grand ambitions to expand their influence into the Tohoku region of Honshu. They had learned from their father about the bullion transfer to the Hanawa mine. They also knew that it was buried in a cave-in that occurred in 1945 and has never been recovered.

They decided to approach North Korea's supreme leader, Kim Jong-il, to see if a collaboration was possible."

Frankie had to interrupt. "Kim Jong-il? As in, the tin-pot dictator?" This was getting crazier by the minute.

Kazuo nodded and continued. "A deal was struck by which the Democratic People's Republic of Korea would supply arms and muscle to the Tsuchiya yakuza in its drive to displace our organization and assume control of parts of Akita, Iwate, and Miyagi," Tomonaga said. "In return, the North Koreans would be allowed access to the old mine, where they believed they could employ advanced high-speed drilling equipment to recover the bullion. The value at today's prices is estimated at between three and five billion dollars, a tidy sum for a regime as corrupt and impoverished as North Korea."

The oyabun sneered before resuming his story.

"Can't even feed its own people," Tomonaga said, although a translation was hardly necessary. "So there you have it. Probably more than you bargained for, but it's important that you know what is happening here and why we have taken precautions. No doubt you noticed the presence of armed kyodai as you arrived. We believe the threat is imminent. I will arrange for your safe transportation back to Sendai. Matsuhata-san, you should immediately collect Noriko and Kume and leave for Tokyo. You will be told when it's safe to return. Masterson-san, I assume that is your Gulfstream at the airport."

As Gary nodded, Frankie stood up. The part that concerned American POWs transferred from the Philippines to work the old mine was bothering him. He wondered if those prisoners might possibly have included Frío and his brother, Ramón. *And this old mob boss with the patch over one eye, the tuerto, said he was a guard. Too many coincidences.*

With palms outstretched, Frankie opened his mouth to speak but was cut short when the crump of a muffled explosion shook the room. Then the lights went out, leaving only the flickering fire to cast shadows.

As the hum of an emergency generator commenced and the lights came back on, Tomonaga answered a call on his cell phone. Then he crisply began giving orders in Japanese and English. He turned to Frankie and Ellen. "Too late to leave now. We are closing the steel front doors. The enemy has arrived sooner than expected, and our kyodai and *shatei* are already engaged at the outer defenses near the roadside. The attackers appear to be North Korean commandos armed with automatic weapons and rocket-propelled grenades. Our men have good cover, but we didn't have time to bring up our large-caliber guns from Sendai yesterday. We are outgunned and outnumbered. Our defenders are fifteen strong. They estimate that the attackers number between twenty-five and thirty."

Frankie glanced at Ellen, who stared back, her sky-blue eyes wide with alarm. He turned to Kojo and saw he was shaking like a leaf. He caught sight of the elderly Japanese woman who had served them earlier. She was flat-footed and frozen in place, perhaps reliving some kind of trauma from decades long past.

"Too many civilians," Frankie muttered. "And I'm one of 'em." He got Tomonaga's attention. "Where can I take them?"

"Kitchen." Tomonaga said something in rapid-fire Japanese to the old woman. "She'll lead you there." He stopped Frankie and pointed to Soichiro, also seemingly transfixed by the sound of explosions and gunfire outside. "Take him, too."

Frankie nodded and, teaming with Ellen to gather Soichiro and Kojo, followed the old woman down a pair of corridors, the first one familiar, deeper into the bunker. A moment later they entered what looked like a commercial kitchen, complete with swinging doors. Frankie spotted the stove top where breakfast had been cooked. Dirty dishes had been stacked haphazardly near a stainless steel serving tray.

Kojo was the last to enter, and as the group followed the old woman into a well-stocked pantry on the far side of the kitchen, Frankie wondered what had become of Masterson. He wasn't exactly a soldier, either. *He better not try to play hero.*

As removed from the fighting as he and the others were, Frankie could still hear the sound of automatic gunfire. Explosions rocked the bunker at regular intervals. Mortars? RPGs? He couldn't quite tell. But he knew enough to know they might not remain safely hidden in the pantry if the attackers made it into the bunker.

He took Ellen's hand and whispered hoarsely, "I'm sorry I dragged you into this."

Ellen shrugged her shoulders. "You can apologize later— *after* we get out of this mess."

Just then a concussive blast—louder than those that had preceded it—shook the building, and suddenly the gunfire sounded close at hand and no longer muffled. Repeated blasts from a shotgun stood out against automatic rifle and small-arms fire.

"They're in the building," Frankie whispered.

Soichiro hurried to the pantry door and cracked it just as the main kitchen doors could be heard swinging open. He turned back to the others. "Only one," he said in heavily accented English. "Heavily armed."

Frankie reached for Soichiro's shoulder but was too late. The silver-haired man opened the door just wide enough to slip noiselessly into the main kitchen.

"Son of a bitch," Frankie muttered under his breath, and before he knew it, he was following Soichiro into harm's way.

A black-clad commando armed with a stockless AK-47 had his back to them and was using the barrel of his rifle to open the huge storage cupboards under the kitchen's island. He turned just as Soichiro came at him with his right hand raised to deliver an incapacitating blow.

The next few seconds went by in a blur for Frankie, and by the time he was cognizant again, he realized he was holding a still-vibrating serving tray in both hands and the commando was lying on his back on the tiled floor. Frankie's ears were still ringing from the gunfire, and he looked to his right and saw a bleeding Soichiro, also prone, a few feet from the commando.

The commando, tricked out in all black, began to stir, and Frankie spotted the man's AK-47, which had skidded across the floor upon impact. Frankie had just enough time to hurry to it and turn. He felt it recoil and the muzzle jump as he squeezed the trigger, and the charging commando crumpled to the floor for good.

"Dad!" Ellen rushed to Frankie.

He held her close with his free arm, which, like the rest of him, was taut. "I didn't have a choice. He came at me." Frankie couldn't take his eyes off the dead commando and the spreading pool of blood.

"I know."

Kojo knelt down beside Soichiro and looked up at the others, clearly unsure what to do. Frankie glanced around and realized Kazuo's elderly assistant had disappeared. He began searching the cupboards for paper towels, napkins—anything to stanch the bleeding. But before he could find anything, the old woman returned with compresses and a roll of gauze.

She moves fast, Frankie thought. He gazed down quietly at Soichiro as she treated his shoulder, which was covered in blood.

Then he heard it.

"Is that swordplay?" he whispered in disbelief.

Ellen's eyes widened as they listened down the hallway.

Frankie couldn't believe his ears. The distinctive sound of metal against metal echoed from the main conference room.

"You stay here," he told Ellen and the others.

"Don't you dare!" Ellen whispered in a scolding voice.

He didn't turn around to argue with her. Instead, armed with the AK-47, he hurried out of the kitchen and down the corridor, following a trail of bodies to the conference room. By the time he had arrived, the swords had fallen silent. Standing over a decapitated body and holding a *shin gunto* sword with the Imperial chrysanthemum on the pommel was Tomonaga, sweat dripping down his face, jacket having long since been removed. Kazuo lay on his side in the corner beside an over-turned chair.

"Hey, Frankie."

Frankie wheeled to his left and spotted Gary Masterson seated with his back against the wall and his legs extended. Blood oozed from beneath his rib cage. He was armed with a sawed-off shotgun.

"You made quite a bit of noise with that thing," Frankie quipped.

"I did," Gary said, his dimple showing as he smiled weakly.

Frankie recognized the feverish look on his face. He was at risk of going into shock. He'd need help soon, or things might go south.

Frankie turned to call for Ellen, but she was already rushing toward Gary.

She knelt, applied a compress to his wound, and then looked up at Frankie, her eyes shooting daggers. "Can we go home now?"

Frankie nodded soberly. He would never forgive himself for putting his daughter in harm's way. Was this what his obsession had led to? Another battle to occupy his nightmares?

Soichiro entered the room with a bandage on his shoulder. Kazuo's surprisingly spry assistant was supporting most of his weight. Her expression remained stoic as she guided him to where Kazuo lay dying of his wounds.

Frankie knelt with them beside Kazuo.

The oyabun eyed the AK-47, now slung over Frankie's shoulder. "Thank you, comrade in arms. You didn't have to join the fight, but you did."

"I didn't do much," Frankie protested.

"Maybe." Kazuo motioned Frankie to come closer. "You remind me of a man I knew during the war, a brave man, an Amerika-jin samurai."

Frankie drew back, confused. Who was Kazuo talking about? Was he delusional?

Kazuo turned to Soichiro and spoke softly in Japanese, while the old woman looked on but said nothing.

In the time it took Frankie to hurry to the kitchen to retrieve a crate of bottled water from the pantry, Kazuo breathed his last. Soichiro sat beside his dead body.

The old woman was already assisting Ellen with another makeshift field dressing. Gary, thankfully, appeared to have stabilized.

Frankie glanced down at his mismatched shoes, which he'd forgotten about since their abduction. Then he noticed the time on his watch. A mere eighteen minutes had passed since the beginning of the attack. Judging by the ache in his thigh and the sticky sweat gluing the back of his shirt to his skin, it felt like it had lasted much longer. An unnerving silence had taken hold, but it soon gave way to blaring sirens and the whapping of helicopter blades. A Japanese SWAT team was on its way.

As excited commands were issued from a bullhorn outside, Frankie handed one of the bottles to Soichiro.

Soichiro took a sip and then grasped Frankie's forearm and whispered, "*Arigato gozaimasu.*"

Frankie smiled and squeezed his hand. "*De nada.*"

Chapter 40

Reunion

Friday, February 1, 2002

Tohoku University Hospital

Frankie was in Soichiro's room in the ICU, two doors down from Gary's, when he saw her.

He had nodded off briefly, lulled to sleep by the quiet hum of machines, and when he looked up from his chair, his gaze met hers. She stood in the doorway, and for a brief moment, he was cast into the past, to a life long gone, to a place he'd never imagined he would return. She stared back at him, eyes full of doubt. She still had the same petite figure, though fuller; the same symmetrical, oval-shaped face, though bearing the weight of so many decades; the same elegant beauty, now augmented by the nobility of her advancing years. She wore a long black skirt, a cream-colored blouse, and a black sweater fastened with only the top button.

Before he could speak, a younger woman appeared off Noriko's right shoulder. She was just as she'd looked in the photo Gary had shown Frankie back in Okinawa: tall, slender, stylish. Her medium-length pixie cut framed a delicate, round face. She had legs a mile long. *Kume.* She held her mother's arm, her eyes hidden behind dark sunglasses. Behind them were two policemen in Kevlar, automatic weapons at the ready.

Soichiro, who was still attached to an IV, stirred from his drug-induced rest. "Nori-chan! Kume-san! Please, come close."

Frankie stood abruptly to make room for Noriko and Kume as they rushed to Soichiro's bedside.

Soichiro's delight at seeing his wife and daughter appeared boundless, no doubt enhanced in part by the morphine in his bloodstream. Noriko held his hand and brushed her lips against his. He touched her face with his free hand. His other hand was confined in a sling, ostensibly there to limit his movement and thus protect his shoulder.

Noriko spoke to him in rapid-fire Japanese, the affection and admonition evident in her voice.

Frankie turned to leave, determined not to spoil such a tender reunion. The only thing outdueling his racing heart was his thigh, which was presently screaming at him. He needed another Advil.

"Frankie-san," Soichiro said in broken English. "You stay." He said something in Japanese to Kume, who turned awkwardly to face Frankie.

"My father doesn't want you to go," she said and removed her sunglasses, revealing beautiful, red-rimmed eyes.

Frankie couldn't help wincing at her use of the word *father*. Kume was his biological daughter, but her heart belonged to the man who had raised her. *Just as it should be*, he told himself. He smiled awkwardly. "Are you sure?"

"My wife," Soichiro said, once again struggling to put his thoughts into English. "She call me a silly old war-horse. Say this what happens when I be with gangsters. Say I could have been killed."

"She's right," Frankie said with a smile. "We both got lucky."

"Not luck," Soichiro said. "Fate."

Frankie smiled again, and as he did, he caught Noriko gazing at him with an odd mixture of curiosity and coolness. She offered him an understated bow and then exchanged words with her husband.

When the conversation dragged on, Kume stepped in to translate. "My father says he owes you his life."

Soichiro wasn't finished, and Frankie could tell by the tears rolling down Noriko's cheeks that something had touched her deeply.

"Now what's he saying?" Frankie asked.

"He says the drugs are making him feel light-headed," Kume said with a laugh. Her smile disappeared, replaced by a wistful frown. "He also says Midorikawa-san was happy to die like a samurai, not an invalid. Before he passed, he told my father he was at peace and that he would soon see Michiko, his bride he lost during the war. He wanted my father to convey to my mother his apologies for all the crude remarks he made over the years. That's why she's crying now."

So that was what Kazuo had said to Soichiro in his final moments, Frankie thought. He noticed Kume's quivering lower lip. He had a hunch she'd rarely seen her mother cry before—if ever. The two women hugged Soichiro just as a medical team arrived. Soichiro was going to be transferred to a hospital in Tokyo, where he would spend his recovery. His injury had been less serious than Gary's multiple wounds, which meant he was already fit for travel.

Frankie nodded to Soichiro. "I'll see you in Tokyo."

Soichiro, still enveloped by his wife and daughter, nodded back weakly.

Frankie waited until the medical team had transferred Soichiro to a gurney and rolled him out of the room. Then tentatively, sheepishly, he turned to Noriko and Kume. After spotting the crucifix around Noriko's neck, he made a gesture as though to reach for it, but Noriko covered it with her hand.

He turned to Kume. "I've never met you, but Gary has said many wonderful things about you. What your fiancé did back there . . ." Frankie resisted the urge to castigate the man for his courage. "Well, from the sounds of it, he was something else."

Gary had been more or less unconscious since arriving at the hospital, but Frankie had spoken with him before he was loaded onto a medevac. Apparently, he had insisted on joining the fight back at the bunker. Tomonaga had handed him a shotgun, and Gary, acting on pure adrenaline, had taken out two of the commandoes after they breached the bunker and entered the conference room. But in the process of defending Kazuo, Gary had taken three bullets to the abdomen. Two had passed clean through. The other had required surgery last night to remove it. Soon he would follow Soichiro to Tokyo for his recovery. His prognosis appeared good.

Kume smiled through her tears. "Thanks." She watched her mother warily.

Frankie addressed them both. "I have no good reason to suddenly appear like this and upend your life. Soichiro was right. My purpose in coming was selfish, to alleviate a great sense of shame over what I did fifty-five years ago. I had no idea it would haunt me for all these years."

Noriko's face showed no emotion. She glanced at Kume and then returned her steady gaze to Frankie. "I remember you were called Dos Equis." She traced two imaginary *X*s in the air with her finger and then waved the hand dismissively. "When you left, it felt as though you had died. I mourned. It took a long time to get over the feeling of loss, of being abandoned. But I made myself believe that it had all been a fantasy—a make-believe world where heroes lived and endings were always happy. I learned a valuable lesson: that the world is harsh, especially when one has the duty to care for a new life." She paused as if searching for the right words.

Frankie stood mute, unable to hide his despair.

Noriko turned to Kume. "And for that reason, my daughter, I have not been the mother you deserved. I buried the past, where stories didn't end happily ever after. Every time I looked at you, I saw the features of the man who had saved and then demolished my world. And I resented you for that. I couldn't tell you about your American father, and I hated that you wanted to know. Still, I wanted to protect you from the fear and sadness and heartbreak I had experienced. And in Gary Masterson, I saw the very personification of that. For all of this, I am so, so very sorry."

Frankie's tongue felt numb, thick. What could he say? He considered leaving so the two women could hash out the past together.

But as he turned to go, Noriko turned back to him and reached for his arm. "I understand that you have suffered, and perhaps your intention in coming was selfish. But I think you also wanted to assure yourself that mine had been a happy ending, after all. I prefer to think that was the real reason."

Frankie nodded abjectly. "It's true. And I wanted to tell you, in person, that I'm sorry. I also wanted you to understand that you meant more to me than you think—and that I did love you."

With a whimsical tilt of her head, Noriko offered a demure smile. "I knew that. And you should know that, for whatever wrong you feel you committed, I forgive you. Some-times things are so obvious that they are easy to miss. You saved me once, in Okinawa, when I might easily have died along with my classmates in the Student Medical Corps. You literally brought me back to life and gave me hope. It was that hope and good fortune that permitted me to meet Soichiro, my husband, a good and honorable man who I love very much. He has been a wonderful father to Kume.

"And now you have saved me a second time. You saved the life of my husband, and for that I owe you everything." With outstretched arms, she approached Frankie, who by then was emotionally spent. She beckoned to Kume to join them, saying, "My daughter, meet your American father."

Frankie's eyes filled with tears, the tension in his body draining away as he swayed, hugging Noriko and his daughter.

Chapter 41

Comeuppance

While her father was stable enough to be transferred to Tokyo, Kume's fiancé was facing a longer recovery. Gary had lost a frightening amount of blood in yesterday's ordeal and, after being rushed to the hospital, had endured several hours of complicated surgery to remove the bullet and repair his insides. She stared down at his pale face and wished he hadn't proven her fears correct.

"Always ready to jump in with both feet," she whispered.

She took a seat in the hard plastic chair beside his bed and reflected on his years of living dangerously. There had been the racing phase, when his love affair with speed had nearly put him in a coffin. And there had been the more recent playboy phase. Adventurers. Athletes. From the sounds of it, he'd made a habit of courting beautiful women—all younger than him— willing to live life in the fast lane.

But she knew he'd always been chasing her. Their infant son's death had driven them apart, the despair too toxic to share. But somewhere deep inside she'd known she still loved him—and that he still loved her. His marriage proposal, though seemingly delivered on a lark, had been a long time in coming.

Her eyes wandered from Gary's damp forehead to the cool white ceiling and the overhead lighting, currently dimmed. The steady din just outside Gary's room—shoes squeaking on the tile floor, carts with wobbly wheels zooming past, voices echoing down the corridors—seemed to stop at the door. Here, beside her husband-to-be, Kume felt a strange sense of calm. She'd lost him once. She didn't plan to do so ever again.

Frankie glanced at Ellen, who had nodded off in her chair beside him in the waiting room, and then at the two armed guards posted nearby. They were just doing their job, he knew, but that didn't make it any easier to accept their lingering presence. The two men, neatly groomed and standing erect, wore navy-blue Kevlar vests over their light blue dress shirts and stared straight ahead at the bank of windows on the far wall. Nothing was visible outside beyond the well-lit entryway; the sun had gone down about an hour earlier, leaving in its wake a blue-black landscape.

The Japanese authorities were insisting that Frankie wasn't under arrest—not yet, anyway. But the fact that he *might* be in legal jeopardy for simply defending himself and his daughter, among others, left him grinding his teeth. He hardly knew the Japanese language, much less the country's laws or customs, but he knew steer manure when he smelled it. Something stunk. The authorities so far had been tightlipped about the battle back at Kazuo's bunker and were treating him with an unsettling degree of suspicion.

Frankie leaned back and closed his eyes, but before he could fall asleep in the chair, whose rigid armrests were conspiring to prevent rest anyway, he sensed a hand on his shoulder and started.

"Catching up on your beauty sleep?"

He straightened and found himself staring up at Iwo Joe and Tony Wagner.

Joe's eyes were full of mirth. Tony's? Nothing but concern. The man hurried straight to Ellen, who was rousing on the chair next to Frankie.

"You wanna grab a bite to eat?" Joe asked, rubbing his protruding belly.

"Sure," Frankie said and nodded to the two lovebirds next to him. "So long as we can pry them apart."

Tony, having knelt in front of Ellen, held her face in his hands. His brown eyes searched hers. "I'm so glad you're okay."

"I'm fine," she said before delivering a passionate kiss that made Frankie and Joe turn away.

Frankie didn't know whether to be touched or find the nearest bathroom.

The four eventually made their way to the hospital's twenty-four-hour cafeteria, a brightly lit space with a picture menu above the self-service food counter, and once again, Frankie found himself staring at an unappetizing meal.

"I think I'm going to die," he complained as he pondered the dish of rice and raw fish.

Ellen was wolfing down hers with chopsticks while Tony looked on in amusement. "Don't be such a baby," she responded. "The food here is actually pretty good."

"So Masterson's going to be okay?" Joe asked Frankie.

Frankie nodded and picked at his rice. "I don't think he'll be playing tennis anytime soon, but yeah, they dug out the bullet and stitched him up. Should be sending him to Tokyo in a few days." He thought a moment. "I wish someone would tell us what's going on. The cops just say that the investigation is continuing, but no charges have been brought. And those kids from the consular office, why can't they give us a straight story? 'Yes, Mr. Castillo,'" Frankie mimicked. "'We're working on getting your passports back. Yes, the State Department in Washington is fully aware of the situation. Rest assured we're doing all we can.'"

Joe acknowledged the armed guards, who had followed them to the café and were standing beside the entrance.

"You like our tail?" Frankie asked. "They go wherever we go."

Joe ran a hand over his balding head. "Rumor has it you two are Mexican cartel operators in league with Hokkaido yakuza. Supposedly you started a heavy gunfight to push aside another yakuza and move into the territory. I know, you can't make this stuff up. It's all about politics—and keeping North Korea out of the picture."

Ellen put down her chopsticks and frowned. "So what do you suggest? Do you know any good criminal defense lawyers? What the hell is the State Department doing? Does anyone around here want to know the truth?"

"Well, Kojo, for one," Joe said. "He went to the police authorities, who wouldn't listen, and so he told me he plans to go see the Tokyo bureau chief for the *Washington Post*. He wants to tell the whole story. Pretty brave. The government could make life difficult for him."

Frankie cocked his head in surprise. "I didn't know the fellow had it in him. He could have hightailed it out of there and never looked back after the shooting stopped. Tell him if things go bad for him over here, I've got a job for him in construction back in New Mexico—that is assuming I'm not making license plates in Japan."

Joe motioned to Tony. "Tony here says he knows someone who might be able to help."

Tony nodded. "I have some JAG friends who can give me some leads on good Japanese defense lawyers, and I'd be willing to bet that your new yakuza friends could recommend some pretty good lawyers, if things come to that. But for now, I suggest you just cool your heels. Let's see if any of the wheels in motion produce any results. You have to think that Tokyo is in a quandary. They know the truth, but the NoKo involvement isn't something they want out on the front page. The government isn't ready to quash the fairy-tale tabloid stuff until they come up with a better face-saving narrative that doesn't rile Pyongyang. They still have some maneuvering room, since at this point, there's been no official statement released about the episode. But pressure for Tokyo to say something is building."

Son of a bitch, Frankie thought. *The guy knows his stuff.*

Joe turned to Frankie. "That's good advice. Outside of engineering a jailbreak, I don't see any other choice. In the meantime, try some of the sushi. Don't fight it. You might end up liking it."

Later that night, after Joe and Tony had left for the evening, Frankie was relieved when an administrator arranged for him and Ellen to occupy one of the hospital's unused suites. They had to share a bathroom, and only a curtain separated their "rooms." But at least he'd be sleeping on a bed tonight—*after*

he took a shower. He couldn't wait to wash off the previous thirty-six hours.

First, though, he needed to face the moment he'd been dreading since yesterday's adventure.

He stepped through the curtain, still partially open, and waved his cell phone at Ellen. "It's time I called your mother. I'll stay here. I may need you nearby."

Ellen looked up from the contents of her overnight bag, which she'd strewn across her bed and was currently reorganizing, and nodded but said nothing. While confiscating their passports from Tomonaga, the police had been kind enough to retrieve their belongings from the hotel and bring them to the hospital.

Frankie heard the phone trilling and realized, too late, that it was six a.m. back home. *Oh well,* he thought. *At least I didn't wake her with another nightmare.* He smiled bitterly. This *was* a nightmare.

Melanie's voice came on, thick with drowsy disorientation. "Frankie, is it you?"

In spite of himself, he felt his voice catch. "Yes, gorgeous. It's me."

He could hear the rustling of bedcovers and Melanie scrambling to full wakefulness. "Where are you? Are you and Ellen okay?"

"Yes, we're okay. We've been involved in some unplanned excitement. I'll put Ellen on in a minute. But for now, I need to have your full attention, because what I have to say is important." Frankie drew a deep breath and began. "I've kept a secret I've told no one since I came home from the war. It's about a woman."

He heard Melanie inhale sharply with a slight squeak.

"She was a native Okinawan girl I helped after the battle ended. She and I grew close. I was her protector. We became

331

intimate. I knew it was wrong because you were home waiting for me. She probably thought I would stay with her, but I had to leave." Frankie paused and watched his hand that was clenching and unclenching. He pictured the face of Noriko on the dock that day the picture was taken. "I left her behind and tried not to think about it. I was going home. For the next fifty years, I buried it, and it never crossed my mind.

"Then a few years ago, the dreams began. They were torture because I knew—really knew deep inside—that it wasn't PTSD or stuff like that. It was my conscience saying to me that I had done a great wrong. Then the Frío business brought it to the surface, and I realized that I had no choice. I needed to find the girl, Noriko, or at least find out what had happened to her."

Melanie was silent for several seconds. "So you concocted this cock-and-bull story about seeing the old battlefield and putting the ghosts to rest."

Frankie clenched his jaw. "Yes."

"And did you find Noriko?"

"Yes, love. I found her. But not before I found out that she had a daughter, *my* daughter, that she never told me about. I met her, too. Her name is Kume, and she's beautiful."

"Well, I hear that's what happens when you fuck around with someone. But it must have been heartwarming having a little family reunion." Melanie's sarcasm felt like a splash of acid. "So what are your plans, Frankie-san? Do you intend to stay or come home?"

Frankie could feel the air going out of the room, but he was determined to finish. "Yes, of course I plan to come home. But that's where it gets complicated." He explained the train of events that had resulted in the gun battle and the subsequent problem with the Japanese authorities.

"Are you under arrest?"

"No. We haven't been charged with anything. But they're holding our passports. It's sort of like house arrest."

"So how long will that be?"

"I have no idea."

"Let me talk to Ellen."

Frankie handed the phone over to their daughter. He felt deflated by Melanie's coldness. He desperately wanted a drink. He listened to Ellen explaining the fight and his involvement.

"Love you, Mom," Ellen said. "Everything's going to be fine." She handed the phone back to Frankie, one eyebrow arched. She was clearly enjoying his comeuppance.

"It's a lot to deal with, and I'll need some time," Melanie said. "At least now I know. You *have* told me everything, haven't you?"

"Yes," Frankie answered with a sigh. "That's all."

Gary, to Frankie's astonishment, was already up and moving two days later. Frankie and Kume joined him Sunday morning for a short stroll down the corridor, wheeled IV pole in tow. Some of the color had returned to his face, but judging by his shuffling steps and shallow breaths, he was still a long way from getting his strength back.

"Gotta hand it to you, white boy," Frankie said, "you're pretty tough for someone who wears a suit all day."

Gary offered a feeble smile and nodded to his fiancée. "It helps to have someone in your corner."

Kume tucked her arm under his. "You okay?"

"Doc says I can handle this," Gary said with his chin up.

Frankie was still getting used to the notion of having another daughter. He'd had a handful of interactions with Kume at the hospital and had felt excited one minute and awkward the next. Ellen, on the other hand, seemed to have bonded almost instantly with Kume. The two had spent several hours talking in the waiting room and had even gone out for a couple of meals. Meanwhile, the word from Noriko, who had followed her husband to the hospital in Tokyo, was that Soichiro was fit to be tied. The old man had already tired of being a patient, apparently.

Gary paused when they reached the far end of the corridor. "Kume tells me you're in legal limbo." He hesitated. "Come to think of it, I may be, too, I suppose."

"At least you aren't under armed guard," Frankie observed.

This brought a faint chuckle. "I guess they don't see me as a flight risk at the moment." He glanced at the two uniformed officers who had been following Frankie around. They had stopped a discreet distance away. Gary lowered his voice. "I may be able to help."

Frankie shook his head. "I appreciate it, but you need to focus on your recovery."

Gary frowned in irritation. "Nonsense. I've already spoken with a friend in DC. I asked him to pull some strings."

"Oh?" Frankie was skeptical. He'd heard similar things from Tony and even Joe over the past two days, but so far no one had been able to break the logjam that was keeping them from leaving. Their lousy timing didn't help. Since Friday afternoon, everyone who might have been able to assist them had clocked off for the weekend, which meant nothing could be done until Monday morning at the earliest.

Regardless, the problem, as far as Frankie understood it, could be boiled down to politics. There was nothing he hated more. The shootout had created a potential international embarrassment for the Japanese, and Frankie was an unwitting pawn in whatever machinations were going on behind closed doors. Would he end up being charged? What about Ellen? Would the authorities cook up some story so they could charge her with something, too?

"His name's Nathan Goldman," Gary said. "Trust me when I say he has some clout."

"Who is he?" Frankie asked.

"Just an old friend of mine who happens to work at the State Department."

"Uh-huh." Frankie was far from convinced. "What's he do there?"

"Undersecretary, Asian affairs."

Frankie raised an eyebrow. "Well, at least he knows the neighborhood."

Gary started back the way they'd come, a look of resolution on his face. "Have a little faith, Frankie." He turned to Kume with a crooked smile. "Sometimes things work out the way they're supposed to."

Chapter 42

La Cueva Dorada

Monday, April 1, 2002

Capitán, New Mexico

The date struck Frankie as ironic. Exactly fifty-seven years earlier, he had boarded the lurching amtrac for the opening attack on Okinawa. It had been Easter Sunday. Some of the GIs had preferred to think of it as April Fool's Day.

Now it was time to bury the ghosts of World War II.

Andrew Mondragón greeted Frankie and Melanie at the door of the small, roughhewn home set against the backdrop of the Sacramento Mountains. "You really didn't have to bring my grandfather's memoir back to me personally," he said, though he seemed genuinely pleased that Frankie had insisted on delivering the document himself.

"As a matter of fact," Frankie replied, "I think it was necessary. What Frío Mondragón wrote in his account of Japanese captivity provided key clues to discovering what happened to my brother. For that, I can hardly repay you. Besides, you said there was something else you wanted to show me."

"Indeed there is, but please let me show you around first." Andrew led them inside, and the bright sunlight disappeared, replaced by warm incandescent light and the faint scent of burning rounds in a woodstove.

They sat together in a small living room dominated by wood. Wide-knot pine paneling. Fir floors. Oak furniture.

"This is where I grew up, as did my father and his father, my grandfather Porfírio. The house has stood for over a hundred years, since the time just following the Lincoln County War. Our great-great-grandfather built the house himself. According to family legend, he let Billy the Kid hide out here after the Kid made his famous escape from jail in Lincoln. Because he killed a deputy during that escape, Governor Wallace had put a bounty on his head. In the end, it didn't matter. Several months later, Pat Garrett finally tracked him down and shot him from ambush in Fort Sumner. And that was the beginning of the legend."

Frankie smiled. "It was pretty clear in your grandfather's narrative that he took great pride in the family history dating back to that period. It also helps explain some of the swagger in the story, his becoming a crack pistolero, and waging what amounted to a personal war against the Japanese on Bataan. But what puzzles me is why he felt it necessary to put it all on paper so many years later. I did my part toward the end of the war, saw some pretty bad things just like a lot of GIs, but I never once thought of writing about it."

"Maybe what I have to show you next will help answer that." Andrew rose and walked over to the roll top desk in the corner of the room. He took a small key from his pocket, unlocked the top, slid it back, and reached behind a false sliding panel to a hidden compartment. "When I first found my grandfather's manuscript, it was here in the bottom drawer. I wasn't aware that he had hidden something more in a secret slot in the desk. I discovered it quite by accident after we had begun communicating." He withdrew a small, yellowed package wrapped in twine from the desk. "This surprised me. Took my breath away, actually.

"But first, a little background. Grandfather Frío returned home a very different young man from the boy who went away to war. He suffered chronic illnesses, mostly brought on by diet deficiencies and tropical fevers. Unlike many veterans of the camps, who never could get enough to eat once they were back home and consequently ballooned to obesity, my grandfather stayed pretty lean the rest of his life. But he was plagued by demons. Today they'd call it PTSD, but back then, they just called it combat fatigue.

"He would go into terrible depressions and disappear, sometimes for days. Often he would be found wandering through the mountains, walking old trails he had explored as a boy. His mother worried constantly, even taking the precaution of having a neighbor remove the old Winchester from the closet for safekeeping. He shunned contact with other veterans and never was an active member of the American Legion. Interestingly, I never remember him taking a drink. Alcohol was not a refuge for him.

"He managed to pull himself together enough to apply for a job as a deputy sheriff for Lincoln County. Veterans like him were given first shot at government jobs, so he was hired. Frío served in the sheriff's department for the rest of his working life, married my grandmother, Gloria Mondragón Trujillo, and they raised three kids. I'm the youngest of seven grandchildren.

"My earliest memories of my grandfather were of a larger-than-life man in a sharp sheriff's uniform and a big revolver on his hip. He spoke little, but when he did, we kids listened. It never occurred to me that his long silences and faraway stare were unusual in any way. It wasn't until later that I realized they were masking inner turmoil and a deep sense of guilt.

"I think this is what you needed to see." Andrew untied the package and handed it to Frankie.

Frankie felt Melanie move closer to him as he calmly unfolded the old paper. A flood of memories surged in Frankie's mind: images of himself in olive drab, his mother placing the gold chain around his neck from which dangled a crucifix identical to the one that now rested in his hand. It was worn, the face of the corpus nearly featureless, and had clearly been through rough times. *Ramón's crucifix.*

The ink had run and was blotched in places, as though the writer had shed tears as he wrote. Frankie read the page with a deep, audible sigh and then handed it to Melanie.

The writing was brief:

> *The gold crucifix belonged to my friend, Sergeant Ramón Castillo. It was a gift from his mother when he was sent to the Philippines in 1941. Ramón cherished and carried it through the war and imprisonment, hiding it from his captors by sleight of hand and sometimes by swallowing it. It was never discovered. Toward the end of the war, Ramón was very ill, and must have believed he would not survive. He gave it to me and begged me to be sure that it made it home. It should be returned to his family by whoever finds this. I am ashamed that I have not returned it myself.*
>
> *Ramón was a hero and the greatest man I ever knew. He saved my life at least three times and the lives*

of others countless times, often at great personal cost. I wish I could have been as brave as Ramón, but to my shame, I wasn't. Ramón died while trying to save a fellow prisoner during a collapse at the mine where we prisoners were forced to work. He called for my help, but I turned my back and ran, leaving him and the other man to die in la cueva dorada.

It has been hard to live with this. Many times, I considered ending my own life for being such a coward. When Ramón's family contacted me after the war, I did not answer their letter, so deep was my shame. My hope is that an all-forgiving Providence will be merciful to me as I offer this, my heartfelt apology to Ramón's family.

Porfirio Mondragón
May 20, 1960

Melanie used her sleeve to wipe the tears from her face.

Andrew nodded solemnly. "I want you to have this," he said to Frankie. "The letter and the crucifix. It would fulfill the wishes of both your brother and my grandfather."

For a long moment, Frankie was at a loss for words. Now it all made sense. The mention of the "cueva dorada," a *golden cave* where Ramón, Frío, and other American prisoners had been forced to work. And the story about the Imperial gold bars and the cave-in at the mine told by Kazuo Midorikawa, the one-eyed guard. A *tuerto.* Was that why, as he lay dying after the fight, the old mobster had grabbed Frankie by the arm and said that he reminded him of a man he had known in the war, a brave man, an Amerika-jin samurai?

The old bastard must have known!

Frankie accepted Andrew's offer and embraced the younger man. Melanie and Frankie left as the setting sun was casting long shadows from the deep purple of the San Andres Mountains. The drive back to Las Cruces was unusually silent, as Frankie, lost in thought, fondled the old religious talisman. He couldn't get *la cueva dorada* out of his mind.

Monday, April 8, 2002

Las Cruces, New Mexico

Frankie always felt a little guilty when he visited the graves, as if somehow he didn't do it often enough. But today was different. He had a bundle of good news to discuss with Mama Elena.

He stepped out of the Ford truck, hitched up his pants, winced at the twinge in the thigh, and reached back for the flowers. Spring was definitely in the air now. The daffodils were blooming, and there was pale green life bursting in the cottonwoods. Even the little Japanese maples were sporting a shade of reddish maroon.

As he stood before her headstone, Frankie felt overcome with pride and sadness. "Mama, you were right. How did you know? We all thought you were just wishing it to be—a stubborn mother who couldn't accept the obvious. Papa, God rest him, humored you, but he had already made his peace with Ramón. And me—I just couldn't be bothered with a story that obviously had ended with my brother's death. But today I've come to tell you that Ramón died a hero. He died trying to rescue another soldier during a cave-in. I know this for a fact because of information I personally received from a prison guard and a former prisoner.

"See this? It's the crucifix you gave him when he went off to war. It has finally come home."

Frankie laid the gold crucifix on the headstone, where the sun caught the image and projected a cruciform reflection back at Frankie's chest. For an eerie moment, Frankie could swear he could hear the sound of an organ playing.

He stood up with a groan. "Oh. And Mama. You have another granddaughter. But that's a story for another time."

He placed the roses on the headstone. Then he picked up the crucifix and placed the chain around his own neck. Somewhere deep within a collapsed mine, Ramón lay buried. But unlike this place, Ramón's tomb was off-limits. Frankie had pondered a trip to the Akita mine in Japan, where he could see and touch the granite slab with all the inscriptions and his brother's writing. But Tomonaga had replied in an e-mail that such a visit would not be possible. The mine had been closed and sealed for years. And due to the recent incident, the place was now cordoned off from public access.

Frankie stood, thankful that he could at least still visit his parents' resting place, and limped back to the truck.

Chapter 43

Organ Music

Seven Months Later

Thanksgiving Day, November 28, 2002

Mesilla, New Mexico

"I'd like to propose a toast," Frankie said as he raised his glass of hard cider. He gazed across the table at his family, which, like his heart, was bulging at the seams.

Melanie, his rock the past five-plus decades, sat at the far end of the table, her graying hair pulled back, her cheeks giving off a rosy glow. She had stood by him through the worst and, despite being kept so long in the dark, had stuck around to celebrate with him in lighter times. They'd been on their own odyssey of sorts since his and Ellen's return, but Melanie, to her immense credit, had slowly, grudgingly softened toward him. The life they had built together was bigger than either of them, bigger than any of their problems.

To Melanie's left, Kume and Gary sat side by side, each the owner of a knowing smile. Gary looked posh in a dark Armani jacket that contrasted neatly with the streaks of silver in his hair, and Kume, dressed in a smart black skirt and boldly patterned silk blouse, looked like she'd just stepped off a runway, as usual. *Très chic.* The two, having survived more than their share of heartache, were slated to wed next spring in Sendai, which meant that Frankie had gained more than another daughter; he was about to become a father-in-law.

It was hard to believe that, just last February, Gary had nearly bled out at the foot of Mount Izumiga Dake in Japan. Today, in the golden glow of the late afternoon sun pouring through the dining room windows, he looked no worse for the experience. He had, more than anyone, paved the way for Frankie's and Ellen's return to the States after the shootout at the bunker. While Joe and Kojo had tried—unsuccessfully— to lobby Japanese officials, Gary, fresh off surgery, had simply made a phone call to Nathan Goldman, his friend in Washington. To Frankie's astonishment, he and Ellen were hurried onto a plane home a few days later. Gary hadn't been exaggerating about Goldman's pull, which from the sound of it extended all the way to the White House. No charges were ever filed by the Japanese authorities, who, after some deliberation, had come clean with the public on the exact nature of the battle that had occurred at the bunker.

Kazuo's fable of the legendary cache of gold, however, had been conveniently omitted. Frankie later discerned just enough from a cryptic e-mail exchange with Gary to realize that the gold story might have been part of an elaborate ruse orchestrated by Tokyo to entrap and embarrass the North Korean government—and the US State Department had been privy to the situation throughout. Frankie, Ellen, and Gary had nearly derailed the whole thing, which explained why Goldman had been so instrumental in freeing them. Nate had confided to Gary that he'd been present when the president had placed a call to Japanese Prime Minister Koizumi, and after a bit of high level horse trading that included releasing fifty late model F-16 fighters to the Japanese Air Self- Defense Force, the Castillos and Gary were on their way home. Frankie, though, preferred to think that he personally was responsible for keeping Pyongyang from developing a third-stage booster for a nuclear ICBM capable of reaching the United States.

To Melanie's right, Ellen and Tony beamed, glasses held high. Tony had cut his hair—as a concession to Frankie, according to Ellen. Frankie had tried hard to dislike the man, but the task had proven impossible. Tony, despite his colorful past and Bohemian streak, treated Ellen like a princess. Lately he'd begun discussing plans to leave LA and open his own practice in Las Cruces. Cocky, charming, and head-over-heels for Ellen, he had so far said and done all the right things. Frankie had a hunch he might be giving away more than one daughter next year.

Flanking Frankie and seated directly across from one another were none other than Soichiro and Noriko, honored houseguests since their arrival Monday. If Soichiro and Frankie had been inseparable since their arrival, Frankie knew he owed their newfound friendship to Ellen and Kume, who had been thick as thieves since meeting for the first time at the hospital last spring. The two women had brought everyone closer together, including their parents. Frankie had done his best to make jokes in broken Japanese, and Soichiro, bless his heart, had laughed at every one of them. Noriko and Melanie, meanwhile, were getting along like two aging sisters. Wise matriarchs, they seemed to regard the ongoing bonding around them with a mixture of pride and amusement.

"To family," Frankie finally said with his glass held high. "Because family . . ." He felt his voice falter as his mind wandered the past. That was when he noticed an odd sensation: the pain in his right thigh had all but disappeared. He cocked his head in surprise and then continued. "Because the people who matter most to me in this world are right here at this table. I'm thankful for you all more than you'll ever know."

"To family!" the others cheered.

They'd barely finished clinking their glasses when Soichiro raised his to signify another toast. "In my country, we say, '*Kanpai*.' It mean 'empty cup.' But . . ." He offered a mischievous smile as his bushy eyebrows danced below his full head of silver hair. "My cup never empty."

"Kanpai!" everyone said through laughter.

Frankie found the joy bittersweet—and doubted he was the only one. Two months earlier, he'd received word that Joe Petrini had died from heart failure. Phone calls to Takeo and Ayaka had revealed that the family was handling the loss as best they could, but the news had nevertheless hit Frankie hard. He'd insisted on establishing a college scholarship fund for the Petrini grandkids. Several months earlier, back in May, Soichiro had contacted Frankie to let him know that Yoko had died. She'd passed exactly a month after Kazuo. It seemed almost fitting. The old woman had seen much and, with the oyabun now gone, perhaps had felt she'd fulfilled her duty to Michiko. Everyone, it seemed, had lost—and gained—someone in what had been the most tumultuous year for Frankie since the war.

Frankie leaned back and patted his belly. As he took in the spectacle before—they'd nearly wiped out Melanie's traditional Thanksgiving spread, including the candied yams and the cranberry sauce—he wondered why he never learned. Every year he forgot to make room for dessert, yet every year he felt compelled to somehow finish at least one slice of pumpkin pie. Last night, though, he'd overheard the women conspiring to "mix things up."

Sure enough, Ellen and Kume disappeared into the kitchen momentarily, only to return carrying a pair of baskets.

Ellen remained standing after they'd placed the baskets in the center of the table. Her sky-blue eyes settled momentarily on Melanie. "It was hard as hell for her to let go, but Mom agreed to let me and Kume make dessert. This is Soichiro's favorite."

Soichiro's face lit up. "*Sata andagi?*"

Ellen and Kume nodded.

"It's a popular dessert in Okinawa," Kume explained.

Tony was the first to dig in, and Frankie watched as he teased something from the cloth napkin covering the basket closest to him. It looked like a doughnut hole. Tony tossed the whole thing into his mouth without hesitation and then grinned as he wiped what looked like sugar from his very recently, neatly trimmed beard. "It's good."

Ellen shook her head in mock disgust. "Don't talk with your mouth full, baby."

Soon enough, everyone was biting into one, including Frankie, whose teeth broke through the crispy exterior and made contact with a doughy center. "Tony's right. It's good." Frankie had no idea where he'd find the room, but he mentally committed himself to having at least two more. "Really good."

Frankie turned to Noriko and saw her smiling at him with her eyes. Those eyes—the same deep pools of vulnerability that had bewitched him so many years ago—no longer made him twinge inside. With her lips turned up slightly and her gaze radiating forgiveness, she looked the way he felt: at peace with the world around them. And in that moment, he found the courage to finally *fully* forgive himself. Wondering what could have been done in the past, he realized, was an impediment to deciding what should be done *now*. He would soldier on as a husband and father, and in the years to come, he could continue to atone for the mistakes of his youth by putting to good use the wisdom he gained with each new day.

As dusk fell, Frankie's big Ford truck was the lone vehicle in the parking lot at the Bataan Memorial Monument. He and Soichiro occupied a bench and stared up at the tall bronze figures without saying a word. Three bedraggled soldiers, one worse off than the others and being propped up by his comrades, were frozen in time, bathed in the warm glow from the up-lighting. Cars streamed by on the busy road nearby, their headlights and taillights passing by in a tangled blur behind the monument.

Soichiro, bundled up in a scarf and a double-breasted wool jacket, retrieved an old Zippo lighter from an inside pocket of the jacket and handed it to Frankie.

"What's this?" Frankie asked as he eyed the old relic, which was adorned with the marines' globe-and-anchor emblem and inscribed with the initials *BE*.

"This belong to Midorikawa-san."

"Kazuo?"

Soichiro nodded. "He take from US Marine on Guadalcanal. I do not want it. Maybe . . . maybe you find marine's name and return to his family."

Frankie stared at the lighter, which suddenly felt heavier in his hand. "I'll do my best."

He heaved a heavy sigh. It had been quite a day. The only thing missing had been an appearance by Andrew Mondragón, but the young man had been unable to accept Frankie's invitation to Thanksgiving. The last time Frankie had spoken with him, Andrew had promised to tell everyone in his clan "the incredible story of Frío and Ramón." He had even suggested in a thoughtful tone that he might write a book about it someday—with Frankie's help.

Soichiro abruptly cocked his head as though listening for a sound and stared up at the dark sky. "You hear that?" he said with a puzzled look on his face. "Sound like music from organ."

Frankie put his arm around Soichiro and chuckled. "I didn't hear anything."

Together they walked slowly back to the truck. Frankie produced a bottle of Old Grand-Dad, and the two friends drank from the bottle.

End Note

A novel is, in most cases, an imagined story with imaginary characters set in the midst of a present or past reality. Much research is required to make such a story plausible, and many sources are accessed in the pursuit of authenticity. While not exhaustive, the following are books well worth considering by anyone interested in taking a "deeper dive" into the times and events underlying *Searching For Noriko*.

To better understand the history of southern New Mexico during the years preceding statehood—a colorful if violent time—one would profit by reading the 1882 memoir by Pat E. Garrett, *The Authentic Life of Billy the Kid*; *Tularosa: Last of the Frontier West* by C. L. Sonnichsen; and *The Two Alberts: Fountain and Fall* by Gordon R. Owen.

Much has been written about the horrors of the "Bataan Death March" and the treatment of U.S. soldiers captured by the Imperial Japanese Army. Among the best sources are *Ghost Soldiers* by Hampton Sides, *Undefeated* by Bill Sloan, *God's Warrior* by Dorothy Cave, *Unbroken* by Laura Hillenbrand and *Voices of the Pacific* by Adam Makos.

Finally, in Studs Terkel's words, "unless we know of Okinawa and its beleaguered people, we know precious little of World War II." While there are many first person accounts and histories of various military units involved in the battle, George Feifer's *The Battle of Okinawa: The Blood and the Bomb* stands alone as an epic, comprehensive chronicle of that terrible three month fight. The book is unflinching in its portrayal of the attacking Allies and Japanese defenders—bravery, cruelty and stupidity on all sides. One begins to comprehend, after the slaughter, why the decision was reached to use the Bomb.

About the Author

Al Dawson is a retired lawyer living in West Palm Beach with his wife Jane and a feral cat named Wee Thomas. A southwesterner by birth, he studied for the priesthood, was a collegiate gymnast, earned a JD at New York Law School and practiced law with several firms and trade associations. Father of Sean, Neil and Erin, he loves motorcycles, tennis, fine wine and traveling with Jane.

Made in the USA
Columbia, SC
30 June 2020